RAVES FOR *OCCAM'S RAZOR*, ARCHER MAYOR, AND JOE GUNTHER

W9-BXW-134

"By practicing his craft with dazzling skill and digging for the deeper moral issues . . . Mayor has made an honorable art form of the regional mystery."
—*New York Times Book Review*

"The strength of this durable series has always been its insularity: local settings, sharp small-town characterizations, homegrown police procedures."
—*Kirkus Reviews*

"Gunther's most interesting case to date. Mayor's major strength is his ability to etch personalities in their settings so that they are as vivid as a video."
—*St. Petersburg Times*

"Mayor, one of the masters of regional crime fiction, wields OCCAM'S RAZOR with a sure hand. . . . As crisp and chilling as the New England winter in which it is set."
—*January Magazine*

"A wonderfully complex plot . . . seamless. . . . Another fine entry in an outstanding series."
—*Mystery News*

"A believable, appealing hero."
—*Cleveland Plain Dealer*

"Mayor has packed a lot of material into this book, taking the reader on a fascinating journey through the criminal mind. . . . A very sharp piece of reading, with nary a dull moment."
—*Shelf Life*

Other Books by Archer Mayor

ARCHER MAYOR

Occam's Razor

WARNER BOOKS

A Time Warner Company

WARNER BOOKS EDITION

Cover design by Rachel McClain
Cover illustration by Mark Elliot

Warner Books, Inc.
1271 Avenue of the Americas
New York, NY 10020

Visit our Web site at
www.twbookmark.com

 A Time Warner Company

Printed in the United States of America

Originally published in hardcover by The Mysterious Press.
First Paperback Printing: October 2000

10 9 8 7 6 5 4 3 2 1

To the men and women of NewBrook Fire and Rescue.
Thank you for your knowledge,
your compassion, and your friendship.

Acknowledgments

To write my books, I rely heavily upon a great number of people inhabiting walks of life I can only appreciate from a distance. I see what they do, express an interest in having it reflected in my work, and watch them open themselves up to sometimes hours of interviewing, just so I can get my facts straight. It is an act of generosity, committed time and time again, for which I am forever grateful. To all you readers who appreciate the verisimilitude of my work, it is these people you should thank.

To list them all by name, however, might embarrass some, cause trouble for others, and make me wonder if I hadn't left someone out by mistake.

Instead, therefore, as in the past, I will merely thank them all anonymously, or thank the organizations for which they work, stressing that any mistakes or misrepresentations should be seen as being mine alone.

The Brattleboro Police Department
The Office of the Windham County State's Attorney
The Office of the Windham County Public Defender
The Office of the Vermont Attorney General
The Vermont Medical Examiner's Office
The Vermont State Agency of Natural Resources

The Vermont State Police

Office of the Governor, State of Vermont

The State of Vermont Agency of Administration

The Criminal Justice Services Division (Department of Public Safety)

The senators, representatives, and staff of the Vermont Legislature

The Bradford M. Field Memorial Library of Leverett, Massachusetts

The employees of the Vermont State House

The employees and management of Thunder Road racetrack and the many dedicated men and women who serve (or once served) the State of Vermont in various capacities (or reported on its activities for the media) and were willing to share the memories.

To all of you who think the fictional characters in the following story are in any way reflective of anyone real, you are in error, though no one I know ever believes that.

Occam's Razor

Chapter One

It was colder without the snow, and felt darker as a result. Even with the starlight and the feeble seepage from the streetlamps around the corner, my eyes took longer to adjust than I expected.

The police officer at the bottom of the Arch Street alley looked up at me quizzically as I hesitated beside the car, my hands burrowing deep inside my pockets. "You okay, Lieutenant?" He was stringing a yellow "Police Line" tape across the way.

I shuddered and nodded, walking down the paved incline, careful of its neglected, broken surface. "Sure, Bobby. Still half asleep."

He lifted the tape to let me pass. "Know what you mean. I been on nights for a week already. Still can't get used to it."

He was fresh from the academy, eager and curious, and, if statistics were any guide, destined to learn the ropes with us and then either enter the private sector, disillusioned and bored, or angle a job with the state police, assuming he passed their scrutiny.

"Who's here already?" I asked him.

"Detectives Klesczewski and Tyler. Officer Lavoie's with them. Sheila Kelly's closing the other end off."

I smiled at his titling everyone except Sheila. It wasn't sexist. She'd been his supervisor before we'd let him loose on his own. She was the reverse of the trend, ten years with the Burlington PD, come to us in search of a slightly mellower pace. Bobby Miller looked to her as a kid might to an older sister.

I continued to the corner, where the Main Street buildings above and behind me showed their backs to the train tracks and the Connecticut River beyond. Typical of many old red-brick New England towns, Brattleboro, Vermont, faced away from the serenity and beauty of the river, having chosen well over a hundred and fifty years ago to regard both it and the railroad paralleling it as unsightly commercial conduits. In its heyday, this stretch of ground, unseen by the gentry, had been a coarse and bustling string of loading docks and receiving bays, feeding businesses two floors above, whose windows had glittered with the primped and polished end results.

Now the area was forlorn and ignored, a parking place for Dumpsters, the homeless, and teenagers seeking illicit time alone. High overhead, out of sight in the gloom, dotting the curved, fortresslike wall following the river's bend, were hundreds of dingy rear apartments, an increasing number of which were being transformed into tastefully renovated lofts or rendered into peaceful, sunlit havens by the town's excess of psychologists and therapists—drawn to the very scenery that their predecessors had ignored. Most, however, still belonged to the marginally solvent—welfare dwellers holed up in small, dark, cluttered dens, surrounded by commerce and benefiting from none of it.

With theatrical abruptness, a tripod-mounted halogen lamp burst the darkness ahead of me with a brief electrical hiss. It was facing away from me, down and across the tracks, so the effect wasn't blinding, but more fancifully melodramatic. Its harsh light destroyed any subtlety or nuance, revealing everything in its arc in angular, brittle starkness—while consigning everything outside it to simple nonexistence. The soiled, damaged brick walls, the cinder-stained gravel of the railroad bed, the parallel crescent of gleaming tracks, and the flat black slab of river water beyond—all were briefly frozen in that initial flash of light, like a startled, disheveled partygoer caught in the glare of an instant camera. And just as quickly, it all became mere background to the item at center stage—and the reason for our gathering in the middle of a freezing January night.

Perpendicular to the outermost track, his feet toward the river, lay a man in a thick, long, dirty coat. He had no head or hands—they'd all been resting on the track when the last train had passed by, and what was left of them didn't merit much description. But they lent the scene its one source of bright color, and to the entire picture a grim sense of purpose.

Standing over the body was Ron Klesczewski, that night's detective on call. J. P. Tyler, our forensics man, had just plugged in the lamp.

He moved away from its glare and joined me in the darkness, like a technician stepping offstage to check his work. "I didn't see calling the paramedics. Got hold of everybody else—the ME, the SA's office, more backup. Gail not on tonight?"

Gail Zigman was a deputy state's attorney, and the woman I lived with. "No," I answered. "I forgot to ask who was when I left." I gestured with my chin down the tracks. "What've we got?"

Tyler shrugged. "Little early to tell, and I don't want to do too much before the ME gets here, but it looks like a bum who ran out of rope."

"Suicide?" I asked mildly.

"Probably. Although you don't usually find them with their hands on the track."

Before moving any closer, I said, more to myself than to him, "Unless he was already dead."

Three hours later, with the sky still black at winter's insistence, I brought a cup of coffee into Tony Brandt's office and settled tiredly into one of his guest chairs.

Brandt was our chief of police and had been for years on end. A born administrator, a natural politician, and a cop his entire professional life, he was probably far more skilled than we deserved. I wondered sometimes if he'd ever realize how much better he could do than a twenty-four-person police force, or when someone like the governor might wake up and draft him to work in Montpelier as the head of some huge agency. It was ironic that we lost less-talented people than Tony all the time but kept hold of a man whose blueprint for community policing was slowly being emulated across the entire country.

But there was a canniness to Tony Brandt that implied that none of this was accidental. A good friend to many and affable to most, he remained both private and quietly driven, leaving the impression that he was looking at us all—and at himself in our company—in some kind of grand context.

He now sat back in his chair, his feet up on his desk, his hands interlocked behind his head. He looked at me impassively through frameless bifocals. "This something to worry about?"

It was an interesting choice of words—a politically savvy variation on the question I'd asked Tyler earlier.

"Could be. It looks like suicide. No signs of a struggle, no other obvious trauma to the body. No one we've canvassed so far has owned up to hearing anything. It might be that easy."

"Except . . ." he suggested.

I held up my hand in protest. "No, no. Except nothing. That's all we've got so far. He's been shipped up to Burlington for an autopsy, Tyler's still poking around the scene, and the canvass is ongoing. Any one of a couple of hundred people could've seen or heard something. I'm just saying we're not done yet."

He watched me without comment while I sipped from my cup, knowing what he'd say next. We went back far enough to find comfort in such oblique communication.

"What's really on your mind?"

I placed the cup on the corner of his desk. "He *might* be a suicide. He might also have been tossed from a flying saucer, and his blood replaced with food dye. But as suicides go, it's a little unusual. He had nothing in his pockets—and I mean nothing at all—and while his clothes were filthy, his underpants were snowy white."

He knew better than to debate the worth of such evidence. "Okay. Keep me informed."

I climbed the stairs slowly, one hand on the banister, by now feeling the lack of sleep. I'd entered the building from the front, using a nondescript door to the right of a clothing store. The double row of weathered, ornate buildings lining Brattleboro's main drag often reminded me of two ancient beached battleships—huge, rusty, and abandoned by modern needs, but also too big and reminiscent of past glories to be replaced. By design and through countless renovations, therefore, they'd been renovated, modernized, and brought up to code until no two floors looked alike, making passage through their innards like an archaeological field trip.

This particular building was clearer-cut than some, and less invaded by yuppies. Above the clothing store, a start-up lawyer and a downscale barber shared the second floor. Farther up were apartments only, inhabited by those whose life options hovered between few and none. If I hadn't already known this from too many past visits, the fetid odor now enveloping me left little room for doubt. One thing about winter—it does stifle any impulse to throw open a window to the fresh air.

Ron Kleszewski's head appeared over the railing of the top-floor landing—clean-shaven, fresh-faced, even after having been up most of the night. "Hi, Joe. It's up here."

He vanished again, allowing me to continue climbing in solitude. Ron had almost resigned a few years ago, after a particularly traumatic shoot-out with some heavily armed Asians. Tentative to begin with, he'd turned inward for a short time thereafter, not coming to work, ignoring his young, pregnant wife. In those days, he'd been my second-in-command, a position I'd realized then had only added to his stress. Giving him time—and his responsibilities to Sammie Martens—had done the trick. He'd reemerged much as before, if anything more solid, and had resumed being our premier logistics man—chasing paperwork, checking records, and keeping the department's revamped computer system up to date.

There were several apartments feeding onto the top landing, but only one with its door wide open, at the end of a long, narrow corridor leading straight to the rear of the building. I headed that way, following the sound of voices.

I had four detectives under my command, Sammie and Willy Kunkle being the two I had yet to see this morning. I knew they were out there working. But just as it was typical of Ron to have called me about the woman I was about to meet, so was it that neither Willy nor Sam had even bothered to check in, much less give me an update. Totally unalike in other respects, they were as passionately independent as Ron was a team player. On those rare occasions when all four were acting up, I felt like the single mother of a dysfunctional family.

Klesczewski reappeared in the doorway and ushered me across the threshold, introducing me to a blade-faced old woman propped up in the far corner of a ratty sofa.

"Mrs. Edith Rudd. Lieutenant Gunther."

We eyed each other across the close, cluttered room and nodded politely.

Ron kept his voice pleasantly upbeat. "Edith has been telling me she might have something to add to our investigation, but she wanted to make sure she only spoke to the man in charge."

Great, I thought.

"That you?" Her voice took me back to my first viewing of *The Wizard of Oz* and the Wicked Witch of the West. She certainly seemed to have the same aversion to water.

"Yes, ma'am."

I crossed over to her, grabbing a chair from under the kitchen table as I went. The apartment was an efficiency, each wall staking claim to a different domestic function—bedroom, living room, kitchen, or bathroom—and each losing its identity just a foot or two into the room, where a generalized heaping of disassociated jetsam defeated all rhyme or reason. It looked like a neighborhood tag sale right after the last shopper had torn it apart.

I placed the chair opposite her and sat down. "What would you like to tell me?"

She shook her head emphatically, as I feared she might. "Not so fast. I don't want to do this again. I tell you once, here and now, and that's an end to it."

I tried looking sympathetic. "We'll try to make it work that way, but since I don't know what you're going to tell me, I can't make any promises."

It was like throwing meat to a wolf. She leaned forward, her face pinched around a pair of glittering eyes. "Just what I thought. They do that at the hospital, too. I'm no whiner. It takes a lot to get me down. So when I call for help, I'm in real pain. And I don't trust them to begin with, so why would I go see them unless I was really hurting?"

I nodded without comment, since I had no idea what she was talking about.

"But when they come in here from the ambulance, putting their hands all over me, they always ask me a bunch of stupid questions like they think I'm making it up. You think they even listen to what I'm saying?"

"Yes, I do," I had to admit.

She held up a yellow, skinny finger. "Well, you don't

know much. They may write down a lot of stuff, but the doctors at the ER throw it out. You know why?"

I remained rigidly uncommitted.

It didn't matter. She stared at me as if I'd just called her a liar. "So they can ask me the same dumb questions all over again. I asked them why they do it, and they told me they wanted to make sure I didn't leave anything out. Can you believe that? Like it's my fault they won't listen."

I got the point. I held up my hand like a traffic cop and spoke loudly to interrupt her. "Tonight, I promise no one will ever ask you the same questions again."

She stopped in midsentence. "You do?"

I glanced at Ron, who looked as startled as she did.

"Yes," I said. "Now, what did you see or hear that might help us out?"

Her entire demeanor changed from the outraged citizen to the confidential source. Her body relaxed, curving toward me, and she turned her head slightly away from Ron, as if excluding him from the conversation.

"It was creepy," she said softly.

"I bet it was." I matched her whisper. "Can you describe it?"

She motioned to me to lean into the acrid odor surrounding her like a fog. Our noses were almost touching by now. "I thought it was aliens at first. It was their talking that woke me up. They had a big bright light, bright enough to bounce right off that ceiling." She glanced up sideways, reliving the moment. "I could see that man, with no head and no hands, and them around him. And then they began doing things to him . . ."

She paused as Ron edged toward the front door,

shaking his head with disgust. "What?" Her voice had regained its querulous pitch.

"That was us," he told her.

Edith Rudd straightened and looked at me, startled and uncertain. "What?" she repeated, this time sounding more like a surprised child.

I reached out and laid my hand on hers. "What you saw was the police trying to figure out what happened," I explained, as Ron left the room, no doubt hoping to escape his own embarrassment. "We needed that light to see better."

She continued watching my eyes, and I held her gaze, smiling slightly. Suddenly her tears welled up. "It looked so terrible."

"I know, Mrs. Rudd. I'm sorry you had to see it, and I'm sorry we woke you up."

She glanced away to the floor and sighed, her whole body trembling slightly with the effort. "Thank you," she almost whispered.

I squeezed her hand, feeling the sharpness of her knuckles under my thumb. "Thank *you* for trying to help."

She looked back at me then. "What's your name again?"

"Joe Gunther."

"I was awake before then—before the light came on. I wasn't really sleeping."

I nodded encouragingly. "Bad night?"

"I have a lot of them. I was looking out the window at the stars in the river when I saw them. They pulled him out of a car and put him on the tracks, just the way you found him."

"He didn't resist?"

"I think he was dead already. They laid him out like he was a sofa pillow."

"How many?"

"Three that I could see."

I gestured to the nearby window, narrow and smudged, and raised my eyebrows. "You mind?"

I rose and peered through the glass. The apartment was almost directly above where we'd spent the early morning hours.

"Were you able to recognize or see any of them clearly?" I asked her.

She shook her head. "They were all in coats and hats. And it was dark."

"How about when any of them passed in front of the headlights? Did you see anything unusual then?"

"There were no headlights. That's why I started looking in the first place. Cars drive along the tracks at night all the time—dopers, prostitutes, you name it. But they all use their headlights till they park. When I noticed this one being so secretive, I got curious." She stopped again and rubbed her cheek with her palm. "I wish I hadn't."

"What time was this, Mrs. Rudd?"

"Around one, I guess."

"Did you hear anything?"

There was dead silence in the room. I heard Ron's footsteps returning from the landing, and hoped he wouldn't alter the mood. But he was hypersensitive by now, and stopped before coming into view.

Finally Edith Rudd sat back in her seat, as if suddenly releasing an enormous weight. "I heard the train."

I returned to my chair. "My God. You saw it happen?"

She seemed more sure of herself now, almost surprised at how easy it had been. "The train blocked the view, but I saw the before and after."

"And the men in the car?"

"They'd left by then. The train comes by at one-thirty every night. They waited a little while after laying him out, probably checking to see if anyone saw them, but then they drove off."

"What kind of car was it?"

A small flash of irritation crossed her face, and I sensed she was recovering. "It was nighttime."

I smiled and shook my head, trying to regain her confidence. "No, no. I'm sorry. I didn't mean what make or model," I lied. "I wondered if you could tell whether it was a station wagon or a sedan, light or dark, large or small—something like that."

"Oh. Let's see. I guess it was a large sedan, I suppose dark-colored, but there I'm not so sure."

I rose to my feet and shook her hand. "Thank you, Mrs. Rudd. You've been a big help. Are you sure you're feeling okay? This must've been a shock."

She answered by struggling out of the sofa's grip and escorting me to the door, tapping me on the elbow as we went. "I'm fine. I'm a tough old bird."

I paused at the door, aware of Ron fading out of earshot down the hall again. "Why did you tell us that tall tale earlier? You knew it was us down there with the light. I bet you even recognized me."

She smiled coquettishly, revealing a row of darkened, misshapen teeth, and tilted her head in Ron's direction. "I could tell he didn't like me. And he called me Edith, just like the nurses and ambulance people."

Chapter Two

Ron Kleszewski stopped me at the bottom of the stairs, just shy of the building's front door. We could see through the glass the first wave of morning traffic filling the streets, passing before us in quick, familiar flashes.

"I screwed up. I should've read her better."

I laughed and shook my head, having told him on the way down what Edith Rudd had seen. "I don't think so. If I'd been the first one in, she would've handed me what you got—pure luck of the draw. She had to tell one of us the truth. It was piled up inside her like water behind a dam. You know if the canvass has dug up anyone else?"

He unclipped a portable radio from his belt. "I'll find out."

I stopped him. "It'll keep—I was just wondering. I'm going back to the office. We'll all compare notes around lunchtime, anyhow."

We parted company on the sidewalk, Ron heading for the next door on the block, and I walking north, through Brattleboro's heart, toward the Municipal Center at the far end of Main Street.

I needed to do more, however, than just jar my sleepless brain with a brisk walk in the bone-chilling air. I found it useful, when I needed to think, to get away from home and office both and to wander the streets I'd patrolled since first becoming a cop. For decades now, I'd watched Brattleboro going through its growing pains, from the post-World War backwater days to the arrival in the sixties of the interstate and the hippies, both of which had infused the town with their separate brands of vitality. There were communities like this that were all but dead in the water, and others so bent on making a buck that they'd turned themselves into strip malls. But Brattleboro, with its mixture of old and new, homegrown and flatlander, rich and poor, conservative and liberal, had acquired an opinionated, contradictory, irritating, but life-saving energy that seemed destined to defeat the doldrums that had doomed so many other towns.

The interstate, and Brattleboro's proximity to the Massachusetts border, had brought darker things, too, of course, and I was wondering if what Edith Rudd had seen last night wasn't one of them. In the past ten years, our homicide rate had climbed to one a year, and sometimes more. The disintegration of the cities to our south, Vermont's reputation for being friendly to the down-and-out, and the role of this town as an employment hub all conspired to make it an incubator for illegal activity. Increasingly, we'd had to deal with everything from youth gangs to drug sales and school violence. Whacking some poor rummy and placing him on the train tracks still made us sit up straight, but it no longer stood out as it would have ten years ago.

It also didn't make a whole lot of sense.

Why kill a bum, when, since he was delivered by car, pocket change and/or spontaneity probably hadn't had much to do with it? Why place him on the tracks, perhaps already dead, and make such an effort to destroy his head and hands? Why disguise him as a bum in the first place, when, as I was beginning to suspect from his clean underwear, he wasn't a bum at all?

For some reason—and at great risk—the man's body had been deposited where it would quickly be found, while pains had been taken to keep his identity a secret.

By the time I reached the Municipal Center, my nose and cheeks had gone numb, a problem quickly remedied by the wall of hot, desert-dry air that smacked me in the face as soon as I opened the front door.

Well over a hundred years old, like its brethren down the street, the building had been repeatedly chopped up by successive tenants, each one in need of a completely different floor plan. Heating this constantly changing environment had, I believed—despite protests to the contrary—finally defeated the people in charge, who had settled on the time-proven principle that if you make it hot enough at the bottom, the top will eventually get warm.

Unfortunately, the police department was located on the ground floor, with its holding cells, locker room, and gym in the basement. Had we been Bedouin Arabs, this might've been ideal, but we weren't, and it wasn't.

Shedding my outer clothing as I walked down the central hallway, intending to enter one of the two side doors leading to the detective bureau on the right, I was stopped by a uniformed officer exiting the patrol division's large communal office area on the left.

"Joe, you got a sec?"

I took my hand off the doorknob. "Sure. What's up?"

Marshall Smith had been with us almost ten years, longer than most, and yet had maintained a newcomer's hesitancy, as if ready to accept the first invitation to go away. "I just got back from a call at the parking lot between Bickford's and the railroad tracks. There's a wrinkle to it Captain Manierre thought you should hear."

"Be my guest," I said, twisting the doorknob.

Smith held back. I noticed then he was still dressed for the weather. "Actually, I was wondering if you had time to take a look at it now."

I began putting my coat back on. "Why not?"

We left by the double doors at the rear of the building, which gave onto a large parking lot we shared with the State Office Building across the way.

"So what're we going to?" I asked as we aimed for one of several white patrol cars lined up in a neat row—a highly visible symbol of police spending that never failed to catch flak at the annual town meeting.

Marshall swung in behind the wheel of one of them. "It's an abandoned truck—a ten-wheeler dump unit."

He started the already warm engine and headed toward the street. The heater immediately began blowing hot air across our faces. "The manager at Bickford's noticed it a few days ago," he resumed. "People leave their vehicles there all the time, usually because they're carpooling, but rarely more than overnight. And nobody leaves a truck for that long. There's too much money wrapped up in it. They're guessing it might've been there for almost a week."

"This a company rig?" I asked as we gained speed up the Putney Road, which starts out as one of the high-class sections of town, but then becomes, over the confluence of the West and Connecticut rivers, a commercial strip as uniquely Vermont as a Coca-Cola can.

"Not so you can tell. There's nothing on the door, no papers inside the cab. Since there're no license plates, I ran the vehicle identification number through the computer and found it was leased from Timson Long Haul outside Leverett, Mass, but the guy I talked to there wasn't too helpful. Said he didn't have his records handy, and that he'd have to dig around and call me back. He's probably cooking up something bogus right now. I was doing an off-line search of the registration through NCIC, just to see what I could find, when Ron radioed in saying you were heading for the office."

I mentally reviewed what he'd done so far, looking for something to add. As far as I could tell, there was no reason for me to be in this car. Some departments insisted on detectives running all investigations. We didn't work that way. Brandt firmly believed that in order to hang on to our patrol officers—since the detective squad had no turnover to speak of—they should be given every opportunity to process cases on their own. Smith seemed to have been doing a good job of just that.

We'd swept by most of the malls, gas stations, and fast food places on the strip and were nearing the town's northernmost interstate exit when I felt obliged to admit as much. "Sounds like you've got everything pretty well locked down."

Smith glanced at me and smiled. "That's because I saved the best till last."

He swung right at the traffic light, onto Route 9 heading for New Hampshire across the bridge, and then immediately pulled into the parking lot beyond Bickford's Restaurant on the corner, a place I frequented as often as I could, but which Gail wouldn't even enter, given her refined vegetarian palate.

The truck—an old Mack, stained and moth-eaten by rust—stood against the far bank, as if trying to disappear into the brush just beyond it. Smith rolled to a stop nearby and got out.

"Here's the kicker," he said, and walked to the rear of the dump body. He pointed to a pool of dark liquid at his feet. "Don't touch it, but give it a whiff."

I did so gingerly, straightening back up immediately, my nostrils stinging despite the frigid air. "Jesus Christ. What is it?"

"Beats me, but I doubt it's legal. That's all that's left, by the way—that and a few puddles in the back. They already got rid of whatever they were carrying."

"I hope to hell you were careful crawling around this thing," I told him.

"I was, believe me."

I stepped away and surveyed the truck generally. As Smith had said, the plates were missing, front and rear, but otherwise it looked like any one of a thousand anonymous, battle-scarred units you see driving around every day. Which may have been exactly the point.

I opened the driver's door and hoisted myself up level to the worn, cracked seat. Smith appeared below me.

"I'm guessing you searched in here?" I asked him.

"For the driver's log, routing slips, or a bill of lading. I didn't tear it apart when I didn't hit pay dirt, though. Wasn't sure if you'd want J.P. to check it out with his bag of tricks."

Standing on the running board, I leaned in and looked around, simply taking in my surroundings. If the driver of this truck was like everyone else I knew, he'd made his vehicle an extension of his home, filled with creature comforts, accessories, and trash. But there were only a few items, and all curiously impersonal— a pack of gum, a few empty soda cans, several maps with nothing written or marked on them.

"Find anything?" Marshall asked after several minutes of this, either to stem his own boredom or take his mind off the cold.

I plucked one of the soda cans off the floor by its pop-top ring and held it up to the light. Its shiny surface was clean of fingerprints. "It's what I'm not finding that's interesting. This guy went to some effort not to leave anything we could trace."

The sun visors yielded nothing, nor the door pockets, nor what passed for a glove box. I flattened out and checked the floor under the seat, finding it abnormally clean. Finally, I ran my fingers along the wedge where the seat met the back. I found some wrappers, a couple of never-used seat belt anchors, and a single scrap of paper with writing on it.

I read it and anticipated Smith's question. "It's a set of directions. You better call ANR."

Vermont's Agency of Natural Resources is the third largest in the state. It includes the departments of Fish and Wildlife; Forests, Parks and Recreation; and Environmental Conservation, as well as a chemical analysis facility near but separate from the state forensics lab, and some eight hundred employees. Over the years, Vermont has laid claim to being one of the most environmentally aware states in the union. The Legislature, prompted and/or supported by a variety of governors, has passed an enormous number of laws controlling what can and cannot be done to the Vermont countryside, hoping to maintain our deservedly famous rural appearance, and creating a chronic—and largely artificial—rift between tree-huggers and pro-business types. In the process, a few snags have cropped up, some of which have been unintended consequences. The truck Marshall Smith had introduced me to was a case in point. By making waste disposal such a complicated, expensive, strictly licensed enterprise, our vigilant environmentalists had inadvertently created a booming black market in illegal dumping.

And waste disposal wasn't the sole focal point. Everything from water runoffs to backyard burn barrels to the appearance of new construction had also become regulated. By this point, the Agency of Natural Resources was being called upon to investigate up to fourteen hundred complaints every year—with only eight field agents to handle the load.

Not just beleaguered, these eight felt themselves estranged as well. While they weren't certified law enforcement officers, and thus had no powers of arrest, they were still seen as cops by the people they pursued—but as nit-picking, sandal-wearing bureaucrats by the cops. And they'd been shuttled around like orphans as well. Spurned by Fish and Wildlife—the very police force within their own agency—they'd been attached to the attorney general's office for a while, then to the newly formed Environmental Court, except, of course, when they could bring a case to the feds. It all went a good way in explaining why, if and when one of the ANR investigators finally did show up at a site, he tended to act a little wary, at least until he could gauge his reception.

It therefore struck me as a minor miracle, once Marshall Smith had phoned the agency, that he was told they'd send someone down later that afternoon. We'd either gotten lucky or we'd struck a nerve. I told Smith to set up some security for the truck and radioed for a patrol car to take me back to the office.

As interesting as this had been, it wasn't as pressing as what was going on downtown.

Sammie Martens was small, slight, ambitious, and as high-strung as anyone I knew over eight years old. A survivor of a less than ideal upbringing, a successful and decorated veteran of some very rigorous military training—back when the brass was trying to prove women couldn't cut it in combat—Sam had made short work of the patrol side of our department, being promoted to sergeant and transferred to the detective squad just a few years after hiring on. I didn't doubt she aspired to more—my job, the chief's, and probably beyond—but I also knew her to have a fierce loyalty to those she trusted and admired. She'd risked her job for me in the past, without expectation of reward, making it clear it was merely part of the package when it came to her brand of friendship.

She and Willy Kunkle, the fourth member of my squad, were waiting in my cramped cubicle of an office to give me an update. It had now been twelve hours since we'd found the body on the tracks.

"Phase one of the canvass is complete," Sammie said. "We hit every apartment or business that has a window overlooking the scene, and in all but about four cases, we found somebody to talk to. The ones with nobody home will be followed up, and where we were told a family member or whatever wasn't in when we visited, we took their names so we can chase 'em down later. But it's not looking too promising, and from what Ron told me about your talk with Edith Rudd, you already got the basic gist. Nobody saw anything except three nondescript guys in a car with no lights. The victim always looked either dead, drugged, or unconscious, the car was always described as a dark sedan with no visible license plates, and nobody heard a single sound during the whole routine—no shouts, no shots, no nothing. Like they were ghosts."

"Or just slightly better at their job than the average idiot we deal with," Willy added sourly.

Perpetually down at the mouth, hypercritical, and dismissive of everyone else's efforts, Willy Kunkle made an effort to be unpleasant. An alcoholic veteran of the Vietnam War who'd abused his wife until she ditched him and neglected his job until he was almost fired, he'd been ironically turned around—somewhat—by a sniper bullet on a case some ten years ago. Now saddled with a withered, crippled left arm, whose hand he kept stuffed in his trousers pocket, he'd taken his smoldering rage and focused it against the people he was being paid to pursue. About as antithetical to the concept of community policing as Tony Brandt's worst nightmare, Kunkle nevertheless had a knack for getting at least one segment of our population to cooperate—successfully enough that none of us wanted to know his methods. Strangely, given his otherwise rebellious personality, Willy could also exhibit a fierce loyalty, and had joined Sammie in risking his job for me back when the attorney general's office was out to end my career. But where her motivation had been to place justice above the law, his had simply been to give the system a kick in the ass.

Well used to his one-liners, Sammie continued unperturbed. "The other point everyone pretty much agrees on is the timing. They put the body on the tracks about half an hour before the train came through."

"What about the train?" I asked. "Did the crew see anything?"

She shook her head. "I called. It was news to them. They've kicked off their own internal investigation, and the feds'll probably get pulled into it 'cause of the jurisdictional thing. But I got the engineer on the line before he'd been told to clam up, and he says he didn't see a thing."

"Probably drunk, stoned, asleep, or all three," Willy commented. "Those guys are amazing—overpaid, underworked, and total losers."

This time, Sammie ignored the stupidity of the remark but did address the subject matter. "He did sound nervous—maybe 'cause he was under scrutiny, maybe 'cause he did foul up. They are supposed to keep one eye on the track, especially at crossings and in congested areas."

"Did you get the feeling any of the witnesses you interviewed might've been playing dumb?" I asked.

Sam began shaking her head, but Willy cut in with a laugh. "Dumb, maybe, but definitely good-looking. I bet she'd like to question him a whole lot more privately."

Sammie hit his good arm with the back of her hand— a solid blow that made me wince in sympathy. Kunkle just kept laughing.

"Asshole," she muttered.

I silently raised my eyebrows at her.

She turned bright red—a first, to my knowledge. "We interviewed four guys who were having an all-night poker game. One of them saw the car out the window on his way to the bathroom. He didn't see the body being dumped, and only remembered it because the headlights were out." She glared at Willy and added, "It's a total dead end."

"That's not what you told me," he said with a leer.

She made to hit him again, but this time he quickly moved out of range, fast and smooth.

"Okay, okay," I said. "Enough. What about my question?"

"I don't think so," she said firmly, fighting to regain her composure. "But we haven't finished yet. Could be one of the people we're still looking for is missing for good reason."

I waved toward the door. "All right. Put it all down on paper. And let me know what develops."

I listened to them arguing as they disappeared into the labyrinth of sound-absorbent panels that divided the squad room into tiny private work areas. In the years I'd known her, I'd never once seen Sammie refer to, or keep company with, any male companion. By all appearances, she'd handed her life over to the department, to such an extent that I'd even recommended she acquire some outside interests. She'd looked at me as if I'd lost my mind.

But it was an interesting turn of events, if Willy was even remotely on target, which from Sammie's reaction I was guessing he was. Not only had she finally succumbed to some man's charms, but she'd done so at the drop of a hat, and in the middle of a murder investigation.

I'd never doubted her loyalty, her competence, or her ability. I'd had occasion to question her judgment, although not in a long while. And I definitely wished her some happiness in her private life. What concerned me right now was that this new and sudden heartthrob had been found at a midweek, all-night poker game—not an inspiring sign.

I hoped she knew what she was getting into, and made a mental note to discreetly keep tabs on her, as both a boss and a friend.

Chapter Three

It was four o'clock when Patrick Mason showed up from the Agency of Natural Resources, looking tired and a little bored, as if reluctantly prepared for yet another delicate jurisdictional dance with a hypersensitive police department. Traditionally, cops can't get rid of hazardous materials cases fast enough. But possession of any case is instinctively territorial in this profession, so yielding control—even of something he doesn't want—can sometimes stick in the point man's craw.

I therefore did my best to set all such misgivings to rest, meeting Mason out in the hallway by the dispatch window where he'd announced himself. "Thanks for getting here so fast. I'm looking forward to working with you," I said, shaking his hand warmly.

Although seemingly in his twenties, with a smooth, pink face and enviably thick black hair, he had the look of a man who'd been sweet-talked before.

He raised his eyebrows slightly. "You are?"

I had been assigned to enough special units in my time to appreciate the skepticism. I smiled at him. "You can draw your own conclusions later." I motioned toward the door he'd just used and brandished the overcoat I was carrying in my hand. "We might as well start with the truck. It's still parked where we found it."

We traded small talk on the drive to Bickford's, and I discovered that Pat Mason had much the same background ascribed to his much-maligned colleagues on the nonenforcement side of ANR—privileged upbringing, environmental studies in college, some Greenpeace-style early political activism. Yet he held those very colleagues largely in contempt. He described them as gung-ho at inventing new rules and regs, tucked away in their offices but having no idea how or whether those edicts were working—and having little sympathy for the tiny squad trying to enforce them. I also found out he was in his late thirties and had been investigating for ANR for over ten years. He'd just been transferred from the north of the state, which explained why we'd never met.

Mason brightened when we pulled up next to the battered Mack truck, however, seeing in its appearance, I guessed, something of what a doctor must detect in a sick patient—the opportunity to get down to some real work.

"How long's it been here?" he asked, reaching into his back seat and pulling out a bulging canvas briefcase.

"Several days. We don't know for sure."

We slid out of the car's warm embrace and approached the truck. "You know why it was abandoned?"

"It broke down."

We both stopped by the puddle under the Mack's rear gate, where Mason, apparently unimpressed by the sharp odor, crouched down, placed his case on the ground beside him, and opened it up. Inside were a variety of vials and small bottles, stoppered test tubes, and packs of swabs. He rummaged among them, selecting what he needed, and collected a sample from the dark ooze before him.

After several minutes of this, he rose and glanced up at the dump body's rim. "Anyone been inside that?"

"We looked over the headboard from the cab, just to see what was there. That's as close as any of us wanted to get."

Mason smiled grimly and returned to his car. "Smart."

He quickly outfitted himself in a billowy white jumpsuit, booties, gloves, and a respirator, speaking as he did so. "Pretty toxic stuff, so far. Probably a cocktail mix of solvents, oils, and God knows what. The lab boys'll have to sort it out. My guess is it was either in drums or more likely, crushed bales, which would explain how it got mixed together. Course, some of it's just old-fashioned engine oil. It's that time of year."

"Meaning what?" I asked.

"When they carry these loads in winter, a lot of it sticks to the bed if they don't coat it with oil. Even these idiots know enough not to want to wade in there kicking it loose."

He finished suiting up and waddled like an albino penguin back to the truck. With surprising dexterity, he scaled its side, paused on the rim, and vanished from view. I heard him land with a hollow, resonating thud on the inside.

"You okay?" I shouted, worried about the oil he'd mentioned.

His voice sounded distant and muffled through the respirator. "Okay."

Half an hour later, from the relative warmth of Pat Mason's car, I saw him reappear, his white suit smeared and dripping, holding several more samples in his fist. He disrobed standing on a small cloth square, and then stuffed both the square and his suit into a clearly labeled, red plastic bag, which he carefully stowed in his trunk.

"What's the verdict?" I asked him as he went through this much-rehearsed ritual.

"Well, whoever they are, they're guilty as sin. They even had remnants of medical waste back there—worth its weight in gold when it comes to disposing it. And I was right about the load being baled. That's why there was so much leakage. They bundle up all sorts of junk—construction debris, motors full of PCP, medical waste, you name it, and then they pour additional liquid waste all over it. During the trip, it either gets absorbed, drips out the back unnoticed except by the poor bastard tailgating, or simply evaporates into the wind."

"Where do they get it?" I asked, not having had to deal much with this type of crime. Brattleboro was considered a poor dumping spot, eighty percent of Vermont being sparsely populated and covered with forestland.

"Surprisingly, it's often from legitimate sources," he explained, storing his collection of samples into his canvas case. "Places like hospitals and construction sites get contacted by supposedly legit haulers. They might do a cursory check of the hauling license and paperwork, but they don't know how to tell a fake from the real thing. So they pay whoever it is a huge amount of money—in perfectly good faith."

"What kind of money?"

He paused, stretched, and looked up at the gray clouds overhead. So far this winter, it hadn't snowed once. "Well, let's see. One case we worked on not too long ago had a transfer station sending roll-offs to a construction site at fifteen hundred dollars a pop. When the station took back the full roll-offs later, they separated the contents, made money turning lumber into illegal bark mulch, which they dyed dark brown and sold to gardening supply stores, and more money on the scrap metal, which they sold legitimately. The rest they had trucked off, paying six hundred per roll-off, except that since the contents of each container had by now been compacted, they could fit the equivalent of maybe seven roll-offs into a single truck, which brought the total paid to the trucker to around forty-two hundred. That trucker in turn added to his profit by picking up some liquid waste, which he cocktailed into the load he already had, and then he cruised around till he found a recipient—in this case a landowner—hungry enough that he didn't care he was filling his water table with pure shit. The landowner got two hundred a load. The trucker pocketed the rest. Everybody came out with a lot of spare change, most of it tax-free."

"Except the landowner," I said.

Mason laughed. "Don't kid yourself. The one I'm talking about made forty thousand dollars in two months, just for standing by his back gate in the middle of the night with a flashlight in his hand. This doesn't happen just every once in a while. It's an ongoing business."

I pulled the scrap of paper I'd found in the truck cab from my pocket, now encased in transparent plastic. "This may be just what you're after, then. Directions to a farm near here. It was wedged between the seat cushions."

He took it from me and studied it closely. "You know this place?"

"I've driven by it. I don't know the owner. You up for a visit?"

Pat Mason smiled, returning the scrap of paper. "With you along as backup, sure. Some of these guys can get a little testy."

I circled around to the car's passenger side. "My pleasure."

We headed north on Route 5, out of Brattleboro and toward the Dummerston town line. Technically, I might have contacted the county sheriff to let him know I was stepping onto his turf, but—also technically—this was now an ANR investigation, and I was going along by invitation, which, since any certified police officer in Vermont has jurisdiction throughout the state, I could do with a clear conscience.

"Do you think what you just described is what we're looking at here?" I asked Mason, as we exchanged the congestion of the Putney Road for the gentle curves of its extension into the countryside.

"Gauging from the age and shape of the truck, I'd say it's something more low-key—something like what another bunch was doing till we nailed 'em last month. Rented a U-Haul truck, got paid by local gas stations to get rid of their excess used tires—at two bucks per—and either paid someone fifty dollars to absorb it all, or—and this is how we found them through the paper-work they left behind—rented a storage unit, filled it with the tires, and walked away with over a thousand bucks in profits.

"Given the load I just sampled, though, I'd say we're

dealing with someone working between those two extremes, where the money's in the midrange. Which still ain't too bad, by the way—medical waste is more expensive than low-level nuclear stuff nowadays. I know one legitimate operator who gets about five hundred dollars to dispose of a single fifty-gallon drum of it. Even cocktailed, there might've been several of those drums in that truck."

We ended up on a dirt lane, winding up a steep hill with woods on one side and fields on the other. Vermont is one amazing, lumpy crazy quilt of highways, roads, paths, and trails, all heading off somewhere, often with authority, sometimes just to peter out for no apparent reason.

In this case, we came to a gate held shut by a piece of wood stapled to a loop of barbed wire. I got out, let Mason drive through, and closed the gate behind us. Over the top of a cleared hill and to the right eventually appeared a broken-back barn with one wall caved in, standing drunkenly next to a sagging wooden house that seemed to be sinking into the earth beneath it.

A bent, leathery man emerged from the house as we approached, our car slowly lurching over the pits and ruts of what was little more than a grassy path by now.

He waited for us to get out of the car, his gnarled hands empty by his sides, a mournful, bitter look on his face.

We both showed him our credentials. I let Mason do the talking.

"I'm Patrick Mason, of the Agency of Natural Resources Enforcement Division. This is Lieutenant Joe Gunther, of the Brattleboro Police. Could we have a few words with you?"

The man paused before answering, looking disgustedly from one of us to the other as if deciding who was the lower life-form. "You already have."

"You own this property?" Mason asked, unfazed.

"Not if you count the bank."

"How many acres do you have?"

"Hundred seventy."

"All under cultivation?"

"Some."

"But not enough." Mason assumed. "Must be tough to make ends meet."

The farmer didn't answer, but his expression made it clear he wasn't in the mood for sympathy.

"What's your name?"

"Norm Blood."

"Well, Mr. Blood, we'd like to see where you're letting those trucks dump their loads, especially the one about four or five nights ago."

His tone of voice did the trick—as if this conversation were just the latest in a long string they'd already had on the same subject. It left no room for guile.

Norm Blood shifted from anger to resignation. "You bastards. What do you give a damn?"

Mason, unrepentant, merely answered, "We can use my car."

I placed my portable radio on the kitchen table without a sound, as quiet as I'd been while negotiating the building's collection of locks. The security lights had come on when I'd nosed into the driveway, as always, but Gail's office faced in a different direction, and from the lack of any sounds upstairs, I assumed she hadn't noticed.

I was saddened by the small surge of relief that gave me. There had been a time when I'd have pounded upstairs to find out what she was up to, or when she'd have kept an ear peeled for my arrival, so we could share a late-night snack.

But there'd been little of that lately. The early novelty of living together had fallen prey to a distracting metamorphosis I wasn't sure she'd even noticed.

Gail and I had met more years ago than I could remember, at a political rally for one of our Washington senators. She'd been an enormously successful Realtor for years by then—a big change from the New York hippie who'd come to Vermont to explore her soul in a marijuana daze. But the transition hadn't undermined her fundamental beliefs. She'd maintained an ideological anchor line to her wealthy, liberal upbringing, getting on the boards of most of the left-leaning nonprofit organizations dedicated to salvaging society's downtrodden. In fact, her hooking up with me had struck most of her friends as consorting with the enemy.

But we had made a good pair, despite our difference in years, backgrounds, experiences, and goals—a weirdly successful catamaran of a couple, demonstrated by the fact that for years we'd comfortably lived apart, while retaining the same chemistry that drew most couples under a shared roof.

I walked through the dark, silent house—it was almost ten o'clock by now—and settled onto the living room couch, my feet on the coffee table, my head against the cushions, looking out onto a moon-bathed wooden deck with a tree through its middle, stars glimmering through its skeletal branches. A tableau in variations of wintry blue—freezing cold.

Gail had been raped a few years ago. The man responsible had been caught, and Gail had weathered the emotional and psychological upheaval with her usual levelheaded strength, bartering for her sanity and survival with a carefully considered array of needs, wants, and hopes. She'd traded her physical independence for the security of living with me, her freewheeling lifestyle for an assortment of alarm systems. But she'd also examined what she'd done with her life, and had come to some major decisions—dusting off a law degree she'd never utilized, passing the Vermont bar, and becoming a deputy state's attorney. What had started as an extraordinary reaction to a traumatic loss had led to a driving ambition to do more than make money and sit on the boards of well-meaning groups. It had ignited a desire to reinvent herself.

I had rarely seen her more self-fulfilled. Working for the SA, swamped daily with cases, sorting through the lives clogging the legal system, she was discovering things about herself she'd never expected. Her brain had become adrenalized, and despite the long hours, the grueling pace, and the depressing nature of many of her cases, she was thriving—confirmed in the choices she'd been forced to make.

But I'd been sensing a drag line threatening this resurrection—the slow metamorphosis I was assuming she hadn't noticed yet. To my sorrow, I was also pretty confident that when the time came, she'd be strong enough to recognize it for what it was, and leave it behind.

That drag line was me, of course. Older, less driven, not as bright or quick on my feet as she, I was one of the few remaining things she'd have to shake loose if her momentum were to be preserved. I'd come to believe we'd become each other's best friend, and didn't expect that to end. But our history together had rarely been conventional, and now that it *had* been that for

the few years we'd shared this house, I didn't expect
it to last. She was slowly drifting off, as yet unaware,
and I was sadly watching—pain laced with relief—as
the gap inched even wider.

Not that such insight was helping me prepare for
the inevitable, of course. I was keeping my mouth shut,
hoping against the mounting evidence that I was making this whole thing up.

I rose from the couch, resolved to stop these self-
eroding reflections, and went upstairs.

I found her as I often did, half buried in a huge
armchair, surrounded by paperwork in a small office
down the hall from our bedroom. She tilted her face
back to receive a kiss and smiled at me, her eyes warm.

"You must be bushed."

"I could do with some sleep," I admitted, settling
on the floor opposite her, my back against the wall. I
thought she looked beautiful, her hair tangled, the reading light next to her throwing the angles of her face
into relief.

"I heard about it in the office. It sounded horrible."

"Not too bad, really. The train did such a job on
him, there wasn't much left."

"Any leads yet?"

I shook my head. "I'm oh-for-two today. Had an illegal dumping case that came up empty, too. We got
the guy who received the stuff—filled a whole ravine
with all sorts of poison, over several years—but he
says he doesn't know who delivered it. He's an older
man, in lousy health, trying to hang on to a family
farm on the skids. I'd love to cut him a deal so we
could swim upstream and nail the people behind it, but
I don't think it'll happen."

"Is he too scared to talk?" Gail asked, her professional curiosity stirring.

"I don't think so. The dumping was always at night. He never knew any of the drivers. Sometimes didn't even see them. And the arrangements were made on the phone. He's just the one left holding the bag, pure and simple."

I rubbed my eyes and stood back up, heading for bed. "It's not up to me anyway. It's an ANR case now. And maybe we'll get a lead on the train track guy from the medical examiner tomorrow—either that or a witness we haven't talked to yet. It's still pretty early."

I paused at the door by her chair and looked down at her. "Something interesting did come up, though. Kunkle claims Sammie's fallen for someone she met during the canvass."

Gail smiled. "It's about time. You know him?"

"No," I admitted. "I'd like to, though. Be interesting to see who could turn her head so fast, after all this time."

Gail looked reflective and echoed my own concerns. "Yeah. Does seem a little unlikely. Hope she's thinking straight."

I kissed her again and told her I'd see her later in bed. She said she'd be done in a while. Then I wandered down the darkened hallway, mixed feelings buried deep, hoping against odds I was wrong, and wondering how much time I had left.

Chapter Four

The Retreat Meadows are one of Brattleboro's most attractive misnomers. Meadows no longer, they are actually a single large body of shallow water where the West River spills into the Connecticut on the northern edge of downtown.

There had been meadowland there once, of course, but a downstream dam built years ago had raised both rivers and forced the floodplain to forever submerge. The Retreat part of the name came from the facility overlooking the water—a highly regarded psychiatric and addiction treatment center that looked more like a small college than a place for those in crisis.

The Meadows are quite extensive, dotted with islands, fringed with reed banks, and looking for all intents and purposes like a lake of ancient lineage. They are also one of Brattleboro's primary attractions, popular in the summer for boating and fishing, and frequented in winter by skaters and a haphazard village of ice fishing shanties.

Ice fishing is one of those peculiar northern pastimes, born of necessity and maintained through habit.

Once in a long while, someone will actually drill a hole, plant a stool by its edge, and drop in a line, utterly dependent on good weather and thick clothing. The standard, however, has moved beyond such a primitive approach. Shanties, most often home-built, occupy a sliding scale of sophistication, from surrounding the fisherman on his stool with four plywood walls and a roof, to giving him a wood-burning stove, a stereo system, a wooden floor, a cot, and several windows to enjoy the view outside. Many men claim their shanties, and the vast amounts of time they spend in them, have enhanced the serenity of their marriages.

I'd been told it was just such a man I was to visit.

Sammie had put me on to him, he being one of her missing potential witnesses. His wife had been instructed to tell him to call us when he came in. Whether she had and he hadn't, or whether he'd simply never returned home, I wasn't above making house calls on a sheet of ice.

His refuge wasn't hard to find—small, red, with a shed-type roof and a crescent moon carved in the door. No windows. "Just like an outhouse," as his wife had said.

I knocked on the rattly door, conscious of how quiet it was out in the middle of the lake, the town's heartbeat reduced to a muted, distant hum. I was unsure how it felt exactly—either like being among a scattering of chess pieces on an enormous pale board, or, paradoxically, being a bird in flight. The unadulterated distance from the shore and all it represented made me feel strangely remote—a thousand feet above the surface, hovering over a cloud.

"Who is it?" The voice emanating from the moon was low and throaty, as if the man inside had a cold.

"Mr. Renaud? It's Joe Gunther. Brattleboro Police," I said softly, aware of the shanties nearby leaning slightly toward us, listening in.

"For Christ's sake."

The door flew back on its leather hinges, almost knocking me over. My feet skittered on the smooth ice as I regained my balance. Edward Renaud stood before me, unapologetic, filling the narrow doorway with a huge, bulbous frame, clad entirely in black-and-red-checked wool, including a hat with earflaps.

"I got a license."

"I'm sure you do," I said, extending a hand. "I'm not here about that."

He took hold of my hand with the tips of his blunt fingers, as if cutting down on the amount of washing he'd have to do later.

"I was wondering if I could ask you about last night," I added.

He looked at me for a moment and then stepped back into the gloom of the shanty. "I gotta watch the line."

I crossed the threshold into a small, dark, curiously comforting space and closed the door behind me, less for privacy and more to sample the environment this man so obviously enjoyed.

A narrow bench ran the length of three of the shanty's walls. Renaud's massive bulk filled one side entirely. I settled gingerly near the door, feeling dwarfed. The fishing hole between us was black and mysterious, but the ice around it glowed softly with the prismed morning sun, filling the tiny space with a faintly religious aura.

"It's nice in here," I commented.

"I like it." Renaud had the voice of someone whose

lungs are never totally free of fluids. Judging from his appearance, I had no doubt his heart was running on reserve.

"You were home last night?"

"Yeah."

"Did you see anything unusual out your back window, around one in the morning?"

"Who says I did?"

I couldn't decide if he was being coy for the hell of it, wanted me to rat on his wife, or if he was genuinely concerned someone might've seen him and wished him ill. In any case, I got the feeling he knew exactly what I was after.

I tried for neutrality. "We're asking everyone in your neighborhood."

Given my doubts, his response couldn't have been more bland. "Yeah, I did. Car came up along the tracks. Three guys did something around the side I couldn't see, and then they left."

"Could you see what they were up to?"

"No. A corner of the building's in the way. I could only see half the car."

"So you heard about it later?"

"My wife told me somebody got squashed by the train."

"What was it that caught your eye? And what were you doing up that late anyhow?"

"Taking a leak. Their lights were off. Seemed funny."

I hoped he'd been playing me like a fish from the start. "Did you get a good look at the car?"

"Dark blue Crown Vic. Four-door," he said without hesitation. "Maybe mid-nineties."

"And a license plate?"

"Only half of one. PCH. Made me think of perch."

He pointed to the hole in the ice, smiling slightly in triumph, feeling suddenly generous. "Like them down there. I saw it 'cause the car drove toward me when it left, and I could just make out the first half. The rest was numbers, but that's all I could tell."

"Did you see any of the men?"

He shook his large head. "Too dark."

I stood up reluctantly, seduced by the shanty's tranquillity, and pushed the door open to the now blinding light. "Thank you, Mr. Renaud. You've been a big help."

He stayed still, his eyes fixed on the hole. "Sure."

I gently closed the door so as not to disturb his meditation any further.

"Jesus H. Christ."

I entered our detective bureau from the small conference room next door. Willy Kunkle, feet up on his desk, newspaper across his lap, was shaking his head in disgust. Tyler was sitting at an adjacent workstation, typically not saying a word.

"Frigging politicians," Willy continued. "Never miss a chance to get some mileage off somebody else's misery."

I hesitated to ask, not being overly fond of such conversations, but then figured it might be worse if I ignored him. "What's up?"

"You know that cluster fuck they had up north, where the kids got whacked? Now the governor and our own Jim Reynolds are jumping up and down, claiming *something's got to be done,* quote-unquote. God help us. They're babbling about maybe the whole system needs to be changed."

Jim Reynolds was a local attorney trying to make his mark as a state senator. Gail liked him and thought he might go places. I agreed with his general philosophy, but he didn't impress me much otherwise—there was too much calculation deep in his eyes to make me think his own self-interest didn't count above all else.

Which is what made Kunkle's comment that much more interesting. "What whole system?"

"You and me—I quote, 'Governor Howell and Commissioner of Public Safety Stanton have asked Senator Reynolds to be the point man on a series of public hearings concerning the feasibility and advisability of revamping Vermont's entire law enforcement structure.' "

Kunkle tossed the paper onto the tabletop. "Howell's also quoted asking why, if New York City has eight million people and two police forces, does Vermont, with one-fifteenth the population, have some sixty-eight different police agencies?"

I paused at my office door. "That's not such a dumb question."

Kunkle opened his mouth to respond, but then closed it when Tyler said quietly, "Reynolds was in the dailies week before last."

We both looked at him. The dailies are the reports filed in the computer by all shift officers, for the edification of the rest of us. They cover everything from homicides to stray animals and allow us to share the town's vital signs.

"Why?" I asked him.

"His office was broken into. Nothing missing, according to him. A patrol passed by the back door in the middle of the night and saw it had been jimmied. They probably scared away whoever it was."

Neither one of us had anything to say to that.

"Is Ron around?" I asked instead.

"Not yet," Willy answered, as Tyler lapsed back to contemplating his paperwork. "He's got the late shift again."

I handed Willy a slip of paper with "PCH" written on it. "That's a partial plate on a late-model, dark blue Ford Crown Victoria. When he gets in, see if he can get DMV to chase it down, will you?"

Kunkle looked at it appraisingly. "This the car from last night?"

"According to Edward Renaud." I turned to J.P. "You get anything like tire marks or anything from near the railroad tracks?"

He frowned. "Nope. Looks like they came, they dumped, and they left without a trace. I tried collecting enough of the skull to get an idea what the guy looked like, but I didn't get far. I shipped the pieces up north anyway—let them play with it. I was hoping for a finger at least, but the train really did a job. His hands couldn't have been better positioned. I looked all over the place. The only angle I got left is to check local dog owners—see if some pooch brought home a little tidbit."

Kunkle dropped his legs to the floor. "God Almighty, J.P. You ought to get out more. I'm going for coffee."

I retreated to my office, an eight-foot-square corner closet with two windows looking onto the parking lot and a third separating me from the squad room. Tyler followed me in with a sheet of paper in his hand.

"This was faxed in from the ME's office early this morning. A complete report's coming by mail."

I took it from him and glanced at the illegible signature at the bottom. "Hillstrom didn't do it?" I asked, slightly disappointed.

"On a teaching sabbatical for the year. That's Bernie Short."

"Okay. Thanks."

Bernard Short was Beverly Hillstrom's relatively new deputy. A nice guy and a good pathologist, he hadn't yet instilled in me the trust I had for his boss. Hillstrom and I went back a long way, and we fed each other's mania for scratching at the details, regardless of protocols, cost overruns, or time allotments. From what I'd been told, it wasn't a relationship she shared with many others, which made me all the more grateful for the attention.

I scanned the preliminary report with limited expectations and was therefore doubly surprised by its contents. I reached for the phone and dialed the ME's office in Burlington.

"Hey, Bernie, how're you holding up?" I asked him, once Short had been put on the line.

His answer was disarmingly honest. "Nervous as hell. I'm sweating bullets I'll mess something up. Good thing the office folks here know how everything runs."

"Well," I reassured him, "if the prelim you just sent me on that John Doe is any indication, you're doing all right. You wrote you found evidence of chloracne in the genital area, indicating a possible exposure to harsh, chlorine-based chemicals. Could you expand on that a little? I've got something cooking down here where that might make sense."

"Oh, sure. Actually, it kind of surprised me. It's not something you see a lot. The only other case I've ever handled was when I was doing my residency. A factory worker checked into the hospital after splashing himself with a liquid dioxin—some kind of oil. He wiped it off at the time and didn't think anything more about it, but less than a week later, he came down with severe chloracne—rash, oozing sores, skin discoloration, epidermal hardening. It was pretty nasty."

"And that's what this John Doe had?"

Bernie Short equivocated a little. "He had chloracne. I don't know how he got it. I did look at his sebaceous glands under the microscope. They were hardened, which fits the scenario, and his liver showed signs of degeneration. I've ordered a special tox scan, so we should know for sure in a few weeks."

I quickly reread the report in my hand. "You also mention telltale bruising in the left scapular area. What's that about?"

His enthusiasm picked up immediately. "That was pretty neat. I'm looking forward to showing it to Dr. Hillstrom when she gets back. When I rolled him over, I noticed a very mild discoloration just below the left shoulder blade. Usually, you just note something like that—get it in the record. But I wanted to try something Dr. Hillstrom had mentioned. Bruising is bleeding under the skin, of course, but if the blow's perimortem—around the time of death—the blood doesn't have time to spread out and make that characteristic blue-black appearance. So I cut around what little bruising I could see and peeled the outer layer of skin back. There I found a near-perfect footprint. I took a picture of it—it'll be in the full report."

"Nice work, Bernie," I said with genuine warmth. "I hope Dr. Hillstrom gives you a gold star. By the way, were you able to pinpoint cause of death? I have witnesses who make it sound like he might've been dead before the train hit him."

The hesitation on the other end told me I'd pushed

him too hard, which I regretted, given what he'd just delivered.

"Those are actually two questions in one," he answered gamely, though his disappointment was obvious. "And I'm afraid you won't be able to do much by either one of them. *Cause* of death might have been anything from a baseball bat to the train, to a shotgun blast to the head—impossible to tell . . . Well," he suddenly paused, "probably not a shotgun—at least not one firing pellets. I checked the surviving skull fragments and found no sign of them. Might've been a deer slug, of course . . . Anyhow, he didn't die from whatever agent caused the chloracne. *Time* of death is a little iffy, too. My guess is that he was alive either when or moments before the train hit him—the pulpified tissue was markedly hemorrhagic, and according to your field notes, there was a lot of blood on the ground where the body was recovered."

I filled the sudden silence that followed this long-winded equivocation with, "But you're not going to commit a hundred percent to saying he died when the train hit him?"

He sounded embarrassed. "I think he did, but Dr. Hillstrom would probably insist on my sticking to the old adage, 'He died between when he was last seen alive and when he was first found dead.' I'm sorry if that's not terribly helpful."

"Don't worry about it," I told him. "I'll let the lawyers worry about that if it ever gets to court. You've been a big help."

He sounded relieved. "Okay. Well, call anytime."

"I do have one last question. In the prelim, you mention the standard 'well-nourished male, normal in overall appearance.' Would that fit the average street person?"

"Not one who'd been following that lifestyle for a while, but you got to start sometime. I just assumed he was a beginner and that the usual signs hadn't surfaced yet."

"So I wasn't out of line thinking that his clean underwear was at odds with his beaten-up clothes."

Short didn't answer for a couple of beats. "That's a discrepancy I didn't think about. His socks looked regular, too—I mean compared to some I've seen."

I smiled at the phone, childishly pleased at having a gut reaction borne out. "Good talking to you, Bernie, and thanks again."

I hung up and shouted into the squad room, "Is Ron in yet?"

Klesczewski appeared still wearing his coat. "Morning. You bellowed?"

I glanced at the new phone on my desk. We'd been equipped some time ago with a new communications system, including voice mail, intercom, and a half dozen other features I hadn't bothered to learn. Typically, J.P. and Ron had mastered it overnight, Willy and I had barely acknowledged its arrival, and Sammie was somewhere in between.

I gave him an apologetic look. "Sorry. Old habit. I just talked to the ME. Our John Doe was exposed to some nasty chemical shortly before he died. It didn't kill him, but it did screw him up—running sores and all." I handed him Bernie's preliminary report. "Dr. Short called it a dioxin. You hear about that abandoned truck at Bickford's?"

His eyes widened. "Were those dioxins, too?"

"Could be. Contact Pat Mason at ANR and tell him

we may have found a connection to his case. Also, if their lab wants to compare what he found in the truck bed to the clothes the ME sent to the state forensics lab, they might find something—unless, like we think, his clothes were switched before he was killed."

Klesczewski nodded. "Will do."

"Short also said he lifted a footprint from the dead man's skin. He was pretty enthusiastic about it. If it's as good as he says, maybe we could use it as evidence later. Did Tyler tell you about the partial license plate Renaud claimed he saw?"

"Yeah. I was just about to call DMV about it." He hesitated, and then added, "Willy also told me about the governor's plan to overhaul law enforcement."

I looked at him more closely, surprised by the change of subject. "I think it was vaguer than that. Wasn't he talking about floating the idea at a few public hearings first, using Reynolds as a bird dog?"

"I suppose. Still, it's a pretty radical idea, isn't it?"

In several ways, Ron Klesczewski was the youngest member of the squad, although Sammie was his junior by a couple of years. Tough in a fight, and as good as anyone I knew with a computer, a phone link, and a data bank, he remained almost endearingly innocent. It was not an affectation, but he was aware of how he projected, and had been known to use it for mileage with strangers. During interrogations, I'd seen suspects become almost eager to talk to him, figuring he needed all the help he could get.

This time, however, he was genuinely curious. "I'm not so sure it is," I told him. "Our type of law enforcement grew up in stages, on a strictly need basis. When we were all a bunch of farmers, the odd sheriff or constable was enough to do the trick, as were the small PDs later on, but now that we're seeing some of what they get every day in New York and Boston, that piecemeal kind of approach can cause problems, just like it did up north."

I was alluding to what Willy had called a "cluster fuck" earlier, which, as usual with him, was both overly blunt and entirely accurate. A man named Amos Melcourt, under investigation by one small municipal department for sexual abuse and suspected of a string of burglaries by the state police, had been visited by a part-time deputy sheriff on a third, minor violation. Inside Melcourt's house, the deputy had seen three TV sets stacked up in the living room but hadn't thought they might be hot, and therefore hadn't blown the whistle. A week later, Melcourt kidnapped and molested three children, killing two of them before being shot by police.

It had happened less than a month ago, and the finger-pointing had been escalating ever since. In point of fact, it was an outrage. The sexual abuse investigation should have been shared among all agencies, the state police's suspicions—and the list of stolen property—should have been more aggressively circulated, and that poor miserable part-time deputy should have been better trained, or at least not been made to interview someone whose malevolence he couldn't gauge.

Adding to the bureaucratic embarrassments was the revelation later that Amos Melcourt had kept a room in his house filled with pedophilic pornography, among which were photos of the three kids he later kidnapped, along with maps and a timetable of their daily routine. It had been made painfully and irrefutably clear by the press that had the deputy recognized the TVs as stolen property, a search warrant could have been issued, the secret room discovered, and the clear intent to do harm to minors established. Melcourt would now have been behind bars, instead of six feet underground, along with his two small victims.

To people like Willy, it was all water over the dam. As he regularly put it when confronted with such horror stories, "Shit happens." To me, it was a clear indication that wake-up calls like the one being issued by Governor Howell and Reynolds were both appropriate and timely.

"It's not that I think the whole system should be thrown out," I explained to Ron. "For one thing, you couldn't get rid of the sheriffs without amending the state constitution. But we do need to improve the way we keep each other informed."

"We have computer-linked data bases, like VLETS and VIBRS and the others," Ron countered.

"As long as the funding's there," I conceded. "But those computers didn't work with Melcourt. Not everyone in law enforcement's as handy as you are with those things. And a lot of the older or more conservative cops still see their turf as private property. Remember what that one sergeant said when he was asked why his department had kept their investigation of Melcourt to themselves?"

Ron nodded. "They didn't want to lose it to the state police."

"Which is exactly what should have happened. But the state police can get pretty superior, too, sometimes, going on about the traditions of the glorious Green-and-Gold. That can get under people's skin."

"They probably are the best in the state," Ron muttered, a little unhappily.

"I don't argue with that," I agreed. "And they've

been bending over backwards recently to share their assets and data, but that hasn't always been true. Years back, one of their people told the Senate Government Operations Committee on the record that all sheriffs should be abolished and that all local cops were wood-chucks. Ancient history now, and just one jackass's opinion, but that kind of crack doesn't easily fade away. And when you're the biggest guy in the schoolyard, it's usually smart to be the most generous—unfortunately, that's a hard lesson to learn."

We were both silent for a moment, Ron absorbing what I'd just said, and I embarrassed for running my mouth. I hadn't realized until then how the Melcourt mess had gotten under my skin. Subconsciously, I adopted Willy's attitude of simply being thankful it hadn't been us caught in the limelight. But Ron's curiosity had forced me to admit that some kind of overhaul was in fact past due.

I glanced out the window at the cold, gray sky, for-getful of Ron still standing awkwardly in the doorway—suddenly aware that another bulwark I counted on for stability was threatening to shift.

That Gail's gradual evolution would cost me her company was no more assured than that the governor and his pet senator would put an end to my job, but the possibilities were there, palpably close, and they filled me with something akin to fear.

Chapter Five

Investigations, even headline grabbers like a man being hit by a train, proceed at a curiously slow pace. Trained as we are by television and the movies, we expect things to move at breakneck speed and for things like lab reports and forensics analyses to appear on demand.

They don't.

There are certain things that happen quickly, of course. The scene is thoroughly picked over, all witnesses located and interviewed, all evidence processed and forwarded appropriately. But then—frustratingly—you sometimes have to stop and wait, with all your instincts receptive, like a hunter in the forest outwaiting the game he knows to be standing stock-still nearby.

Such a pause occurred during the two days following our discovery of the bum on the tracks. Matching the chemicals from the abandoned truck to the tox scan being done on his blood was going to take time, as were the variety of tests J.P. had ordered on the odds and ends he'd found at the scene. That we were prepared for. Running "PCH" through the computers at

Motor Vehicles and not getting a hit was much more frustrating.

As was searching for anything more about the three men who had dumped the body.

I put Willy in charge of beating the bushes on that one, not only because it was his particular expertise, but also because Sammie, for the first time ever, called in sick.

I called her at home as soon as I heard, since along with everyone else I assumed only death could keep her off the job. She did sound terrible on the phone, and told me she'd be out for a couple of days only, but I thought she was a little cagey about the nature of her illness, and I was irritated by her reluctance to see a doctor. Since things were less than frantic at work, however—for the moment—I decided not to pursue it. Considering all she'd given this department, I had little cause for complaint, and God knows she had sick days due. But I was suspicious about what was really going on, especially since Kunkle, after I asked him what he knew about it, gave me an angrier-than-usual brush-off. Issues of privacy notwithstanding, I wasn't going to give this too much more time before asking for an explanation.

Fortunately, my attention was soon diverted. On the third day, both Tyler and Klesczewski, from different directions, kicked the investigation back into motion.

Tyler appeared at my office first, triumphantly holding a fingerprint card in his hand, which he brandished before me like an award. It was the standard form with ten available slots, one for each fingertip, with only one of the slots filled with the familiar loops and swirls of a print. "I found it," he proclaimed. "One fresh fingertip. Not a hundred yards from where the body was."

"Some animal grab it like you thought?"

"Hard to tell. And it's not guaranteed. Dumb as it sounds, we don't know for sure if it is John Doe's, and we definitely don't know if John Doe ever had his prints taken, or if the one print will be enough to bring a file out of the computer, but it's better than nothing. I sent the finger itself up to Waterbury for a DNA comparison with the body, so that can be settled at least, and I was about to see what the AFIS computer could do with that." He gestured at the card he'd placed on my desk.

I returned it to him. "Nice work. You actually been looking for that all this time?"

He smiled, a little embarrassed. "I just couldn't shake the idea there had to be leftovers somewhere. The people who put him there counted on train wheels being like meat grinders. But they're also sharp-edged and narrow, and kick up a lot of wind as they pass. I was hoping maybe all that energy moved one of the hands slightly. I couldn't believe nothing was left behind except mush."

"You did well. Let's hope it pans out."

Ron Klesczewski came next, an hour later. "Remember that off-line NCIC check I was doing on the truck's registration?" he asked, not expecting me to answer. "Well, it paid off. A month ago, a state trooper in Connecticut stopped the truck for a broken light. He let the driver go, but recorded the plate number and the rest."

He handed me a typed sheet of paper and kept speaking, "Philip Resnick, New Jersey, DOB 4/8/51. I fed the name into the computer. He's got priors for grand theft auto in his home state. Also disposing of stolen property, breaking and entering with intent to burgle, consorting with known felons while on probation, and a bunch of recent motor vehicle violations, all related to truck usage."

"Any of it tied to hazardous materials?" I asked.

"Yup. Two. But no convictions. I haven't had time to call up the locals for more details."

"So he's our guy?"

Ron's enthusiasm slipped a notch. "Maybe. The truck's leased, and it's had more than one driver. I *think* Resnick was the latest, but the NCIC check also came up with some earlier entries listing other drivers. So I can't swear to it. Not yet."

"That's okay. Let Tyler know. Maybe the name'll help him find a match to that fingerprint. Still nothing on the PCH partial Ed Renaud claims he saw?"

Ron shook his head. "I'm not sure where to go with that."

"Try changing the letters—P to B—something like that. I always think D and O look the same from a distance. Maybe Ed was slightly off somewhere."

Ron nodded and smiled ruefully. "Okay. Guess I'll find out how patient DMV is."

I sat back in my chair, feeling good. Things were coming together gradually, logically, and with the curious harmony that touched almost every case eventually. This was the point I enjoyed the most, where I still wasn't sure where we were headed, but could sense the coordinates slowly organizing, like a flight of birds gathering into a pattern.

But there were still oddities threatening the symmetry. It looked as if Philip Resnick had been the driver of the truck, that he'd recently dumped a load of toxic waste, and that he'd been contaminated in the process. But his death remained unexplained, as did the reason why those three men dispatched him the way they did, combining stealth and carelessness so randomly. I was used to the fact that most of the crooks we dealt with had low IQs, but there'd been none of the usual stupidity here.

Tyler's finding that finger was a stroke of luck, as was Ron's discovery of Resnick's identity, which the three men in the car had apparently worked hard to keep secret. But their efforts seemed contradictory. Why the elaborate charade, making Resnick into a bum and depositing him where he'd be found within hours? Why not simply tie a cinder block to his body and dump him in a pond? Or bury him in the woods?

The good feeling I'd enjoyed minutes earlier drained away. It seemed our efforts—perhaps even our successes—were being orchestrated somehow, making the man on the tracks a part of something bigger.

Maybe something ongoing.

So much for any metaphorical flock of birds uniting in perfect harmony.

The phone rang as if in response to my worsening mood.

"Joe. How're you doin'?"

Stanley Katz was the editor of the *Brattleboro Reformer,* the daily newspaper. Both he and it had gone through some serious ups and downs over the years, the fallout being that the *Reformer* occasionally read like a real newspaper's second cousin.

Which wasn't entirely the paper's fault. The police department had many of the same problems, and not just because money was tight. Brattleboro itself was partly responsible, being neither big enough to support a muscular PD and a thriving paper, nor small enough to do without them.

Also, the *Reformer* had been bought and sold a number of times over the previous decade, finally to its own employees, which is how Katz, an erstwhile police beat reporter, had ended up at the helm. Self-ownership had proved to be good in principle, injecting pride into those who wanted to live here anyway, but for the younger, more restless, upwardly mobile junior workers, there were just too many other better-paying jobs elsewhere.

Just as with us.

"I'm fine, Stanley. What's up?" I asked him, wary as always. We had disagreed often enough in the past to make a friendship unlikely, although we'd been known to cooperate, sometimes to the brink of what was legal.

"Just wondering about any movement on the dead bum case."

I doubted it was that simple—he didn't seem interested in his own question. "What did the chief tell you?"

He avoided answering. "Nothing's happened for days. People are getting curious."

"We're waiting for lab reports. Nobody we've found saw anything useful."

"I heard you've got an abandoned truck near Bickford's, too."

I hesitated. I could tell this was what he was after, which made me wonder what he already knew. It also meant we both hoped the other had something interesting to offer.

I began vaguely. "Yup—gave it to ANR. Pat Mason's handling it. Call him."

I knew he already had, and the response he'd received.

Katz tried again. "Too bad about Norm Blood. It's a guarantee he'll lose that farm."

"Probably."

"Lot of family in the area. Makes for a good local story. Sad one, though. You hear of any other local names connected to it?"

Here it comes, I thought. "Nope. We handed it over pretty fast. Haz mat's not our thing."

"How 'bout Jim Reynolds?" His words came out in a small rush, as if he'd suddenly tired of his own game.

I was startled, and didn't immediately respond. I remembered Tyler's mentioning Reynolds's office being broken into. Given his prominence as a state senator and a local attorney, I now realized I should have followed that up.

I decided to play it straight. "Can't help you, Stan. Reynolds never came up. Why?"

I could feel him wavering, wondering how much to admit. "I got a call. Guy said there might be a connection."

"To the truck or Norm Blood?" I asked.

Now I sensed embarrassment. Apparently, Katz had been hoping for a totally different kind of conversation from this.

"Neither, really, just to haz mat in general. I figured it was the truck, 'cause that's the only case I know about right now. You been working on anything else concerning illegal dumping?"

"Nope. That's it. What did your informant say, exactly?"

He sounded almost relieved to stop playing cat-and-mouse. "He didn't identify himself. He requested me by name, and asked if I'd heard Jim Reynolds was up to his waist in illegal dumping. I said no, and he told me I better hop to it or the *Rutland Herald* was going to eat my lunch—again."

The *Herald* was arguably the best paper in Vermont, and the fact that it regularly scooped the *Reformer* on Brattleboro stories was one reason it had earned that reputation. Katz himself had once defected to them briefly, just before the *Reformer*'s last owner had sold out to the employees, who in turn had wooed Stanley back.

"What did Pat Mason say?" I asked.

"A generalized 'no comment.'"

I paused again, my brain teeming with questions Katz couldn't answer. "Well, Stanley, I don't know what to tell you. We haven't heard a peep about Reynolds."

His disappointment turned to bitterness. "But you'll put me first on the phone list when you do, right?"

I considered trying to smooth his feathers. He had, after all, made me a gift of sorts. But I changed my mind. "All in good time, Stanley."

After the phone died in my ear, I dialed Tyler on the intercom.

"Who filed the report on that break-in at Reynolds's office?"

"Bobby Miller. I just saw him in the Officers' Room."

"Thanks."

I left my cubicle, crossed the building's central corridor, and entered the department's other half through an unmarked side door that led directly into the communal area we'd dubbed the Officers' Room. There were several desks scattered about, each one crowned with a beige computer. In one corner was the patrol captain's lair, glassed in like my own, in another was a fridge and a counter with a coffee machine, a microwave, and an assortment of cups, plates, and other kitchen debris. Bobby Miller, coming on duty, was loading up on caffeine.

I tapped him on the shoulder.

His face lit up when he recognized me, which wasn't guaranteed with all the uniforms, our department being pretty typical when it came to rivalry with the plain-clothes cops. "Hi, Lieutenant. How're you doin'?"

"Fine. I wondered if I could pick your brain about a call a few weeks ago."

"Sure." He finished pouring cream into his coffee and took it and a doughnut over to a small conference table nearby. "This okay?"

I took a doughnut myself and sat opposite him. "You were in on the office break-in at Jim Reynolds's, right?"

He nodded, his mouth full.

"How did that go?"

He swallowed, took a sip of coffee, and then shrugged. "Nothing much to it. I saw the back door was slightly open when I drove through the parking lot, so I called for backup. Pierre Lavoie showed up about three minutes later, and we both checked it out. The office sits by itself on a patch of lawn, with the sidewalk out front and the parking lot in back, so it didn't take much to go around the outside and see what was what.

"By that time, Sheila had joined us, so we all three went inside. As far as we could tell, things looked pretty intact. There was one filing cabinet in an inner office that had a couple of drawers open, but that was it."

"No stolen computers or radios or anything else?"

Finishing a second sip, he shook his head. "Nope. It all looked normal. We called Reynolds at home right after, so he could confirm if anything was missing. He got there about fifteen minutes later."

"Did you see anyone near the building before you noticed the door, like a lookout, or maybe the burglar pretending to be a pedestrian walking away?"

Miller looked unhappy with himself. "I thought about that later. I was coming from the west, which means I drove past the front of the building, up its far side, and then into the parking lot. If whoever was inside saw me right off, he would've had time to head out the back. I did notice a car driving down the street next to the lot, away from the main drag, but it was only after I was writing the whole thing up that I wondered where it had come from. Given the direction it was heading, I should've seen it just before I pulled in, either in my lane or approaching from opposite. So it must've been already parked on that street, waiting. I didn't think about it at the time, though, so I have no idea what kind of car it was. I just saw the taillights out of the corner of my eye."

I thought it likely he was right, but I didn't want to make him feel any worse by rubbing it in.

I moved on instead. "What was Reynolds like on the phone? Were you the one who talked to him?"

"Yeah. He wasn't happy. Kept asking if anything was missing. I told him that's why we were calling him. But he was different once he got there. After he gave the place a quick once-over, he acted like it was no big deal."

"You mention the open filing cabinet?"

"Specifically. I figured a lawyer would be more antsy about that than a missing fax machine or whatever. You want my personal opinion, he was more upset than he wanted us to know. When I first showed him the open drawers, it was like he was glued to the spot, he was so surprised. That's why his change of mood was so weird—like it was forced."

I thought for a minute about what he'd told me, allowing him time to take another bite of doughnut. After he'd finished, I asked, "Bobby, do you have any idea what was in those drawers?"

He hesitated before answering. "Not really. There wasn't much point in our poking around in them. I did take a glance, though. I think they were case files— old ones. I remember noticing that the tabs on the manila folders were bent and a little dirty, like they'd seen a lot of use. But I suppose that could be true for ongoing cases, too, considering how long it takes to get through the system . . . I guess I don't really know. Sorry."

I stood up. "Don't be. That's all I needed."

To his questioning look, I added, "His name's come up in something else. Seemed like twice in a couple of weeks was quite a coincidence."

Bobby Miller was apparently satisfied with that, since he went back to his doughnut without comment.

I, however, was more curious than ever. I doubted the Reynolds break-in was any standard smash-and-grab. The contents of that filing cabinet had to have been the motive. The question therefore became: Did the thief have time to do what he'd set out to do, or had he been interrupted prematurely? Was Reynolds's change of mood a feint, or did he see at a glance that he had nothing to fear?

Jim Reynolds had worked in this town for over fifteen years, exclusively as a criminal defense attorney. He and Gail's boss had faced off in a number of high-profile cases, and even when he'd lost—which was rare—he'd squeezed out every legal option available to him, earning him the nonflattering nickname in our office of "Robo-lawyer."

He had also become one of the town's high-profile citizens, joining the right groups, associating with the right heavy hitters, so that when he'd finally run for state senate, after brief stints on the school and select boards, both the announcement and subsequent victory had been all but preordained.

What had been surprising was how little we'd heard from him since, given the attention-grabbing foreplay. Admittedly, politicians in Vermont operate a little differently from those elsewhere. We run a true citizen-legislature, which generally only runs from January to April or May. Most of our legislators have outside jobs, since the best they can hope for as politicians, including extras, isn't much more than $13,000 a year. Only the governor, the lieutenant governor, and the speaker of the House get paid year-around.

So it's true that neither the Jim Reynoldses nor their House counterparts have the opportunities or the budgets to make the headlines their full-time colleagues do in other states. Correspondingly, because of this double existence, it is also a fact that relatively few attorneys run for state office, since it cuts so seriously into their schedules and incomes.

I'd therefore thought that having achieved what he'd wanted politically, Jim Reynolds had suddenly found himself running a part-time practice while being a part-time legislator—dividing by half any chance to be truly effective. Gail gave him more credit. She felt he was just biding his time, waiting for the right issue.

It looked like she'd been right.

He was nearing the end of his second two-year term.

Legislative sessions straddle a biennium, and this January had marked the start of the second half, called the "adjournment session." Reynolds was the chair of the powerful Judiciary Committee, but he'd failed to win the pro-tem position, which in practice is the Senate's top dog—the lieutenant governor's title of "president" notwithstanding—and I'd argued with Gail earlier that his enthusiasm might be running out.

Until Amos Melcourt had killed those two kids, of course. Now it looked like Reynolds had found himself a life raft, and with it, the backing of the governor and his head of Public Safety, Dave Stanton. Since Willy Kunkle had sourly revealed all this in the office several days ago, one of the promised public hearings on revamping statewide law enforcement had taken place in Rutland—to rave reviews. People had turned out in droves, almost every police agency had been used to mop the floor, and Reynolds was beginning to look like the spearpoint of change.

All of which reminded me of Watergate, and made me wonder if a simple botched break-in might be more than it appeared.

Chapter Six

I didn't get the chance to mull over the break-in of Jim Reynolds's office any longer than it took me to leave Bobby Miller to his doughnut, cross to my side of the building, and come face-to-face with Harriet Fritter, the squad's administrative assistant and a doting grandmother several times over. "There you are. I've been looking all over for you."

"I was in the Officers' Room—ten minutes tops."

"There's been a killing on White Birch Avenue. A woman stabbed with a knife." Her face suddenly hardened. "And a baby, too."

I squeezed her shoulder in sympathy and continued to my office to fetch my coat. "Everyone there now?"

"The first units, just barely. It came in as a missing persons first."

I returned down the hallway, struggling into my parka. "Okay. You know the drill. Round up who we need. They have a suspect yet?"

"Not that I heard."

White Birch Avenue is located in the southeast quadrant of town, a flat plateau dominated by a contrasting mixture of three cemeteries, the high school, the town garage, a sedate middle-class neighborhood, and some of the poorest housing we've got. Depending on where you are in this area, you have no inkling of the existence of its other parts, such is the division from one section to the next.

White Birch is barely a hundred yards long. Connected to South Main and dead-ending at the gates of Saint Michael's Cemetery, it is narrow and shady to the point of being overgrown, tucked away out of sight and out of the public's general consciousness. The homes along its length run from fairly run-down to flat-out decrepit. It is not at the bottom of Brattleboro's food chain, but it is not far removed.

I reached it in under four minutes.

The scene was much more active than the railroad tracks had been in the middle of the night. There, the assumption had been that a bum had committed suicide. Here, there were no doubts what had happened, and as Harriet had demonstrated, a child's involvement had cranked up emotions to the utmost. South Main Street was jammed with ambulances, squad cars, and private vehicles with either red or blue flashing lights, even though the first of these couldn't have been summoned more than ten minutes earlier, and most weren't necessary now. The late afternoon light hovered between day and night, making the colorful, pulsating display all the more festive in a world of uniform gray.

I parked at a distance and walked to White Birch, which already had yellow tape barring it from the growing crowd. I was happy things had been so quickly contained.

A young woman detached herself from the pack as

I approached—Alice Simms, the cops-'n'-courts reporter for the *Reformer*.

"Joe, any idea what happened?"

I smiled and shook my head. "Give me a few minutes. I'll issue a statement later."

I passed by her, ignored the others—an assemblage of off-duty cops, firefighters, rescue personnel, and neighborhood gawkers—and ducked under the tape.

Ahead of me the narrow street led straight to the cemetery's closed chain-link gate. One squad car and a second ambulance were parked opposite a small, dark green one-story house, sagging and stained, with a haphazard collection of junk littering its scrappy front yard. There were probably twenty thousand houses just like this one scattered all across the state.

Ward Washburn, one of our veteran patrolmen, met me on the porch.

"Who's inside?" I asked him.

"Ron, a two-woman team from Rescue, Inc., and Dave Raymo. He was first on scene." He pointed over my shoulder. "Here come Willy and Tyler."

I glanced in their direction. "Good. They do a lot of tramping around in there?"

"Not sure. I heard Ron telling 'em all to keep to a narrow path, and they're all wearing gloves."

"Okay. Make sure you get someone guarding the back, and seal the place up tight. I don't want anyone messing this up."

"What about the ME and whoever the SA sends over?"

"They should put on containment suits. By the way, you string up that police line?"

Washburn's thin, lined face allowed a faint smile. "Yeah."

"Nice job. Fast thinking."

I climbed back down the steps to greet J.P.

"Been inside yet?" he asked before I could open my mouth.

I shook my head. "I was waiting for those." I pointed at the new bag he was carrying, full of the thin white overalls, booties, and caps he was hoping we'd start wearing to keep crime scenes pristine. This was the first chance we'd had to try them out—there hadn't been any point at the railroad tracks.

He dropped the bag onto the frozen grass as I keyed the mike to my radio, simultaneously reaching for a suit. "Ron, it's Joe—why don't you get everyone out here so we can seal the scene?"

Moments later, the front door squealed open and four people stepped out—two women wearing dark blue jump suits and carrying bulky medical kits, followed by Dave Raymo and Klesczewski.

Ron indicated the two women as he approached. "Joe, this is Cindy Berger and Melissa Snow of Rescue, Inc. Melissa's a paramedic and the crew chief."

I shook hands and addressed Melissa Snow. "How did this go down?"

Dave Raymo interrupted. "I called 'em."

I didn't like Raymo much. He was more interested in the trappings of being a cop than the job itself. He had a special grip on his pistol, a fetish for tight-fitting leather gloves, a goofy haircut somewhere between a flat top and a Mohawk, and a swagger I thought grotesque for a public servant. He'd come to us from Massachusetts a half year ago, and I suspected he'd be moving on before another year went by.

"I got a call to check out a missing person complaint," he continued. "Some old lady said her daughter wasn't answering the door or the phone or anything else, and she was worried something had happened. When I got here, I looked through the windows, saw the body on the floor, called for backup and Rescue, and then we entered the premises. When the ambulance got here, I already knew they wouldn't be needed, but I thought what the hey, and had 'em check both bodies out. CYA, you know?"

There was a breeziness about his manner that made me doubt his story. "So you also found the child?" I asked, clumsily pulling the overalls on over my coat.

Raymo hesitated and finally blurted. "Yeah, I saw the crib."

Melissa Snow explained further. "I found him in the back bedroom. I noticed some toys lying around and went looking."

I glanced from one to the other, registering what wasn't being said, and decided to deal with it later. "This might sound dumb," I said to her, "but you're sure both people are dead?"

Raymo rolled his eyes. "Wait'll you see 'em."

We both ignored him. Snow answered, "The child is cold and stiff—I'm guessing hypothermia there. The woman's head is almost severed from her body, and the blood's frozen."

"Where's the victim's mother?" I asked Raymo.

He jerked his thumb at the nearest patrol car. "I put her in my unit."

"She okay?"

"Yeah. She didn't see anything—too short to reach the window. You can't see the real gory stuff from there anyhow—that's why I called Rescue. Wasn't sure she was dead."

I crossed the lawn and climbed the rickety porch

steps again, accompanied by Willy and J.P., all three of us looking like bulky ghosts. Ron stayed behind. "Did either of you touch anything inside?" I called out to both women as an afterthought.

They shook their heads, Melissa adding, "We were wearing gloves anyway."

"Okay. Thank you very much. We might be asking you for fingerprints, hair samples, and shoe impressions later. Just so you know."

As they left, I gestured to Ron. "Could you check out the mother? See how she's doing and get a statement."

He nodded as I pointed to Raymo. "Switch cars with Washburn and go back to the office to write up your report. We won't be needing you anymore."

His expression showed he took my full meaning. He turned away without comment and stalked off, stiff with anger.

Willy laughed softly. "Asshole."

I wasn't in the mood. "Then don't start acting like him."

He smiled and held the door open for me, unrepentant. "Yes, Mother. You know he's going back on patrol—show you who's boss."

"I know."

The building's interior was as cold as the outside, although much better lit. We stood in a short, narrow entrance hall as J.P. unfurled a roll of brown construction paper and began laying it before us like a red carpet, ensuring nothing of value would be picked up by our shoes and carried out of the house. It was a little compulsive, given that we were already wearing surgical booties, but he didn't get to do this often.

The woman was lying between an obviously ransacked living room and the kitchen, still as a fallen mannequin. As described by Melissa Snow, her head was almost detached, and blood surrounded her like hemorrhaged syrup. The biting cold seemed suddenly to sink in deeper.

J.P. took a series of photographs before getting to one knee, just clear of the frozen pool. "Multiple stab wounds to the chest," he reported, not bothering to look back at us, his head enveloped in vapor from his breath. "Defensive cuts to the hands and forearms. Fingernails look intact—might be some of her attacker's tissue there. Hard to tell right now." He glanced up at the walls. "Given the blood-spatter pattern, it looks like she put up a fight, but never ran. It all happened right here."

Willy Kunkle was flashing a light into the darker corners nearby. "Probably an acquaintance attack, and she was either a real slob, or somebody was looking for something."

"Any weapon?" I asked J.P., flexing my cold fingers inside their thin latex gloves.

He took a slight hop over the body into the kitchen beyond. "Nothing obvious," he said, looking around. He began taking more pictures.

Catering to his tidiness, I took the roll of paper and prodded it down the hallway to the back of the house with the tip of my white-swathed boot, leaving Willy and J.P. behind.

Past a communal bathroom and some disgorged closets, there were two bedrooms, both with lights on. One was obviously an adult's—a woman's clothing was strewn about; cosmetics, jewelry, and a hair dryer were scattered across a scarred bureau and a night table. The bed appeared permanently unmade, but again, all the drawers and closets looked like they'd been rifled. The other room was the child's. I entered it first.

The baby lay in its crib, a beaten-up hand-me-down planted in the middle of the room. Melissa Snow had implied it was a boy. Its one thin blanket appeared slightly disturbed, so I assumed for the moment she'd checked that fact out personally. The room didn't reflect any signs of care or affection. The walls were bare of decorations, even the torn-out magazine pictures I'd seen in other such homes. The blanket was dirty, as were the floor and windows, and the rest of the floor was buried under boxes, suitcases, and laundry bags, of the kind usually reserved for attics or garages—and all, as elsewhere, having clearly been tossed around. There was so much junk that the crib looked imperiled in its midst, as if four crests of rolling flotsam were about to close in on it from all sides and swallow it whole like a small boat beneath a tidal wave.

I heard heavy, hurried footsteps approaching down the hall, and turned as an out-of-breath Sammie Martens appeared at the door, still pulling her gloves up over the cuffs of her overalls.

"Sorry I'm late," she said.

I looked at her carefully and took my time responding. "I thought you were on the sick list."

Her face, already pink from the cold and exertion, deepened in color. "I'm feeling a lot better."

"Does this mean you'll be sticking around?"

She opened her mouth to answer and then paused. I could tell, however, that her immediate reaction had been anger. "Yes. Sorry if I caused any problems."

I stepped aside so she could get a full view of the dead baby. "You haven't, Sam. I just want to know if we can count on you."

This time, the anger showed. "I never let you down before."

I motioned her to approach the crib. "The paramedic thinks hypothermia. There's a wood stove in the front—probably the only source of heat. You see Ron when you came in?"

"In the unit, talking with some woman." Her eyes were fixed on the crib's contents.

I gestured up the hallway. "The victim's mother, supposedly. I'm hoping she'll know something about all this—a few names, at least." I glanced back at the baby, as peaceful as if it were still asleep, aside from a waxy pallor. "Christ. What a world," I murmured.

Sammie hesitated and then said, "I am sorry, Joe. I know I've been a little flaky."

I looked up at her, embarrassed myself. "Don't worry about it. I came down too hard on you. We can talk later. I'll leave you three to it for now and have Ron organize the canvass, neighbor interviews, record checks, and everything else. Make sure J.P. covers all the angles, okay? There's no rush. I'll make sure someone comes by later with hot coffee and something to eat."

Back outside, I stripped off my containment suit, balled it up, and stuffed it into a red garbage bag J.P. had left for that purpose. Ron got out of the car, leading a woman in her forties by the elbow.

"Lieutenant, this is June Dutelle."

I shook her hand, noticing as I did so that she seemed curiously remote from her surroundings, as if she'd been delivered to the wrong airport and couldn't speak the language. "Glad to meet you," I told her. "Sorry it's under such circumstances. Why don't we go back into the car? I'm freezing."

We all three returned to the warm embrace of the patrol car, seeing through its windows the tired old house beside us, its peeling, battered hulk flickering in the strobes like an advertisement of the grief within. From the front seat, I leaned forward and killed the flashing lights. Ron and June Dutelle were sitting in the back.

"Mrs. Dutelle was telling me," Ron began, "that she'd been having trouble locating her daughter Brenda for over a day. She didn't answer the phone, missed a date they'd set up, and didn't come to the door when Mrs. Dutelle knocked on it."

I couldn't resist smiling at his stilted use of her name, remembering Edith Rudd. "Do you prefer June or Mrs. Dutelle?" I asked her.

She smiled timidly. "June's fine. Dutelle was my husband's name."

I just barely heard Ron sigh. "When your daughter didn't answer the door, why didn't you walk in to see what was up?"

"That was a rule she had," June answered. "She set boundaries. She said that if more mothers and daughters did the same thing, there wouldn't be so much trouble between them. I was never allowed inside unless I was invited. Course, all those boundaries were for me. I never closed any doors to her." Her voice gained an edge of irritation. "Any time of night or day, I was always willing to baby-sit, sometimes with no notice at all. Brenda would just appear and drop him off, dirty diaper and all."

"She worked odd hours?"

June Dutelle laughed bitterly. "Her idea of work was to stand in line at the welfare office. This was when she wanted to see her friends and didn't want a baby hanging around her neck, ruining things."

"I take it the boy's father isn't in the picture?"

Her eyes widened. "Jimmy hasn't been near any of us since Brenda first got pregnant."

"What's Jimmy's full name?" Ron asked quietly.

"James. A. Croteau. Lived in Burlington, last I heard."

"So your daughter's name is Dutelle?"

June shook her head sadly. "Oh, no. They got married. Lasted about a month. I suppose she still is married, legally."

Ron shot me a glance at June's use of the present tense.

"This is a pretty expensive house for a single person on welfare," I noted. "Did you help her out with the rent?"

The older woman's face shut down. "You should see the hole I live in. Brenda has her own money—I don't know how. I didn't want to know."

"Who did she hang out with?" I asked.

June looked through the side window for a moment. Her voice was wistful when she answered. "I don't know that, either. Not really. Those boundaries she talked about went a long way. I was just the baby-sitter, when you get down to it."

I let her silence fill the small space inside the car, until its own weight prompted her to continue. "She has a girlfriend named Janice Litchfield. She's a wild one. I hold her responsible for most of what Brenda got into. Then there's Jamie Good, who's anything but."

Ron gave a slight shake of his head as he wrote down the names in his notepad. We all knew Jamie Good.

"The others," June continued, "I don't remember. They come and go. Most of the time, I never hear their names anyway. Janice and Jamie were the most regular. They go back years—all went to school together."

"From what you just said," I commented, "I'm guessing Brenda got herself into a jam, once or twice?"

When June Dutelle turned back to face me, her face was damp with tears. She'd gotten so practiced at suppressing her feelings, I hadn't noticed her slide from shock into grief.

"Well," she barely whispered, "I guess that's over now."

Through the rear window behind her, I saw two shadows approaching up the street. "It's okay," I said softly. "We can finish this later. Do you have someone at home to keep you company? Or someone who can stay the night?"

She nodded. "I'll be okay."

"Ron here will see about getting you home. I take it you drove here?"

"Yes."

"That's all right. We'll have someone bring your car home, too. I don't want you driving yourself right now."

"Thank you."

I slipped out of the car and met the two people I'd recognized through the window: the local assistant medical examiner, a GP in real life named Alfred Gould, and Carol Green, one of Gail's fellow deputies from the State's Attorney's office.

"Is it just my imagination," I asked her, out of earshot of the car, "or are you the only one they allow out after hours?"

She gave me a tired smile. "Just lucky, Joe. Besides, it's just barely quitting time. Is this as bad as it sounds?"

I escorted them both to J.P.'s pile of equipment. "'Fraid so, and we're doing it by the numbers, so I'd appreciate your both suiting up and staying on the paper carpet J.P.'s laid out inside."

Gould put down his bag to comply, asking, "How fresh are they?"

"A day or so. There's no heat in the house, so they're both frozen solid. The hypothesis right now is the stove died after the mother was killed. Whoever did her in may not have even known about the child till later— not that he cared even then."

Carol pulled one leg of the overalls on angrily. "Yeah, well, if you guys catch the son-of-a-bitch, he's going to find out we don't give a damn what he knew or didn't know. He's got two murders on his hands, like it or not."

"This blind justice talking?" I asked, half in jest, a little startled by her vehemence.

"Not if I can help it," she answered.

Chapter Seven

The *Reformer*'s Alice Simms was going to hold me to my promise. She intercepted me as I tried to duck under the police line as far from the thinned-out crowd as I could get.

"Walk you to your car, Joe?"

"Sure. Still too early to say much, though."

"Try me."

I gave her little more than what she and a few hundred other eavesdroppers had already heard over the scanner. "Appears to be a double homicide, woman and infant, unknown manner and cause, unknown identities, unknown time, unknown suspect or suspects."

"You find a weapon?"

"Not so far, but we've barely begun looking—don't want to rush things," I added, hoping the philosophy might be catching.

It wasn't, of course. "Was it a gun, a knife? What?" She was walking and writing in a notepad at the same time. Her head ducked down, her hair covering her face, she was headed straight for a telephone pole. I grabbed her elbow and guided her clear. "Watch your step."

She looked up quickly. "Could it be a murder/suicide?"

I conceded that much. "Not the way it's looking right now."

"So, a double murder."

"I didn't say that."

She stopped and dropped her hands to her sides. "Well, say something, for crying out loud. Whose house is it, at least?"

I shook my head. "You're moving too fast." I checked my watch. "You've got five hours till deadline, more if you push it. Let me do the basic homework, so we don't both look like idiots later, okay? I'll call you, I promise."

She grudgingly went along with it, although I knew she'd pursue other sources in the meantime. She snapped her pad closed and let me leave in peace.

Heading back to the office, however, I decided to test Willy's theory about Dave Raymo, who was supposed to be laboring in front of a keyboard, writing his report. I reached for the radio under my dash and called him up.

He answered tersely, his tone of voice betraying his surprise at being found out so quickly.

"Meet me at the bottom of Main and Canal," I told him. "The Food Co-op parking lot."

Predictably, I got there first, although I didn't doubt he was waiting around a nearby corner, convincing himself that such a taunt would successfully salvage some juvenile pride—it was the kind of head game he held too dear. I merely left the engine running, thankful for a good heater, and watched the early evening crowd slowly converge on the co-op.

He arrived eventually, his left elbow incongruously resting on the driver's side windowsill—a casual look except for the obvious fact that he must have been freezing half to death.

He rolled to a stop so that our windows were opposite one another, forcing me to expose myself to the cold as he'd chosen to.

"What's up?" he asked, his voice flat, adding with feigned nonchalance, "I had something I had to do before headin' back to the barn."

"I don't think you want to be feeding me an attitude right now."

He pursed his lips and kept silent.

"Maybe you can use your screwing around to some benefit," I told him. "Before the night's over we'll have interviewed the Rescue crew, our own dispatch, the backup team you called, and all the neighbors on that street. We'll have a pretty good idea what really happened when you first showed up. So now's your chance—you want to change your story before it's too late and you've made it part of the record? You told me you called Rescue and backup, and then 'we' went in. Who did you mean by 'we'?"

He knew there was only one way out. "I went in alone," he confessed angrily. "I didn't wait for the others. I thought the woman might need help in there. I didn't want to waste time."

"What about the Rescue crew? Why weren't they warned it was a homicide—to stay at a distance?"

His voice climbed a note, just shy of a whine. "They showed up too fast. I was still checking the house out. I had to make sure it was safe."

"So they just walked in, totally unaware?"

After a pause, he admitted, "Yeah—just as I was checking out the kid's room. That's why I missed him. It didn't even look like a nursery—I thought it was all storage."

I sympathized with him there, at least. "You know what might have happened if someone had been waiting inside—to you and the Rescue folks both?"

A flash of irritation crossed his face. "I know, I know. It won't happen again."

I resisted the urge to reach out and twist his ear like a child's. "That's between you and your supervisor. I want to know exactly what you saw when you entered that building."

"What're you after?" he asked suspiciously.

"What you're going to be putting into your report, Dave. The truth. What you saw, smelled, heard—everything that happened."

He scowled, which came easily to him. "I didn't hear or smell anything. Everyone was dead. And I didn't touch anything."

"How 'bout the lighting? Did you or the Rescue people turn on any lights to see better?"

"No."

"Not even the baby's room? Why have a bright overhead light on in a room with a sleeping baby?"

All suspicion drained from his face and he shook his head. "No. That is weird. That room should've been dark. The whole place was lit up like a Christmas tree."

I put my car into gear, confirmed in my guess that the killer—or killers—had searched the place from one end to the other. "Okay, Dave. I'm glad you didn't get yourself killed—or anyone else."

The surliness returned. "Thanks," he said, and hit

the gas, squealing out of the parking lot ahead of me in some parody of male dominance.

I found a message to call Bobby Miller when I returned to the office. He was on the same shift as Raymo, and so presumably out in his cruiser somewhere. I told dispatch to let him know I was back.

The phone rang five minutes later.

"Lieutenant? Something came up this afternoon I thought you should know about. Right after I went on duty, I got a call from Winthrop Johnston. You know him? He said you were old friends."

"We are. He's a PI. Ex-state trooper."

"Right—that's what he told me. He wanted to know about the break-in at Jim Reynolds's place."

I stood without moving for several seconds, digesting this. Jim Reynolds was becoming a radar blip that wouldn't fade. "What did you tell him?"

"Nothing. I said I'd have to clear it with you. He was real nice about it. Said he understood and that he'd wait for you to call him. He made it sound like it was just a boring piece of paper shuffling he was doing, but it struck me as a funny coincidence."

"Me, too. He didn't say what he was after?"

"Nope."

I thanked him, hung up, and dialed Johnston's number from a list I had taped to my desk—not of snitches, whose names I kept more securely tucked away, but of bankers, business leaders, artists, teachers, and one private investigator—all keen observers, all well traveled, and all willing to act as sounding boards if they thought the questions I had made sense.

Winthrop Johnston, universally known as Win, had been born in Hardwick, in northern Vermont, attended the University of Vermont, and had worked with the state police for thirteen years before deciding to go independent. He'd been a PI for over a decade, working out of Putney, just north of Brattleboro, and had established a reputation as a straight arrow, walking the tightrope between actual broken laws and legal improprieties with a surefootedness often lacking in his colleagues.

He answered on the third ring.

"Win, It's Joe Gunther. Bobby Miller tells me you have some questions about Jim Reynolds."

"No," he answered carefully. "Not Reynolds. Just about the break-in at his office."

"Can I ask why you want to know?" The question wasn't as futile as it always appears on television. On TV, everything a private cop does is mantled by client confidentiality. In reality, PIs know they have to work closely with police, and also know that making an issue over trivialities is both irritating and undermining.

Johnston didn't disappoint. "He hired me to find out who did it."

"Is he missing anything?"

"Not that I know of. What was your take on it?"

I had nothing to lose by being honest with him in turn, since I had nothing to begin with, anyway. "Can't figure it out. He denied anything was missing, and we couldn't tell if anything might've been added."

Johnston sounded mildly surprised, which he may or may not have been in fact. "Like what?"

"Cute, Win. Rumor has it the man wouldn't mind being governor. *Was* anything added?"

Win chuckled, then said, "Okay, he is worried, but I don't think it's because anything happened. My guess is he hired me because he wants it to stop there. If I get lucky, I'm basically supposed to say, 'We know who you are and we know what you did,' and hope that ends it."

I took him at his word, at least for the moment. "Then I wish I could help you. Since there was nothing gone and no suspect in sight, we've pretty much dropped it. Bobby did notice a car heading off down the side street, but all he saw were taillights. His guess was he scared off whoever had broken in, and I think he's probably right."

"Okay, Joe," Win conceded after a moment. "I appreciate the help."

I sat staring at the phone for a long time after he'd hung up, remembering Stan Katz's call to me earlier, along with something Bobby Miller had told me which I hadn't passed on to Win Johnston—that the filing cabinet which appeared to have been rifled contained old, dog-eared files.

I finally shook my head and returned to the matter at hand. Jim Reynolds would have to stand in line.

I didn't lie to Alice Simms, but when I did finally call her, I figured she had about thirty minutes to write her story and still make the deadline. That didn't allow for a long question/answer session—a detail she assumed I'd planned from the start.

"You don't get public servant of the year for this," she told me testily once she got on the phone.

"You want it early and sketchy or late and fleshed-out?"

"Knowing you guys, it'll probably be late and sketchy. What've you got?"

I cleared my throat and read from the SA-sanctioned statement I'd scribbled down following our ten P.M.

squad meeting. "This afternoon, at five forty-six the Bratt PD was called to investigate a missing person complaint at the home of Brenda Croteau, aged twenty-three, living at number thirty-eight-B White Birch Avenue. The complaint had been filed by Ms. Croteau's mother, June Dutelle, also of Brattleboro. Upon seeing what appeared to be a prostrate woman through one of the residence's windows, officers entered the building and discovered Ms. Croteau's dead body, and that of her infant son, Sean. It appears right now that Ms. Croteau was the victim of a knife attack, while her son died of exposure after the home's wood stove burned out."

I stopped, hearing Alice's rapid typing in the background. "Going too fast?"

"Not hardly."

"Okay. The victim's mother stated that she'd been trying to locate her daughter for the last thirty-six hours, which lack of success stimulated her call to police. Brenda Croteau was married to James A. Croteau just over a year ago, although the couple has not lived together since before Sean's birth."

"How old was the kid?" Alice asked.

"Five months," I answered, and resumed my monotone. "Mr. Croteau is not a suspect at this time—"

"Why not?" she interrupted again.

"Mr. Croteau is not a suspect at this time," I repeated, "but police are conducting a thorough investigation, and expectations are high that a solution will be reached in due course."

"For Christ's sake. We're all going to *die* in 'due course.' What's that supposed to mean?"

I continued reading. "Several leads are being developed based on evidence left at the scene and the manner of Ms. Croteau's death. However, if anyone with knowledge of any of these individuals or of any events connected to or leading up to this crime would contact the police department, their cooperation would be greatly appreciated."

"You write all that?" she asked, sounding incredulous.

I was slightly offended. "To help you out, yes. You want to clean it up, feel free. And you can add that autopsy results will be forthcoming."

"I will. Can I ask you some questions, or is that all I'm going to get?"

"You won't get much more. What're you after?"

She laughed. "Well, for starters, what the hell happened? Was it a rape, a robbery, or what? Did she know the guy? What was she involved in that got her killed? And what about the hubby? He got ruled out pretty quick."

"Off the record, he was in Burlington, with an alibi."

"An alibi? You said the baby died of hypothermia after the stove died out, which means a lot of time's gone by between now and when she died. How could he have an alibi?"

"Again off the record, because he's in jail."

There was dead silence at the other end, followed by, "I guess that would do it. He could've hired someone."

"Okay, Alice. That's it. We'll be in touch."

I heard her say something, but didn't catch it since the phone was already halfway back to its cradle.

Gail smiled at me from across my office—about five feet. She'd dropped by to see how I was doing.

"Alice unhappy with your press release?"

I sat back in my chair and locked my fingers behind my head. "I can't blame her, but it's a catch-22. They get pissed because we're so closemouthed. We get pissed because they don't show any discretion. I know it's old-fashioned, but I keep thinking back to when people like Eisenhower could trust journalists to keep quiet about D-Day and the Manhattan Project."

"You can thank Vietnam for ending that," Gail said. "Was that really true, what you told her about wrapping things up fast because of evidence left at the scene?"

I shook my head. "No. I gilded the lily a bit there. J.P. found a bloody smudge that looked like it came from someone's knee. He also dusted for fingerprints, but it looks like half the Russian army's passed through that house. We didn't find a weapon or a nosy next-door neighbor, and we didn't get anything from the victim's mother. And you heard what I said about the hubby."

Gail frowned. "Sounds like you're up a creek."

"I doubt it," I answered. "Brenda hung out with a rough crowd. We'll get something from one of them. Generally all you have to do is ask enough questions, and sooner or later somebody spills the beans. These ain't Ph.D.'s, and there is no honor among thieves. What we're guessing is that she was fixing dinner, let her assailant in, and they got into an argument in the kitchen. There was a cutting board near where she died, but no knife. Tomorrow, when it's light, we'll comb the neighborhood. I'm hoping we'll find it in the bushes somewhere, complete with prints. If past history's any guide, I won't have lied to Alice about wrapping this up soon."

Gail gave me a long, considered look. "I'd hate to see you eat those words."

I shrugged. "I might. Alice asked if hubby could've hired a hit man. It could get complicated. This is only if the pattern stays typical."

Gail changed the subject. "You heard from Sammie?"

"Yeah. She's back on board. Turned up all out of breath at the scene. Pissed me off, to be honest. If the call had been for a cat up a tree, she'd still be on the sick list. I was going to talk to her about it."

"Don't."

"Why not?"

"She's earned the privilege to have a private life. Everybody else has one, goes on vacations, takes recreational sick days—except you, maybe. She's never done any of those. She's just becoming normal—and hoping her male colleagues will allow her that right. I think you'd be a real jerk to call her on the carpet."

She was right. Sammie had spoiled us rotten. But I wished Gail hadn't put it in just those words. To feel like a jerk was a whole lot less painful than being called one out loud.

"I won't." I held up my right hand. "Promise."

Gail stretched and rubbed her eyes. She'd come here from her office, and I knew she was planning at least a couple more hours of study time at home. "You going to pull an all-nighter?" she asked.

I checked my watch. "Could be. We've invited some of Brenda Croteau's old playmates in for a grilling session. Might take a while."

She got up and gave me a kiss. "Okay. See ya later."

I watched her go, caught between wanting to leave with her and knowing it wouldn't make any difference. Throughout our relationship, our jobs had paradoxically become the same haven other people made out of spending time off together, or having a family. Fundamentally, we were two loners, and if, as I feared, we were to go our separate ways, it would probably be as natural a transition as when a normal couple decides to move into a smaller apartment after the kids leave home.

No big deal.

Chapter Eight

Based on what June Dutelle had told us about her daughter's friends, we decided to pull in both Janice Litchfield and Jamie Good for questioning that night. A phone conversation with Brenda Croteau's husband, James—safely tucked away in the Burlington jail—also added Dwayne Matthews to the list, supposedly Brenda's current boyfriend.

In what amounted to a drawing of straws, I got Janice Litchfield. Willy and Sam got the other two. Ron and J.P. were sent to bed, so at least somebody would be conscious the next day.

The police department only has one official interrogation room, the traditional small box with a one-way mirror. Since we knew Jamie the best, he being a repeat customer, he got the box, and Willy along with it. Janice Litchfield and I ended up in a small cubbyhole used by the department's office manager.

Litchfield was in her mid-twenties, thin to the point of scrawniness, and equipped with spiky purple hair and all the standard hardware accessories, from tongue and eyebrow posts to a half dozen earrings running up each lobe. She also sported a rose tattoo on her temple, which I rather liked.

I had her sit in a straight-backed chair in the corner, while I remained standing.

"Would you like me to call you Janice or Miss Litchfield?" I asked her.

She was sitting slouched over and knock-kneed, scratching at one set of painted nails with the other. "I don't care."

"All right. We'll make it Janice. You want a soda or some coffee?"

"No."

"Anyone tell you why we asked you to come here tonight?"

"No—I figured it was about Brenda."

"How did you hear about that?"

"I just heard. Everybody did. It's all over town."

"They saying who did it?"

"No."

"You have any ideas about that?"

"No."

I reached back in time. "How long have you known Brenda?"

"Since before high school."

"Middle school or around the neighborhood?"

"Middle school. I knew about her when we were kids, but I didn't know her."

"What was she like?"

Janice hunched her shoulders slightly, eyes still glued to her fingertips. As far as I knew, she hadn't looked at me once yet. "Normal—you know."

I had no idea what defined normal here, although I had my suspicions. "You describe her as a follower or a leader?"

"Kind of a leader, I guess."

"How was she with boys?"

"Pretty tough. She didn't take no shit from them."

"That get her into trouble with them?"

"Nah. They kind of like that—sometimes."

"Until they don't get what they want?"

She looked up quickly, and just as quickly dropped her gaze. But I'd seen the smile. "You mean sex? That wasn't a problem. She wanted it, too. She just didn't let them control her."

I picked up a feeling of envy there. "So what happened after high school? You two keep in touch?"

"Sure. We were best friends."

"You must be pretty sad she's dead, then."

The fingers suddenly stopped their nervous dance. Her head tucked in just a fraction more. "Sure."

I paused, considering my course. "Must be scary," I finally said.

She didn't answer.

"The two of you did some risky things together."

She nodded, almost imperceptibly.

"You worried that's what got her killed?"

"Sort of." It was barely a whisper.

"You may be right, Janice."

Silence filled the room. I crouched next to her so I could look up into her face. Her expression was rigid with concentration. "Janice, I'd like to stop whoever did this from doing it again. What were you and Brenda up to that might've killed her?"

Her eyes slid over to me at last, her chin trembling slightly. She sounded bewildered. "It could've been anything."

Of that, unfortunately, I had no doubt. For the next hour, I extracted details of a life as haphazardly brutal and careless as any in the urban front lines to our south. We kid ourselves in Vermont that because of the trees, fields, and our thinned-out, monochrome population, life is somehow saner up here. But it isn't architecture, density, or racial mix that breeds despair and self-destruction. It's the training and instincts we supply our young at home, and there Janice Litchfield and Brenda Croteau and a few thousand others like them had been as shortchanged in bucolic Vermont as any shattered child in the ghetto.

By the end of my session with Janice, I was armed with a long list of names, and a sense of confusion as deep as her own. Given what I'd learned, Brenda could have been killed for drugs, sex, money, or because the type of coffee she drank wasn't the right brand. I was certainly no longer wondering how she could afford to live beyond the means of a welfare recipient.

Later, close to midnight, Willy, Sam, and I met around the long table in the conference room adjacent to the squad room. Each of us had pads of paper covered with notes.

"Okay," I began. "Willy, why don't you start off?"

Kunkle looked like he'd just stepped into something disagreeable. "If there was any justice, Jamie Good would be a permanent boy-toy in some federal pen. That guy is the slimiest piece of shit I ever met."

"Meaning he gave you nothin'," Sammie interpreted.

"I wanted to rip his head off."

"Were he and Brenda tight?" I asked.

"He said they knew each other, had slept together, done drugs together. But that's like asking puppies if they piss on the same newspaper. He said it didn't mean a thing, and I believe him. I know his type, and I know him personally. He was having fun in there. I don't think he killed her."

"He know who did?"

"He'd like to. That's the one thing that got him down. He would've loved to have held that over my head, but he couldn't."

"Or didn't," I suggested.

"He's not that self-restrained," Willy countered, "and I know him well. Much as I hate to admit it, I think he's clean."

We both looked at Sammie.

"I can't say the same about Dwayne Matthews," she admitted. "He says they were getting along fine, that he last saw her day before yesterday, around noon, at her house, but he's cagey. Denies ever doing drugs, although we got him down as a probable dealer, said he didn't have a record, till I put it in front of him."

"What kinds of stuff?" Willy asked.

"Penny-ante—disorderly, assault, petty theft, B&E, possession—usual kinds of recreation. Nothing armed, nothing lethal, nothing that had upward mobility written on it. We've never actually caught him at anything."

"Janice told me Brenda was into everything that moved," I said, "and usually got paid for it. Did Dwayne share that opinion?"

"Not really," Sammie answered. "He called her a wild chick, but it was hard to tell if he meant sexually, criminally, or socially. He was real evasive. He did say he thought she drank too much and overdid it with dope. Gave me some sanctimonious shit about how he'd told her it was a bad influence on the baby."

"I did a record check on Brenda," Willy said. "Maybe Dwayne was vague because he didn't know where to start. Her sheet covers prostitution, drunk and disorderly, possession of and selling a controlled substance, assault, probation violations, receiving stolen goods. My kind of woman."

"That would explain hanging out with Jamie Good," Sam muttered.

"Neither of you knew about her before?" I asked. "With a reputation like that?"

"It's from here and there," Willy explained. "She traveled around, mostly in-state. Good's a hometown boy. Brenda was a wanderer."

I wondered if we'd end up going outside of Brattleboro for our solution. Generally, these types of crimes occurred close to the nest, but Brenda's restless background left that door wide open.

First things first, though. I tapped my pad with my fingertip. "Let's compare the names each of them gave us. See if we can come up with some kind of family tree. Maybe someone'll stand out."

There are two major groupings for homicides: the slam-dunks and the who-dun-its. The slam-dunks, luckily for us and unhappily for fiction writers, are by far the most common. Someone gets pissed off, lashes out, and either waits remorsefully for us to arrive or at most hightails it home, leaving ten witnesses behind to point the way. With these, we sift through an excess of testimony, making sure the perpetual contradictions are explained (he was left-handed, he was right-handed; he was fat and short; he was tall and skinny). Basically, it amounts to legalistic traffic control, done in close cooperation with the prosecutors inheriting the ball.

Who-dun-its are much rarer. With them, we're left on our own, interviewing people who don't want to talk to us, conjuring up scenarios based on evidence and not wishful thinking. There's also a sense of lost time, lost opportunity, and ever-vanishing prospects. Who-dun-its are like being adrift in a rowboat, with the tide pulling you out to sea. Unless something turns up to reverse the trend, all that's left is to watch the shore slowly sink into the horizon. In the movies, who-dun-its are action-packed, thrillingly progressive, and ultimately successful. In reality, they are slow, plodding, and often end up nowhere. If a bad guy in this country has the smarts to knock someone off with just a modicum of discretion, chances are pretty good he'll never be caught. All the science, the networking, and the inspiration don't come to much if you don't have a name to begin with.

Which was why we were comparing notes.

It was routine in an interview especially—versus an interrogation, where you were usually pursuing a confession—to throw as broad a net of questions as possible. Who do you know, who did you see, who did you hear being talked about—were all questions designed to sift suspects like a colander. Sam, Willy, and I spent two hours sifting, formulating how each name connected to the rest, so we could get a better glimpse of the world Brenda Croteau inhabited before she died.

It is usually pretty dry work, so I was encouraged when, at Willy's mention of Frankie Harris, Sammie grew wide-eyed.

"What is it?" I asked her.

Willy, who'd continued reading aloud, paused, saw her face, and repeated, "Frankie Harris—yeah . . . that does ring a bell."

Sammie's voice was strained. "He was at the poker party."

I watched them both closely as Willy momentarily

froze. "Overlooking the railroad tracks? The night the bum got whacked?"

"More than that," he agreed, with none of his usual malice.

It was the party where Sammie had met her current flame. "What's your new friend's name, Sam?"

She flushed and said angrily, "It's not Harris. It's Andy Padgett."

The quiet in the room fell like a loud noise in church—everyone noticing it, and pretending they hadn't. Frankie Harris, after all, was no longer just a name being mentioned in the context of one killing, but of two. We all had to wonder what Andy Padgett might have to say about that, especially given his sudden interest in a cop.

I tried skirting the issue. "Tell me what we've got on Mr. Harris," I told Willy.

For once, he was happy to cooperate. "According to Jamie, Harris was one of Brenda's johns, but one she liked. He was a regular. He's also clean—I ran him through the computer." He paused slightly, still watching Sammie, whose eyes were glued to her notes. "I remember him from when we did the first canvass. Quiet guy, maybe early fifties." He pulled his pad from his back pocket and flipped through its pages. "Yeah. Here he is. Typesetter, fifty-one, unmarried, lives on Frost Street. He was the one who said he saw the car with no headlights through the window, on his way to take a leak."

"Sammie?" I asked. "Anything to add?"

Her voice still showed her discomfort. "I remember him. Seemed legit."

"Have you and Andy discussed him at all?"

"Only that night. I don't think they know each other

that well. It was one of the other guys' birthday. He was the connection between Andy and Harris."

Willy referred back to his pad. "Donald Carter, divorced, now aged thirty-one, two DUIs, a disorderly stemming from a domestic dispute, and a disturbing the peace with loud music, all spanning the past eight years. Nothing within the past several months, when he got clipped for the second DUI. No jail time. Claimed he never saw or heard a thing, not even the train. It was his apartment, so he's learned to tune it out, according to him. I think he'd tucked away enough that night to make him deaf anyway."

"Anything to add to Carter?" I asked Sammie.

"Andy's mentioned him," she admitted reluctantly. "They work together at Naughton Lumber, in the mill."

Naughton Lumber was a huge operation north of town, turning felled trees into lumber, molding, plywood, and pulp. One of the town's larger employers, it was notoriously unscrupulous about whom it hired.

In the awkward pause following her statement, Sammie grew angry again. "So what? Willy's probably related to half the people doing life in St. Albans. Doesn't mean he's crooked."

Willy laughed. "Don't be so sure."

It was a typical crack, although once again I sensed him casting her a protective mantle. He and Sammie had always worked well together, while bitching like cats and dogs. He had a respect for her he'd never shown Ron, for example. But I'd never seen him shield her from anything—her or anyone else, for that matter.

"No one's saying anything against Andy," I told her. "But we have to look into this, don't you think?"

"He doesn't know Frankie Harris that well," she repeated. "That's all I'm saying. And I don't know how

Carter knows him. Maybe they went to school together or something."

"Harris is twenty years older than Carter," I reminded her.

She pushed away from the table and stood up suddenly. "For Christ's sake. I knew this would happen. I didn't expect it from you."

She stalked out of the room, leaving her notes behind. I rose, grabbed her pad, pointed a finger at Willy, said, "Stay put. I want to talk to you," and gave chase.

I caught up to her just shy of the front door, taking her by the elbow. "Sammie. Slow down."

She didn't fight me off, but turned and leaned back against the wall, her face contorted by fury, embarrassment, and frustration. "Damn," she said.

I gave her the pad, moving my hand from her elbow to her shoulder and looking her straight in the eyes. "Sam. What the hell's going on?"

She averted her gaze. "I don't know. I'm tired. It's a little confusing, is all."

"Being in love?"

She looked at me then, checking for any mockery, finding none. "I don't know what hit me. I barely know him, but I can't stop thinking about him. It was like an electrical connection or something."

"It's okay," I said. "It's perfectly normal. Maybe you got it worse than some, but you're also overdue. And nobody's dumping on you because of it, least of all me."

Her brow knitted. "That's not the way it felt at the crime scene earlier."

I shook my head. "I was pissed at you for showing up healthy when you'd told me you were sick. It made you look devious, and I was already mad at Raymo for playing cowboy. I'm not angry you've finally found someone to fall in love with."

She pursed her lips and said quietly, "I don't know if it is love."

I smiled at her. "Sex, then. I don't care. Whatever it is, it's good for the soul. It's also nobody's business but your own. I'm not going to tell you people won't talk, or aren't talking already. Not only did this happen pretty fast, and in an unusual context, but it's also out of character for the Sammie we're used to—a Sammie you *trained* us to be used to. You've got to expect some flak for that, just like anyone else would get."

She sighed once heavily and then nodded. "I suppose."

I let her go. "You want to pretend to be like one of the boys, they're going to treat you that way—sophomoric as it sounds. It doesn't mean they're really going after you. On the contrary."

"I know, I know," she agreed, calming down. "I've seen it enough times. It's just hard being on the receiving end."

"It would've helped if you hadn't been so coy about it, taking sick days."

She smiled ironically. "You really believe that?"

I conceded the point. "Okay. You would've caught shit anyhow. But now the cat's out of the bag. You can relax. All right?"

"All right. Sorry I blew up."

"Don't be. It's been a hell of a day, this thing came out of left field, and," I added, raising my eyebrows suggestively, "I don't imagine you've been getting much sleep lately."

She laughed and punched me in the arm. "Lay off. You want me back in there?"

"No. Hit the sack, rest up, and I'll see you later. Check in when you're ready. I'll finish with Willy and kick him loose, too. We've all done enough for tonight."

I watched her go and then returned to the conference room. Willy was tilting back in his chair and gave me a lewd smile. "Sort out her love life?"

I ignored him, sat down, and asked, "Tell me about Andy Padgett."

He gave me an exasperated laugh. "What do I know? She met the guy, sparks went off, they been making like rabbits ever since."

"You telling me you didn't run *him* through the computer?"

His small notepad was still lying open before him, but I noticed that this time he didn't bother consulting it. "Age twenty-eight, been working at Naughton for three years, drove a truck for Rugby before that, unloaded groceries at C&S right out of high school, which he attended here. Lives in a trailer in West Bratt. Never been married, no kids, one dog. Owns a pickup and a Harley. No record outside a disturbing the peace when he was in high school, and an equipment violation when he was driving rigs, which went back to the owner."

I was struck by Padgett's having once been a truck driver. "What was your gut reaction when you met him, before he and Sam became an item?"

"Just a regular guy. Nothing special."

I left it at that, sensing his discomfort. "What about the fourth member of this poker party. Who was he?"

Willy reached for his pad. "James Lyon, married, three kids, age thirty, works at Span-Lastic. Plays on a softball team with Carter—that's how they're friends.

He's clean as a whistle. I wrote down 'nervous' in my notes, but I don't know if it means much. We do that to people, especially virgins."

I rubbed my eyes. "What do you think about Frankie Harris being connected to both Brenda Croteau and the railroad killing?"

"Could be a coincidence," Willy equivocated, then added reluctantly, "but we'd be nuts to just assume it."

"Yeah," I agreed. "You better really look into him—family, friends, co-workers, the works. Also, get together with Sam later and chase down the list of common denominators we compiled tonight—put them under the same microscope. If the law of averages has anything to do with this, Brenda got killed over drugs, money, or both. June Dutelle might be more helpful there, too, if we press her a little harder."

I paused, and Willy got up. "That it?"

"Yeah. We'll be crawling all over White Birch Avenue for evidence when it gets light. You're good at that, so if you can make it, I'd appreciate it, but make sure you get some sleep first."

He gathered up his notes. "You got it."

I stayed where I was for a while, thinking. Not about Phil Resnick, who was maybe the dead trucker, or Brenda Croteau, or her cast of dubious friends. I found myself wondering about Willy and Sam. Something was cooking there, at least on Willy's part. Not only had he ignored his notes while recalling Andy Padgett's particulars, he'd also known he had a dog.

That depth of knowledge wasn't available through a criminal records computer.

Chapter Nine

Generally, winter's brief daylight hours only aggravate people's moods in Vermont. The morning after my meeting with Willy and Sam, however, I was all too happy to get two hours of extra sleep before I knew J.P. and his crew—by dawn's tardy light—would be out searching White Birch Avenue.

I drove there straight from home and found them already setting up. Tyler had a team of ten people, including, I noticed, both Sam and Willy. He was equipping them out of the van he'd brought for the purpose, keeping track of his assignments in a three-ring binder.

"What's the plan?" I asked him during a lull, noticing he was wearing earmuffs and fingerless gloves, like one of Scrooge's underpaid scribes.

"Three teams: one inside the house to pick up where we stopped last night; another combing about a ten-yard perimeter around the outside walls; and the last working from one end of the street to the other. With this many people, it shouldn't take too long—maybe most of the morning. I'll let you know before then if we find anything interesting, though."

I smiled. "That your subtle way of telling me to buzz off?"

He didn't see the humor, looking at me with round, slightly surprised eyes. "No. Ron radioed here about five minutes ago. Said he just missed you at home. He's got something at the office he wants you to see."

Anyone else would have tacked on a note of curiosity, especially in the midst of two felony cases. Not Tyler. He took most of life as a series of facts or events that could either be analyzed or tucked away for future reference. I'd watched his family grow over the years—a wife and two children, now both teenagers—fully expecting at least one of them to sprout green hair and go slightly bonkers. But so far, they all seemed content to emulate him, going through life doing good, doing well, and not making much of a fuss.

I didn't mind being dismissed. Poking through trash-strewn bushes or a frozen, blood-splattered house wasn't my idea of fun. I preferred picking people's brains to going through their leftovers, even though it was the latter that often clinched the case in court.

I didn't even reach the office before I discovered what was on Ron's mind. He came running out into the parking lot without a coat and met me as I swung out of my car.

"I got something you should hear," he said, his rapid breathing encircling his head with fog.

"You'll freeze to death before you can tell me. Let's go inside."

"I heard back from DMV on that plate number I've been trying to unscramble. I don't know why they took so long, but the number is registered to Jim Reynolds."

I stopped dead in my tracks. "Reynolds? How'd they come up with that?"

Ron was already beginning to shiver. "Ed Renaud said he saw a dark blue Ford Crown Victoria with a plate beginning with PCH. Reynolds owns that exact car, license number PDH-835. There are some with PCH which aren't Crown Vics, and Crown Vics that don't have PCH, but only Reynolds's has anything even close to PCH."

I took pity on him and finished walking to the PD's back door, quickly punching in the combination and ushering him through. "You talk to him yet?"

"No. I only just got it." He hesitated, and then added, "Plus, I didn't want to jump the gun, especially after this." He pulled a newspaper from his pocket and unfolded it so I could read the headline.

"Reynolds: No More Mayberry RFD." And in smaller type, "Senator Proposes Bill to Revamp Vermont Law Enforcement."

"Tell me what it says," I said as I peeled off my coat, collected my mail and messages, and headed for our squad room on the other side of the building.

He fell into step behind me. "It's the same thing he's been test-flying at those public hearings for the governor—to replace us with a single police force."

"The state police?" I asked, cutting through the Officers' Room to grab a cup of coffee.

"Not according to this. It would be a whole new entity."

I walked into the main corridor. "What about the sheriffs?"

"It doesn't say. None of that really matters anyway. All he's done is refer the bill to his own Judiciary Committee. It doesn't mean it'll survive the week. The reason I brought it up is that it's a hot potato, it's anti-local law enforcement, and if we hit him on this railroad death without being damn sure of ourselves, we'll get creamed by the press for smearing him to protect our turf."

We cut through the administrative office and the conference room, and stepped into our own bailiwick. I looked around at the clustered desk cubicles, now all abandoned because of the White Birch Avenue search. "What do you propose?" I asked him.

"Big-time background check," he answered unsurprisingly, computers and their paper trails being to him what forensics were to Tyler.

I nodded by way of agreement. "Okay, but discreetly. He hired Win Johnston to watch his back, so Win'll have his nose to the wind. Stick to either public records or closed police sources. No interviewing of family or friends. Okay?"

He was pleased by my instant endorsement. "Sure. Okay. I'll get right on it."

I went back across the way to bring the chief up to date.

Tony Brandt recommended a different tack. After I updated him on Reynolds's office break-in, his hiring of Winthrop Johnston, the sighting of his car at a probable murder scene, and the call I'd gotten about him from Stan Katz, Tony opted for the direct approach.

"He's running for the state's top job, for Christ's sake, or he will be as soon as he makes enough hay out of this bill. I think you should hit him with what we got, even vague as it is. That way, he can't complain later he didn't know of our suspicions from the get-go. It pulls the politics right out of it."

He leaned forward for emphasis. "Plus, if he is guilty, one brief chat with you will make him sweat bullets like nobody's business, especially when you tell him you're there because Katz pointed the way. He may even solve this thing for us—which also means you better assign people to watch his wife and secretary ahead of time, just in case that conversation leads to any sudden flurry of activity there. We don't need a certain automobile to spontaneously catch fire by accident, do we?"

I had to respect Tony's zeal, especially since I knew he'd voted for the man. I rose to my feet. "Okay. I'll keep you informed."

The drive to Montpelier takes under two hours—north along Interstate 91, halfway up the state's eastern edge, and then northwest on I-89 through the middle of the Green Mountains. It is a trip epitomizing the Vermont so well-known to the rest of the country—deep, ancient, river-cut valleys slicing through dramatic waves of forested mountains, dappled here and there by white-coated clapboard villages and the ever-rarer cow-appointed field. Even looking as it did now—made drab and scabby by winter's blight without the face-saving grace of a pristine coat of snow—one could sense the richness awaiting spring and summer. Vermont is not a wilderness like what stretches for untold miles out west amid the Rockies. This is land as much carved by humans as by glaciers long gone. A stroll in the densest woods will yield countless stone walls built by farmers who went broke around the time of the Civil War. Vermont, touted today as a bastion of undisturbed nature, has been worked and reworked by inhabitants who at one time had eighty percent of it under cultivation, but who have never really figured out how to exploit it to their own best advantage. At every election, along with the standard arguments about education, taxation, and jobs, the debate about how to use Vermont's photogenic acreage rages on—all while tourism remains the state's largest industry.

That was one reason this sudden interest in law enforcement was so peculiar. Never before had the subject been of much use to politicians, who, as long as they paid lip service to the state police and sheriffs—otherwise generally neglected—could all but ignore the rest of us with impunity. Few people in government cared how municipalities dealt with crime, and those who did were content to think that the state police or a few federally funded task forces were enough to keep chaos in check. The almost seventy agencies being talked about now had been largely left to themselves to standardize communications, integrate databases, and join the growing national trend to fully share information. The state police, for all the flak they got for being elitist, aloof, and self-serving, were actually responsible for many of these breakthroughs, but there remained a lot of bad blood for past transgressions never forgiven or forgotten. It was unfortunately typical that the preventable deaths of a few children had been necessary to get the topic on the political agenda. It would also be typical, I thought, if the whole subject just as conveniently disappeared once the current electoral season ran its course.

Which was why I had mixed feelings about Jim Reynolds coming under our scrutiny in such an odd manner. In a world where political leaders were increasingly susceptible to ruin through bad PR alone, I wondered about the timing of this discovery.

Not that history hasn't taught us how arrogant, stupid, greedy, and short-sighted the political animal can be.

Montpelier is located right in the middle of the Greens, straddling two rivers, which periodically dam up with gigantic ice floes and flood downtown with freezing water. A purely political creation, it cannot tout the commerce of Burlington, the skiing of Stowe, or the granite quarries of Barre as its reason for being. It thrives because, in 1805, it won out in the battle over what town would become the state capital.

In this context, it is fitting that Montpelier's two most prominent features are a gaudy, tiny, gold-domed capitol building, and the lurking presence of a tree-cloaked, gargantuan life insurance company, perched atop a hill and overlooking the town like some faceless, obscurely threatening capitalist shadow. The one had all the slightly absurd sparkle of democratic pomp and hopefulness, often confused with power, while the other oozed of money and influence, about whose clout few had any doubts.

In between them lay a modest, bustling town of white-trimmed red brick buildings, accessorized here and there with the inevitable monolithic government structure—gray, bland, and built of granite. Montpelier is cradled in the palm of a cluster of hills, and exudes a feeling of warmth and community, although, in fact, it is missing some of a normal town's sense of balance. Heavy on restaurants, bars, hotels and inns—befitting a transient population used to being catered to—it lacks some of the basics that a similarly sized permanent crowd might have naturally expected, like a shoe store.

One stubbornly provincial detail has been maintained, however. Despite the seasonal onslaught of cars, flocking to the State House like bees to a hive, parking stinks. If I hadn't uncovered all of Montpelier's nooks and crannies from prior visits, I would have discovered them by the time I finally squeezed my car into a dubiously legal spot a half mile from my destination.

The walk was pleasant, though. It was brain-numbing cold, but aside from having to rub my nose now and then to revive its circulation, I didn't pay it much heed. It is said that Vermont is annually visited by nine months of winter and three more of damn poor sledding. While it's really not that bad, we've learned to take poor weather in stride.

It was also sunny, which made the approach to the capitol building particularly gratifying. One of only fourteen state legislative domes to be coated in gold, Vermont's is all the more astonishing because of the structure it caps. The State House is perhaps the smallest of its ilk in the nation, and while handsome, is rather plain, making its topknot as quaintly out of place as a silk derby on a farmer.

Constructed of light gray granite, the building is the awkward result of a tangled birth. Actually the third incarnation of a legislative home, after the fiery deaths of its predecessors, it is fronted with an enormous columned Greek portico—all that's left of structure number two—which now looks as if it had been glued on as a classy afterthought. Adding to the lopsidedness, the dome does not sit back, like a lord in a rowboat, but instead crowds to the front, making the decorative columns look more like buttresses put in place to keep the dome from falling into the front yard.

As if in homage to a debate-based form of government, many of these peculiarities rose from bitter arguments between the original Boston architect and his practical-minded, stubborn superintendent.

The end result, however, belittles such visual snags, for the State House is in the end a jewel box of a building, reflecting all the excesses and ambition of a diminutive rural state long lost in the wake of a bustling nation's consciousness. Where Albany and Washington, DC, have their perfectly proportioned, cold temples by the handful, it seems fitting that Vermont's sole offering—much cherished and restored—looks as if it has been constructed of dearly purchased, high-quality spare parts. It is a reflection of pride and pragmatism commingled.

As I entered the unguarded side door—there is only one security officer in the building, and no metal detectors—I was reminded of another, more blatant example of the philosophy underlying this true house of the people: The legislators have no offices of their own. Of the hundred and fifty representatives and thirty senators, only two—the speaker and the president pro tem—have private places to call their own, complete with secretaries. Everyone else has an antique desk in either the House or Senate chamber, a large, shared, computer-equipped common room, a cramped committee room, or a briefcase on the lap. If you want to find the people you elected, there are few places they can hide, and even fewer subordinates to run interference for them. It's always been one aspect of democracy I've liked the most.

It also made locating James Reynolds fairly easy. All I had to do was wend my way through the milling crowd of lobbyists, lawmakers, and assorted others, climb one of the two ornate iron staircases to the second floor, and walk over to the glass-paned double doors leading into the startlingly small Senate chamber. I immediately saw my quarry sitting at a long, curved row of connected school desks, furiously scribbling on a yellow legal pad as one of his colleagues was pawing the air in midspeech.

I cracked open the door, motioned to one of the door keepers, and handed him a note, "For Senator Reynolds."

He nodded and crossed the chamber, delivering my message. Reynolds thanked him, glanced at what I'd written, looked up at me with a surprised expression, and immediately left his desk.

He met me at the door, grabbed my arm, and propelled me toward a second, narrower staircase leading up to the visitors' gallery overlooking the chamber. "Too noisy here," he said, a broad smile contrasting with the tenseness in his voice. "I know somewhere quieter we can talk."

At the top of the stairs, he steered me away from the galleries toward a small, low, locked panel that looked like a discreet closet door. He dug into his pocket and extracted a key. "I'm not supposed to have this, but you take what you can in this job."

The small door opened onto a rough wooden corridor, lined with electrical boxes, ductwork, and bundles of wiring, and to a second opening to the right, leading up a final set of stairs, made of bare, unfinished two-by-sixes.

We finally emerged through the floor of the State House dome, which towered a good sixty feet above us in a giddying grid of raw trusses and crude bracing—in startling contrast to its sleek, gilded exterior. Encircling us were twelve tall decorative windows, alive with the buzzing of hundreds of trapped flies, incongruously out of season, beating against the warm, sunlit glass. A rough wooden catwalk crisscrossed overhead to a final small door, almost invisible at the top.

"They sometimes bring school groups up here to show them how it was put together." He gestured directly overhead. "There's a little balcony way up there, too—it's quite a view."

I didn't answer, waiting for the public persona to settle down to normal. Looking around, I saw dozens of names scribbled on the rough lumber surfaces surrounding us—simple signatures of people who apparently thought the most impact they could have on this building and its occasionally self-inflated inhabitants was to furtively leave their mark in an unseen place.

Reynolds glanced at the note he still held in his hand. He was a big man—broad, tall, trunklike in build, with a thick mane of unruly hair. In court and on the stump, he used that to his advantage, frequently raising both arms to better resemble a bear, while occasionally flashing a boyish smile as if to show he wasn't without heart. It was a physical demonstration of the ambiguity that helped make him all things to all people—and which hinted at a lack of sincerity to those who got too close or looked too hard.

He waved the note at me. "What did you mean by this?"

I'd taken Brandt's recommendation to heart. The note had read, "I'd like to know why your name keeps cropping up," and I'd signed it, "Lt. Joe Gunther—Brattleboro Police," to put the question into context.

I extracted it from his fingers and placed it in my pocket. "Mostly I just wanted to get your attention.

It is true, though, and Tony Brandt thought we better talk."

His expression was unhappy and guarded. "Maybe you should be a little more specific," he said slowly.

"There was a break-in at your office you downplayed at the time, but later hired Win Johnston to investigate. I got a call saying you might be involved in the illegal dumping of hazardous waste—right after we discovered a broken-down empty truck that had just made a midnight delivery in Dummerston. And finally, your Crown Victoria was seen at the end of Arch Street, carrying three men who deposited a body on the railroad tracks, which was then pulverized by the night freight."

Up to the end, his face wore the neutral expression I'd seen him use in court. But the last item got a reaction. His eyes grew wide and incredulous. "When the hell was *that* supposed to have happened?"

I gave him the date we'd decided upon. "January sixth."

He shook his head. "That's bullshit. I was up here that night."

"With anybody? In the middle of the night?"

He became angry. "What the hell's that mean? I have an apartment downtown. I was alone. I don't use that car, anyhow. It's my wife's and she keeps it in Bratt. My car's got Senate plates."

"You could have driven home and back, with nobody the wiser."

He stared at me, his mouth half open. He reached behind him and groped for the railing at the top of the stairs, leaning heavily against it. "This is like a bad movie. I thought that guy was a bum who committed suicide."

I was impressed. Hitting someone out of the blue could have all sorts of unintended benefits, especially with lawyers, who were trained to recover quickly. Honest-to-goodness bafflement was a rarity.

"That's what we've let the press believe so far. But we have witnesses to the contrary."

The politician in him began to revive. He looked at me closely. "How many people think it was my car?"

"Just my squad. It won't stay there for long, though. Never does."

He rubbed his forehead. "Jesus H. Christ. How the hell . . . ? Does my wife know? Did you talk to her yet?"

I shook my head. "Thought I'd see you first. The car's registered in your name."

He waved a hand absentmindedly. "They all are. Who was the victim, if he wasn't a bum?"

I decided to keep that to myself. "We don't know yet. We're still checking."

Reynolds rose and began pacing the wide expanse amid the windows, further stirring up the flies. "Look, I can tell you right now I have no idea what this is about. But I know what kind of impact it's going to have. I'll do all I can to help, and you can count on my wife for the same cooperation." He stopped before me. "But will you at least try to keep a lid on it until you've got something solid? It's not just the embarrassment. I'm doing something downstairs I hope'll change this entire state—make it safer for its citizens and create a better place for you to do your work. It's precedent-setting. If we get this bill passed, it'll be a real sign we're no longer tied down by traditions and habits that date back to the horse and buggy. And we could do it. Vermont more than any other state in the

Union has proven how bipartisan pragmatism can be made to work for the good of all. We can get the job done if we don't let the kinds of bastard that're behind this get to us."

I held up my hand. "No offense, Senator, but I don't really care. It doesn't change how I do my job."

He tucked his head and smiled apologetically, even shuffled a foot. "Sorry. Got carried away. You can't believe how that hit—what you just told me. There's nothing to it, but it could sink me all the same."

"What about hiring Johnston?"

He hesitated. "That was for protection. I didn't find anything missing after that break-in, but I wanted to know who did it and why."

"One of our officers noticed a couple of file drawers were open, as if someone had been rifling through them."

He dismissed that with a wave of his hand. "Sloppy housekeeping on my part. I left them open by mistake."

"Doesn't your secretary tidy up before she leaves?"

He laughed. "I'm the one who usually closes up. She works regular hours. Believe me, mine's no nine-to-five job." He shook his head. "Look, nothing happened at the office—don't waste your time. It's the other thing that worries me—politics can get pretty dirty, even here, if the stakes are high enough. And they couldn't get much higher."

"Meaning seeing your car at the railroad tracks is a setup?"

"I don't know what it means," he answered carefully. "I know it didn't happen, or if it did, it was without my knowledge. Assuming your witness actually did see my car—and you better check his reliability—it means someone's very serious about getting me out of the way. The same goes for that rumor about me being involved in illegal dumping."

He straightened slowly, almost imperceptibly, until I was fully and belatedly aware of his towering over me. "It would be a shame, given what I'm trying to do here, to have your department used as an instrument of libel. Once the truth came out, the fallout would be enormous."

There was a long pause, during which I merely looked him in the eye. Then he turned on his heel and went back downstairs.

It had bordered on being a personal threat. I'd seen him in action before. It wasn't a bluff.

Chapter Ten

I got back to Brattleboro by late afternoon and found Tony Brandt sitting in his office, talking on the phone. He waved me to a seat, quickly concluded his conversation, and put his feet up on his desk—his preferred position of contemplation.

"He confess?"

I laughed. "Right. No—I'll give him that much. If he is guilty, he hides it well. He looked totally bowled over, then he got curious, then he pulled the I'll-sue-your-ass card out of the deck. He says forces from the Dark Side are out to get him, and we better watch out we don't become their unwitting handmaiden. He also told me he's probably the best thing that'll ever happen to us in our lifetime."

"Us? You mean the cops?"

"And everyone else. Brave New World is right around the corner, assuming he gets that bill passed."

"You tell him what his chances are?"

"I figured I was there to listen. He's an impressive guy."

Tony gazed at me thoughtfully. "So are a lot of bas-tards."

"I thought you voted for him."

"I did. But he's a defense lawyer and a politician and he's put everything on the table with this thing. Defining the Dark Side might depend on your point of view here. I know a lot of people who'd love for him to disappear."

I'd already expressed how I thought some sort of streamlining of all these police agencies might make sense. I was curious to hear the educated other side, especially from someone I trusted.

"Like who?" I asked.

"Basically anyone who's fought hard to get where they are. The state police at the top of the heap, the chiefs with their cherished turfs, the sheriffs with their town and state contracts, all the boards of selectmen fearing loss of local control, the right-wingers and the tree-huggers screaming socialism or fascism, depend-ing. It's almost hard to think of anyone who *would* be for this bill."

"That include you?"

"Not necessarily. A bunch of other places have made it work—including small countries—and they're bigger and busier than we are. But common sense doesn't al-ways apply—most people agree education should no longer be funded with property taxes. Doesn't mean it'll ever change. There are a few things in life we're just plain stuck with, and in Vermont, one of them's the local cop, as redundant, expensive, and inefficient as that may be."

"So Reynolds is screwed."

He laughed softly and raised his eyebrows. "Who

knows? A hundred years ago, nobody thought women would get the vote."

I got up and moved to the door. "There are a lot more of them than there is of him—even with his ego. One thing I did get, by the way, was that this scares the hell out of him."

"I don't doubt it. You think he's involved at all?"

I paused on the threshold. "His car being seen at the tracks seemed to hit him out of the blue. Hiring Win as a bird dog sounded reasonable to me. But he blew off the dumping accusation pretty fast—there may be something to it."

"What're you going to do now?" he asked me.

"Check in with Sammie and the others. See what they came up with today. Then I was planning to visit Mrs. Reynolds."

Tony nodded his approval. "Good. How's Sammie doing, by the way?"

I hesitated, surprised he knew anything was wrong. "Okay."

He smiled conspiratorially. "I have my sources, Joe. She's good people—we both know that. She's also young."

He left it at that. "I know," I agreed. "I'm keeping an eye on it."

"One last thing," he added. "Let Kunkle and Sam handle the Croteau killing. I want you to keep on Reynolds. We need to know if your witness is all wet on pinning his car to the scene, or what really happened if he's not. This one could do us damage, Joe. Okay? The press could have a field day."

It was a rare request from a boss who usually let his department heads rule their roosts. But I sensed he was right. Despite the current popular appeal of the

Croteau killing over the railroad death, Reynolds was a celebrity, and could tilt that balance in a heartbeat.

J. P. Tyler was in his element, sitting cross-legged on the floor, surrounded by paper evidence envelopes, videotapes, Polaroid photographs, a plaster casting, and several brown paper bags, with a clipboard balanced on his knees.

"Have a good day?" I asked him, careful to keep outside his circle of possessions.

He looked up and smiled broadly, a rare show of happiness. "Pretty good."

"Find the murder weapon?" I guessed.

He tapped one of the bags by his side with a pencil. "Butcher knife—ten-inch blade. One of a set of five the victim had in her kitchen. It's got prints on it. I checked by blowing iodine fumes across the handle, but I want to send it to Waterbury so they can do a complete job on it." He rooted around through a pile of photographs and handed me a shot of the handle covered with purple fingerprints. Blowing iodine gas across a surface will often make prints briefly appear—usually long enough to take a picture. The remarkable thing was that these prints were clear. Hollywood notwithstanding, that was not usually the case.

I handed it back. "You been able to compare them to anyone yet?"

He was back to inventorying and didn't look up. "Nope, except the victim, of course. They aren't hers, or at least not all of them are. I'm driving up to the forensics lab tonight so I can get a clear copy of at least one of them and run it through their AFIS machine. Assuming that's okay with you."

"Sure." AFIS stood for Automated Fingerprint Identification System, and in simple terms consisted of a fancy copier hooked to a growing national computer database. You could put the image of a print or some-one's actual hand on the glass and have the digitally translated results compared to what an increasing num-ber of agencies had on file, including the FBI. There was supposed to have been one of these "live scan sta-tions" in every county of the state by now, and all across New Hampshire and Maine as well. But some-where the works had been gummed up, and we were still waiting.

J.P. continued, "We found the knife about halfway up the street, in the bushes to the left. Placement sug-gests it was thrown from a car."

"The plaster mold?"

"Yup—tire track, opposite where the knife was. It was fresh, showed a little skidding, and it was off the edge of the road, in the dirt, as if the driver swerved over to throw something out."

He looked up at my lack of response. "All right, all right—*possibly*. I know it may have nothing to do with it—might've even been the ambulance or one of us. Still, it looked interesting, and it would be sweet if it fit a pattern down the line."

I granted him that. "True enough. How 'bout in the house?"

He jerked a thumb over his shoulder. "Ron's han-dling that. I collected some hairs, fibers, and more prints than I know what to do with. I don't think I'll even run them unless I need to."

"And what you thought might be the impression of the killer's knee in her blood?"

He looked less pleased with that. "Denim blue jeans.

The direction of the weave only tells me what it's not—a pair of Levis, for instance—but that's about it so far."

I rounded one of the cubicle corners. Ron was at his desk, doing a tidier, more condensed job than J.P., poring over small stacks of letters, papers, and files.

He looked up as I appeared. "How was Montpeculiar?"

The standard nickname for our capital, especially when the Legislature was in session. "Crawling with people. Only got a denial from Reynolds about his car, though. He says it's his wife's, anyway. I'm going to talk with her later. What've you got?"

He sat back in his chair. "A gold mine—I think. Maybe not for this case, but a real who's who of area dealers, users, hookers, johns, you name it. She kept a journal of sorts." He reached out and tapped a fat ledger book with his fingertip. "She seemed to think she was a budding writer or something. This thing's full of rambling notes, lists of names, pages that look like diary entries or flights of fancy. It's hard to tell, it's so jumbled up. Also, the handwriting's so bad in places you can barely tell if it's English, and it reads like she was on drugs. Other places, it's like an accountant's notes—listing johns and prices. I recognized a few names, but I'm not so sure some of this isn't make-believe. Hard to tell what's real and what's not. Got blackmail material, if she was into that."

"Find anything that points to her killer?"

"Not in so many words. But if she ever did put the squeeze on anyone, they might want her dead. Besides the criminal activity, there're some pretty prominent guys here—married men Stan Katz would love to write about. To me, though, what's interesting is what's *not* here—several pages have been ripped out."

"That what you think happened?"

"It fits—guy confronts her, kills her, turns on the lights and tears the place apart looking for this, rips out the incriminating pages, and splits. If he did a good job, though, finding him'll be tough. We'd have to talk to everyone she knew, show them what names we can extract from the journal, and hope somebody can think of who's missing. Could take a while, ruffle a whole lot of feathers, and end up nowhere."

"Frankie Harris come up at all?"

Ron flipped open the file and pawed through several pages. "Yeah. The guy at the poker game. Sammie told me about that connection. There is an entry here someplace . . ." He extracted a single sheet covered with dense, cramped handwriting. "This is it. A whole section on him. It's a little kinky—goes into some detail. But she liked him. Sort of a father figure, from what I could tell, if you're into screwing your father."

I leaned forward and glanced at it. I could see why he was having trouble deciphering it. Sentences appeared as if cut from confetti, some long, convoluted, and grotesquely poetical, others with all the flair of an affidavit. But I saw what he meant—what wasn't pornographic seemed dewy with sentiment. No sense of threat from Frankie Harris. In my mind's eye, I could envision Brenda Croteau late at night, a bottle by her side and a joint between her lips, writing feverishly, at some times conjuring up a reality far different from her own, at others listing names and actions like a speed cop recording license plates.

I had no doubt her killer had once been among them, if only as a passing reference. But Ron was right—he had his work cut out for him.

I returned the sheet of paper. "Once you've figured out all the players, compare them with what Willy, Sam, and I got from Brenda's playmates. Maybe we'll get lucky somehow. Otherwise, it looks like we're going to be talking to half of Brattleboro before we're done."

Ron sighed and stared at the pile before him. "You don't think we'll get a break here?"

I knew how he felt. "A lot depends on J.P. and that knife. You know where Willy is? I got a job for him."

Jim and Laura Reynolds lived in a modern home on New England Drive, a dead-end street paralleling a very busy Western Avenue—just beyond where the interstate slices West Brattleboro off from Brattleboro. A few decades ago, New England Drive was conjured up by someone wanting to sell off several parcels of increasingly valuable, highly taxed woodland. It was an attractive street, within earshot of the heavy traffic but shielded by the thick pine trees that had once covered the whole area. I wondered how long it might be before whoever owned the intervening acreage decided to duplicate history and deprive these newcomers of their illusional privacy.

The Reynoldses had obviously considered that, and had placed their house at the dead end of the road, strategically blocked in by both their own trees and some very careful landscaping. As soon as I entered the curved driveway, I felt removed from the rest of the neighborhood and almost embraced by the forest, as if in tasteful hibernation.

Willy saw it differently.

"Jesus," he said sourly. "It's like being in an upscale cemetery."

I rolled down my window as a police officer appeared from the underbrush, dressed in heavily insulated camouflage.

"Anything?" I asked him.

"Nothing unusual," he said. "The Crown Vic hasn't moved once since we been posted here, and the family's comings and goings have looked totally normal."

I nodded. If Reynolds had told his wife or secretary to do any criminal housecleaning after I told him we were interested in him, they'd either ignored him or had been very subtle about it. That's one thing we were hoping to find out tonight.

"Okay—thanks. You can call it quits now. We've got a warrant to dig through it."

It was just getting dark by the time we parked in front of an enormous garage—gloomy enough so that the motion-detection lights on the house flickered feebly to life.

The front door opened as we emerged from my car, and a slim woman in expensive clothes poked her head out. "Lieutenant Gunther?"

I waved to her, impressed by how well she and her husband communicated. "Mrs. Reynolds?"

"Yes, yes. Jim told me you'd probably be dropping by. Do come in. It's freezing out here."

We climbed the steps and passed through into a mudroom as large and well-appointed as a living room. I introduced Willy, who looked around suspiciously, ignoring her proffered hand.

"Let me take your coats," she said awkwardly, taking mine by the collar as I shrugged myself free. Standing close to her, I smelled something like bottled fresh air. It made me feel slightly unwashed. Willy kept his coat on.

She ushered us through another door and into a library/

den that made the mudroom proportionally small. "Would you like some coffee or tea to take the chill off?"

As admired as I knew these manners should be, I was already tiring of them, and decided to leave the chill where it was. I ignored the chair she indicated and turned down her offer. "No, thanks. I guess the senator told you why we'd be coming?"

She smiled pleasantly, looking slightly vague. "He said my car was seen somewhere it wasn't—a case of mistaken identity or something."

Willy let out a small snort, no doubt imagining how that conversation really went. "You could say that," I said. "Three men were seen dumping a body out of it in the middle of the night onto the railroad tracks."

She crossed her arms across her chest. "I read about that in the paper. But I can assure you my car had nothing to do with it."

"You were here that night? Alone?"

"Yes, I was, with the children, and we have an au pair living here, too. They're all out getting a pizza right now, but you can ask them when they return. Nothing happened to the Crown Victoria that night. In fact, it's been in the garage for almost a month. We have a third car—an Explorer. That's what I drive this time of year. We use the Crown Victoria for long trips in the summer. It's a good highway car."

"Yeah. Mine, too," Willy muttered.

"Could we take a look at it?" I asked, fearful he'd start building up steam.

"Of course." She crossed the room toward the distant kitchen. "The garage is right through here. It's heated, so you won't need your coat."

Willy headed back to the front door. "I'll get the stuff. Meet you there."

Laura Reynolds hesitated, momentarily confused.

I pulled an envelope from my pocket and handed it to her. "This is a search warrant for the car, just to keep things aboveboard. In case we find anything."

She took it as if I'd handed her a dead squirrel and dropped it on the nearest counter. Her voice showed its first quiver of strain. "I'm sure you won't."

Now it was my turn to be well mannered, bowing slightly and indicating the door. "Please. Lead the way."

The garage was an immaculate four-car unit, as big as a home, cleaner than a morgue. Its size was emphasized by there being only one vehicle in its midst—the gleaming dark sedan of interest. Willy pounded on a side door with his foot and I let him in, noticing as I did so that it was locked from the inside with a deadbolt. Willy was lugging one of J.P.'s evidence-collecting kits, which he deposited with a reverberating crash on the smooth concrete floor.

"And you're sure you haven't driven the car since the night in question?" I asked Laura Reynolds, who was staring at Willy, seemingly transfixed.

Her voice sounded small and frail in the sterile room. "No. I already told you. It's a summer car."

Willy snapped on a single latex glove with his teeth—moving as smoothly as if he'd been born with one arm—opened the kit and the car doors in turn, and set to work.

"What is he looking for?" she finally asked after a minute of silence.

"Anything helpful," I answered. "Blood, hair, clothing fibers."

Her hand touched her smooth forehead for an instant, as if making sure it was still there. I noticed she was shivering slightly. "You know," she said, "this is just beginning to sink in. You actually believe we might have had something to do with this man's death, don't you?"

"Not necessarily." I took her elbow and steered her back toward the main part of the house. "Why don't we go back inside? It's not all that warm in here, and Detective Kunkle will be a while."

She complied without a word.

Back inside the house, she paused between the living room and the kitchen, seemingly at a loss. I kept quiet, wondering what might be building up inside her.

She finally turned to me and asked, almost shyly, "What does all this mean?"

"That's what we're trying to find out."

A furrow appeared between her eyes, as if I'd said something totally off-color. "No. I mean, what does this mean for us—Jim and me?"

I purposefully played dumb. "If we find something?"

Her face tightened. "You won't."

"I'm sure you hope that, Mrs. Reynolds. But you may not know where that car's been lately."

"Of course I do," she answered angrily. "I told you that. It's been in that garage for weeks. It couldn't have been anywhere else. The doors lock automatically, the garage is alarmed, and one or the other of us has been here most of the time anyhow."

I just looked at her.

Her eyes widened slightly at the unstated possibility. "Jim? You can't be serious. You people are out of your minds. This must be a political thing. That's what it is. Some stupid story concocted by his enemies. It's incredible—like something out of Kafka."

I gestured to her to continue into the living room and take a seat. "Mrs. Reynolds, we don't know *what* this is yet. We were told by several witnesses that your car was seen at the tracks and it's our job to check that out. There's no conspiracy on our part here. That's not how we work. I would like you to tell me a few things, though."

"Like what? I told you all I know."

I sat opposite her, my elbows on my knees, trying to look as solicitous as possible. "This isn't the only event that's struck you as odd lately, is it? Like the recent break-in at your husband's office."

She looked confused. "A break-in? Jim told me it was teenagers trying to jimmy the door. They didn't actually break in, did they?"

"When did you last see your husband, Mrs. Reynolds?"

"Last weekend. He has an apartment in Montpelier. At the start of the session, he can only get away on weekends. Why?"

"It was a break-in. He claims nothing was stolen, but we think his files were tampered with. It makes me wonder what else he might be shielding you from. I mean, he must work under a lot of pressure, given his two jobs. Is he pretty protective of you and the kids?"

Her eyes were darting between my face, my hands, the furniture, the distant window. Throwing her several loaded messages at once seemed to have generated some doubts.

"I don't know. I suppose so."

"Why do you think he didn't tell you about the break-in? He got the call about the back door being forced open here at home, didn't he?"

She nodded. "Yes." Her voice had lost most of its perfect hostess lilt.

"I heard he was pretty upset."

"He was. Very."

"This is an important time for him, isn't it? With this new bill?"

"Yes."

"He been tense? Preoccupied?"

"Of course."

"Mrs. Reynolds, do you ever worry about him? Some of the clients he's had over the years, some of the people he has to deal with to get things done in Montpelier."

"There have been a few unpleasant ones . . ." She stopped, seemed to clear her head, and then spoke again more forcefully. "Look, I don't know what you're trying to do here. Jim is a good man, who's doing the best he can to help this state out. He's risking a lot with this bill, and he's doing it for people like you. I don't know what this is all about, but I know Jim isn't a part of it."

I got up and moved to the window. The light from the house lay dimly on the driveway. Beyond, the darkness of the trees made it feel like we were floating in outer space.

I spoke to my own reflection. "Mrs. Reynolds, I want to be perfectly honest with you. I like your husband. I voted for him, the woman I live with campaigned for him, and even though he's a defense attorney, we have a lot of respect for him at the police department. He fights hard but fair."

I turned toward her. "So don't think I'm going after him because we're political opposites. If anything, I'd like to lend him a hand. But I have to do my job, and what he's been up to lately has raised some questions."

"What do you think he *has* been up to?" she asked,

her face coloring. "All I've heard is something about his office being broken into and our car being somewhere it wasn't. This is crazy."

I held up a finger. "He hired a private investigator to look into the break-in, and we have several witnesses to the car."

Her mouth opened slightly. "A private investigator?"

"Yes. Winthrop Johnston. Good man. Very discreet."

There was a long pause before she asked, "What are you saying?"

"Only that your husband has a lot of irons in the fire, that he hasn't been entirely straight with you, for whatever reasons, and that I have some concerns about what may be going on."

"Like what?"

I spread my hands out to both sides. "I don't know. Maybe you can help me there. Have you had any worries about him recently?"

She looked thoughtful for a moment. "He's been very tense. I thought it was because of the bill. He's betting his political future on it."

"What about at the office? He's had to cut back on his practice. That must affect your income."

She waved that away, her voice slightly bitter. "I have money. We don't need the income. He works so he can feel he's not a kept man. It's not my choice we barely get to spend time together."

There was a sudden flash of light in the window next to me, and the motion-detection lights exposed a big Ford Explorer angling into the driveway and pausing in front of the garage doors. Laura Reynolds stood up, the tension of an instant ago replaced by the perfect smile. She crossed the room to stand next to me. "It's the children with supper."

With obvious relief, she headed for the kitchen and the garage beyond. Then she stopped abruptly and looked back at me. "What are you going to tell them?"

I didn't hesitate. "That we're investigating an accident and wanted to make sure your car was okay."

Her smile warmed then, perhaps for the first time since we'd met. "Thank you."

I waited until we were retreating down New England Drive, having met the kids, the au pair, and the two dogs, before asking Willy, "So what did you find?"

"Zilch. No blood, no scratches or tears, no signs of anything hinky. There was even some dust on the steering wheel, as well as on the garage floor behind the tires, and the license plate screws look like they never been touched. That car hasn't moved in weeks."

"You take a picture of it?"

"A dozen of 'em."

This time around, I met Ed Renaud at home—a far cry from the dark, cool sanctity of his fishing shanty. Reverberating with the blast of a television sitcom, and tinged with a sour blend of poverty, neglect, and lost hopes, his crowded walk-up apartment was ample enough justification for a fondness for outdoor recreation.

I didn't ask to be let inside. The landing was close enough. I dug into my pocket and retrieved one of Willy's Polaroids.

"Mr. Renaud, you told me last time you got a pretty good look at the car carrying those three men. You think you'd recognize it again from a photo?"

He thoughtfully dug at a tooth with a fingernail. "I guess so."

I handed him the picture.

He glanced at it for no more than ten seconds and returned it. "That ain't it. The license is right . . . Well, I guess I screwed that up a bit. I thought it looked like 'PERCH,' but now I see it again, I know that's what I seen. But the car's wrong."

I watched his face carefully. "Mr. Renaud, you said it was a dark blue Ford Crown Victoria."

"It was. But that thing's got one of those fake rag-tops." He took the photo back and stabbed it with his finger. "See? The one I saw had a shiny roof. I remember the reflection coming off it. This ain't it."

He paused and pulled at his chin. "Don't understand how that plate ended up on it, though, 'cause I'm sure *it's* right."

I returned the Polaroid to my pocket. "I guess that's for us to find out."

Chapter Eleven

I found Gail in the tub, surrounded by music and soap bubbles, looking like a vision from a Doris Day movie. She was pink and hot and smelled as fresh as a baby.

"God, that looks nice," I said as I leaned over to kiss her.

She smiled up at me. "There's room for two."

I began shaking my head.

"Why not?" she interrupted. "I'm not getting out till I'm good and pruny, and you look like you could use it."

I considered her offer for three seconds and then loosened my tie.

The water was so hot it hurt to enter it. But as soon as I'd done so, I had no regrets.

"Tough day?" she asked, after I'd settled in with much groaning, sliding my thighs over hers and my toes just under her armpits, my skin burning with the slightest movement.

"More like a waste of time. What can you tell me about Jim and Laura Reynolds?"

I hadn't shared our recent interest in Reynolds with

her. I'd thought it might put her in an awkward position, since they were friends and political allies. But given how Ed Renaud had just cleared their car of being at the train tracks, I wasn't so sure Jim Reynolds was in the hot seat I'd thought he was.

"They on your radar scope for some reason?" she asked.

"I think someone's trying to put him there. One of their cars was reported seen at that railroad killing, but now it looks like it might've been a substitute look-alike, equipped with his license plates. It's smelling like some strange kind of frame-up."

"I guess," she agreed. "So what do you want to know?"

"General stuff. Gut reactions. Whatever you can tell me about both of them."

"You met her?"

"Yeah—tonight. I'd seen her before, but this was the first time face-to-face. She's very poised—to begin with."

Gail laughed. "And then?"

"I got the feeling she was underwhelmed by his ambition."

"She hates it," Gail said flatly. "But he's a hard man to push around. Very competitive. I've talked to her about it—she plays the doting wife well, and I was curious how and why she did it. She didn't hold back once we got friendly. She loves him very much, and she's willing to put up with the bullshit for now, hoping to get her turn later. I think she's kidding herself, but that's the plan."

"A retirement in Santa Fe with concerts, tennis courts, and visits from the grandchildren?" I asked.

"Something like that. I don't think she understands how committed he is."

My chin was barely clear of the water by now, which meant that only half her face was visible above a field of billowing soap bubbles. My entire body was slowly relaxing.

"And how committed is he?" I asked.

"Very. Jim Reynolds's altruism is the real McCoy. It's not just ambition or insecurity or misplaced machismo that makes him both a politician and a defense lawyer. For one thing, he's bright enough to have gone to Boston or New York and made a zillion bucks working for cigarette companies or something. He believes in what he says, no matter how corny the Willy Kunkles of the world think that sounds. It's one reason he came up with this law enforcement bill, even if it means it'll make his life tougher as a lawyer. Selfishly, he'd be better off leaving the system alone, since it allows him a whole variety of loopholes to jump through."

"Except he won't be working as a lawyer," I commented. "If things work out for him, he'll be governor, and won't have to give a damn."

To her credit, Gail didn't get defensive. "Okay," she conceded, "I'll admit he's also a self-serving, conceited egomaniac who's going to wind up disappointing his long-suffering wife. If he does pull off this miracle and become top dog, he'll probably be aiming for something higher before he's three terms into it. She'll end up alone in Santa Fe and he'll be in DC. He is a politician, after all. He needs the attention. He needs people to tell him they love him."

"Could all that make him crooked, if he got desperate enough? He hadn't been making much of a statewide name for himself before this."

Again, she avoided the expected denial, merely tilting her head reflectively and admitting, "Maybe."

I laughed. "So much for Ivanhoe."

She scowled at me, provoked at last. "I never said he was that. I said he backed his ideals with action. What idealist hasn't run over a few people because he convinced himself it wasn't too high a price? And who are you or I or anyone else to say they're wrong? It's a pretty blurry line between stepping on people's toes for the right reason and running them over with ambition. I don't see Jim Reynolds ever committing an immoral or illegal act for purely selfish reasons. I *could* see him doing it thinking the ends justified the means."

"Sounds pretty arrogant," I said.

"He is that," she agreed. "He's also a real believer, which is why Laura's going to have to make up her mind to either make her peace or run for the hills." She paused and then added, "Not that it'll ever reach that stage—not with Mark Mullen standing ready to clip Jim's wings."

"The speaker?" I asked, surprised. I'd never heard Mullen's and Reynolds's names in the same sentence before. "What's he got to do with it?"

"They're eyeing the same gold ring. You watch. He's not going to let Reynolds ride that bill to the governorship. Somehow or another, when it gets to the House, Mullen will take it over—kill it, amend it, abandon it in committee—'let it hang on the wall,' as they say up there. But he'll remove Reynolds's fingerprints from it. Mullen hasn't spent thirty-plus years in the House without knowing how things work. And with Howell retiring, he feels he's earned a promotion."

I wiped the sweat from my face with a wet hand. "This may be more than I need to know right now."

Gail smiled and returned to more immediate issues. "So you think Laura may be trying to hobble Jim's horse?"

I laughed. "By framing her own husband? Interesting idea. I suppose she has the means to set it up— she said she was rich."

"Very. All inherited. Believe it or not, they met on a ski slope. He was the rugged, handsome instructor, on vacation from law school. She was the wealthy snow bunny working hard to drive her father nuts. That part probably worked, but she hadn't banked on Jim having dreams of his own." She paused and then added, "I doubt she figured on falling in love with him like she did, either. She may hate the life, but she's devoted to the man. That's where your theory hits the rocks."

I laughed. "My theory? This is your little movie. I don't have the slightest idea what's going on. I do know Stan Katz has his nose in the wind, though, so whatever it is, it's not going to stay private for long."

She made a disgusted face. "Great. That'll really help clear things up."

"He called me to ask if Reynolds had any ties to illegal dumping."

She surprised me by not rejecting the notion out of hand. "As in hazardous materials?"

"Yeah. Why?"

She answered slowly—and enigmatically, "He's represented a lot of people over the years. One of them might be thinking he didn't get his money's worth. That's where I'd look."

The thought had crossed my mind. As had the fact that Jim Reynolds—despite Gail's opinion and his own wife's support—might be a whole lot less pure than the driven snow.

Snow, as it turned out, was on everyone's mind the next morning. Having held off entirely through a bitterly cold, bleak Christmas season, it seemed winter was trying to make amends all in one day. Looking out the window as I dressed, I couldn't even see the garage. Slowly falling in thick, heavy flakes, it reminded me of a flurry of cherry blossoms torn suddenly from their stems. But a flurry without stop.

I went downstairs and paused on the back doorstep, taking it in. This kind of snowstorm—dense, silent, and windless—has an effect unlike any other weather phenomenon. Rather than producing sound, it absorbs it; instead of displaying great havoc, it cuts off your sight. And yet it permeates every sense, less like an act of nature and more like a spiritual event. Most people walk around in such a snowfall as if blessed with new insight—or at least lost in childlike wonder.

Gail, on the other hand, was having none of it. Appearing next to me moments later, she merely glanced up, scowled, and said, "This'll sure screw up traffic," and disappeared into the whitewash like a thought fading from memory, heading for her car.

I followed her example a few minutes later, driving off without working my windshield wipers. The snow was dry, and the motion of the vehicle was enough to clear the glass, which allowed me to enjoy the snow-clad stillness unimpeded. I could almost imagine not being in a car at all, but traveling in a dreamlike state through some hopeless romantic's version of utopia.

Except, of course, that Gail had been right. Not far from the house, I passed the first abandoned car in a ditch, and after that was confronted by a series of traffic jams, confused drivers, and irritated plow operators. The scanner in my car murmured an endless stream of directives to ambulances, wreckers, and squad cars to aid those lost, hurt, and broken-down. The town I'd left the day before had been visited by a quiet, otherworldly, beatific disaster.

When I finally reached it, the office was a command center under siege, the dispatch room manned by a double shift, the hallways filled with milling, snow-dusted officers tracking muddy footprints behind them, and the air resonating with the sound of ringing phones and squawking radios. And yet, beneath it all, there was a lightheartedness. No one, it seems, can really take a storm like this too seriously, even in the midst of chaos and discomfort. Too many memories of sledding, snowballs, and the taste of it on your tongue get in the way.

Predictably, the detective squad was sparsely populated. Harriet was there, as was Ron. Willy, as expected, was not. Sammie, the sudden enigma, was also missing, no doubt bundled up with her newfound joy under a comforter.

My one concern was Tyler. "Where's J.P.?" I asked Harriet.

"Returning from Waterbury. He radioed in a while ago. He's on the interstate, not far north of here, but he's having a tough time. Things are almost at a standstill. The weather report's predicting three feet—a record-breaker."

"He did say the lab came through big time," Ron added from his desk. "Course, he was up there all night bugging them."

He looked it when he arrived an hour later—disheveled, in need of a shave, and with bloodshot eyes. But smiling.

He dumped an overstuffed briefcase on his desk and collapsed into a chair without removing his coat. "The print on the knife belongs to one Owen Tharp, aged nineteen. Last known address: Brookside Terrace. Supposedly lives there with an aunt, Judith Tharp Giroux. He's unemployed, was being monitored by SRS until two years ago, and has been tested ADD, among other things. SRS told me his parents never married, his father's unknown, and his mother died of alcoholism about eight years ago. He's been in foster homes since he was three, never stayed in one for more than a few years, and didn't finish high school."

He paused to take a breath.

"Any criminal record?" I asked, saddened by the familiarity of this litany.

"You bet. Burglary, destruction of private property, criminal trespass, assault, possession of malt beverages, public disorderliness, and a shit-load of other stuff, mostly committed in Springfield and Bellows Falls, where he grew up. He did juvie time, too, but I couldn't find out what for. My contact would only bend the rules so far."

SRS was the state's Department of Social and Rehabilitation Services, largely designed to help those of Vermont's children who were in peril. It was a swamped organization that was predictably either lauded or damned, depending on one's viewpoint. I wouldn't have worked there to save my life. They got my respect, though, even if their procedures sometimes drove me crazy.

"One other thing," J.P. added with a broad smile. "Just in case you were thinking of an arrest warrant.

The lab pegged that plaster cast I took of the tire impression to a cheap Taiwanese brand, sized to fit something small, and equipped with the kind of knobby tread a teenager might put on a pickup. Aunt Judith is registered as owning an '88 Chevy Luv pickup, pale blue."

I turned to Ron Klesczewski. "The names Owen Tharp or Judith Giroux appear in any of those lists you been tabulating?"

He nodded, reaching for a thick folder. "Tharp's does. I remembered it 'cause it sounded funny." He started pawing through sheets of paper, pausing now and then to read. "Here it is," he finally said. "Janice Litchfield mentioned him as a hanger-on. Nothing beyond that."

"See if you can get her in here."

Janice Litchfield had regained her composure since our last conversation. Now she was as brassy as the hardware puncturing what body parts I could see.

This time, I put her in the interrogation box.

"Why'd you pull me in again?" she demanded, sitting on a metal chair like she'd been dropped from ten feet.

I was walking back and forth before her. "We were wondering if you'd thought of anything new that might help us nail Brenda's killer."

She began studying her bitten, flaking nails again. "I told you what I know."

"You gave us some names. That was a start. You think of any others?"

"No."

"You said you and Brenda were involved in some

pretty risky things, any of which could've gone sour. Anything there that might've gotten her killed?"

"No."

I stopped pacing. "You were also worried you might end up the same way."

She flared up slightly. "She was stupid. I always had more brains than her. She was asking for it."

"How?"

"Shootin' her mouth off. Dissin' the wrong people."

I pulled a piece of paper from my pocket and consulted it. "Which people?"

"Just people." She was sullen.

"Like Jamie Good?"

"Sure. For one."

I picked a name at random, although a familiar one. "Billy Conyer?"

"She liked Billy."

"Walter Freund?"

"Yeah."

"Frankie Harris?"

She looked up. "Frankie's an old guy. He's no threat."

"They saw a lot of each other. Maybe she pissed him off somehow."

She just shook her head.

"Owen Tharp?"

This time, she laughed. "*Owen?* You gotta be kidding. Owen's like a puppy dog, hanging around, diving for scraps. He wouldn't scare nobody."

"He know Brenda?"

She shrugged. "Everybody knows everybody."

"They do drugs together? Have sex?"

"Owen's always broke. That's why he lives with that old bitch."

"Judith Giroux?"

"Whatever."

"You seen him around lately?"

She narrowed her eyes suspiciously. "Why're you so interested in Owen? He's like nowhere."

"Maybe, but you're not the only one being brought in for questioning, Janice. We're talking to everybody, from the top dogs to the nobodies."

"Well, you're starting with a nobody there."

"So when did you last see him?"

"I don't know. A few days. He's around, though. Ask Walter, if you're so interested. He's more Walter's pet than anyone's."

I moved on. "You ever see Owen get mad?"

Janice's nervous hands became still.

"You have, haven't you?" I pressed.

"Sure." But her surliness had lost its edge.

"Tell me about it."

She looked up with something like wonder. "It was weird—like he flipped out. Walter was raggin' him, like we all do. Owen invites it, the way he is. But this time he blew up. Came at Walter like he was going to kill him."

"How?"

There was silence in the small bare room. I thought suddenly of the mantle of thick snow that was slowly enveloping the building, smothering everything beneath it.

"He grabbed a pen," she finally said quietly. "Tried to use it like a knife."

"What did Walter do?"

"He laughed."

*   *   *

Brookside Terrace is a combination low-cost housing development/condominium complex, which looks about as awkward as it sounds. Consisting of a scattering of brown-painted wooden structures reminiscent of either a run-down motel or a cheap ski-slope apartment building, it is tucked into a hillside and pinned there by the Whetstone Brook, which cuts across its front on its way through Brattleboro. Paralleling the water along the opposite bank is Route 9—variously called High Street, Western Avenue, and the Marlboro Road. As Vermont's only southern, quasi-straight, horizontal traffic corridor, Route 9 is at the best of times crowded, and during rush hours, a nightmare. Thus the cheaper units at Brookside Terrace get the combined joys of little sunlight, limited access, long waits at the stop sign, and the pleasant, soothing, year-round sound of rushing water—punctuated by squealing tires and the roar of traffic.

Not that there was much of that when we approached the area in the early afternoon. The snow had continued unabated, and although the plows were beginning to catch up, at least on the primary thruways, traffic had pretty much called it quits. The snow's one-dimensional whitewash had reduced visibility like an offshore fog bank, making distinguishing a car from the road beneath it a challenge.

There were three of us—Ron, myself, and Sammie, who had appeared at the office two hours late. I'd also arranged to have a patrol car with two uniformed officers stand by at the gas station down the road, despite the storm-related workload having gotten so bad that an extra shift had been called on duty.

Owen Tharp and his aunt lived in a long, low unit of apartments right by the edge of the brook—the first building to the left off the access bridge. I'd had Sammie telephone not fifteen minutes earlier, pretending she was from SRS, to talk to Owen about some made-up bureaucratic detail. Judith had answered first, confirming they were both at home, and Sammie had kept it brief and innocuous, closing with a comment about the weather. Owen had complained about the long-range buses being canceled that day.

Which had told us to either move fast or miss him altogether.

Ron and I took the front door of the apartment, sending Sam around back to keep an eye on the rear.

I knocked, standing to one side out of habit, Ron across from me. We didn't have our guns out. Most arrests, especially of people with Owen's largely meek reputation, are fairly dull affairs—low-key conversations ending with handcuffs and a depressing walk to the back of a car.

This one didn't start out any differently. After a minute's wait, the door handle turned, and we were greeted by a thin woman with her hair tied back, her face sharp and unpleasant, a cigarette between her fingers.

"What do you want?"

I let Ron do the talking. "Police, ma'am. Is Owen Tharp here?"

"Why?" she asked querulously, stepping more fully into the door.

That was all I needed. As Ron answered, "We have a warrant for his arrest," I pushed by Judith Giroux and entered the dark apartment, closely followed by Ron.

"Hey," Giroux yelled, grasping at the wall for bal-

ance, and knocking over a lamp. "You can't do that."
And in a louder voice, *"Run, Owen, run."*

We both heard a muffled crash from the back and
charged in that direction, cautious at the doorways, guns
now out. I keyed the mike of my portable radio and
shouted at Sammie to watch out.

There was no response.

We entered a messy bedroom, slowly filling with
freezing air from a wide-open window.

"Damn," I muttered, and carefully poked my head
outside.

Sammie was lying sprawled on her back, half in the
water, nearby but barely visible in the unremitting
snowfall.

"Sammie. You okay?"

She waved at me. "He went downstream. I slipped
on a fucking rock."

She fell again trying to stand.

I gave Ron a boost out the window and then joined
him at the water's edge. Whetstone Brook ran year-
around, violently in spots, and—especially downstream—sometimes between steep, ravinelike banks.

"Was he armed?" I asked Sammie as she joined us,
soaked from the waist down.

"Not that I saw." Her face was flushed with fury.

"All units," I radioed. "Suspect has fled east along
Whetstone Brook. Unknown whether he's armed or not.
Approach with extreme caution."

Sammie was no longer interested in caution.
Drenched and probably freezing already, she plunged
off in pursuit down the middle of the streambed, stag-
gering on the uncertain footing.

Ron glanced at me quickly. I let out a sigh of frustration. "Guess we better keep her company."

Our progress was predictably slow. Blinded by snow, deafened by the water's roar, and confused by the hidden terrain, we tried keeping to the bank, stumbling every few feet, bruising our freezing hands on the slippery rocks. It quickly became impossible to differentiate between solid ground and water under the snow's crust, and we both were soon wet to the knees, beginning a thermal clock that our bodies could only fight for so long. Sammie was probably already totally numb, but I wasn't counting on that to slow her down.

As we went, I kept updating dispatch by radio, suggesting places where intercept teams could get to the water. But the weather, the traffic, and the number of accidents around town were limiting our stretched resources. The backup unit I'd had standing by had been notified too late to be of immediate use, and while they were now driving east to head off Owen farther downstream, I wasn't sure they'd be successful, blue lights or not.

The terrain got worse. The banks steepened and the streambed narrowed, forcing us deeper into the faster-running water. Now all three of us were soaked, and the initial sting of cold had become a violent throbbing, making numbness a blessing and frostbite a real possibility. I'd waited too long to call off what never should have started in the first place.

Complicating this, however, was Sammie. Barely visible ahead of us, making no pretense of fighting the rapids, she'd allowed herself finally to be simply swept along. Either because of the cold or her own hard-headedness, she'd gone beyond being rational.

"Ron," I shouted over the water's roar. "We got to get her out. To hell with Owen."

Ron nodded, and to my utter astonishment, plunged

headlong into the water, like a lifeguard into the summer surf.

We had struggled to just shy of the Williams Street bend in the stream, where an abrupt drop-off creates a quasi-chasm in the midst of a rocky, tree-choked glen. Although this spot is near the heart of one of the largest towns in Vermont, there was no evidence anywhere that we were within a hundred miles of civilization.

Except, just before the falls, for a narrow, low-slung metal trestle, carrying a six-inch sewage pipe from one bank to the other.

As I gingerly drew within sight of it, unwilling to yield to the water's rage as had my colleagues, I saw them both—along with Owen Tharp—draped or pinned against the overpass like bugs on a windshield wiper. Sammie had one arm hooked through the metalwork and the other arm around Owen's neck, while Ron was keeping both of them from being carried over the edge to the rocks below.

I updated the others by radio and, moving like an awkward, antiquated robot, tried to help Ron keep everyone alive.

Chapter Twelve

The three of us were in Sammie's hospital room the next morning when Willy Kunkle walked in. We'd been kept overnight for observation—including Owen, under guard—to assure that our cold-water adventure hadn't led to more than a craving for lots of hot coffee. Fortunately, it had not.

"Don't you look cute," Willy observed of our hospital gowns. "Sam, climb out of bed so I can see if that's one of those tie-across-the-back models."

Sammie still hadn't regained her sense of humor since losing Tharp to a slippery stone. "Up yours."

"How's Owen?" I asked diplomatically.

Willy was unusually cheerful. "He's fine, and getting VIP treatment, since he totally spilled his guts. He's already in our lockup, waiting for arraignment."

"He confessed?" Ron asked.

"Yup. Last night, after the docs let us at him. Described where he left the body, the knife he used, and where he threw it by the side of the road. J.P. and me checked his apartment and gave Judith the third degree—there's a lovely woman, by the way—and she even handed over some bloody clothes she was going to get rid of."

"Anything fitting the knee-print we found next to Brenda's body?" I asked.

"Don't know. J.P.'s hoarding it. All I saw was a jacket with a smeared cuff and a shoe with a couple of drops on it. Looked like Owen must've split before it got real messy."

"The arraignment's this afternoon?" Ron asked, always conscious of deadlines. "You been able to get the paperwork ready?"

Kunkle looked at him scornfully. "Scared you might be replaced, Ronnie? Actually, it was so easy, I wonder why you make such a big deal out of it all the time. Job security, I guess."

I cut him off as Ron's face reddened. "Why did he do it?"

Willy perched on the edge of Sammie's bed. "That part's a little melodramatic, but then I think Owen's a few bricks shy of a load. He says he had a girlfriend a couple of years back who died of some bad dope. He didn't know it was Brenda then that supplied her, but when he found out, he got good and hopped up and went over to confront her. She told him to pound sand and he sliced-'n'-diced her—just like that."

"Who told him it was Brenda?"

"No one. He said he discovered it for himself—that she'd poisoned the stuff."

"He know about the kid in the back room?"

"Negative. Not that it matters. It's a two-for-one sale, according to the SA—Felony Murder Rule."

Thinking of the election later in the year, I asked, "The SA going to handle it himself?"

Willy smiled. "Nope. Your love-mate is, with him looking over her shoulder, of course."

"Gail?" I blurted out.

"Unless you switched partners. Derby wants to spend his quality time rallying votes. Rumor has it James Dunn wants the office back in November. Total bull-shit, of course—everyone hates Dunn—but Derby's got sweaty palms. Plus, he thinks if he lets one of his deputies handle it, it'll show off the office's depth—he's fighting the image of being a headline hog as well as a micro-manager, just like Dunn used to be. Looks like the public defender's office is going to assign Reggie McNeil from their side. Should be fun for Gail, given Reggie's habits."

McNeil had made a reputation of using anything and everything in defense of his clients—sometimes to the point of getting his wrist slapped by his boss, the defender general. This zeal did not endear him to anyone I knew in law enforcement.

"How do you know McNeil's got it? Wouldn't that happen at the arraignment?" I asked, surprised.

"Right after Owen fessed up"—Willy gave Ron a meaningful look—"which was right after we Miran-dized him nice and legal—I guess he suddenly got cold feet. Maybe it was hearing himself out loud or some-thing. Anyhow, he clammed up—a little late—and said he wanted a lawyer. Asked for McNeil personally. Not that that scumbag isn't a household name to every loser in town."

"McNeil is such a jerk . . ." Sammie began joining in, but came to a full stop, her mouth half open and her eyes on the door.

We all followed her gaze and saw a tall, slim man with long dark hair, dressed in a thigh-length leather jacket. He had high cheekbones, a permanent five o'clock shadow, a strong chin, and penetrating eyes. To my jaundiced eye, he looked like a wannabe fashion model, touched by just enough cheapness to ruin the effect.

"Andy," Sammie said in a slightly strangled voice.

Andy Padgett looked uncomfortably at the bunch of us, obviously caught unawares by our presence.

"Hey, babe," he said cautiously, his voice muted.

Willy turned to Sammie in mock outrage. "You never let *me* call you that. How's he get away with it?"

Sammie's lips barely moved. "Fuck off, Willy."

I got up and crossed over to shake Padgett's hand, hoping to dilute the tension. Gail and Ron's wife had dropped by to see us the night before, and we'd all had a good time. I felt badly now that Sammie's chance at the same kind of comfort was being ruined. "Hi. I'm Joe Gunther. Glad to meet you. This is Ron Klesczewski. Willy Kunkle I think you already know."

Padgett's grip was brief. His eyes only briefly met mine. "Yeah. Hi."

"Sammie's said good things about you."

He took a half step backward, still speaking in a murmur, obviously not buying my patter. "Great. She's okay. Look, I don't want to interrupt." He raised his hand to her. "I'll catch you later."

Willy laughed. "Well, warm your hands up ahead of time. She's a little frigid right now."

Sammie punched him in his bad shoulder. "You are such an asshole. I'll see you at home, Andy. Thanks for coming."

Padgett vanished as if a rope had yanked him clear of the doorway.

"Must've been late for another poker game," Willy said, relentless to the end.

Sammie pushed him clear off the bed. "Get out, Willy. What the hell did he ever do to you?"

Willy moved to the door. Under the smirk, he was simmering. "Nothing yet. He better hope he doesn't, either."

"Jesus," she exclaimed, but her target had already left.

A doctor filled the doorway instead, stopping dead in his tracks at the assembled hostile stares. He glanced at Kunkle's departing back, invisible to us, and then asked generally, "Is everything all right?"

For some reason, we all looked at Sammie.

She was pale with rage. "Not hardly."

"So—good news?" I asked him hopefully, my voice sounding loud in the quiet room.

He took my cue, ignoring the tension, and allowed that since we'd apparently survived the night with no obvious ill effects, we were free to go.

But back in the room I'd shared with Ron, changing into my clothes and preparing to leave, I found my thoughts weren't on the weird three-way tug-of-war between Sam, Willy, and Andy Padgett. That, as I saw it, had been something they'd have to work out on their own. Instead, I was grappling with the abrupt end of an intense investigation, made all the more dramatic by Owen's unexpected confession.

We'd still be involved in the case, of course. After the arraignment, both sides would retire to their corners, build up witness lists, read each other's mail about evidence, and jockey around for advantage. And we'd be called to help in some of that—tying off the odd loose end. But as I tucked my few belongings under my arm and headed for the door, I still felt like I'd been left on the dock to wave a ship good-bye.

I should've known better.

With Gail anointed the lead lawyer in the prosecution against Owen Tharp, it was deemed a bad idea to have too many of my fingerprints on the case. While not married, we were a well-known couple, a connection which had come up in court before. It was obvious baloney—the police and the state's attorney's office were supposed to work in tandem—but on high-profile cases like this, it was best not to give the defense any more than we had to.

And it wasn't as if I had nothing else to do—a point driven home as soon as I'd sat down at my desk.

Harriet Fritter, after asking about my health and telling me to act my age, dumped a thick pile of paperwork before me and told me Stan Katz had been in hot pursuit by phone.

I held off calling him back for a while, digging through the pile instead—half wondering if Harriet hadn't subversively set me up to do just that—when Ron appeared in my doorway.

"I heard back from New Jersey on Phil Resnick—the guy we're hoping was our dead truck driver?"

I nodded to keep him going.

"Well, it's a definite hit. They sent me prints, and one of them not only matches the finger J.P. found, but Waterbury just confirmed it through their data bank. It wasn't on AFIS, but they used some other method. That's why it took so long—that and the fact it was only one finger."

"Phil Resnick," I mused. "What else did New Jersey tell you?"

"That he was Mob-connected. Not family himself—with that last name—but more of a freelancer."

"Trucking haz mat?"

"Yup," he confirmed, "throughout New England."

He handed me a grainy black-and-white facsimile of a photograph of a round-faced, ugly man, apparently trying to melt the camera lens with his eyes.

I studied the face for a few moments. "Makes you wonder if any other department up around here ever had dealings with him."

Ron smiled. "I just finished putting it on the wire—every PD from Maine to upper New York State, including Massachusetts. God knows what we'll hear back, or when, but it can't hurt. Sounds like the guy'd been doing this for quite a while."

That rang two bells in my brain. "According to Bobby Miller, the only thing disturbed in Jim Reynolds's office was a cabinet filled with old files. And Gail said a few days ago that she wouldn't put it past one of Reynolds's old clients to want to get even with him, especially if he'd lost their case."

Ron just looked at me, his eyebrows arched.

"Do me a favor," I asked him. "Dig through the court records, back to when Reynolds started working here, and pull anything dealing with hazardous materials, illegal trucking, Phil Resnick, environmental offenses, and anything else like it." I checked my watch. "Who's going to the intel meeting this morning? We might as well give them a heads up, too."

"I was planning to go," he admitted, "but I don't have anything to present. Why don't you give them this while I start on Reynolds's court records?"

*   *   *

Regional police intelligence meetings were held once a month in a conference room at Rescue, Inc., the area's primary ambulance squad. They could have been held at our department, but the theory was to give all those attending a sense of neutral ground.

The principle behind the meetings was simple: to get as many representatives from as many diverse agencies as possible into one room every four weeks to present, update, and exchange information. Depending on the time of year, and the luck of the draw, attendees could number from as few as five to as many as twenty. They were sheriff's deputies, federal agents, state police from Vermont, New Hampshire, and Massachusetts, municipal cops from any one of dozens of surrounding communities, parole and probation officers from the Department of Corrections, investigators from state's attorney's offices, and people from liquor enforcement, the Agency of Natural Resources, and even outfits like the National Guard. The organizations they represented ranged from departments with a few officers to the United States government, and the topics discussed from stolen tires to foreign terrorists threatening to poison whole cities. Nobody was treated differently from anybody else, and all information received equal attention. Sending a bulletin out to surrounding departments— as Ron had just done concerning Phil Resnick—was worthwhile and routine, but it was hard to beat a direct sell if you wanted to have your message clearly heard.

Pure chance had timed the monthly meeting for today. And by going, I could stave off talking to Stan Katz that much longer.

There were about ten of us by the time we settled down, having turned the parking lot into a convention of squad cars and suspiciously bland sedans, all sprouting antennae, and all precariously huddled next to towering eight-foot snowbanks.

Henry Roberts of the Windham County Sheriff's Office—polite, precise in manner, and always immaculately turned out—ran the meeting, having each of us speak in a clockwise rotation around the table, while desperately keeping notes on a laptop computer.

By the time my turn came, we'd all received xeroxed mug shots of a check kiter, a car booster, and a welfare defrauder, had been asked to keep an eye out for a suspected coke dealer, a religious right-wing gunrunner, and a two-brother team of bunko artists, and had covered our notepads with lists of names, birth dates, known associates, license plate numbers, and vehicle descriptions.

"Sorry I don't have anything quite as lively as everyone else," I began. "My suspect's not only dead, but missing a head and both hands."

"The railroad bum?" one of them asked.

"Yes and no," I answered. "We had doubts he was a bum from the start. Now we've found out he was a New Jersey-based truck driver with Mob connections named Philip Resnick." I passed around copies I'd made of Ron's fuzzy photograph. "Date of birth 4/8/51. His past accomplishments are listed below the picture. We're pretty sure he was transporting a haz mat cocktail that he dumped at Norm Blood's farm just before his truck broke down and he had to abandon it near Bickford's. My first question is: Has anyone here ever seen him or heard about him?"

There was a momentary pause around the room: "Any local connections other than Blood?" someone finally asked.

"Not really," I answered. "The truck was leased from

Timson Long Haul near Leverett, Massachusetts, but the guy we talked to there couldn't find his paperwork and wasn't inclined to look. Supposedly, Resnick was just one of several people who'd leased the same rig recently, so we're thinking Timson might be a dead end. If the Mob is tied into this, it's unlikely they'd make it that easy for us to find them."

A plainclothes state trooper from Massachusetts named Peter Manning disagreed. "We've had dealings with Timson before," he said. "He's definitely crooked, but he's also probably a pure freelancer—he's never appeared on any of our Mafia watch lists. He makes a profit, though. Leverett's hardly the place for a trucking company, and his place is a dump, but he keeps plugging along year after year, like he was located in downtown Boston. You want to give him a visit, I'd be happy to ride shotgun. The only thing we've caught him red-handed at over the years is either routine vehicle maintenance shit or some minor book cooking. But his name keeps coming up with this haz mat stuff, and I'd love to let him know we're still watching."

I nodded my thanks. "You got a deal. I'll call you in a few days."

Later, back in my office, I stared dolefully at yet another pink phone message from Katz, the latest in a stack of four. I didn't actually know what he was after, but it didn't really matter. It was the general predictability of our conversations I dreaded more than their actual content.

This time, however, he surprised me.

"You at your office?" he asked right after I'd identified myself.

"Yeah."

"We have to meet—now—somewhere neutral."

There was an edge to his voice I'd only rarely heard before. "If by neutral you mean private, how 'bout past where Corrections hang their hats? The snowplows have a turnaround just beyond their parking lot."

"I'll see you there."

Katz was hyperactive by nature. It had helped make him the journalist he was, which, in all fairness, was honorable—if as irritating as a canker sore. But the level of energy I'd just heard on the phone was several notches above his norm, so I set out to meet him with some real curiosity.

The Corrections Department's parole and probation offices occupied the basement of a flamboyantly pink office building that had once housed a chocolate factory. It was located on a flat strip of land between the high bank supporting the Putney Road and the same Retreat Meadows floodplain where Ed Renaud and I had shared our meditative chat in the fishing shanty.

The building is almost the last structure on a dead-end road, and as I'd pointed out to Katz, the snowplows have turned the area just past its parking lot into a round amphitheater of piled-up snow, visually isolated from any neighbors, but with a view of the frozen Meadows.

As a result, when we met there ten minutes later, it looked oddly like a half-completed stage set—two cars parked in an empty, featureless half bowl of white space, faced with a seemingly flat picture-postcard image hanging before us like a drop.

I left my car to join Katz in his—a rusting, ten-year-old Japanese pickup with chained-together cinder blocks in the back to give it traction in the snow. As soon as I'd closed the door behind me, I regretted my manners.

The tiny cab stank of rancid fast food and stale cigarettes, both aggravated by an overactive heater.

Despite the cold, I cracked my window a few inches and turned up my collar. "What's on your mind, Stanley?"

He sat staring out at the view for a few seconds, as if collecting his thoughts. "We've known each other a long time, right?"

I didn't bother answering.

"And we've helped each other out now and then. You've given me stuff under the counter. I've sat on a story or two. I mean, all the cops-versus-press bullshit aside, we've always gotten along pretty well, haven't we?"

He expected an answer this time. And despite his being someone I'd never think of inviting over for supper, at least I couldn't argue his basic point. "I suppose so."

As anemic as it was, that seemed to settle his mind. "I'm in a bit of a jam. Not a legal one." He quickly cut me a glance. "More like an ethical one. Remember when I asked you about Jim Reynolds?"

Again, I stayed silent, this time holding my breath.

"Well, I got another anonymous call about him—a little more serious."

"Same guy?"

"I couldn't be sure. It was a man's voice, but muffled like the first one."

He hesitated. I filled the gap. "What did he say?"

He twisted in his seat to look at me. "It's pretty big, Joe, even without Reynolds being who he is and this being an election year. It's big enough that I'm going to be digging into it like nobody's business."

"You want to know what we have on him?" I

guessed. "Use me to see if you might be on to something?"

"I want to know where you stand with him first."

I stared at him in surprise. "*Stand* with him? I barely know the guy. You asking if I'd shield him?"

My incredulity spoke for me. He looked slightly embarrassed. "I had to ask, Joe. You blew off the illegal dumping when I mentioned it. Gail does have close ties to him . . ."

"Tell me what you got," I told him angrily, "or I'm out of here." I put my hand on the door handle, impatient with his dancing around.

"The man on the phone said Reynolds was connected to the woman who was knifed to death."

That stopped me. "How?"

"You know of no such connection?"

I hesitated before answering, suddenly wary of what might be lurking out of sight. I decided to play it straight. "None at all."

"But you are checking him out?"

I sidestepped a bit, sticking to what was already in the public record. There was no chance in hell I was going to tell him about the presumably bogus sighting of Reynolds's car at the railroad tracks. "His office was broken into a while back. We are looking into that, although we have no suspects, no leads, and nothing reported stolen or missing."

He understood I wanted him to read between the lines there. "That must be a little delicate, poking around where you're not invited." He paused and then muttered, as if to himself, "I don't remember that item being in our police blotter column."

"It was right up there with a barking dog complaint. The current theory is that one of our patrols scared off whoever it was before he even got inside. You said it yourself, Stan, it's a political year—hotter'n most. Could be your caller is up to dirty tricks."

"Tying a candidate to a murder?" he asked, his voice rising. "Suggesting I'm being used? Who says you're not doing the same thing right now?"

I suddenly became resensitized to the heat and stench of the cab. I wanted to get out of this conversation. "Stan, I'm not sure what we're doing here. I could've told you on the phone we have nothing linking Reynolds to Croteau's murder."

"Then why are you still poking into a burglary that wasn't? Why were you checking out Reynolds's car at his house?"

I rolled the window all the way down. So much for the buddy-buddy routine. "Who told you that?"

"Never mind. I know you were there, and that Willy brought J.P.'s bag of toys with him. What were you looking for?"

"Something that didn't pan out." He opened his mouth to say something, but I kept talking. "Stanley, we do a lot of things nobody ever hears about. People call us anonymously, too, you know? They tell us they saw a crime, or committed one, or know someone who did. We check 'em all out, no matter how bogus they sound—just like the one that brought us to Reynolds's garage."

He pretended to look at something far out on the ice. "If it was a dead end, why don't you tell me what it was?"

"Because it's not news, Stan. It's none of your business."

He suddenly flared up and hit the steering wheel with the flat of his hand. "Bullshit. I get two separate calls that Reynolds is dirty, his office is broken into, I know you guys have been checking him out, and the whole town is in a tizzy with two homicides, one of which I've been told is linked to him. And I'm supposed to ignore that?"

"I wouldn't be writing any stories about it."

He ran his fingers through his hair and sighed heavily, finally smiling at me wearily. "That's why I'm here, Joe. I'm not writing any stories. I want to do the right thing, not play into some game his opponents are setting up. The press gets manipulated enough as it is. I want to write the truth."

I opened the door to get out. "I'd help you if I could, Stan. Right now, the truth is we came up with nothing when we looked at his car, so the reasons why we did so in the first place are irrelevant. And we have absolutely nothing linking Reynolds to the Croteau killing. As Jack Derby already announced, we have a confessed suspect in custody for that, and we're going to trial with it."

He rolled his own window down as I circled his hood to return to my car. "You don't put a man's car through the forensics wringer for a fender-bender. If Reynolds is clean on the Croteau thing, then maybe you're trying to tie him to the bum. Is that what's happening?"

I considered leaving it at that, with an unstated "no comment." But I knew Stan too well—it would have been like pouring gasoline on an ember.

Instead, I leaned against his door in a friendly gesture. "Look, I know you want some answers. And I know that, being who he is, Reynolds brings a lot of weight to all this. So I'm not trying to blow you off. I mean, you're right about our scratching each other's back now and then. It's worked out for both of us. But we move slower than you do, Stan. We have to. You've got readers wanting sexy news, not state's attorneys ready to kick your ass at the first mistake. It makes us more cautious."

"I wouldn't print anything I couldn't stand behind," he said stiffly. "That's why I called you."

"I know that. I also know you're not going to end it here. You're going to chase after every other source you can think of."

"So?" he asked.

I held up my hand. "So great. I'm just telling you to watch out . . . Off the record?"

He raised his eyebrows. "What?"

"We are looking into Reynolds, for what I won't tell you right now. But I am smelling a rat in motion somewhere, which is what's making me extra careful. You're going to do what you do—you always have—but I gotta tell you: On this one, watch your step. Don't get used."

I couldn't read his expression, and didn't wait around for explanations.

I stopped by Ron's desk and waited for him to finish typing on his computer.

"What's up?" he asked almost immediately.

"Remember I asked you a while back to look into Reynolds's past?"

"The court cases? Yeah, I got that going . . ."

He was stopped by my shaking my head. "No, no. I meant earlier—anything on VIBRS or even our internal files. Any mention at all?"

He looked at me oddly. "Couldn't find a thing.

Maybe a parking ticket or two, but that was it. Why? You got something?"

I didn't make a habit of withholding information from my officers, but I comforted myself this time that what I had didn't even qualify as such—yet. "No. His name just keeps coming up. Have you had a chance to tear into Brenda's journal—line by line?"

"Pretty much. It hasn't been a high priority, what with her killer in jail. I thought I'd use it more as a future intel source than as ammo against Owen. He's barely mentioned."

"What about Reynolds? Does he come up?"

Ron shook his head, giving that look again. "Nope. Not a peep."

"How 'bout code names or pseudonyms?"

His brow furrowed. "Nothing that obvious. She used a lot of first names, though. I suppose they could be codes."

I got up, disappointed. "Okay. Thanks anyway."

"How'd the arraignment go?" I asked Gail that night.

She put her briefcase on the floor, kicked off her snow boots, dumped her coat on one kitchen chair, and collapsed into another. "Fine. McNeil whined about his client's confused state, his ties to the community, his financial constraints. Judge Harrowsmith couldn't have cared less. I asked for no bail, and that's what we got. Good thing Owen called about bus schedules just before you grabbed him. I think that clinched it for Harrowsmith. We have any boiling water ready?"

I knew her well enough to have done just that. Without asking, I fixed her a steaming cup of green tea and set it on the table beside her. She took advantage of my proximity to kiss me as I leaned forward.

"Thanks," she said. "You get a chance to talk with Owen?"

"No. By the time I got out of the hospital, he'd already been sucked into the pipeline. Why?"

She paused to sip her tea, wincing slightly at its heat. "God, that feels good. I don't know—he looked pretty pathetic. Hardly the knife-wielding sort."

A cold feeling entered my mind as I recalled Katz's suspicions about Reynolds. "You had dinner yet?" I asked.

"We had a pizza brought up—again. That's one reason this tastes so good. Cuts through the grease."

"You seen the evidence we have against him?" I asked her cautiously.

She interrupted a second sip to answer quickly, "Oh, yeah. I don't have any doubts he did it, and we have Janice Litchfield's statement about him attacking someone with a pen a while back. He just looked a little incongruous, you know? Like the kind of kid always ignored by the in-crowd."

I took my own cup of coffee and sat next to her, as we often did late at night. "You think that's the line McNeil's going to use? Diminished capacity or something?"

"Probably. Who knows? He's only had about fifteen minutes with him so far. It's too early to tell. He'll start digging around and collecting witnesses and asking for delays, like he always does, hoping he can wait long enough for either the furor to die down or for us to drop the ball somehow. And sure as hell he'll try to get that confession thrown out."

"You think he can?" Again, I was wondering what Katz might be doing in the meantime, unwittingly or not, to undermine the process. Not to mention where those missing journal pages might be.

She shook her head. "I talked to Willy about it. I wish he hadn't been the one to get it. He leaves such a lousy impression with juries. But he had J.P. with him, and it sounds like it was straight as a string. It should hold up. What worries me is that since it came after that chase, McNeil'll argue Owen was too weak and disoriented to know what he was saying—and since he did ask for a lawyer right after he confessed, it shows he was confused."

I smiled at her scrutiny of the angles. She hadn't been a deputy SA for very long, and had started out, as most of them did, in family court, where any potential mistakes occurred mostly behind closed doors. This was big-league stuff at last, and I could almost touch her enthusiasm.

"How's Derby to work with on this?"

"Great. He's giving me lots of leeway. He handed virtually my entire case load off to the others, so I can really keep focused. I think it'll be fine."

"Scuttlebutt has it he'll be chasing votes most of the time anyway," I said mildly. "James Dunn supposedly wants back in."

But she saw through the veil. "Oh, I know what people think. I'm a woman, I have strong local connections and a useful political past, and this case is a no-brainer. I can live with that perception." She drained her cup and smiled at me. "Because I also know Jack Derby owes me. He feels guilty for giving me the shaft when you got into trouble with the attorney general's office—treating me like a pariah just because he was worried about bad press. He knows I deserved better."

She paused and added, "He didn't come up with the idea of using me entirely on his own, you know."

I nodded deeply in her direction in a mock salute. "I should never have thought otherwise. And I'm sure you'll knock 'em dead."

But I had my concerns, both real and imagined.

Chapter Thirteen

Leverett, Massachusetts, is between Amherst and the Vermont border on one axis, and Interstate 91 and the Quabbin Reservoir on the other, which puts it neither in a popular recreational area nor along the interstate's heavily commercial corridor. Once home of the largest general store in the county—a hundred and fifty years ago—Leverett township covers some twenty square miles and contains four minute villages, almost no businesses at all, and just under two thousand commuters, retired hippies, stay-at-home workers, and a few retirees.

As Peter Manning had mentioned at the intel meeting the week before, it was an odd place to headquarter a trucking company.

Manning was with me now, riding shotgun as he'd promised he would, but outfitted in his absurdly resplendent state police uniform, complete with shiny black riding boots, peaked cap, and patent leather Sam Browne belt. If we'd been in his cruiser, I would have felt like a refugee being escorted out of the country.

Since I was driving my car, however, it looked more like I'd kidnapped the lion tamer from a circus act.

The six-foot-four Manning obviously picked up on my quick fashion appraisal. He cast me a sideward glance as I negotiated the narrow, snowbanked roads leading into the heart of Leverett, and smiled. "I'm hoping," he explained, "that the guy we're about to visit shows more respect for the uniform than he has for anyone wearing it."

"You shouldn't have any problems, then. Who is he, anyway?"

"Charlie Timson. He's actually a pretty good guy, for a sleazeball. Twenty or thirty years ago, he probably would've been just another good-ol'-boy, playing cards with the sheriff every Saturday night. But what with trucking regs, insurance rates, and environmental laws, he either had to move to a more urban area or follow the line of least resistance."

"You made it sound worse at the intel meeting," I commented.

"It's not good." Manning sighed. "But we've just gotten used to it. No one's as innocent as they used to be. This part of the state was once like Vermont. Not much of Boston's shit ever reached us. Now we're ankle-deep in it, and it's getting deeper fast. Springfield's where Boston used to be, and Holyoke, Northampton, Pittsfield, and the rest are all going down the tubes." He waved a hand at the passing trees outside. "I mean, look around. This is Leverett, for Christ's sake. The only income is from property taxes. And here we are, looking for a bad guy."

He suddenly turned to look at me. "You ever been down here?"

"No," I admitted.

"Old hippies on the north side, Amherst commuters to the south, divided by a row of hills. That's Leverett in a nutshell." He pointed ahead. "You want to take a left here."

The roads were twisting and hemmed in by dense forest. Leverett seemed like a total wilderness.

"Timson operates just north of Rattlesnake Gutter. The Gutter's like a deep ravine between two mountains, except for there's no streambed. Nothing. I heard that fourteen thousand years ago, when the last ice age was wrapping up, hundreds of square miles of glacier water were backed up just north of here, looking for a way out. It finally broke through and formed a miniature Grand Canyon. But when it was over, all that was left was a river chasm with no river—a gutter. Neat, huh?"

I smiled at his contagious enthusiasm. "We going to see it?" I asked.

But he shook his head sadly. "There's a road down the middle of it, but they don't clear it during winter. Probably worried some plow operator'll take the Nestea plunge off one of the cliffs. Too bad we had that storm, or I could've showed it to you. Slow down here. Timson's place is right around the corner."

We came upon an old, rusting, corrugated building laden with snow, its dooryard haphazardly plowed so that only one of three truck bays was cleared. The place looked abandoned, with no vehicles or people in sight. I parked uncertainly near a snowbank and killed the engine.

"You sure he's here?" I asked Manning.

He opened his door to a blast of arctic air. "Oh, yeah. He holes up inside like a hibernating bear."

I was only half out of the car when the bear in question appeared through a small door cut into the building's side, dressed in an oil-smeared parka randomly hemmed with frayed duct tape. He looked like a creation gone missing somewhere between Jack London and John Steinbeck.

Charlie Timson was short, round, broad-shouldered, and stamped by a life of hard, rough work. But he was also graced by the thin polish of a working-class entrepreneur. The resentment I saw in his blunt face as he appraised Peter was almost instantly masked by the broad smile and proffered handshake of a man who had only slowly come to appreciate the advantages of a feigned friendly greeting over an extended middle finger.

"What can I do for you?" he asked in a consciously neutral voice.

Peter and I had earlier decided that I'd take the lead, leaving him to play the implied muscle.

"Charlie Timson? I'm Lieutenant Joe Gunther, of the Brattleboro Police Department. This is Sergeant Peter Manning. We were wondering if we could ask you a few questions."

His small, careful eyes widened slightly. "Brattleboro? Haven't been up there in a while." He made no move to invite us inside, no doubt hoping to keep things short.

"This actually concerns one of your trucks."

He acted out a lapse of memory, scratching his head. "Oh, right—the ten-wheeler. What a pain in the ass."

"It may be a little more than that. You mind if we step inside?"

He checked his watch and sighed irritably. "I don't have much time. You know I'm not responsible for whatever people do with those trucks, right? It's in the lease. I don't know anything about what happened up there, except that until I get it back, I'm out one truck. I told that to whoever called me from your office."

"Things have developed since then," I explained.

That was Manning's unspecified cue. As Timson opened his mouth, presumably to stave us off in another way, Peter stepped up next to me, towering over both of us, and stared down at him. "Cut the crap, Charlie. It's a murder now."

Nothing came out of Timson's open mouth for a moment. When it did, it had no punch left to it. "I'm not involved in that."

"Then invite us in," I suggested.

Without another word, he turned on his heel and led the way into the ramshackle building.

The interior was a huge metal cavern—dark, echoing, and inhabited by the half-seen enormous shadows of an assortment of trucks, backhoes, and service equipment. Parked against one wall, a trailer was incongruously perched on its wheels, as if ready for instant flight, its windows providing the only light.

The building was almost as cold as the outside.

"Not doing much work these days?" Peter asked Timson's back.

Marching toward the trailer, Timson didn't bother turning to look at him. "I do just fine."

The office beyond the trailer's flimsy door looked like a gang of vandals had ripped it apart. The chairs were torn and stained, the carpeting was in shreds, there were holes in the wall paneling, and paper was strewn everywhere. Timson wandered through it unaffected, heading for a battered metal desk at the far end, behind which he barricaded himself in a squealing chair. Peter and I remained standing.

Timson's voice regained its previous strength. "So what's this bullshit about a murder? I didn't hear nothin' about it."

"The driver of your truck was killed," I told him, "which naturally makes us a little curious about your role in the whole deal."

His features contorted into a dark scowl, but again Manning interrupted him. "Charlie, think about what's happening here. It's not about poor maintenance, or sloppy records, or playing shell games with your trucks. A man's head was crushed under a locomotive. The rig he'd been driving was loaded with haz mat, probably supplied by the Mob. I'm not saying you know anything about that, but if you don't think we can't use it to drag your butt in front of a judge, you've been living on another planet."

"I *don't* know anything," he complained, spreading his arms wide. "I swear. You saw what I got in the shop. The leases I sign out sometimes don't come back for years. The customers do the inspections, the maintenance, and everything else. I just send 'em a check, or deduct it from their lease. Somebody wants a truck, and I got a lease running out, I send 'em to where it is and do the paperwork by mail. I got something like twenty rigs out there, and *I* lease over half of those myself, for Christ's sake. I never see any of 'em till some shit like this comes down."

"You've had enough time to check your records since one of my men called you," I said. "Who did you contract that truck out to?"

Timson shook his head. "I told you then, I don't got it to look up. I can't find those records. I did try—looked all over the place, but you can see what . . ."

His voice trailed off as Peter grasped the edge of

his desk, and pivoted it to one side as if he were opening a door, exposing Timson on his creaky chair as though he were a hedgehog perched on a stool.

"What the hell're you doing?" he asked nervously, grasping the chair's arms.

Manning stepped into the void the desk had filled and stood so close to Timson their knees were almost touching. Timson's head cranked far backward to look up into Manning's face.

"You can't do this, you know?" His voice sounded strangled.

Manning ignored him. "I thought we had an understanding, Charlie. We're investigating a homicide, and you're a member of the public, eager to help us do our job." He pulled a long legal document and laid it on the other man's lap.

"That's a Duces Tecum warrant to search these premises for any paperwork concerning that truck. It'll give you all the cover you need to hide from the people you're really worried about. We were just hoping you'd spare us stripping this place of every scrap of paper in it—including all licenses and operating permits—and taking the next six months to carefully go through it, looking for what you could hand over in two minutes."

"I'd sooner lose some money than my life," he said.

Manning was unsympathetic. "We issue the right press release, you won't have that choice. Your playmates don't like messes, Charlie, and you ain't one of the family, so to speak."

Timson's face darkened. "Get out of my way, asshole," he growled at Peter, trying to summon a few shreds of self-respect.

Manning stepped back. Timson got to his feet, and

then surprised us by lumbering up onto his desk and reaching for one of the acoustic tiles overhead. He popped it back with his fist, groped around its edges for a moment, and retrieved a single brown manila envelope.

He handed it to me before climbing back down. "There. That's all of it. And you found it on your own."

Manning smiled. "You got anything else interesting up there?"

"Fuck you."

I opened the envelope and studied its contents.

"Could you do that someplace else?" he asked peevishly. "I got things to do."

"It says here the truck was last leased to Katahdin Trucking of Portland, Maine. Any chance that even exists?"

His answer for once sounded reasonable. "I'm supposed to know that?"

Back in the car, Manning indicated the envelope. "That going to do you any good?"

"Not much," I admitted. "Katahdin Trucking is probably only the second layer in God knows how many more, and I bet the deeper we dig, the harder it'll be to find even this much.

"It's not totally useless, though," I added. "At least we know we're dealing with something organized." I paused and thought once more of Jim Reynolds's open filing cabinet, filled with old cases.

"And maybe something with history."

My next meeting with Jim Reynolds didn't come at my instigation, however. Shortly after my trip to Massachusetts, I was summoned to Tony Brandt's office.

"Run down what we've got on the senator," he requested after I'd settled into one of his chairs.

"Not much yet," I admitted. "But suspicions are growing. His name comes up every time we turn around. Somebody's calling Katz, too, trying to link Reynolds to both illegal dumping—and by inference Phil Resnick's death—and to Brenda Croteau."

Brandt raised his eyebrows. "Anything to it?"

"Don't know. It might be the same people who got us all excited about the Crown Vic—playing political hardball. I have Ron looking into Reynolds's past, but so far he's come up empty. I'll keep at it, though."

Brandt studied me a moment. "You sound like there might be something there."

I gave him an equivocating wobble of the hand, tilting it back and forth. "It's more like an itch I can't reach. You heard about the one solid connection we did find between the two cases, right?"

Brandt thought a moment. "Yeah—what's his name? The poker player who was also one of Brenda's customers."

"Frankie Harris. I'm just thinking that if there's one, there could be others. After all, we still don't know what we're dealing with here. The Owen Tharp case looks simple enough, but with Resnick, I have no idea. Three men execute a Mob-connected illegal dumper from New Jersey on the railroad tracks in the middle of the night, using a dummied-up copy of a car belonging to one of our state senators. What the hell's that all about? And I can't get that office break-in out of my head, either. Unfortunately, about all I've got are questions," I paused a moment, watching his face. "Why do you ask?"

"Reynolds's Judiciary Committee is about to vote

out his bill—they're taking testimony from supporters and giving it as much armor as they can before sending it out into the world. I wanted to know if we were sitting on some smoking bomb that would make that whole exercise a waste of time."

"Not that I know of," I answered carefully, adding, "Why would we care anyway?"

Brandt gave me an enigmatic smile. "Ah. Well, it's not just what they're doing in Montpelier—it's what I've been asked to do for them, and where I'm hoping you'll help me out. Reynolds is being pretty careful with this bill, despite all the 'bold and radical' crap in the press. For one, he made sure it was introduced by his committee, and not by him alone—which gives it more clout—and now he wants to make sure the same committee gives it a dress rehearsal with as many tough questions as they can raise. Also, I think that by dragging that process out just a little, Reynolds is hoping to orchestrate it so that the other Senate committees that get to consider it won't have much time to do so. My guess is he's shooting to have the bill reach the House just before Town Meeting Day in March, so the speaker and his minions will get the message on the village level that the people are behind it."

I appreciated the civics lesson, but dreaded whatever was lurking behind it. I waited silently, not making it too easy for him, knowing I wouldn't like what I was about to hear.

I didn't. Brandt cleared his throat slightly and said, "Anyhow, long story short, they asked me—along with a bunch of other people—to be a committee witness. I was hoping you'd go in my place. I was told it would be pretty informal. More like a think-tank session."

I sat stock-still for a moment, analyzing my emotions. It was a favor he was asking of me, not something I had to do. But it was coming from a man who'd stuck his neck out for me many times in the past, and whom I considered a good friend. Finally, much as I disliked most politics, I was also—like a lot of people—a little curious about its workings.

"You got something else going?" I asked gratuitously, mostly to increase his obvious discomfort.

He shifted in his chair. "No more than anyone else. To be honest, Joe, I'm asking you for two reasons—one pretty straightforward, the other a little more self-serving." He held up his index finger. "One, you've been part of more task forces, special units, and out-of-department assignments than anyone. You know how the interjurisdictional system works, its strong and weak points, and you probably have your fair share of ideas about how to improve it." He raised a second finger. "Two, I've been known to ride a little high in the saddle politically, now and then, and I'm worried if I go up there, they'll start taking shots at me for ancient history and maybe lose track of what they should be doing. I think Reynolds has an interesting idea with this one-department-for-the-whole-state approach. I know it's got problems, and would never fly as such, but this state is long overdue for a change, and I don't want to be a part of anything that screws that up."

I couldn't argue his points, or find cause to turn him down, and I'd satisfied my childish urge to make him squirm. Also, while he'd been talking, I'd realized that since Jim Reynolds was going to be in my sights for a while longer, it wouldn't hurt to see him functioning on his own turf.

I finally nodded and stood up. "Okay, you got a deal. When do I go?"

* * *

The trip to Montpelier this time was completely unlike its predecessor, the passing countryside as draped in crystalline white as it had been brown and drab before. The contrast was more pronounced several miles east of town, at the interstate's highest point crossing the Green Mountains, where a brief rain the previous night had coated every twig of every tree with a shimmering sheath of near-blinding clarity. Driving through this corridor of sparkling, glassy trees, with the deep blue, unsullied sky overhead, pulsating with the sun's cold energy, I felt transported far away from the often discouraging world I normally inhabited. It was with palpable regret that I reached the western downslope of this exposed bit of road and continued to my rendezvous with a room full of politicians.

Montpelier was busier than during my earlier visit, and the parking that much worse, neither of which helped my darkening mood. In contrast to the startlingly clear air, the ring of surrounding snowy hills, and the prominent gold dome of the capitol in their midst—as bright as a sparkler adorning a birthday cake—the town looked gritty and flattened this time, like some bit of soil ingrained in the palm of an enormous celestial hand.

Adding to my apprehension was the presence of several haphazardly parked cars and trucks, all stamped with the logos of various newspapers, radios, and television stations. I started thinking that Tony Brandt might have been a little coy with his reasons for staying home.

The first floor, under the two chambers and the governor's ceremonial office, housed the Senate committee rooms and was as packed with people as a subway during rush hour. Shedding my coat in the sudden heat,

I elbowed my way to the sergeant-at-arms' office to announce my arrival. She made a brief phone call I couldn't hear and told me in a loud voice to stand by the doorway—that someone would soon arrive to escort me to the committee room.

In the ten minutes that took, I watched some of the hurly-burly of a citizen legislature in action.

In most states, the capitol is called the "people's house," or something close to it, although most visitors know there are limits to how much access they have to this purportedly open domain. A trip to these places is not unlike a tour of a museum—grand, quiet, a little stuffy and sterile, and yet imbued with the sense that something significant is occurring just out of sight.

In Vermont's State House, the only museum quality in evidence is in the architecture and the artwork adorning it, which is all the more remarkable for being jammed into such a small building. Otherwise, the whole place was reminiscent of a high-class hotel during a wedding reception or a famous person's wake. People milled all over, talking, laughing, arguing, shaking hands, and grabbing elbows. I recognized a few of them from pictures I saw in the papers, and many more by their attire as workmen, farmers, or well paid lobbyists. But whether in overalls or three-piece suits, they all wandered the halls with comfortable familiarity, knowing that here there were almost no rooms they couldn't enter with impunity. The crowd reinforced the feeling that while most governments exuded a sense of privacy, waste, and special privilege, Vermont's was still small enough—at least in this picturesque, cluttered setting—to seem viable, real, and eminently approachable.

Eventually, a teenage page, dressed in an awkwardly

fitting uniform of green blazer, gray slacks, and over-large black running shoes, tugged on my sleeve and led me down a dark hall to a room marked "Judiciary."

It was small enough—and with high enough walls—to make me feel I was standing at the bottom of a large can. A can so full of people, both sitting and standing, that at first it looked like there was no possible way through them.

Excusing myself repeatedly, however, and choosing my steps with care, I made my way slowly to the large table in the middle and the one empty chair I was obviously supposed to occupy. Surrounding the table in concentric rings were several senators, their assistants, guests, lobbyists, and who knew what else, and finally a row of journalists, standing against the walls and windows, holding pads, tape recorders, cameras, or light-equipped camcorders. It was my first glimpse of just how big the so-called "Reynolds Bill" was playing.

The man himself sat opposite me, flanked by his Senate colleagues. Even sitting he looked oversized, his unruly hair crowning a head more proportioned for statuary than for human anatomy. He identified me, introduced me to the others, and ran down a small list of my achievements. He did not mention that I was here substituting for my boss.

Over the next hour and a half, against a steady background of people shuffling in and out of the undersized, stuffy room—and to the accompaniment of the occasional camera click or whir—I answered questions about law enforcement in Vermont from my personal perspective. It was easier than I'd thought it would be back home, where for the past several days I'd been boning up on practices and protocols. I discovered that these lawmakers were remarkably ignorant of what I did for a living, asking me questions so simple at times that I suspected I was being tested less for my knowledge than for my kindness to the mentally challenged.

This was not true of Jim Reynolds, of course. Being one of the few elected lawyers in the State House, he was used to navigating the waters I traveled. But he was careful not to show that off, and spent most of his time encouraging his colleagues to follow me through an elementary primer of police procedure, using me as his foil in describing a system often redundant, wasteful, inefficient, and costly. It was masterfully done, I had to admit, as I slowly watched my interrogators become increasingly confused by what I was trying to keep simple. Reynolds had a point to make, and he was manipulating everyone but himself into making it.

I had worried that at some point I'd be asked my personal opinion of the bill and its ramifications, but here again, Reynolds showed a subtle control of the tiller. While those kinds of questions did occasionally come up, he always swooped in and convincingly urged that at this early stage such prejudices be put aside. Toward the end, like a well-intentioned trail boss watching his herd simply wandering away, I heard my bland and placid testimony sounding more like a resounding condemnation—all due to Reynolds's carefully worded guidance.

As I picked my way toward the room's exit at last, having been solicitously thanked for my appearance, I could already visualize the next day's headlines, touting me as a clarion for change.

Unfortunately, I didn't get to wait that long. I hadn't placed one foot into the hallway before I was confronted by a short, square state trooper I knew to be big in their labor union—a strong organization within the state's most powerful police force, and as such, a two-headed entity that constantly caught heat from almost every other agency in Vermont. The Vermont state police endured the same barbs suffered by all dominant organizations. Some were deserved, others generated from pure envy, but the value of either was usually lost in prejudicial rhetoric. It no longer mattered who was right anymore, or even that the VSP had recently been making great strides in an effort to be more inclusive. The division had been drawn long ago, and although both the VSP and the rest of us talked constantly about being one big happy family, both also took pride in celebrating one side of that line at the expense of the other. It was but one of the obstacles Reynolds was confronting, and as the short state trooper fell into step beside me, it was the one I was going to have to deal with.

"Jesus, Joe. You trashed us pretty good in there," he said in a low voice.

"If I trashed anyone, it was the whole kit-and-caboodle. You guys run a better ship than most."

"Oh, come on. All those comments about how we work. You made us look like the Pentagon or something, and you're not even one of us."

I stopped and looked at him. "I'm a cop just like you are. The whole point of this exercise is to try to make that the only relevant distinction—not the uniform, not the town, not the budget or the turf battles. I wasn't picking on the VSP—I'm not even sure I mentioned your name. But I sure as hell wasn't going to deny how much waste and redundancy there is across the board."

He looked like I'd slapped him for paying me a

compliment. "What about the efforts we been making to open communications? The computer link-ups, the advisory boards, user groups, task forces, the exchange programs, and all the rest?"

"I told them about that. I even stressed what a positive development it was."

"You made it sound like it wasn't working."

"It's not—not so long as we treat each other like competing rivals."

His eyes widened. "Jesus Christ. It's positive but it's not working? No wonder they had you in there. You sound like one of them."

I half opened my mouth to answer, and then gave it up, saying only, "I gotta go."

It had been a jarring conclusion to a confusing experience, and it left me resenting Tony Brandt for sending me here, and respecting Jim Reynolds for having orchestrated the outcome he'd sought—a conflict of loyalties that galled me instinctively, and one I tried sorting out all the way home.

Chapter Fourteen

Gail was hunkered down in her upstairs armchair like a mole in a burrow, surrounded by pillows and paperwork. "I'm starting to wonder what you look like in daylight," I told her.

"I'm starting to wonder what daylight looks like. How was Montpelier?"

I tried making light of the bitter aftertaste, still lingering after hours in the car. "The usual circus. It was interesting seeing Reynolds at work. Very crafty."

"You made it on the news tonight."

I sat on the floor with my back against the wall. "Great. A colleague from the state police cornered me right after and accused me of fratricide."

She shook her head. "I wouldn't worry. It was just background footage to the reporter's voice-over. They didn't even use your name."

I took off my shoes and wriggled my toes into the thick carpeting, eager to change subjects. "Thank God for small favors. How's it going with the Owen case?"

She made a face. "Could be better. Derby and I are starting to wrangle. He wants me to go hell for leather—

Felony Murder Rule, double homicide, maximum sentence."

"And you don't?" I asked, remembering how Brenda's head had barely been attached to her body.

"I'm not against it, necessarily. I just think we sometimes charge people like you'd hunt deer with a machine gun. It's grandstanding and it's sloppy. We don't know yet what really went on in that house, and what led up to it. It's at sentencing that the penalties should be meted out, once all the cards have been put on the table. That's what separates Vermont from the feds—we have more latitude."

I slid down to rest on my elbows. "Derby must love you, especially during an election year. I didn't think it was the prosecutor's job to worry about motive."

She gave me a sour look. "Don't you start, too. Any idiot knows the jury'll want to hear a motive, whether it's our quote-unquote *job* or not. If we don't pay attention to that, McNeil will eat us for lunch. Besides, intent *is* part of our burden of proof, so whether we like it or not, we're going to have to step onto that thin ice."

"He said he went there to kill her. He'd been waiting for several years to find out who spiked his girlfriend's dope with poison."

"He didn't bring a weapon, he killed her where she stood, and he drove his aunt's truck there to do it. Hardly a plan born of deep thought."

I was silent for a moment, thinking of how tense the situation must have become at her office. I felt a certain sympathy for her boss. Charging a perpetrator with everything and then compromising with a lesser sentence after trial—or better still, using those charges to cut a pretrial deal—was standard practice. I wondered if Gail's social welfare past wasn't getting in her way.

But she was still talking. "My God, Joe, if I'm asking these kinds of questions—first time on a murder trial—don't you think McNeil's been over the same ground thirty times by now? Derby's so desperate to get something locked in by November, he's not thinking straight. Besides, I doubt that confession will make it to trial. I already told you that. You ever read it?"

"Sure."

"Then you saw where he said he first went there to get her to come clean, and only after a little prodding from Kunkle said he wanted to kill her for what she'd done. If McNeil doesn't get it thrown out, it'll only be so he can shove it up our noses in front of the jury and make it look like coercion.

"Plus," she added, "that bloody knee-print never panned out. The stained clothes we got from Owen's aunt didn't include pants, and now she's saying he never wore jeans anyhow."

"That's pretty convenient," I said. "Who says she's telling the truth? The pants could've been jeans, and they might've vanished precisely because they were soaked in blood. It was Brenda's DNA on what little the aunt did hand over, wasn't it?"

"Yeah," Gail admitted without enthusiasm, and then added more hopefully, "but not much. A bit on his jacket and a few drops on one shoe."

"Boy," I said softly after a long pause, "doesn't sound like you and Derby are even working the same case. Could Owen get off?"

"Of course he *could*," she answered angrily. "Just ask anyone who thinks O. J. Simpson was guilty. The point is, you enter a case like this with something other than blood in your eye. Jack basically wants to throw a rope over some tree branch and ride off into the sunset to general applause. It ain't going to work that way unless he wakes up."

I got to my feet, shoes in hand, and kissed her again—this was the second debate of the day I didn't want to touch. "Sorry you're having a tough time. He'll probably settle down once McNeil begins showing what he's up to. You haven't even seen his witness list yet, have you?"

"No," she admitted glumly. "But when we do, your squad better expect a phone call. I know in my gut we're going to be digging into Owen's past deeper than they will at the Pearly Gates." She suddenly reached up and grabbed my wrist. "Speaking of which, could you do me a favor? Call Hillstrom's office and find out if it actually was poison that killed Owen's girl-friend—Lisa Wooten."

"You got it," I said. But mundane as it sounded, the request hit me as somehow wrong. I just couldn't put my finger on it.

The next morning, I met with Sammie, Ron, and Willy. Several weeks had gone by since Philip Resnick had been pulped by the train, and we were no closer to finding his killers than we had been that first night. On the bright side, the car, the three men, Resnick's identity, and his connection to the abandoned truck hadn't made it into the papers yet, which were still referring to the victim as an unidentified vagrant.

Which they wouldn't be doing for much longer.

"We still think Reynolds is involved?" Willy asked with characteristic bluntness.

I looked at Ron for an answer.

"If he is, he's being very cagey," Ron answered.

"Cagey?" Sam butted in. "You really think he framed himself with a bogus copy of his own car, just to throw off suspicion? It's unreal."

"I agree," Ron resumed. "But it still may be possible. Speaking of which, a Crown Vic matching Renaud's second description was reported stolen in Keene, just before Resnick was killed. Also, I looked over Brenda's journal again, seeing if I could find a pattern to those missing pages, but the whole thing's just too chaotic to begin with."

I sat back and rubbed my eyes. "Damn, this is frustrating. An office break-in where nothing's missing, a car at the crime scene that turns out not to have been there, a few missing pages in a dead woman's journal that might've mentioned anybody. I mean, I can write off the phone calls to Katz as political highjinks, but some of this stuff has *got* to have something to it. Reynolds just keeps coming up."

"Or we're being led to think that way," Sammie said quietly.

Willy crushed a plastic coffee cup he'd been nursing and threw it into the trash. "We missed out when his office was broken into. If one of us had been there, we might have gotten a look at those files."

I turned to Ron again. "You been able to go over his old court records yet?"

He gave me a tired look. "I looked, but there're hundreds of 'em. He's a hardworking man. So I stuck to checking for index references to Resnick or Timson or hazardous materials or trucking—and got nowhere. The only other option is to open the files and go over them page by page."

There was a gloomy break in the conversation. "How 'bout Katahdin?" I finally asked.

"I tried it." He didn't need to explain further.

I sat up slowly, a sudden thought stirring. "Where's Reynolds licensed to practice?"

Ron pawed through some notes. "Vermont, New Hampshire—" He suddenly stopped. "And Maine."

All three of them looked up at me.

"Get hold of the Portland court clerk," I told Ron. "See if he hasn't been over there defending Katahdin Trucking. And Sammie, I want you to get back in touch with the New Jersey people Ron called earlier about Resnick, and find out everything you can about him— not his criminal record, but his family, colleagues, drinking buddies, personal habits. Anything you can. I want a family tree of associates we can compare to anyone we might have on file."

Deputy Medical Examiner Bernie Short sounded tired on the phone. "What can I do for you, Joe?"

"Get some sleep, would be a wild guess."

"Yeah, well, forget that."

"How much longer till Beverly gets back?"

"Too long. Late summer."

"I'll cut to the chase, then," I said. "Your office did a Lisa Wooten a few years ago, from down here." I gave him the exact date and reference number. "All I can find in my files is 'drug overdose,' but we're working a case right now where someone's claiming the stuff that did her in was deliberately poisoned. Can you give me the details?"

His voice remained flat. "Hold on."

He was back on the line in surprisingly short order. "Nope. Heroin cut with confectioner's sugar. Usually what happens is they try to kick the habit for a while, lower their tolerance for the stuff, and then shoot up with the dose they were used to, but can no longer handle. Boom, they're dead."

"So, definitely no poison?"

"You want a copy of this?" he asked instead.

"The SA's office might," I told him. "I'll let them know. By the way, you couldn't tell if the dose that killed her was bigger than her norm, could you, assuming she hadn't tried to kick the habit?"

His answer was short, but eloquent: "Nope."

I hung up and redialed. "I did your bidding on Lisa Wooten," I told Gail when she picked up. "I'm afraid you're not going to like it."

"Tell me."

"She was a straight overdose. Bernie Short said the only adulterant was sugar. Whoever told Owen Tharp that Brenda poisoned Lisa's dope was lying."

"Shit." The line went dead.

I hung up slowly. I didn't blame her—I even held myself partly responsible. She'd just committed a cardinal error—uncovering a fact beneficial to the defense—and I hadn't been sharp enough to see it coming. Reggie McNeil would probably have dug it up eventually, but the fact that this little exculpatory tidbit had been a gift from the prosecution was a card he was sure to play up. If Owen had been deliberately lied to in order to get him motivated to kill Brenda, it could be made to weigh heavily in any jury's considerations.

Jack Derby was not going to be pleased.

My contemplation of Gail's fate was cut short by a shadow falling across my desk. "Daydreaming, Joe?"

Al Hammond—tall, distinguished, gray-haired, and

the Windham County sheriff since God was a teenager—stood on my threshold smiling.

I offered him a chair. "Haven't seen you in a while. What've you been up to?"

"Watching television," he said pleasantly, his eyes very steady.

"Meaning you saw me on the news?"

"Saw you and had the transcript faxed down to me. You really backing this idea?"

His tone was stiffly noncommittal. I decided to play the same game. "What did your reading tell you?"

"It didn't tell me you were against it."

"I'm not—not until it's something other than a vague proposal on its way through a bunch of committees. I'm not necessarily for it, either."

"You think the concept of a single police force is a good thing?" This time, his voice gave him away, if only slightly, not that I needed a road sign. Sheriffs were political by statute, and this one seemed to have been born that way.

"I think almost seventy different agencies are too many. But you're safe. Why do you care?"

"Because being in the constitution and surviving as a reality are two different things, as you damn well know. We could be reduced to a crosswalk officer per county and still be in the constitution."

I baited him a little. "So it's about turf?"

Those cool, gray eyes narrowed slightly. "It's about function. Nothing exists for long if nobody needs it. Sheriffs predate every other police agency in this state. For good reason."

"Welfare fraud investigators are four pay grades below a Vermont state police sergeant," I countered. "When Welfare was told to tighten their belts, they handed investigations over to the VSP. But what was good for their budget turned out bad for the state's. In a few counties, VSP is scheduling fraud investigations during overtime hours, and allowing anyone eligible to conduct them. I know a captain who is legitimately taking advantage of that, and for a lot more money than Welfare was paying in the first place. Does that make sense to you?"

"A single agency would have the same problems. Plus, you're talking about the state police—hardly the paragon of efficiency."

I tried again, hoping to avoid the standard inaccurate target-shooting at the VSP. "Amos Melcourt killed those three kids up north because a part-time deputy sheriff was put where he shouldn't have been, supposedly because money was too tight to allow for anything better. That wouldn't be true in a more centralized system with a state-mandated budget."

Hammond opened his mouth to respond, but I interrupted. "Al, I'm not picking any fights here. All I'm saying is that just because something worked during the Revolutionary War doesn't mean it should stay the same into the twenty-first century. These seventy-odd departments have about one thousand full-time cops working for them. It's not much, but it means different uniforms, cars, equipment, weapons, training . . . you name it. They say that if every department in Chittenden County alone shared a single dispatch center, they could all save some two million dollars. Think of the money we could have—without raising a single additional penny in taxes—if we could *all* share our resources like that. We're already beginning to use the same computer data, we've been fighting for years to get automated fingerprinting, the FBI has launched a centralized DNA bank, and other states are creating legislation allowing their cops to participate. We're on this train whether we like it or not. I'm just saying we ought to acknowledge the fact and figure out how to make it work for us, whether it's one big department or six regional ones or whatever. We ought to kick it around a bit."

Hammond wasn't interested. He rose to his feet and looked down at me for a moment, finally saying, "It sounds great, Joe. And if you and I and a few others were the people who were doing it, I might even go along. But we're not. It's the likes of Jim Reynolds and Mark Mullen and our jackass Governor Howell that're going to be cobbling this together, and they're going to be working under VSP direction. You mark my words: If this thing goes through—and I'm going to do everything in my power to stop it—it'll have the stamp of the Green-and-Gold all over it."

He stalked out the door, his back ramrod straight, like the state trooper he had been more than twenty years earlier.

Chapter Fifteen

I picked up the phone on the first ring, out of instinct, but was still half asleep when I placed it against my ear.

"Joe? Lieutenant? Hello?"

I opened my eyes. It was still the middle of the night. "What?"

"It's Ron. Sorry I woke you up. I just got a call about that stolen Crown Vic from Keene."

My brain was beginning to function, if not my tongue. "Right."

"They found it in the woods near Marlboro, covered with branches and snow. The three guys must've driven it there right after they killed Resnick, and let Mother Nature take care of the rest."

I looked at the digital clock by the bed. "It's two in the morning, Ron. You telling me somebody just found it?"

"Two cross-country skiers were enjoying a moonlight run, found the car, called the state police, who called me. I'm on call tonight. It might be the break we been after."

I couldn't fault him the wishful thinking. "Okay. Put a man on it till daylight, but call J.P. now and let him know. Ask him if he thinks it might not be a good idea to have the state's mobile crime lab give us an assist, just in the interest of time. But be diplomatic, okay? He can be a little thin-skinned about those guys." I almost hung up, and then caught myself. "Also, get hold of someone with a flatbed truck to transport the car to a closed facility for examination—and a brand-new tarp to wrap it in. J.P.'ll know how to handle it. Tell him I'm real keen on this."

"Will do."

I felt obliged to add, "And thanks for calling."

The big car sat in the borrowed town garage like a stolen artifact of inestimable value, surrounded by men and women garbed entirely in white Tyvek costumes and crouching in the middle of a huge pale paper apron extending to the garage's rough-hewn walls. J.P. and the mobile lab crew had been at it for several hours by the time I arrived. The paper around the car was littered with labeled evidence bags and Polaroid pictures.

J.P. came to meet me as soon as I crossed the threshold. I pointed at the car. "You find anything yet?"

"Yeah. There's no doubt it was the same one at the railroad tracks. The gravel in the tread matches, the bogus license plate reads like Reynolds's, although an obvious fake in good light, and we found blood high on the back seat where they must've propped the victim up during the ride."

"So, two in the back and one driving?"

"Probably. Can't tell for sure. The car's a few years old and the real owner's no neatnik, so it's going to be hard to differentiate what trace evidence belongs to the killer and what doesn't." He gestured to the envelopes I'd noticed earlier. "We found a ton of it, in any case, and a shitload of latents. We're going to have to reference-print everyone who's ever been in this car in order to rule out what we've got. Even if it's possible, I doubt it'll be worth the time or expense."

He then led me to a bench near the back of the bay, to where more evidence bags were piled. He selected one and held it up for me to see. Swathed in its slightly cloudy embrace was an oversized dirty ball peen hammer.

"This is what we think did him in—before the train, of course. Pretty good amount of blood on its business end. Found it in the trunk."

I peered at it closely. "Funny tool to keep in a car."

"It wasn't kept in the car," J.P. confirmed. "I called the owner in Keene. All he had was the usual junk."

He replaced the hammer on the counter and picked up a Polaroid lying beside it. "Here's the kicker, though—if we're lucky."

I recognized it as an extreme close-up shot of the hammer handle's butt end. Stamped in the oil-darkened metal was a short string of numbers.

"Remember that program we ran a few years ago?" J.P. asked. "Where we were trying to get people to mark their valuables and register them with us? I think that's what this is. Makes sense, too. One of these goes for a hundred bucks or so—weighs a ton, all metal construction, primo goods."

I waved the photograph at him. "Can I keep this?"

He let out one of his rare, thin smiles. "I thought you would."

I put it in my pocket. "Nice work—keep your fingers crossed."

Franklin's Machine Shop had been a Brattleboro institution for as long as I could remember. Owned by at least the third generation of Franklins, it had always been on Flat Street—in a small, unassuming one-story warehouse, with windows so greasy they were essentially opaque—and had always restricted its advertising to a single, hubcap-sized metal sign hanging over the wooden sliding front door.

I had been a periodic customer of Franklin's over the decades, especially when I'd needed something either custom-made, or that had stopped being sold elsewhere twenty years earlier. If you needed an old flywheel, for instance, or a replacement drive pulley for an ancient snowblower, Franklin's was the place to shop.

Not that it was a hardware store, of course. There were no display cases or clerks or pristine overhead lighting. In fact, there was barely any lighting at all. Even at the height of a summer's day, the interior of Franklin's remained cavelike, tenebrous, and cool. Like half-seen metal skeletons, huge piles of odds and ends loomed precariously, forming corridors, or were stacked behind and on top of long, scarred, debris-covered wooden worktables. Here and there, stamping machines, drill presses, metal cutters, and who knew what else also stood around like fossilized wallflowers at a soundless party, each accompanied by a single extinguished gooseneck lamp. There was just enough cleared space around these tools for an operator to stand, but generally there was no operator to be seen. If Franklin's had ever had a heyday, it lay as far back in memory as the heavy leather belts that still crisscrossed its ceiling. Nowadays, either Franklin worked alone or he was accompanied by some relative killing time between jobs.

I hadn't known Franklin's real first name until I'd looked it up in our computer just fifteen minutes earlier. Inevitably, he'd always been referred to as Ben, as had his father and grandfather before him. I now knew he was the third in a line of men named Arvid.

As serious as was the reason for my visit, that tidbit wasn't something I was about to ignore.

"Hey, Arvid," I shouted as I entered the shop, noticing only the faintest touch of warmth from a centralized, rumbling upright furnace that looked like a locomotive begging for food.

There was a metallic crash from somewhere in the gloom, and a cigarette-ruined voice shouted back, "If you're not from the IRS, you're some kind of wiseass."

"I'm not from the IRS."

A shadow detached itself from the darkness, looking as oil-stained and solid as the machinery surrounding it, and an old, slightly stooped man with enormous blackened hands and a filthy baseball cap appeared before me. His face showed neither pleasure nor recognition.

"Should've known it was you. You got nothin' better to do than to hassle me?"

We didn't shake hands. It wasn't something really old friends did. "Nope. Been keeping busy?"

"Enough. What d'ya got? Some other cheap piece of junk crap out on you?"

"Not this time. I think we might've found something

belonging to you." I handed him the picture of the ball peen hammer.

He hesitated taking it, carefully wiping his hand on the front of an insulated vest that looked as though it had been washed in oil. Despite the lack of light, he didn't squint to make out the image. He merely glanced at it and returned it to me. "No shit. Never thought that stupid program of yours would work."

"So it is yours?"

He studied me impassively for a moment. "You're here, aren't you?"

"You didn't report it missing."

He turned to a nearby workbench and picked up an oddly configured cylindrical object, possibly part of an old drive shaft, and cradled it in his palm, feeling its cool smoothness with his fingertips. Ben Franklin was rarely without something metal in his hands. It seemed to calm him as the feel of rich earth might a farmer.

"You know how much stuff I got in this place?"

I shook my head.

"Well, I don't neither. For all I know, that thing's been under a pile the whole time. Never knew it'd grown feet."

"You know how long it's been missing?"

"Two months," he said without hesitation.

I let those two words hang in the air a moment. Two faint plumes of near-freezing air escaped from his nostrils as he waited me out.

"You thought enough of this hammer," I finally said, "that you marked it and registered it with our department. Now you say you didn't report it missing because it could've been lost in this mess, even though you know it disappeared exactly two months ago."

He didn't respond.

"We think it was used to kill a man."

His lips compressed, his hands grew still, and he seemed suddenly transfixed by something hovering in the middle distance just over my left shoulder.

"Tell me who took it, Ben."

"You sure you're not yankin' my chain?"

This time, I kept silent.

He sighed, returned the cylinder to the bench top, and stood before me with his big hands by his sides, empty and useless. "My nephew—along with a bunch of other stuff. Billy Conyer. You guys know him."

We did that, but not only because he was a regular customer. He'd also been mentioned by Janice Litchfield as a friend of Brenda Croteau's.

The rooming house where Billy Conyer lived on Elliot Street was one of the worst examples Brattleboro had to offer. A warren of tiny, dark, evil-smelling cubbyholes, it was as famous for its transient inhabitants as for the illegal activities they practiced there. The lighting was haphazard, the plumbing erratic, the heating quirky, the walls looked like Swiss cheese, and the stench was a combination of rotting food, unwashed bodies, and backed-up toilets. It was a place EMTs, firefighters, cops, and building inspectors all got to visit regularly. One hot summer night a few years back, when the local ambulance had gone racing by the nearby firehouse to respond to yet another call at that address, the on-duty firefighters had lined up in front of their open bay doors and saluted the rescue crew by waving fistfuls of rubber gloves at them.

It was that kind of place.

And now it was our turn.

We'd taken our time, made sure the crime lab could

match the blood on the hammer to Phil Resnick's DNA, and had discreetly studied Conyer's habits for several days running, using one of the windows at the firehouse as an observation point.

The night we chose to move was possibly the coldest of the year so far, and dark as the inside of a closet. It was tailor-made for keeping people indoors, their eyes accustomed to the lights within.

There were six of us, including Sammie and me, all dressed in black, sporting thick armored vests and short twelve-gauge shotguns. Willy, dressed as a bum and equipped with a radio, had been stationed on the inside, slumped in a smelly, inert pile in a corner of the hallway leading to Conyer's apartment. We'd watched Conyer enter the building just before midnight, heard Willy report him entering his top-floor room alone, and had seen his light come on behind his tattered shade—and turn back off an hour later.

We'd then waited another thirty minutes, to let him ease off to sleep.

"Any sign of him?" I radioed Willy, who was equipped with an earphone.

"No," came the quiet reply. "I listened at the door five minutes ago. Not a peep."

"Okay. We're in motion."

I gave the prearranged signal, and we all moved from various positions inside and around the building, quietly convening at opposite ends of the hallway Willy was monitoring. At our arrival, he faded back to stand guard outside, along with a couple of other unobtrusively placed uniformed officers.

The heat inside the building was terrific, making us all sweat under our heavy protective gear. As we took our places to either side of Conyer's door, I became aware of how—to a person—our faces were dripping wet in the harsh overhead light.

I nodded to the man near the switch at the staircase. He killed the overhead lights. For a long couple of minutes, there was no sound, no movement, while we waited for our eyesight to adjust to the semidarkness, alleviated only by two bright red exit signs, miraculously still functioning. Then I murmured into my throat mike, "Let's go."

The two men holding the short battering ram between them swung it back once and smashed through Conyer's lock with a single splintering crash. Then they dropped the ram and fell off to either side, pulling out their sidearms, while Sammie and Ward Washburn burst through the door screaming at the top of their lungs.

It was textbook perfect, except that as Sammie shouted, "It's empty," a door halfway down the hall banged open, and Billy Conyer appeared, half naked and with a gun, his face gaunt and his eyes wide, his body glowing red in the light from the exit signs.

Pierre Lavoie had been standing by the light switch at the end of the hall, where he could also guard the top of the stairs. Now he was not only blocking Conyer's escape route, but he was standing where any bullets that missed Conyer might hit him.

I don't know who yelled, *"Don't move."* All of us, from the sound of it. But it still didn't work. Billy Conyer fired twice at me, then swiveled on his bare heel and crouched low to shoot at Pierre.

But Pierre had instantly assessed his own predicament. Instead of trying to return fire—and possibly hitting us—he simply launched himself down the staircase, vanishing as if the earth had swallowed him whole.

Conyer quickly straightened, apparently astonished

by what had happened, presenting us with his glistening back.

"Don't move," I yelled again. *"Police."*

He either wasn't thinking or had seen too many movies. In one of those moments every police officer dreads, will never forget, and will always hold in doubt, Conyer disobeyed and turned. But whether he planned to shoot again or was actually going to surrender and had simply not dropped his gun, none of us would ever know. Faced with a pointed weapon, we all fired in unison, feeling more than hearing the explosions, and watched as his body was thrown to the floor like a rag doll, spattering the walls nearby with blood.

I had no idea of the time when I crept into our bedroom. My head hurt, my brain was in a fog, and my body felt numb. Conyer had been shipped up to Burlington for autopsy, a preliminary post-shoot investigation had been conducted by the state police, the state's attorney's office had been notified, and Jack Derby himself had showed up to be briefed. So far, everyone was calling it righteous, which did little for the soul.

Gail stirred as I tried to remove my clothes quietly in the dark.

"Joe?"

"Yeah. It's okay. Go back to sleep."

"What've you been doing?"

"A little late-night workout with the boys."

She reached out, turned on the light by her side of the bed, and squinted across the room at me. "What's that mean?"

I was sitting on the edge of a chair, with one shoe in my hand. I didn't want to have this conversation. Enough had been said tonight already. I needed to think quietly, if not sleep, and put the image of Conyer collapsing in on himself into that mental cupboard where I kept all its brethren.

"There was a shooting, and a long post-shoot. Everyone's fine, though, except the bad guy."

The squint faded as her eyes adjusted to the light. "*You* don't look so fine. And what's with the 'little late-night workout'? You hate that John Wayne crap."

I stared at her for a long moment, struggling to sort out my reactions. Her initial show of concern was so at odds with this last comment, I wasn't sure where to start.

"Sorry," I said lamely.

"Who was killed?" she then asked.

I sat back, dropped the shoe, and rubbed my eyes, feeling the echoes of question after question lapping against my head like waves on a fragile sand dune. Of all the people I'd spoken to tonight, she was the most important to me, but it took all my reserves to merely say, "Billy Conyer."

Her brow furrowed. "Sounds vaguely familiar."

"Friend of Brenda Croteau."

She sat up angrily. "What? I don't understand. You're not working the Croteau case. What's going on?"

I got up slowly and crossed the room to sit on the bed beside her, resolved to go through it one last time. "We got a lead on who killed Resnick. Turned out to be Conyer. We raided his place tonight—thought it was a one-room apartment. He'd chopped a hole into the apartment next door, and the one beyond that, and that's where he was sleeping. I don't know if it was for security or just because he thought it'd be fun. But when we broke through his door, all we found was an empty room. He came bursting into the hallway two doors down, gun blazing, and we had to take him down. I have no idea how or whether he's connected to your case. When his name first came up, I should have let you know. It slipped my mind. He never played more than a bit role in the Croteau research—I think Janice Litchfield mentioned him once in passing. Sorry if I messed you up."

She put her hand on mine, suddenly more conscious of my state of mind. "I'm the one who's sorry. Talk about misplaced priorities. Was it bad?"

"We used shotguns—pretty ugly."

"Did he shoot at you?"

I nodded. "Marshall caught one in the vest. He was the only one hit. He's fine."

Following a long silence, she murmured, "I can't imagine what that would be like."

God knows Gail had gotten her lumps over the years, either seeing me being patched up in the hospital or suffering herself at the hands of her own assailant. But she'd still always viewed my world as a bit of an abstraction, even now that she was a prosecutor. She didn't share my knowledge of the streets, or of the people inhabiting them. It was an ignorance I had taken for granted until now, but which had lately begun to chafe on me, especially now that she was deciding which of my collars got deals and which went to jail.

Without being fully aware of it, I'd come to see her differently in her new job. From rape victim to fighter to law student to now, she'd built herself over, with motivations and goals far different from those I'd known when we'd met. I'd done what I could to be supportive—moving into this house, in which I'd never felt fully at home, encouraging her when she'd given herself totally to her law studies. But I realized now that the distance I was feeling between us wasn't solely due to her gaining speed and my staying put. It also involved a discomfort on my part with living so close to so much constant energy.

She squeezed my hand to remind me that I hadn't said a word for several minutes. "You okay?"

"I will be," I said. "I've been through shootings before. I just have to give myself a little time to process it."

"I'm sorry I mouthed off."

It was a comment normally deserving of a dismissive, "It's all right," letting the trauma of the shooting act as a cover-up for unspoken feelings. But, paradoxically, I didn't have the strength right now to take a quick and easy out.

"Maybe that's become par for the course lately, on both our parts," I said tentatively, unsure where I was heading, or even why.

Her hand slipped off of mine. "What do you mean?" Her voice was careful.

"That we've changed."

I knew I should say more, but I couldn't find the words.

She surprised me by simply saying, "I know."

I turned from staring at the floor to meet her eyes, astonished that she might have been sharing what I'd thought were one-sided misgivings. "You feel the same way? What happened?"

She looked at me sadly. "Maybe more than we could handle, starting with who we are and where we came from."

I understood what she meant. She was a child of privilege, and I the son of a make-do farmer. We'd come like travelers down separate roads, and had found peace and joy on a common path. Our pasts, and the influences that had forged us, hadn't much mattered in a shared but busily distracting life.

We'd even prided ourselves on surviving tests of fire—the stresses of my job and its dangers, the political wrangles Gail had been sucked into over the years. We'd seen those as the worst of hurdles, easily jumped.

Until we'd hit the rape.

I touched her cheek with my fingertips. "I love you, Gail."

She smiled, barely. "So what do we do?"

I kissed her. "Go to sleep. Trust to instinct. This'll work itself out. I don't know how—I'm not even sure what the problem is, really—but we're friends first and foremost, and I think that'll see us through."

We left it at that, but it was a restless night, filled with things left unsaid.

Chapter Sixteen

The morning after, I could still smell the gunpowder in the stagnant air of the hallway. It was very quiet, the street sounds barely audible through the walls. Yellow police tape had been strung up to isolate the entire floor, adding to the museumlike quality of the place. Conyer's blood had dried to a nondescript brown.

I paused on the landing and looked down the corridor, beyond the coagulated pool and the scars the buckshot had left along the walls, trying to put aside the memories for the job at hand. It was hard to forget the bright flashes from Conyer's pistol, and not knowing if I might suddenly feel the numbing impact of a bullet.

Ron Klesczewski stepped into my line of vision from a side door, snapping me out of my reverie. "Hi, Joe. Heard you were headed this way. You get any sleep?"

From the look in his eyes, it was obvious he knew I hadn't. "No."

He smiled sympathetically. "Well, we may have lost out on a chat with Billy Conyer, but he left enough behind to keep us busy for a while."

I drew abreast of the door we'd forced open just eight hours earlier. Given the outcome of that visit, our search of Conyer's digs had been delayed by the post-shoot team's priorities.

I peered over Ron's shoulder at the room beyond. "I just hope it's enough. I want to get moving on this."

Ron stepped aside and let me in. The room was what we'd come to expect from the neighborhood—dark, stuffy, unclean, stripped of all but the essentials, and filled with the debris of a human being with little care for himself or his environment. Enhancing the flavor, the building's heating system was still in overdrive, making the whole place feel like a sauna perched over a garbage dump. There was a jagged two-foot by four-foot hole in the side wall, which Conyer had created as a backdoor.

Willy stuck his head through the hole and smiled at me. "Hey, there, boss. Decide to join us before noon?"

"Drop it."

He laughed. "Oh-oh. Joe's grumpy. Must've not gotten laid."

He didn't know how close that cut. "What've you found so far, Willy?"

"Mostly just the by-products of a disgusting lifestyle, but we haven't been at it long."

"What's the story on the three rooms? How was he able to cut through the walls with nobody knowing?"

"I checked into that," Ron said from behind me. "It wasn't coincidence they were empty, like we thought last night. Conyer rented the other two under assumed names."

I looked at him closely. "How long ago?"

He glanced at his notepad. "January eighth."

"Two days after Resnick was killed," I said. "Anyone check if he had a bank account?"

Willy laughed. "Yeah. I don't think he was into banks. I got his assets in a suitcase here. Something under five grand."

"We checked the local branches," Ron elaborated, "and we put it out on the wire. But he could've used an alias, like he did for the other two rooms. We might never find out for sure."

I turned back to Willy. "That money in new bills or old?"

"Bit of both."

"New ones banded or loose?"

"Loose."

"Check those for prints. If we get lucky, maybe Conyer's contractor left a fat thumbprint on each as he shelled 'em out. Who's working the friends and relatives angle?" I asked.

Willy's voice took on a slight edge, no doubt matching my own. "Sam. She could probably use some help, if you've finished busting our chops."

I got the hint.

I tried clearing my mind on the short drive to the office, freeing it of last night's shooting, of my conversation with Gail, and of my overall frustration. I knew I'd been overly terse with Ron and Willy. With all of us under pressure and in need of sleep, I was supposed to be setting an example of grace in the face of adversity.

Sammie was at her desk, poring over Ron's notes. I sat in her guest chair, not bothering to remove my coat.

She glanced up. "You look beat."

So much for that effort. "I'm okay. Willy told me you were chasing down Conyer's family and associates."

She pulled a sheet of paper from the file before her. "Yeah. He spent most of his time with the twenty-something crowd—big on bar-hopping, hell-raising, and recreational dope."

"Looks like he was paid to do in Resnick. Willy found a suitcase full of cash."

She stared with renewed interest at the contents of her file. "Huh—well, if he was the lead man, it sure doesn't sound like the guy I've been reading about. One report describes him as a born underling—not a doer. According to his criminal records, he acted out now and then—assault and battery, aggravated assault, destruction of private property—but he never went over the top, and he always got busted in a group, as if he couldn't be aggressive on his own, or needed someone else to lead the way."

"So maybe he was at the bottom of a three-man totem pole."

She sat back, looking thoughtful. "That's what I was thinking. He could've stolen that hammer to qualify as one of the team—like a rite of passage."

"Implying a big brother relationship somewhere," I mused.

Sammie played the devil's advocate. "On the flip side, he did a pretty good Rambo imitation last night. Could be he finally grew some balls and put a gang together—maybe the Mob paid him to hit one of their own."

I shook my head. "I think he was being manipulated and felt he was in too deep to get out. That's why he came out shooting. He must've been scared shitless—

making holes in the walls, keeping his money in a suitcase, and sleeping three apartments over. When a small-
timer becomes a murderer, he usually makes a mess of
it—he doesn't put together a complicated deal like what
we're trying to figure out. I think you're right—someone was pulling his string." I pointed my chin toward
the paperwork. "So what's your plan?"

"Check out the family—and his erstwhile playmates.
He has two brothers who live in town. Another died
of an overdose in Boston two years ago."

"You want me to take them?"

She handed me one of her sheets. "Be my guest."

Brian Conyer worked at the C&S Grocers warehouse
north of town, an enormous enterprise, one of the largest
suppliers of groceries in the Northeast and, depending
on the year, the biggest business in the state of Vermont. Trucks came and went from the warehouse around
the clock, serviced by a small army of loaders, stack-
ers, freezer personnel, hi-lo operators, forklift drivers,
and dozens of others. Given the constant turnover, the
lack of intense prehiring screening, and the low expectations from both management and employees that
the floor jobs had any upward mobility, the whole setup
was predisposed to attract a certain slice of the population. Several of our customers had lain low at C&S
at one time or another, which made it, paradoxically,
one of the police department's bigger allies. By offering jobs to people who might otherwise go into business for themselves, the company helped keep a lid on
the crime rate.

According to a computer check I made before driving to C&S, Billy's brother didn't fit that special category, however. He was like the majority of workers

there: high-school-educated, locally based, low income, and, in all probability, with few illusions that the future would ever look any different.

I found him stacking pallets in the three-story-tall freezer—big enough to fit several houses—dressed in overalls so heavily insulated he looked ready to attack the Antarctic. I made no apologies for escorting him outside the building into the winter cold and around a corner that shielded us from the explosive belches of a row of eighteen-wheelers. If anything, I figured it would be warmer than where I'd found him.

He took off a glove, revealing a large, muscular, scarred hand, dug into his overalls, and pulled out a pack of cigarettes and a lighter. He didn't offer me one. He was broad-shouldered, deep-chested, and apparently not given to idle chitchat. "I guess this is about Billy."

It wasn't a question, and it wasn't phrased with any great interest.

"Yes," I admitted. "When did you hear about it?"

"The radio—this morning. During coffee break."

"When did you come on?"

"Midnight." He inhaled deeply and then mixed smoke and cold breath vapor into a cloud before him. He answered my questioning look by adding, "I'm working overtime right now. 'Nother four hours."

"You haven't called any of your family?"

He didn't answer at first, which I assumed was for my benefit. I sensed Brian prided himself on being tough. "My brother Tim phoned. To let me know."

"How was he taking it?"

Conyer shrugged. "He wasn't crying, if that's what you mean."

"Not a close-knit bunch?"

This time, he smiled ruefully. "My folks didn't work real hard in that department. My dad beat my mom, and we four boys beat on each other. Pretty basic."

"Did you know what Billy was up to lately?"

"Nothin' good."

"I mean for a fact."

He inhaled again, held it a moment, and made like a smoke signal. "For a fact? I didn't know and I didn't care."

Timothy Conyer was in the employees' break room at the back of Sam's, once Brattleboro's largest Army-Navy store, now its largest "outdoor outfitters"—a semantic concession to changing sensitivities. It was still a remarkable place, jammed with everything from wool shirts and dress slacks to ammunition and Swiss army knives. And it still had a section of surplus military goods. There had never been a time when I didn't have something from Sam's in my closet.

Tim Conyer was as slight as his brother Brian was massive, both in body size and demeanor. He rose nervously as I entered, and immediately offered me a cup of coffee.

"Please. Have a seat."

I accepted both offers, adding milk and sugar to my mug. "You know why I'm here?"

"I figured they'd be sending somebody."

"Why's that?"

He gave a quick, automatic smile. "Well, Billy . . . I don't know. Isn't that what you always do?"

I took a sip. It was hot and sweet and very good. "I suppose so. I heard you called Brian about it this morning."

He allowed a small frown. "Yeah. Shouldn't have bothered."

"That's basically what he said. According to him, there was no love lost between any of you."

"He's speaking for himself. We were a family, regardless how good we were at it. Brian just never made the effort."

"Where's he fit in terms of age?"

"The oldest. I'm the youngest. Maybe that has something to do with it. I didn't see everything he did when we were growing up."

"Your dad beating your mom?"

He smiled again, this time sadly. "He told you about that? I'm surprised. He usually writes it off as no big deal. I bet he didn't tell you how it ended. Brian beat the crap out of him one night, and that was that. Dad split to find a different punching bag."

"How did Billy fit into all this?"

Tim stared into the dark pool at the bottom of his own mug. "I always thought he and Robbie were the real victims—too young to defend themselves, too old to be oblivious like me. Bri and I were the lucky ones."

"It was Robbie who died in Boston?"

He looked up at me sharply. "OD'd in Boston. Yeah. I had a nightmare once where I saw my mother and father swinging Robbie by his hands and feet, and then throwing him onto an enormous needle—big as a spike—at the bottom of a ditch, skewering him like a butterfly to a corkboard. I didn't need a shrink to explain that one to me."

"But Billy stayed in town."

"Yeah. His reaction was a little more complicated. He wanted to be a tough guy like Brian, but it didn't come naturally. You could call his bluff pretty easily.

For a while, all he did was hang out with younger kids—he could dominate them. But I guess that didn't do it for him, 'cause later it was just the opposite. He'd spend all his time with older jerks who pretended they were God's gift to cool."

"Like who?"

He glanced around the room vaguely. "Oh, I don't know. Jamie Good, Walter Freund, people like that."

Both names had been mentioned by Janice Litchfield in connection with Brenda Croteau. The bridges between the Resnick homicide and Brenda's were multiplying. "He hang around with Dwayne Matthews?" I asked, figuring I'd start with Croteau's boyfriend.

But I drew a blank. "Who?"

"Janice Litchfield?"

"Oh, sure. He knew Janice. Everyone knows her. That wasn't anything special, though. They were just friends."

"Owen Tharp?"

His eyes widened at a name that was now headline news. "Owen? Is that what this was all about? Billy got killed because of Owen?"

I shook my head emphatically. "I didn't say that. Owen comes from that circle, so did your brother. I just wondered if they knew each other."

"Sure, they did. Owen was one of the younger kids Billy liked to push around."

"Sounds like everyone pushed him around."

Tim Conyer suddenly became pensive. "Yeah. He used to remind me of Robbie that way, sometimes— everybody's punching bag, including his own." He looked at me quizzically. "That's what makes his killing that woman so weird. I never would've thought Owen had that in him."

"Witnesses said he'd lash out sometimes—violently."

Conyer nodded. "I suppose so. I saw it, too. But that was like when my brothers and I were kids. We'd slug it out—sometimes pretty good, too—but there was always a limit."

I finished my coffee. "Tim, we have evidence Billy was involved in the killing of that man on the railroad tracks a while back. That's why we went to see him last night—and why we think he decided to shoot it out. Do you know anything that might explain that? Did he talk recently about some money coming his way, or landing a big score, or maybe making some new friends?"

Tim was already shaking his head. "No. He was excited about something, but he never told me what it was. He probably knew I'd give him flak about it. I used to tell him he was headed for trouble, not that he ever listened."

"How 'bout this last crowd of his—Good and the others? Any of them likely candidates for the railroad tracks killing? There might've been three people in on that."

He looked at me helplessly. "Maybe. I don't know. I have a hard time thinking of anybody killing somebody else. Billy's friends aren't nice people, but I always saw them more as show-offs, not killers."

That night, as if by unspoken arrangement, Gail and I were at home at close to a normal hour. We set about making dinner as usual, dividing the labor, where I sliced and diced and she did arcane things at the stove. At first we spoke tentatively, generally touching on the day's activities, acting as if this were a first date and we two people only vaguely acquainted. There was an oddly competitive feeling about it, as if each of us were daring the other to open an intriguing but ominous package placed between us.

"Gail," I finally began, "I know some of this is probably just in my head. Maybe it's a midlife crisis or something."

We had finally settled down at the small breakfast table in the kitchen, in front of a meal neither one of us had the appetite to eat.

"Midlife crises don't happen to two people simultaneously," she argued. "This isn't just your problem."

I waved an empty fork at the roof over our heads. "Is it this? Living together? We were doing pretty well before."

Her smile was forlorn. "Moving in together wasn't what changed things, Joe."

I was irritated she thought I'd belittle what she'd been through. "I know that. But it's something we can do something about. I can't take back the rape."

Now she looked angry. "The rape isn't yours to do *anything* about. It just happened. It wasn't preventable. But it did happen to me. It affected both of us—I know that—and it cost you, too. But it cost me more."

I replaced the fork carefully, struggling to choose correctly from a tangle of emotional options. "I'm not trying to take ownership of it, Gail. Or play it down. I just meant there has to be a way for us to move onwards—as a couple. It was a life-altering thing, but I don't see why it has to destroy how we feel about each other."

"Was it the rape that started you feeling differently?" she asked, still suspicious.

I knew most of my choices were charged with harm

and hurt. We were like two glasses, filled to the brim, balancing on an unsteady tray held between the both of us.

"It was the rape," I began slowly, "that changed the course of your life. I'd gotten used to the ways things were, and I had trouble keeping pace with the new direction you were taking."

She opened her mouth to say something, but I held up my hand, suddenly clear on what I wanted to say. "Please, hang on. There's no fault implied there. I was amazed at how you rallied—I still am. And even more amazed at how you grew from an event that's ended other women's lives. In fact, it made me feel like I was standing still in the middle of some road, while you were making tracks like there was no tomorrow. Your rebirth, if you want to call it that, left me wondering what *I* had done lately—stuck in the same job, the same town, the same routine. I began wondering what possible worth I could be to you."

"Joe," she began to interrupt, her voice softer, but I stopped her again.

"Let me get this out. I'm not playing for sympathy here. I'm trying to be realistic. For whatever reasons, you've been given a second shot at life, and you're going at it hammer and tongs—as you should. It's not all that different from before, after all—being a Realtor, a selectman, all those board positions you had—but now there's an intensity that wasn't there before. You used to do what you did because life just turned out that way. Now I don't know if I can keep up with you, or if it'll be any good if I try."

One of the things I liked most about Gail was her reluctance to tell people what they wanted to hear. She didn't say she was sorry when she wasn't, didn't offer condolences when she didn't feel them, and didn't dole out sentimental soothings just to make an issue go away.

She could have argued against what I'd just said, but I wasn't surprised she didn't.

"Does this tie into when the AG threw the book at you?" she asked.

I thought about that for a moment. The year before, I'd been framed by people who'd wanted me out of the way, and a young Turk from the attorney general's office had wasted no time playing into their hands. Only a revelation of the truth and a last-minute pardon from the governor had saved my job. Part of the AG's reasoning had been that my living with a younger, richer, upwardly mobile woman—with whom I could no longer keep pace—had made me open to corruption. He'd been wrong on the facts, but he'd cut close to the bone emotionally. I had been feeling outdistanced.

"Partly," I admitted. "One of the reasons we always worked so well together was because we gave each other lots of space. We moved in together because you needed the company—you were wounded. Temporarily. But now that you're healthy again, I'm feeling a little like the nurse who's been allowed to stay on just for sentimental reasons. You're so strong and so motivated and so wrapped up in the things you're doing, I guess I've started to feel a little sorry for myself."

"And you want your old life back," she said.

I shook my head. "That's oversimplifying it. I want to know what *you're* feeling. I want us to find something that works for both of us. I'm not pretending we can just turn the clock back, and I sure as hell don't want us to split up. What I used to feel being with you was an inner calm—a sense of completeness. I just want to know if that can be revived."

There was more welling up inside me—all on the same theme. But I fell silent, knowing that to go on would be either futile or unnecessary—and fearing that I'd said too much already.

Gail got up and circled the small table and pulled me to my feet. She kissed me long and hard, her arms wrapped tightly around me. When she pulled back, her eyes were moist, as were mine, but her voice was recharged with purpose. "I'll never meet another man like you—ever— and I don't plan on losing you now. But I don't want to talk anymore. I want to take you to bed. Okay?"

I nodded and followed her upstairs.

Chapter Seventeen

Ron found me the next morning in the Officers' Room, pouring myself a cup of coffee.

He waved a fax at me. "Finally heard back from the Portland court clerk. Five years ago, Jim Reynolds defended Katahdin Trucking on a case of illegal shipping of hazardous materials."

I took the sheet from him and studied its contents. "I'll be damned."

"That give us enough for a Duces Tecum search of his office yet?"

I shook my head. "He's a defense lawyer—this just proves it. And most of the other things we have, or had, against him still don't amount to much. Even a judge who hated the guy wouldn't cut us papers on this. And Derby sure as hell wouldn't."

Ron looked disappointed.

"Which only means we're jumping the gun slightly," I added to cheer him up. "Find out who in Katahdin was involved. Let's see if we can form a link between Resnick, Katahdin, and Reynolds. That might give us enough to get through his door."

I saw the morning paper lying on the kitchenette table amid the debris of several people's fast-food breakfasts. The headlines were still screaming about the killing of Billy Conyer two nights ago. "I guess they're having a field day," I commented between sips of coffee.

Ron followed my glance. "You read it yet? Katz wrote an article about undue force, violence in general, and the irony of our being more part of the problem than part of the solution."

"Catchy. Sammie in yet? I never got a chance to compare notes with her about Conyer yesterday."

Ron told me she'd come in early, and I followed him back to our squad room.

Sammie didn't look good. She was disheveled, had bags under her eyes, and appeared to have gone all night without sleep.

I sat next to her desk and asked quietly, "You okay?"

Her answer was almost curt. "Fine. What'd you find out from the Conyer brothers?"

"And good morning to you."

She sighed irritably. "Andy and I had a fight last night."

"Gail and I had one the night before."

She looked at me for a long time and then allowed a half smile. "What a drag, huh?"

"I don't know. We made up." I didn't add to what ambiguous effect.

Her shoulders slumped slightly. "I suppose we will, too. I forgot how hard this junk is."

"You haven't had a lot of experience at it, Sam. It does get easier. What happened?"

She hesitated before admitting. "The job got in the way.

You know how I was supposed to check into Conyer's inner circle? Well, Andy cropped up again."

I raised my eyebrows. "Oh?"

"Yeah. I mean, I know he's no choirboy. I also know he doesn't have a record. But he did hang out . . . I guess I should say he does hang out with some guys who do."

I smiled to hide my concern. "So do we. What makes this different?"

"One of Conyer's favorite dives was the Dirty Dollar. Andy's a regular there. They knew each other, and Andy never fessed up to it. The son-of-a-bitch fired a shot at me, and Andy never admitted he knew him. I had to go to the Dollar, poking around, and find it out for myself. I felt like a total jerk."

Her pallor gave way to flushed cheeks as she worked herself up. I had no problem imagining the scene at her place last night. "He might've been hoping you wouldn't find out. Did you find any criminal ties between him and Conyer?"

"No. As far as I could tell, they just drank together sometimes."

"Then that's probably all there was to it. After all, it wouldn't have changed anything if he had told you he'd known Conyer, right? The guy was already dead. What's Andy's take on your job?"

"He doesn't think much of it, and he sure as hell doesn't like Kunkle. And from what he told me, I'm about ready to tear Willy a new asshole myself." She suddenly leaned forward, speaking right into my face. "Andy said Willy's been checking up on him—talking to neighbors, co-workers, hanging out on his street. I couldn't believe it. Like everybody I know's been holding out on me, like I was some fucking retard."

I put my hand on her shoulder. "Whoa. Take a breather. You know that's not true. Come on—sit back."

I pushed her slightly and she settled back in her chair. But her face remained grim.

"Sammie, you checked him out yourself. You just told me so."

Her mouth tightened.

"Willy thinks more of you than he lets on. You're probably the one person on the whole squad he considers a friend."

"Some friend."

"Yeah, some friend. You fall head over heels for a guy you found at an all-night poker game during a homicide investigation. Wouldn't you have been concerned if you'd been Willy? You two are partners, for Christ's sake."

She didn't answer, but I could tell I'd hit home.

"I'll admit he might've gone a little overboard. Tell me that's out of character."

"I suppose," she grumbled.

"Now let me ask you something: In the midst of all the fireworks between you and Andy, did you really settle in your mind if he was or wasn't connected to Conyer? Be honest here, 'cause if you have any doubts, I'd be happy to be the bad guy—finish the research and talk to him directly."

She spoke dully. "They just hung out together. No big deal."

I didn't say anything. The silence stretched between us until she was forced to look up. "Would you mind?"

"Nope. It'll probably make things even tenser at home, though. After Willy, Andy's going to feel we're gunning for him."

She rubbed her forehead harshly. "Damn. It wouldn't

be an issue if he'd just been straight with me . . . No, you go ahead. I don't think you'll find anything, but it's got to be done. If it turns out I was wrong about him, and I gave him special treatment, I'd have to quit my job. I couldn't look anyone in the face."

It was a little melodramatic, reflective of her youth and passion. I merely nodded and said, "Will do. Who else did you find out about yesterday? Conyer's brother Tim said he'd been hanging out with Jamie Good and company, wanting to be around the big boys. Is that the sense you got?"

She nodded, slowly regaining speed. "Yeah, the bartender was pretty good on Conyer. Said he didn't pull much weight. He also said that the last few times he was in, he acted different, saying he was up for a promotion. Nobody paid much attention. I called the garage he worked at. His boss just laughed at the promotion idea—said he didn't know why he hadn't fired Conyer long ago. His work habits were a little irregular."

"So no tight buddies you could find?"

"Not tight like you or me might have, but he did have people he either looked up to or who looked up to him."

"The last being younger people?"

She nodded. "Yeah. Billy's other hangout was the teen center. The folks there thought he was obnoxious, but harmless enough—basically a bad Marlon Brando imitation. I've got leads on a few people who might be able to tell me what Conyer was really up to. It'll just take some time to find 'em."

I got up. "Well, I'll leave you to it, then."

"You going to talk to Andy now?" she asked a little nervously.

"Thought I might as well get it out of the way. I'll try to keep it relaxed."

She frowned. "Not on my account. Just do it right. If he can't live with what I do for a living, I need to know that."

"Okay." I turned to go.

"Joe?"

I looked over my shoulder at her.

"Thanks."

Naughton Lumber was a huge, sprawling place—a combination of enormous long sheds and vast expanses of open ground covered with towering pillars of stacked lumber, each capped with a gray mantle of old snow. Logging trucks, eighteen-wheelers, and forklifts ambled up and down the corridors created by these structures, as did occasional groups of men, warmly dressed in clothes that had been picked at and torn by constant exposure to rough wood. The air was full of the muffled, high-pitched whine of saws and planers, mixed with the sweet tang of raw lumber.

The foreman directed me to the molding shop crew boss, who escorted me to where Andy Padgett was operating a gigantic, threatening, screaming machine. Wearing ear protectors against the din, the crew boss tapped him on the shoulder, pointed to the front of the building, and gestured to both of us to leave.

Before taking the lead, Padgett gave me a hard, appraising look.

We ended up in a snack bar of sorts, built like a parked mobile home against one of the huge shed's walls. It was long like a diner, harshly lit with fluorescent strips, and at the moment totally empty. The walls were obviously heavily insulated, since from the moment we stepped inside, the howling behind us was instantly muffled to the level of industrial white noise.

Padgett stepped up to one of a bank of vending machines lining one wall, removing the earplugs from around his head. "You want something?"

I sat at a Formica-topped table. "No—all set. Thanks."

He fed the machine with change, pushed a button, and watched as a plastic cup noisily filled with hot tea, which he then carefully brought to the table, smiling awkwardly. "Drink this stuff all winter. Damned if I know why. Never touch it the rest of the year."

He sat opposite me and pulled off his watch cap, sprinkling his lap with a fine shower of sawdust. "Guess you're here about Billy Conyer," he commented.

"Yeah," I said mildly. "I heard you knew him."

"Sammie sic you on me?" His tone of voice was pleasant enough, but the smile accompanying it was forced.

"You did kind of sneak up on her—not letting her know."

He busied himself with his cup for a moment, swirling its contents around before bringing it to his lips for a tentative sip. "Yeah," he finally admitted. "Would've spared myself some grief if I had, I guess." He looked at me directly. "I didn't know the guy that well, you know. I told her that. I had a few drinks with him, listened to his bullshit. That was it. He was just another guy at the bar."

"You couldn't have told her that right off? Something like, 'Holy cow, I used to drink with him'?"

"I said I messed up. I don't see what the big deal is. You people are too damned touchy."

"That surprise you?"

"Kunkle's pretty surprising, you bet. She tell you what he did?"

"Yeah, and I'll talk to him about it. He gets a little overprotective."

His thick brows gathered in anger. "Guy's a jerk. Everybody knows it. Makes you all look bad. I'm not too sure what he did was even legal."

"Mr. Padgett," I stopped him, getting a little hot myself. "What he did was make some minor inquiries. Not too surprising, given your coyness with the truth."

He stood up abruptly. "I don't have to take this shit. I'm not some fucking criminal, you know. I didn't do anything wrong."

I waved my hand at him tiredly. "Sit down. My God, why is it everybody's got a burr up their butt today? Talk about being touchy."

He surprised me by smiling. "Sammie run you up the flagpole, too?"

I decided to play along, if only to calm him down. "Why should I be any different?"

He resumed his seat, his pleasant demeanor back in place.

"You know," I told him, "the only reason I'm here is because Sam felt she was too emotionally involved with you to conduct a run-of-the-mill interview herself. It's standard procedure. If you're too tight with a person, you switch off with someone else. That's all that's going on here. You happened to know Billy Conyer and we need to find out what that amounted to."

"Which is nothing."

"These things are like jigsaw puzzles," I persisted, "made up of hundreds of seemingly meaningless pieces. All I want is your one small piece."

He finally relented. "Okay, shoot."

"How long ago did you first meet Billy Conyer?"

"A few years. I don't remember exactly. It was at the Dirty Dollar. And it wasn't a big thing. I just began to notice him as a regular. I tend to drink at the bar, instead of at a table. You get to hear more bullshit that way, talk about the game on the tube, meet people as they come and go for their orders. It's more sociable."

"And Billy did the same?"

"Off and on. He'd rotate from table to table, and then wind up at the bar after everybody had told him to shove off. He was like a bug that way—always in your face, buzzing away."

"You never told him to shove off? Sounds pretty obnoxious."

"Nah. He was harmless. And he could tell a good joke."

"He ever talk about himself—his family, friends, job, any big dreams?"

Padgett looked reflective and took a swig from his now cool tea. "His family. Said he'd had one brother OD, another who was a wimp, a third who walked around like a caveman. He made it funny. Job? I think he worked in a garage. I'm not sure about that."

He paused.

"The bartender mentioned him talking about some good prospects coming his way lately," I said.

He flicked his hand dismissively. "Oh, hell, they all talk like that. It's the lotto, or some relative dying. I never believe it. Is that why he got shot? He rob that guy the paper says he killed?"

I ignored the question. "You said he went from table to table. What was he doing?"

"Schmoozing. That's one thing. When he did hang

out with me at the bar, he'd talk a lot about who so-and-so was, and how they were connected to whatever." He suddenly laughed. "As if it amounted to anything. I mean, shit, to be one of the high-and-mighty at the Dollar, all you need to do is draw a regular welfare check."

"Still," I countered, "a few of them do all right. Jamie Good, for instance."

"Yeah, I suppose."

"Who else?"

"Walter Freund. Jimmy Lyon hung out there whenever his wife would let him. Donnie Carter—the guy I work with. Hell, there're a lot of 'em. But nobody's rich. The real success stories just got jobs, like me."

"You ever drink with Good?"

"Nah. He was a table regular. Liked to have people like Billy hanging around, making him feel special. Billy sucked up to him a lot."

"Freund's name keeps coming up. What's he like?"

"Not as noisy as Good. He's a little creepy. I didn't have nothin' to do with him."

"And Owen Tharp?"

Padgett looked disgusted. "He was pathetic. Made Conyer look like a captain of industry."

"You ever see him lash out?"

"I barely heard him speak. I couldn't believe he knifed that woman. Are you sure you have the right guy for that? Just seems so unbelievable."

When I didn't answer, he looked at his watch. "I gotta get back. This going to take much longer?"

"Just a couple more," I said. "You mentioned both Lyon and Carter. Those were two of the men you were playing poker with that night, weren't they?"

"Yeah, them and Frankie Harris."

"Harris didn't frequent the Dirty Dollar?"

He hesitated a split second. "I might've seen him once or twice. He wasn't a regular." He stood up. "You said a couple. I don't want to get in trouble."

He moved toward the door.

"What about Brenda Croteau?" I asked. "She hung out with that crowd."

He put his hand on the doorknob. "Could be, but I didn't. I only saw 'em when they were drinking at the Dollar. Do me a favor, will you?"

"What's that?"

"Tell Sammie what a good boy I was."

I watched him leave without comment. To be honest, I had no idea what kind of boy he was.

Chapter Eighteen

To a native-born Vermonter, driving across New Hampshire is a little like walking on a rival team's playing field. It's not an infraction of the rules, or even in bad taste, but it does feel kind of funny.

On the map, they look like mirror images of the same real estate—two similarly sized wedges fitting together to form a rough rectangle. New Hampshire has the sea, Vermont, Lake Champlain; New Hampshire's largest towns are near Boston to the south, Vermont's are to the north, not far from Montreal. Both pride themselves on their mountains, their maple sugar, their cows, and their sense of independence.

And both couldn't be further apart.

The rivalry between them predates the Revolutionary War, when New Hampshire claimed sovereignty right up to the New York border, declaring present-day Vermont to be the "New Hampshire Grants." That was actually fine with the few settlers living there, except that in 1764, King George III stuck his foot in it again by giving Vermont to New York, whose governor had taken exception to New Hampshire's high-handedness.

This allowed a very belligerent Ethan Allen—with his Green Mountain Boys and the fortunate timing of the American Revolution—to create in 1777 not just a new state, but a wholly independent republic, which didn't join the Union for another fourteen years.

Referred to colloquially as Vermont from its birth, the new republic was officially named New Connecticut, revealing how ambiguous its residents had become.

Maybe as a result of this contentious start, both New Hampshire and Vermont have forever after eyed one another like suspicious twins, and made great hay about their differences.

It was hard to admit, therefore, that the actual drive across New Hampshire to Portland, Maine—where Ron had set up a meeting with the prosecutor in Reynolds's old case—was more pleasant at this time of year than a similar trip would have been across southern Vermont. At home, the Green and Berkshire mountains link up between Brattleboro and Bennington, making passage across their backs scenic but perilous in all but good weather. New Hampshire is only gently hilly and benign at the same latitude, influenced by the seashore to the east and the Massachusetts plains to the south.

Not that we had bad weather to contend with. The whole region had settled into a routine after that one major storm, with perfectly bearable alternating periods of grayness and sparkling sun. The day Ron and I had chosen for our drive was of the blue-skied, ice-cold variety so favored by skiers and longed for by those going bonkers with cabin fever.

We didn't discuss work at first, taking advantage of the outing to simply enjoy the scenery. Traffic was light and the roads were in good shape, so the feeling encouraged more talk of home and family than of major crimes and office squabbles. Ron had a wife and a small child, of whom he was inordinately proud. Where many male cops referred to their mates as "the wife" on a good day, Ron carried pictures in his wallet, bragged about his small family at the drop of a hat, and made no bones about the delights of going home at the end of the day.

It was a healthy tonic for me to hear him go on about such domestic bliss, and so I encouraged him until we'd passed through Concord on our way to Manchester and then due east.

At which point, making a reasonable transition, he brought up Sammie Martens.

"You think she and Andy are going to become a permanent item?" he asked hopefully.

It had been several days since my chat with Andy Padgett, and I hadn't said a word to anyone about it. I had double-checked some of what he'd told me—speaking with the bartender Sammie had recommended, for instance—but I'd only covered the basics. I hadn't probed deeply, both for my sake and hers, and hadn't found reason to in any case.

I didn't harbor deep suspicions about Padgett. I truly believed him to be as he appeared: someone on the periphery, not my type of human being, and not too wise in his choice of drinking companions—but essentially an innocent.

That being so, I still didn't like him, and protectively hoped Sammie wouldn't try to make a go of him.

"I don't think so," I said lightly.

"Really? She seems pretty stuck on him."

"I think she's making up for lost time."

"Is this the father figure I'm hearing?" he asked with a smile.

I glanced at him appraisingly, impressed less by his insight, which hardly mimicked rocket science, and more by his boldness. To hear Ron Klesczewski speak in a jocular, mocking manner was like hearing Willy Kunkle being compassionate.

"You're feeling your oats."

He laughed. "Probably just getting away for a few hours. Not too often we have this heavy a caseload—which'll only be getting worse."

"With Reynolds? Could be. He's certainly the strangest aspect of all this. The way his name keeps coming up is pretty weird."

"Maybe that's part of his game plan."

"What do you mean?"

"Look at the chronology," Ron said. "The break-in, the abandoned truck, the killing. Each one a little worse than its predecessor. The confusion over that car always struck me as real screwy. It was so elaborate, so stagy, and incredibly risky. If you get a guy like Resnick—from out of state and with a minimal support system—and you bang him over the head, why go to the effort those three guys went to? Especially when the frame can be pulled apart so easily?"

"And your answer is?"

"Maybe Reynolds staged it himself, to make it look like he's being targeted by someone."

"Implying Reynolds killed Resnick?"

"He could have, using hired help. I think the office break-in was for real. The body language Bobby Miller reported sounded right on. But I also think it was more than an interrupted B&E. Which means that maybe something happened that night to make the other stuff necessary."

I couldn't say he was wrong. Neither one of us had

anything concrete to work with. But it sounded far-fetched. "What about the truck breaking down?" I asked. "Forensics said it looked like a straightforward mechanical problem."

"Maybe," he agreed, "but it doesn't explain why Resnick hung around town afterward, his skin burning from chemicals, not going to the ER to be checked out. Why didn't he seek help? What happened that night? Where did he go? Who did he call? It must've been somebody, or those three guys wouldn't have found him. And that means he must've trusted them—or thought he could."

I started shaking my head emphatically. "Ron, for Christ's sake. Listen to yourself. Reynolds is involved in trucking dirty goods. One of his drivers—Resnick—has a breakdown and an accident both, pouring God-knows-what on himself. He therefore calls Reynolds for help. Help, however, consists of three of Reynolds's henchmen, who bean Resnick on the head, drive him to the tracks in a car designed to compromise their own boss, and use a train to kill him. All so we can find the body first and the car later, and declare the whole thing a clumsy frame, thereby taking the one guy we never suspected in the first place off the hot seat? It's crazy."

He remained silent and tight-lipped.

I instantly regretted my outburst. "Ron, look, I'm sorry."

"No big deal."

"You do hear what I'm saying, though, right?"

"Yeah." He sounded more regretful than angry.

"I'll grant you most of what you said," I tried again. "But not with Reynolds as the mastermind. More log-ical would be that the frame was meant to stick—and only fell apart because the people rigging it had a room-temperature IQ."

He conceded the point, suggesting instead, "It still means Resnick holed up somewhere—maybe with a friend—until the others figured out what to do. We find out where that was—or who it was—and we go a long way to solving this."

I couldn't argue with him there.

We were introduced to Kevin Daly in a basement in downtown Portland, in a small room next to what appeared to be the courthouse archives. The room was windowless, undecorated, and quiet, and dominated by a large table with four wooden chairs.

Daly waved his hand at several document boxes neatly arrayed on the table's surface and blithely announced, *"The State of Maine versus Katahdin Trucking.* All yours."

Ron and I both stared at what was obviously several days' worth of reading.

"Mr. Daly," I began slowly. "We were kind of hoping we could do some of this verbally. We won't have enough time otherwise."

He was visibly caught off guard. "Verbally? You're kidding. I don't have any more free time than you do. Try starting with the witness lists and depositions. And the index to the transcript, in case there's anything you want there. That won't take too long. I thought I explained all that to someone over your way."

I backed up a bit. "Okay, I'm sorry—probably just crossed wires. You were the prosecutor?"

He smiled. "Yeah, but I won't be much use to you." He pointed to the boxes. "That was a few hundred cases ago, and no big deal, either. I barely remember it."

"How 'bout the basic charge?" I pressed him.

He cupped his cheek with his hand and stared at the floor for a moment. "Well, like I said on the phone, I think it had something to do with Katahdin lying on their manifests. They'd write down construction debris, and forget to mention a few oil drums. Or they'd log an empty run to a site for a pick-up when they were in fact transporting an illegal shipment for burial at the site—splitting the profits with the job foreman or contractor or whoever—and then getting legitimately paid for carting out a real load. My memory's pretty vague, though. They aren't the only ones we've nailed for something like that, so I may be mixing their case up with someone else's. Do your homework first. If you have any questions after that, maybe I can help you out."

We thanked him for digging out the files, let him go back to his job, and settled down to work, despite Ron's grumbling under his breath, " 'I thought I explained that.' Bullshit he did. I'm the one he talked to. He barely said two words—I asked if we could meet, he said sure."

"Don't worry about it," I said to smooth his feathers. "He probably just forgot and is covering his butt."

Relying on the index to lead us to the trial's highlights, we still spent some six hours reading, discussing, and taking notes about *Katahdin vs. the State of Maine*. The charges were close to what Daly had described, and by the end of our labors I understood why his memory had been so hazy. Katahdin had been found guilty, given a fine and a wrist-slap by the judge, and then allowed to carry on, aside from a few conditions designed to keep them on the straight and narrow. It had amounted to a probation, which I was happy to see still hadn't run out.

I mentioned that to Ron, who merely raised his eyebrows questioningly.

"It means we have something to hold over them when we meet," I explained.

He checked his watch warily. "We're meeting with them?"

I knew he was thinking of the very family he'd been extolling on the way over, and hoping to return to by late tonight. "Ron, what've we gotten out of this so far?" I indicated the piles of scattered documents.

"That Reynolds defended Katahdin and lost?"

"Right. We didn't find anything connected to what we're working on. What we need is a larger picture of Katahdin's operations—something beyond the scope of this court case." I turned a sheet of paper around to face him and put my finger next to a single name on a list of twenty others. "Maybe by having a little chat with this guy."

"Joseph Crowley," Ron read aloud. "One of the dispatchers?"

"And the guy who seemed to be sweating the most during the trial."

Ron looked puzzled. "I don't even remember what he said."

"Exactly. Daly put him on the stand to account for a time-sequence gap in his boss's story, but didn't seem to notice or care that he acted like he was sitting on a keg of dynamite. My guess is Daly already had enough to win his case and didn't want anything complicating an easy prosecution. Crowley must've thought it was his lucky day when he was excused and not asked to explain his guilt."

"Guilt about what?" Ron asked, obviously mystified.

"Doesn't matter," I said. "What counts is that he thinks he got away with something, and he's worried about that dreaded midnight knock on the door."

I got to my feet. "Let's go find Daly."

It wasn't actually midnight—more like ten-thirty—when we rang the front doorbell of Joseph Crowley's house in the Portland suburbs. The timing was both accidental and strategic. The first because it took a while to work through Kevin Daly to the Portland police in discovering Crowley's address; the second because if you want to make a man nervous—especially about something that's been going on at the office—it never hurts to approach him late at night, in front of his family.

He answered the door himself, his wife within sight in an armchair facing the television. He peered at us a moment, adjusting to the darkness outside, blinking like an owl startled from reverie. "Hi. Can I help you?"

Ron and I both flashed our useless, out-of-state credentials, which the poor lighting made impossible to read. I did the talking. "We're police officers, Mr. Crowley. We'd like to ask you a few questions."

His mouth half opened. "Police? About what?"

I saw his wife rise and approach to stand silently beside her husband. She, too, seemed utterly stunned.

"What's the trouble?" she asked of all of us.

"We'd like to talk to Mr. Crowley about certain aspects of his job."

Both their faces went blank.

"Could we come in?" Ron asked from just behind my shoulder.

They both stepped back. Joseph Crowley turned toward his wife and said softly, "Honey, could you make some coffee?"

She silently squeezed his arm and disappeared to the back of the house. Crowley distractedly waved us toward the sofa and chairs grouped around the TV set, while he picked up a remote and killed the set long-distance. The silence replacing the canned dialogue almost made my ears ring.

He sat on the edge of his chair while we made ourselves comfortable. "Is there a problem?"

"That depends," I said. "If we feel you've been straight with us after we're done, then the answer'll be no."

"You remember testifying five years ago?" Ron asked.

If possible, Crowley looked even more depressed than before. "Of course."

"It occurred to us," I resumed, "that at the time, you knew a lot more than you were being asked about—that you were even scared one of the prosecution's questions would open a can of worms you didn't want opened."

"I was completely truthful at that trial."

"I'm sure you were, just like I'm hoping you will be tonight."

"What have they done now?"

I smiled broadly. "God knows, Joseph. Let's hope you don't make us want to find out."

His eyebrows huddled together in confusion. "I don't understand."

Ron said, "We want to know a few things about Katahdin's operations—very confidentially. If we like what we hear, we disappear and nobody knows we've been here. If we don't, we start making wider inquiries.

Given the probation you folks are still under, that should have some meaning to you."

He licked his lips. "I have always cooperated with the authorities. I just didn't know anything that would interest them."

I gave him a hopeful expression. "We don't think you were asked the right questions."

His wife reappeared, carrying a tray with three cups, some milk, sugar, and a pot of coffee. "It's instant," she said quietly. "I hope that's okay."

I ignored her, still looking at Crowley. "If you *were* asked the right questions, you'd still answer them truthfully, wouldn't you, Joseph?"

"Of course."

"Great." Now I addressed his wife. "Instant's great. You're not going to have any?"

She put the tray down and backed away as if it had a stick of dynamite burning in the middle. "No, no. I don't want to be in the way."

"Okay. Thanks for the coffee, then. It was nice meeting you."

"Me, too."

We all waited until she left the room. Nobody made a move toward the coffee.

"Joseph," I began, "in all your years at Katahdin, do you ever remember hearing of an outfit called Timson Long Haul?"

"Yes. Of course. We sometimes lease trucks from them."

"Often?"

"Often enough. I guess I hear their name a few times a month. The business office would know exactly. I'm just a dispatcher."

"Well, we're here right now, so we'll ask you. All right?"

"Sure, sure. I'm sorry."

"It's okay. Tell me, though, is a few times a month a lot or average or what? I'm not familiar with Katahdin's operations."

"It's about average. We don't own a lot of the trucks we lease. That way, if business is down, we aren't stuck with a lot of idle inventory. Timson's been helpful that way for years."

"But they may not own their trucks, either. Isn't that right?"

"Right. It's a funny business that way. People think it's like Avis or something, but trucks cost a fortune to own, and you never seem to have the right mix of sizes anyhow. So we've all come up with this system."

"Gets a little hard, though, keeping track of who owns what."

He looked from one of us to the other in the silence I let hang. Finally he said, "I wouldn't know. I just dispatch."

"So you said. Think about it, though. I lease a truck to Ron here, who leases it to you, who leases it to somebody else. Lot of paperwork going through a lot of offices, some of which aren't very well staffed. Files get lost, numbers misplaced. And there are a pile of numbers, aren't there? VINs, registrations, license plates, CDL numbers, God knows what else. Hard to keep track. Did you know any of the Timson drivers?"

Unconsciously, Crowley had been rubbing his hands together between his knees. He suddenly stopped and placed them firmly on his thighs. "No. I mean, I might have, but not specifically as Timson people. Actually, Timson probably doesn't have any drivers, come to think of it. They just supply trucks. The drivers are up to someone else."

"So drivers come and go regularly, too. You must know some of them pretty well. I mean, dispatchers tend to build special relationships with the guys at the other end of the radio."

"I guess."

Ron suddenly spoke up, making Crowley jump slightly. "You ever know Phil Resnick?"

"Sure."

"Tell us about him," I suggested.

He shrugged awkwardly. "He was just a freelance driver. We never got into personal stuff much."

Neither Ron nor I said a word to that. Crowley began rubbing his hands together again. "I knew he was from New Jersey."

"And Mob-connected?"

He compressed his lips a moment. "I heard rumors."

"You see him often?"

"Off and on. Not lately."

I felt it was time for my stab in the dark. "About the time the trial hit? Maybe just before charges were filed?"

He became very still. My suspicions were that Resnick was the least of Crowley's concerns—that he was sitting on enough company indiscretions to be feeling very vulnerable, and that by asking only about Resnick, especially after all this buildup, I'd make him think he was getting off lightly—again—and thus make him generous as a result.

He took the bait. "He was around then, yeah."

"Did he have any contact with Jim Reynolds?"

He straightened with surprise. "Reynolds? The lawyer?"

Again, we silently let him draw his own conclusions.

After a moment's reflection, his eyes widened. "Yeah. He did."

"Tell us the circumstances."

Crowley sounded almost disappointed. "Not much to tell. During the pretrial routine—which lasted months, by the way—Reynolds was in and out of our office all the time, interviewing all sorts of people. I just remember Resnick being one of them."

"Why him, especially?" I asked.

"'Cause it struck me as funny at the time. First because Resnick was just a freelancer, who really had nothing to do with us, then because I sensed Reynolds did everything he could to avoid him afterwards, supposedly because he'd heard about those Mob connections—and he sure as hell didn't depose him. It was like seeing a kid reaching for a cookie and then being told it'd been baked using horse blood or something. I just remember the contrast."

We stayed the night in a motel outside Portland, hitting the sack almost immediately following our interview with Joseph Crowley and getting up well before daybreak to return home.

The drive was far different from what it had been the day before. Our mood, for one, was bleaker. Not only were we headed back to the confusing mire this case had become, but the complication of Crowley's revelation was more troubling than enlightening. Once more, we'd been handed Jim Reynolds's name in connection with something unsavory, and once again, it had turned out to be little more than an innuendo.

The scenery matched the mood. Surrounded by the

predawn dark and cold, utterly abandoned by other traffic, we chased our own headlights for miles on end as if we were the only people left living on the planet. Past Manchester, after exchanging the interstate for Route 9, the effect was even more dramatic as we drove through the occasional widely spaced town—and found the sole signs of life to have been paradoxically reduced to the rhythmic blinkings of a few traffic signals.

Amid this funereal stillness, the sudden chirping of the cell phone made us both jump.

Since Ron was driving, I picked it up.

"Joe?" Sammie said. "You there?"

I spoke louder than I had answering. "Yeah. What's up?"

"All hell's broken loose. The *Reformer*'s coming out this morning with an article saying we're targeting Reynolds for the Resnick killing. We just got an early edition. Derby's madder'n hell and wants to meet with you and Brandt as soon as you hit the parking lot."

"Is Resnick identified by name?"

"Oh, yeah. And he's been pegged to the haz mat truck. Not only that, but your trip to Maine is mentioned, too."

"Christ," I muttered, and told Sammie, "We're about an hour out."

I hung up and updated Ron.

He thought for a minute before saying, "Remember what Kevin Daly said about explaining the case to someone, quote-unquote, *over your way*? I bet that was Katz or one of his people following my footsteps. As far as I know, I'm the only one Daly talked to from the PD."

"Great," I said, half to myself. "Which means we've sprung a leak somewhere."

Chapter Nineteen

Sammie Martens came out to greet us in the parking lot before Ron had even rolled to a complete stop.

"You want to take a post-trip pee, you better use the hallway bathroom, 'cause Derby's already in the chief's office waiting. You are not to visit your office first, you are not to take off your coat, you are not to pass Go."

"That good, huh?"

"Looks like it. Thought you'd like to see this first." She handed me a copy of the paper, which I shoved into my pocket unread.

"Also," she added, giving me a small folded piece of notepaper, "Willy gave me this for you. Said it might come in handy."

I followed her to the department's side entrance, down the short hallway into the central area between dispatch and the chief's office, and entered the latter without bothering to knock.

Jack Derby rose from his chair. Brandt, behind his desk, stayed put.

"I hear we have problems," I said, removing my coat and hanging it by the door.

"That's putting it mildly," Derby agreed, so tense his teeth almost clenched. "Do you have any idea how Katz got this story?"

"I haven't had a chance to read it yet," I answered blandly, sitting down, and by example forcing him to do the same.

"Well, I have, and it sounds like he was briefed better than I was."

Tony Brandt added in an almost lazy voice, which I imagined only added to Derby's irritation, "I told Jack we'd do an internal—see if we can plug the leak."

Derby scratched his forehead. "I have one felony murder case already under way and another in the pipeline, assuming you find the killer. I do not need to be watching my back while I'm juggling these two, wondering who the hell's going to be sticking it to me next. I do not want guilty people going free because some cop can't resist seeing his anonymous words in print."

It was a little pompous, and more than slightly disingenuous. Both Brandt and I knew perfectly well that any potential future trials were far less imperiled by such leaks than were Derby's hopes for reelection. His passion, as a result, was somewhat disappointing. I'd voted for him when he'd first run for state's attorney, largely because I'd liked his pledge to take politics out of his office. I hadn't actually believed it, of course— I've been around too long for that—but after years of working with the imperious James Dunn, I had hoped for something better in his successor. It was beginning to look as if I'd only ended up with something different.

"What's Jim Reynolds's take on it?" I asked innocently, simultaneously unfolding Willy's note and glancing at its contents.

Derby stared at me as if I'd just fallen on my head. "What the hell do you think it is? He's fit to be tied."

He suddenly stopped dead in his tracks, aware of what I'd lured him into, and quickly added, "At least I imagine he is. I would be, in his place."

He got up again and began pacing. "What the hell is it with Reynolds, anyway? Do you actually have anything on him?"

Brandt looked at me to respond. "We have growing concerns," I said. "His name keeps coming up, like it just did in Portland. Right now, the use of a car like his at the murder scene looks like a clumsy frame, but someone did break into his office, he did know Resnick from that case in Maine, which also involved illegal haz mat, and according to this"—I waved Willy's note in the air—"while he told me he was at his apartment in Montpelier the night Resnick was killed, his nosy neighbor just told Kunkle that his car wasn't in its parking place till just before dawn."

Derby ran both hands through his hair. "Meaning what, for God's sake? That he snuck down here, stole a car that looked like his, fitted it with bogus plates to match his own, and then knocked off a guy in the one section of town that probably has more windows overlooking it than your average New York tenement?"

Neither Brandt nor I said a word.

Derby stopped pacing. "All right, all right. Let's move on. From the reports I've read so far, it looks like both the Resnick and Croteau killings are beginning to rub shoulders. What's going on there?"

"So far, it just looks typical of a small town with a

small underworld, where everybody steps on everybody else's toes. Billy Conyer, for example, who we think was one of the three who killed Resnick, was a friend of Brenda Croteau's. We also have witnesses in one case who feature as acquaintances in the other."

Derby looked irritated. "Great. McNeil's going to have a field day with that." He suddenly stared at me. "Your girlfriend's already giving me enough grief as it is about Tharp's motivation."

I felt my face flush and was about to respond when he cut me off. "Save it, Joe. I shouldn't have said that. I'm getting too worked up here. What's important is that we try to keep things as uncontaminated as possible. I don't want the Tharp case derailed because of some extraneous poking around by you into Resnick or—God forbid—Jim Reynolds. Remember that, okay? Just keep things delineated. And give your people the same message, especially Kunkle. If I hear that someone on either my witness list or McNeil's has been harassed by him, I'll cut him off at the knees."

"We'll conduct the investigation as we see fit," I said, finally allowing my anger to show. "It's not in your purview to tell us who we can and cannot interview."

Out of the corner of my eye, I saw Brandt smiling slightly.

Derby bent toward me, like a teacher addressing an errant student. "I'd be careful there. My 'purview,' as you call it, cuts pretty goddamn wide." He straightened suddenly, as if stung, and ran his hand down across his face. "That's not what I said, anyhow. I said 'harass,' and I referred to extraneous poking around. I did not tell you how to do your job. I know you think I'm being a jerk here—I can see it in your face. I'm young,

I've been a prosecutor for all of three years, and I'm up for reelection soon. That makes me the asshole. Fine. But the buck stops with me—I'm the guy who's supposed to put Tharp in jail. If that doesn't happen because of some mistake from this department, it's still going to be my butt in the sling. That's why I want things done right."

I weighed my options, trying to temper my anger by recognizing that while his style was lousy, his points had some merit. But I finally settled for a simple, "Can I go now?"

He seemed as startled by my lack of reaction as if I'd really let him have it, making his suddenly conciliatory tone all the more awkward. "Of course. I'm sorry I went overboard. I shouldn't blow off steam like that— we're a team, after all. We just have a lot riding on this."

"I'm sure you do," I said as I headed for the door.

I found Willy Kunkle in the squad room, reading a book. "Thanks for the info about the neighbor. What made you think of that?"

Willy marked his place with a thumb. "Old-fashioned police work. Just noticed nobody else had done it."

"Is the neighbor credible?"

"Enough. Retired schoolteacher, working on the great American piece of shit. Stays up half the night looking for inspiration. Seems to do it staring out the window, though, 'cause he knew the habits of everyone within sight. I quizzed him on it."

"Any hint of a girlfriend tucked away?"

"For Reynolds? Nope. I asked. The teacher's never seen anyone other than the Mrs. and the kids and the

standard politicos. And usually the senator stays put
after lights out. That's why this stuck in his memory."

"So his car was parked early on, then vanished, then
reappeared before dawn?"

"Yup. His guess was it was gone from about nine
till four-thirty or so."

"You ask Reynolds about it?"

"I figured that was your job."

Tony Brandt found me in my office about ten minutes
later and made a seat out of one of my low-profile filing cases. "You recovered?"

"Oh, sure. I just wanted to leave him dangling. He's
not the first prosecutor to have a hissy-fit. I just hope
he improves with age."

Brandt nodded in agreement. "Tell me more about
Maine."

"There isn't much more. Looks like Reynolds was
doing his lawyer thing, rounding up witnesses and the
rest, when he came across Resnick, who was doing the
same kind of contract work for Katahdin he was doing
for Timson. The guy we talked to thought Reynolds
probably caught wind of Resnick's Mob connections
and dropped him like a hot rock to make his case look
better. Perfectly reasonable."

Brandt looked disappointed. "What about Reynolds
not being in his apartment the night Resnick died?"

"I just talked to Willy. The source sounds good.
Whether Derby likes it or not, I'm going to have to
ask Reynolds to explain it."

"That's fine," he said. "Just fly low when you do.
Jack asked me to issue a press statement about how
Reynolds is no more a suspect than anyone else we

look at during a case. It would probably help if Katz isn't given any more than is necessary."

"Speaking of which, are you going to look for the leak?"

"Yeah. I'm not at all happy about that, Derby or no Derby. We all use the press now and then to our own advantage, but this was way over the line. If I find the guy, he'll be out of a job. What is your strategy going to be on the Resnick case?"

"Now that I've been given my marching orders?" I asked with a smile.

"Regardless."

"Well, right now it seems like Billy Conyer's our best inroad. Given his homebody personality and habits, at least one of his two co-killers must be local, or at least have local ties. Billy didn't get around much. I was planning to organize an alibi dragnet, put the squeeze on anyone and everyone who had anything to do with him, and see what popped out."

Brandt looked thoughtful for a moment and then said, "That's probably what Derby's most worried about."

"Jesus, Tony—"

"I know, I know. Hold your horses. Do what you've got to. Just warn your troops to tread carefully. Derby may be wet behind the ears politically, but it won't be good for any of us if Owen Tharp's case gets thrown out of court on some technicality. Remember, if you start asking questions of people who're planted in both the Resnick and Tharp cases, and one of them blabs something revealing about Tharp, that's got to be shared, either with Derby or McNeil—if it looks like he could use it." He slid off the filing cabinet and moved to- -

ward the door. "That's the law. So watch out. That's all I'm saying."

I waited until he was gone and then rubbed my face vigorously with my hands, wondering what the hell else could go wrong.

As things turned out, I didn't have to chase down Jim Reynolds to ask him about the night Phil Resnick was murdered. He called me, and he didn't sound pleased.

"What the hell do you think you're doing?"

I took the phone away from my ear and looked at it, wondering how many other politicians were going to rake me over the coals today. I seriously considered hanging up on him.

"Shouldn't you be asking Stan Katz that?" I asked instead. I had since read the article in the *Reformer*. It did make for some serious entertainment. Katz had done the writing himself, much to Alice Simms's irritation, no doubt, and he'd done a good job. It had been suggestive to the very brink of libel, without falling over.

"I'm leaving Katz to my lawyer," he blustered. "I want to find out what your beef is with me. I know a lot of cops are upset about my bill, but I thought you, of all people, were above this kind of character assassination."

I almost laughed at the narcissism of it. I was looking into a homicide, and he thought I had an ax to grind over his bill. "Believe me, Senator, I could care less about what you're doing up there. You want to get together, though, I'd be happy to oblige. I have some more questions to ask you."

There was a surprised and wary silence at the other end. "What about?"

"I'd prefer to do it in person."

Anger crept back into his voice. "Fine. I'll be at the house tonight. Come at eight."

He hung up before I could answer.

Laura Reynolds opened the door, looking less than thrilled to see me. She was polite, though, and took my coat, showed me to the living room, and offered me something to drink. I declined, she happily abandoned me, and I sat alone by a crackling fire, surrounded by tasteful indirect lighting, soft carpeting, and furniture that looked like no child had ever thrown up on it. It was unusually pristine for a house full of kids. Then again, few of my house calls were to places with live-in help and heated garages.

Reynolds let me stew for a while, either testing me or trying to put me in my place. But I was content to enjoy the fire and the comfortable sofa, and spend the night there if necessary.

It wasn't. He appeared fifteen minutes later, with no apology, and sat in a wingback opposite me, crossing his legs in a commanding manner—the lord of all around him.

"What've you got for me now, Lieutenant? My car been seen running people down again?"

"Where were you on the night Resnick died?" I asked bluntly, tiring of the theatrics.

He froze for a split second, and then furrowed his brow. "Ah. You found out about that, did you?"

Brilliant, I thought. He'd headed me off at the pass, skipping a denial altogether.

"Where were you?" I repeated.

"At a clandestine political meeting, the nature of which I'd like not to disclose."

"You won't necessarily have to, if the other person or people involved can corroborate your being there."

He steepled his fingers before his chin and glanced up at the ceiling. "To reveal one would be to reveal the other. I'm afraid that would be too risky, especially given what's already happened. I am sorry."

I merely stared at him.

"Lieutenant, I know you told me earlier you couldn't care less, but what I'm trying to do in Montpelier is to change something running all the way back to the state's beginnings. That isn't going to be easy. There are many people who think I'm right, but most of them can't afford to admit it in public. That means my dealings with them have to take place discreetly, as on the night in question. That was the first such instance, as I'm sure my nosy neighbor told you. But it won't be the last. Be prepared to hear him report all sorts of midnight sorties, because the backroom deal-making has only just begun."

"What was your relationship with Phil Resnick five years ago, during the Katahdin Trucking case?"

He smiled indulgently, getting on my nerves. "Right. The trip to Maine. My 'relationship,' as you call it, consisted of a single interview, during which I asked him about his working for the company. I discovered as a result that he would be playing no part in my defense strategy, and thus I never spoke with him again."

"You found out he was tied to the Mob."

Again, he beat me to it. "Correct," he said simply.

"How was it Katahdin knew to hire you in the first place?"

"I've had experience in environmental law," he said vaguely. "They could have chosen someone else. I never asked."

"Why was your office broken into?"

"That's why I hired Win Johnston. So far, I don't know."

"You must have suspicions. You don't hire a private detective if you think some teenager was trying to steal a computer."

"I'm a lawyer and a politician, and I'm cautious by nature. For all I know, it was a teenager, but I've learned not to make assumptions. That, I might add, is something you should learn."

I stood up. "That's not what I'm doing. I am trying to find out why you're under every rock I kick over."

He waved a hand at me. "If you're leaving, Lieutenant, please don't. I'd like to talk some more. Do you mind?"

I considered his offer. I'd gotten nowhere so far and had been about to leave pissed off and disappointed. Maybe, with a little time and flattery, his ego might get the better of him and let something slip. I sat back down.

Now he was Mister Sociability. "I'm sure my wife offered, but won't you have a drink? A cognac, maybe, or a cup of coffee? I'm going to have a little something."

"Sure. Coffee'd be fine."

He rose, moved toward the back, and called out, "Honey, could you rustle up some coffee for the lieutenant?"

There was no response, which didn't faze him in the slightest. He crossed the room to a large cabinet mounted into the wall and opened a pair of double doors to reveal a full bar. He poured something into an overlarge snifter and regained his seat.

"She shouldn't be long," he said soothingly, placing his drink by his side untouched.

He crossed his legs again. "I wanted to thank you for your testimony the other day. You were very good. You've obviously thought a great deal about your profession."

"I've been at it a while."

"That could be said of a lot of deadhead old-timers. You've learned the system inside out." He suddenly laughed. "From both sides, given what that deputy AG tried to pull last year. You've made it work for you, and you're widely respected as a result."

"It was a governor's pardon that got me off the hook with the AG. I would've been out of a job otherwise."

He dismissed that. "Nonsense. It was common knowledge that one man used the rules of evidence to go after you for his own selfish interests. I happen to know the AG himself lobbied the governor on your behalf—and he wasn't alone, either. You're far more widely regarded than you know or admit. Let me ask you something: Even though it's still being hammered out in committee, what do you think of my bill?"

"I don't think it matters."

His eyes narrowed slightly. "Too much modesty can have the same effect as too little. Didn't your mother ever tell you that?"

"No. But I wasn't being modest anyhow. I don't think it matters because I don't think it'll become law."

He smiled thinly. "Why not?"

"You've taken advantage of some popular momentum due to Amos Melcourt killing those kids. You've also been allowed that momentum by people who're taking their time to stop you dead in your tracks."

"And who are they?"

Laura Reynolds entered the room bearing a small tray with a cup, some sugar, and a little pitcher of milk. She placed it on the table next to me without comment or eye contact.

"Thank you," I said.

She glanced up, gave me a small nod, and left as quietly as she'd come. Reynolds acted as if she'd never been there, staring at me throughout, awaiting his answer—a man used to being served.

I fixed my coffee as I spoke. "You name it. You claim you're thinking in terms of efficiency, the public good, and planning for the future. Almost every cop in uniform thinks of job security. You're threatening that."

"That's not true. The number of police officers won't necessarily change. Just the way they're organized. They'll all be in one department, with their leader ranked at cabinet level, and with the same access to the state budget as any other agency. They'll have better pay, more benefits, and many more opportunities for advancement and diversity. If tagging moose is your thing, and you used to be stuck in the Burlington PD, in this new organization you can just ask for a transfer to the wildlife unit. Equipment will be first-rate, training will be improved, and the political clout will be as never before. It's an absolute win-win situation. Occam's Razor, practically applied."

I wondered if he was trying to put me in my place. "Occam," I answered, "was talking about theological philosophy, not employment concerns."

He made a funny tucked-in gesture with his chin, as if I'd just punched him gently in the chest, which perhaps I had. During my short stint in college, I'd

spent most of my time with my nose buried in books—
including a few on philosophy and ethics.

I used his surprise to press him further. "Are you
saying that part-time deputy sheriff who let Amos Melcourt slip by will have a job?"

A look of irritation crossed his face. "Of course
there will be standards to meet. That's only reasonable.
You can't have any woodchuck who chooses to just
sign up."

"Maybe not, but with the sixty-eight different employment possibilities we have right now, that woodchuck has a better chance of being hired than he would
with your single police force. And all the guys who
are currently in uniform but who might be just barely
hanging on—they're going to fight you with everything
they've got. And that's not even mentioning the pride
factor. You really think the Green-and-Gold are going
to tolerate being anything else? Being forced to be on
a par with someone out of Bellows Falls or Brattleboro or Windsor?"

He shook his head tiredly, obviously bored by the
very debate he'd set in motion. "Look, all that really
doesn't matter. The police, no matter who they are,
don't have a strong constituency in the Legislature.
Once the public hears the details of the final bill and
sees the logic behind it, all that naysaying will be identified as the narrow self-interest it is. The police are
essentially a military organization. They'll do as they're
told."

"They may be military in appearance," I pressed
him, "but they exist because civilians created them. Selectmen and voters all over this state won't be too
thrilled with having their homegrown, handpicked departments replaced with some top-heavy, faceless state

agency, no matter how rational the explanation. Bellows Falls measures a single square mile, and is maybe eight minutes away from one of the larger state police barracks, but year after year they fund their own PD, despite all the statistics that tell them it's nuts. Local control's still a big thing here. Why do you think it took Vermont so long just to get 911 adopted? And that looked like a total no-brainer."

He gave me the indulgent look of a long-suffering parent. "This is not some flash-in-the-pan, election-year notion, Lieutenant, as you know full well. As early as 1990, the Windham Foundation hosted a conference on this topic, and the general consensus from everyone attending—from sheriffs to local cops to the state police—was that this course of action made the most sense in addressing a raft of problems we've been saddled with for decades. In fact, that same year, the various agencies in Chittenden County pooled together to form CUSI, with a focus on sexual assault cases, and it's proven very effective, as has its St. Albans–based counterpart, the Northwest Unit for Special Investigations. Things move slowly, I know, and sometimes it takes a tragedy like what happened up north to give them the push they need, but that doesn't mean they can't eventually happen. You just need enough people to believe in the cause."

I resisted pointing out that while the Windham Foundation meeting he'd mentioned had concluded that policing could be improved using a regional approach—and not a single police agency—everyone in attendance had also agreed that none of them would live long enough to see any of their recommendations become reality.

"In any case, I'd like to make you a proposal," he

continued. "When all this comes to pass, I'd like you to consider a leadership position in this new organization."

I deflected the offer, which I didn't see as his to make in any case. "Have you come up with a name for it yet?"

He smiled broadly. "Tentatively, yes. The Agency for Criminal Justice has been kicked around, but that sounds a little flat to me. I prefer the Vermont Bureau of Investigation—VBI for short."

"Very flashy. Sounds like an army dressed in business suits and barn boots."

He lifted his snifter in a toast. "You can laugh now, but I'll see this thing through. To your health."

I returned the gesture without comment.

Gail was reading in bed when I got home. "Where've you been? I called the office an hour ago."

"Having an out-of-body experience with Jim Reynolds. Strangest conversation I've had in a long time."

She smiled sadly. "That's saying something, given the ones we've been having."

I sat beside her and squeezed her hand. "Those haven't been strange. They've been painful."

She took my hand and kissed it. "So what did you talk about?"

"I went there to give him the third degree. I ended up watching him drink cognac, treat his wife like a servant, and make references to Occam's Razor."

"Who?"

"Exactly what he was hoping I'd say, except I fooled him. William of Occam was a fourteenth century theologian who came up with a theory that said, more or less, that too much bullshit makes for cluttered thinking. And encourages the employment of too many managers, who in turn do their best to keep things cluttered."

She looked at me questioningly.

"Okay, so maybe he used different words and was mostly talking about a bloated clergy. In any case, it's been handed down to us as that favorite of all management tools: Keep It Simple, Stupid—KISS. That's what Reynolds claims his bill is—a massive pruning of redundancies."

"I suppose he's probably right."

I got up and started getting ready for bed. "From what I heard this morning, Derby's apparently trying to get *you* familiarized with William of Occam."

Her eyes narrowed a fraction. "What did he say?"

"That you're giving him hives fretting about Owen Tharp's motivation."

"What did you say?"

"Not a word. To borrow a phrase from the legal profession, it was a spontaneous utterance. I was telling him how the two homicide cases were bumping into each other in terms of crossover witnesses. He said McNeil was going to love exploiting that, and then he nailed me with how my girlfriend was giving him enough trouble as it was."

She didn't bite at the girlfriend crack, admitting instead, "I am."

I paused in midmotion and looked at her. "A lot of trouble?"

She tilted her head slightly. "Could be. You and I have been over this ground before. I don't have any doubts Owen Tharp killed that woman, but I've got some major ones that it was as simple as everyone's hoping. McNeil and I have started trading pretrial information, and there's not much I can see in Owen's past that would make him go to Croteau's house and kill her without cause."

"He had cause. He thought she'd killed his girl-friend."

"Exactly," she said, sitting forward for emphasis. "And we now know from the girlfriend's autopsy he was lied to. In his confession, he didn't say something vague like, 'The dope was poison.' His exact words were, 'Brenda put poison in her dope.' That's a specific accusation. The autopsy doesn't bear it out, Owen wasn't a witness to Lisa's death, and nothing indicated at the time that she'd been murdered. So someone must've fed him that line, thereby directing him like a guided missile toward Brenda Croteau."

I scratched my head. "I don't know, Gail. There's no evidence of that."

"Are you kidding? *Look* at the kid. He's everybody's lapdog. They treat him like shit and he comes back for more—again and again and again. He's the perfect weapon. He craves affection, isn't too bright, and is prone to violent outbursts, and according to the lab results, he was higher than a kite on the night of the killing."

"So why isn't McNeil knocking your door down with a devil-made-him-do-it defense? He could plead diminished capacity, send Owen to a rubber room for a few years of gentle treatment, and have him back on the streets before he turns thirty."

She thought a moment before answering. "Two reasons: one, he just might—it is early yet—and two, his client may be protecting the person who pushed his buttons. If Owen thinks that shooting his mouth off will land a father figure in jail, he's going to do the noble thing. He's a romantic, after all—he already thinks he avenged his sainted girlfriend, and she, for all we know, was a hooker who gave him a single roll in the hay, if that."

By now I was sitting on a chair across the room, one sock in my hand, listening intently, my mind in a turmoil.

"I'm not arguing the point," I said. "It could've happened that way. But what can you do about it? It's not like you have the wrong man in jail. And Derby will have your hide if you open a can of worms this late in the game, especially when all you're working from is a theory."

She stared at the small hill her knees made under the blankets, reflecting on what I'd just said. Then she raised her eyes and gave me a half smile, filled with all the sadness and disappointment we'd been trying to deal with these last few days.

"I guess I need help."

Chapter Twenty

I rose early the next morning, out of long-standing habit, got ready for the day in a bathroom down the hall, from where I wouldn't disturb Gail, and went downstairs to fix a cup of coffee and some toast.

It was still as dark as the middle of the night, making the house more intimate than I ever found it during the day. Somehow, with most of the lights off and all the artwork and elegant furniture obscured, I felt more at ease with my surroundings. Less like a visitor.

I washed my cup in the sink, put on my overcoat, and grabbed the bag where I kept my gun, radio, paperwork, and various odds and ends, and headed outside.

The freezing air grabbed my nostrils like a pair of pliers, making me blink and catch my breath. It was short-lived, as always, and even comforting in an odd way, instilling in many of us who chose to live here a sense that by merely staying alive this time of year, we weren't doing too badly.

I crossed the driveway to the garage, triggering the

usual battery of motion-detector spotlights, which both ruined the mood and replaced the starlight with a confusing tangle of harsh glare and deep shadow. Inside the garage, I pulled my keys from my pocket—and suddenly froze.

Outside the garage, I heard the faint squeak of frozen snow under a carefully placed foot.

I dropped down, circled the car, and waited, crouching behind its passenger-side wheel well, breathing through my mouth, my chin tucked down so no vapor cloud would rise above my barricade and give me away.

I heard someone approach, pause, then turn slightly. After a long silence, a voice said tentatively, "Joe?"

I rose from my hiding place and found Stanley Katz standing awkwardly, looking slightly frightened.

"For Christ's sake, Stan. You ought to know better."

He laughed nervously. "Holy shit. I didn't know where you went. It was weird."

"Keep your voice down. Gail's still asleep. What're you doing here?"

"I wanted to talk to you about Reynolds. You read yesterday's paper?"

"I had it shoved down my throat, thank you very much. What the hell were you thinking?"

He looked offended. "Printing the truth. It was all accurate, wasn't it?"

"My God. Where're you parked?"

He jerked a thumb over his shoulder. "On the street. I've been here half an hour. I wanted to catch you alone."

I started my car to warm it up, but then headed to where he'd indicated. "Let's talk there. My heater takes ten minutes to kick in."

He followed me without comment. Inside his smelly

truck, I asked him, "A man goes into a bar, stays an hour, then leaves. On the way out, he stumbles, falls against another patron, mutters something incomprehensible, and wanders off. What's the conclusion?"

Stanley looked at me quizzically. "He had too much to drink?"

"Wrong. He's a teetotaler. But he was visiting a friend, has a speech defect, and stumbled because he's near-sighted. If you'd written the story the way I first told it, it would be accurate, but everybody reading it would've reached the same conclusion you did."

"Meaning you got nothing on Reynolds."

I was surprised. A younger Stanley Katz would have started preaching along some thin line of logic, defensive to the end. This new cut-to-the-chase, realistic approach was much more appreciated. "Right. I think both you and I are being had. I don't have any proof of it—any more than I have proof against him—but every time I hit him with the little I dig up, he comes back with a perfectly reasonable explanation."

"So he's a good liar."

"Or he's telling the truth. It is possible, Stan. It happens."

Katz thought a moment. "What'd you find in Maine?"

"That he defended a trucking company, bumped into Phil Resnick, and backed off as soon as he heard Resnick had Mob connections in Jersey."

He looked at me wide-eyed. "He does?"

"Down, boy—stay with me, here. Remember that night we visited Reynolds's house and checked his car? It was because we'd heard it had been used to carry Resnick's unconscious body to the tracks. Then we found the real car, dummied up to look like Reynolds's—a clear-cut frame. Same thing with that tip you gave us about Reynolds being involved with Brenda Croteau. There were some pages missing from her journal, but nothing even vaguely linking her to him—on any front. And again with the deal in Maine—smoke but no fire. I think the game plan here is to combine our wild goose chases with the rumors you've been fed so you can write a story you think you're putting together on your own."

He mulled that over. "Either that or you cooked this whole thing up to get me to back off."

"Back off what? We don't have a case against Reynolds. I thought you'd want to know you're being used."

"So big-hearted. Why do you care?"

He had me there. "I'd like to know who your police source is. If he's on the take instead of just being a motor mouth, I want his hide."

But he was already shaking his head. "No way."

I didn't argue with him. I hadn't expected him to agree. "Then do me a favor. Break a tradition—look this gift horse in the mouth. Draw your own conclusions."

"How's my story affected the department?"

I supposed that was something all reporters wanted to know, especially after they thought they'd hit a homer. "You haven't done us any favors, and I think in the long run you'll be wiping egg off your face. Whoever your Deep Throat is, he's going to be feeling some heat."

"What about Derby?"

I looked at him. "Why? You have something personal in this?"

Now he did look defensive. "No, but he's been acting real political lately. I just wanted to know how he'd reacted."

I opened the door to a tidal wave of freezing air. "Ask him yourself."

He rolled down his window as I crossed the street. "What? What did I say? There's nothing wrong with that. What're you so touchy about all of a sudden?"

I didn't bother answering. Aside from thinking his curiosity a little juvenile, I hadn't found it that offensive. It was the suggestion of irresponsibility behind it that had propelled me out of his truck—that and the need to be free of him in general. Much as we scratched each other's back now and then, I didn't want it to become second nature. Besides, I'd done what I'd wanted to do—made Stanley a little pickier about the morsels he was fed, and, more subversively, perhaps compelled him to act as a bird dog on our behalf.

If I could convince him that he'd been used to smear Jim Reynolds, then there was little that would stop him from trying to discover the truth behind the ruse. I'd seen Stanley Katz get angry before, and use a keyboard like a shotgun when his pride was stung.

At the squad meeting that morning, I followed Brandt's recipe of the day before and told everyone our first priority was to analyze Billy Conyer's past with a microscope—chasing down everyone he had contact with and finding out what they were up to—while being very careful not to sabotage the SA's prosecution of Owen Tharp. I made it clear they were to think about what they were asking before they asked it. We each took names, culled from all the sources we'd accumulated from interviews, Brenda's journal, and common knowledge, and set out to create a combination timeline/genealogy of the late Billy Conyer's universe, hoping we could discover who his two colleagues had been, and maybe whoever had turned him into a killer.

Afterward, I signaled Willy Kunkle to follow me into my office.

"Shut the door," I told him as I sat at my desk.

He took his time getting comfortable, tucking his useless left elbow between his body and the arm of my plastic guest chair, as if buying himself time. I imagined he thought he'd earned yet another trip to the doghouse and didn't want to rush things.

"You all set?" I finally asked him.

"Sure. What's wrong?"

"Nothing. I got something extra I thought you might enjoy. All that stuff I just said about not stepping on the SA's toes doesn't apply to you."

He looked at me without comment for a moment, a doubtful half smile on his face. "Meaning what?"

"Meaning I'm going to ask you to stick your neck way out. One point Jack Derby made no bones about yesterday was that he didn't want Kunkle messing things up for him. He was worried that since the Croteau and Resnick cases involved some of the same players, you'd go straight to work displaying all your usual lack of delicacy."

He laughed.

"But what *I* want from you," I continued, "isn't good manners—it's a little subtle subversion. You heard about the tensions between Derby and Gail?"

"Sure. I never thought she was cut out for that job anyhow."

"Be that as it may, she's asked me for a favor only you can help me grant."

The smile widened. "Yeah?"

"Gail doesn't think Owen Tharp acted entirely on his own. That given his personality, he had someone pushing him to kill Croteau."

Willy's reaction was fully expected, echoing the way I'd felt initially. "So what? He killed her anyway—and the baby."

"I know the logic—that just because he's got problems doesn't mitigate his crime. She's not looking to get him off the hook. But she does think he was used like a contract killer—by remote control—and that if all we do is nail Owen, the guy pulling his string will get off."

He was beginning to look very doubtful. "She know something I don't? I didn't hear anything about Owen being used, and I'm the guy he confessed to, remember? He didn't say anything about being under orders."

"I know, I know," I conceded. "This is where you're going to have to cut me some slack. This whole hypothesis is just a gut feeling. Gail's sense of it is that Owen was made so dependent on someone that he was willing to do anything that person told him to do, especially if it was phrased right and he was suitably under the influence, which his urine and blood tests say he was. Gail asked me a while ago to look up the autopsy of Lisa Wooten—the girlfriend he said he was avenging."

"Because Croteau had spiked her dope," he finished.

"Except," I said, "that her dope wasn't spiked. It was a straight overdose."

He didn't speak for a few seconds, digesting what I'd said. I knew this meant more to him than the sum of its parts, since he had been the one to receive Owen Tharp's confession. Unlike the rest of us, he'd heard the inflection behind the words and studied the face of the man uttering them. Instinctively, he'd been burdened with more than mere content. He'd been witness to meaning as well.

I didn't doubt such distinctions had gone unnoticed at the time. Now I was hoping I'd triggered their reconsideration.

One of Willy Kunkle's saving graces—so few in a man in need of so many—was his instinct for human character. He was dismissive, offensive, and occasionally abusive, but largely, I thought, because he'd been saddled with insight so clear as to make life almost unbearable. He saw through cant and affectation and self-service and moral cowardice with ease, and yet—for a lack of training or experience or pure simple faith—could find little with which to fight it. Except rage.

And the anger had been all that most people had been able to see, including Jack Derby. Which was too bad, because Willy, as I think Sammie also understood, knew more about the human animal than almost anyone I'd met. It was his secret and his curse.

It was also what prompted him to finally say, "I hate to admit it, but old Gail may be on to something."

"If you do this, and it leads where she thinks it will, we'll undoubtedly catch unholy hell from her boss. He'll say we were working for Reggie McNeil."

"*You* might be. I'll just be trying to put another bastard in jail."

Over the next few weeks, life became an odd, slow, carefully paced minuet of assembling facts on several segregated levels. The detective squad—helped by the patrol division in dealing with the weekly menus of B and Es, bad check reports, and minor drug busts—constructed a paper trail of Billy Conyer's last few months of life. Willy, while fulfilling his role in this effort, additionally wandered farther afield, examining the growing tentacles that linked Conyer's world to Tharp's, working discreetly, alone, and at odd hours of the day. He and I met occasionally to discuss what he'd discovered, and wonder, like questioning chemists, whether any promising solutions were in the making. Meanwhile, Tony Brandt conducted his own investigation in pursuit of the department's leak, fueling a paranoia that is never far from a police officer's mind in the best of times.

In the background, Gail, who had no idea what Willy and I were up to, tried not to press me when we were at home, where we labored instead to bury our emotional concerns in a predictable domestic routine, using the pretense of overwork to stave off the inevitable reckoning.

The irony to this stage of a major investigation is that it looks so deliberately paced. The popular notion of a police department handling several homicides at once is that everyone works around the clock. In fact, it's usually too much to ask—either of people's passions or the department's budget—to keep up an around-the-clock schedule.

So we all eventually became like workers on an assembly line, busy building parts of what we hoped would be an overall final product. Ron, as usual, managed the information as it arrived, assigning it a roosting spot and keeping track of it on several oversized charts he'd rigged up in the conference room. On a daily basis, we met there and compared notes, watching the charts for changes as devoted stockbrokers might a ticker tape.

This scrutiny had an entertaining side effect. Many of the people we were watching led lives that defied the norm. We grew attached to favorite characters and either cheered or bemoaned their actions as we learned of them—as when, for example, we discovered that Billy Conyers's brother Brian had at least once gone to bed with Brenda Croteau's mother. Soap operas couldn't compete.

Adding to this tangle of loyalties and associations were the moves and countermoves of Gail and Reggie McNeil, who were also involved in much the same research, racing one another to load up on their witness lists, ascertain competency, and determine who would depose whom, and to what purpose.

Owen's confession fell early to this maneuvering, when McNeil filed a motion to suppress on grounds that Owen had been too cold, exhausted, and scared by the likes of Willy Kunkle to know what he was doing.

And all of this played out to a steady drumbeat of newspaper articles, radio reports, and the occasional piece on the nightly TV news, alternating with an equally endless stream of updates on the progress of the Reynolds Bill through the state senate.

Which was reasonable, given that the latter began taking on a life of its own, spreading in notoriety to the Boston media and beyond. Reynolds's rugged likeness cropped up in magazines and TV programs far outside the region, and as the month of March slowly approached—and Vermont's famed plethora of town meetings along with it—the name of Jim Reynolds became increasingly linked to the looming vacancy in the governor's office. The early flurry of concern stimulated by Katz's articles was slowly replaced by a naive overconfidence among Reynolds's growing boosters that his idea might actually become reality—despite the ominous silence on the issue from both the speaker of the House and the various spokesmen from the law enforcement community. My personal feeling remained that like the iceberg awaiting the *Titanic,* some pretty formidable forces were standing ready to stop Reynolds cold in his tracks.

On a brighter note, however, it looked like one of his early obstacles—and ours—would be melting to more manageable size. Stan Katz called me at my office one afternoon, more muted and abashed than I'd ever heard him be.

"What's up?" I asked with real concern, thinking he'd been hit by some personal loss.

In a sense, he had. "I figured you'd like to know who's been feeding me that false information."

"About Reynolds?" I asked, struck by his use of the word "false."

"Yeah. It was one of your boys in blue, like you thought. Cary Bancroft. You might want to tell Brandt. I got him on tape, had one of our photographers take a shot of us meeting—the works."

Bancroft hadn't been with us long, and had made little impression on me. I'd written him off as one of the young transients that traipse through our department virtually without leaving footprints. I sensed now I might have been right about the length of his tenure, but certainly not about his invisibility. This one was going out with a bang.

"Why, Stan? He was making you headlines."

"I did like you said," he admitted, sounding even more depressed. "I looked a gift horse in the mouth. I'm not sure what I did was legal, so I won't give you the details, but I found out his bank account's been getting padded at my expense. He was paid to feed me stories."

"Who by?"

"I don't know. *He* doesn't know. It was the old voice-on-the-phone routine, along with anonymous cash deposits. You want to chase it down, I'd start with the anti-Reynolds crowd, but good luck finding the source. To save a little face, I tried like hell to find out—I've known about this for a few weeks now—but I got nowhere. So it's all yours."

His dark mood precluded my being able to needle him, much as I was tempted. Instead, I tried my best being sympathetic. "Jesus, Stan, I am sorry. You can still make a little hay out of it when Brandt shows him the door—maybe make it into a cautionary tale. It'd be a good story."

But that wasn't what he wanted to hear. "Fuck you, Joe. And if you guys do make a big deal out of this, you'll live to regret it. I'm handing him over 'cause he broke the rules and he made me look like a jerk, but don't push your luck. I'm still as ready as ever to chap your butts if you screw up."

"Very graciously put, Stanley," I said with a laugh. "I'll be sure to pass your compliments along to the chief."

In fact, there was no big flurry surrounding Bancroft's departure. Brandt and Derby both agreed with Katz that discretion was probably best suited to everyone this time, and ended the whole episode with barely a murmur.

As satisfying as it was to have this problem put to rest, however, I was the first to acknowledge that its importance had been diminished by recent events.

Reynolds was on a roll, the rumors that had threatened him early on all but forgotten—a fate I feared our case might suffer unless something broke soon from the underbrush.

Like Willy walking into my office, looking fresh from a meal of proverbial canary.

It had been some time since I'd seen him so well disposed, for despite his efforts—or because he'd had to be uncharacteristically light-handed—he'd been having a tough time getting the cooperation he was used to. Also, he hadn't been alone. With the SA's office, Reggie McNeil, and the media all out there digging, not to mention half the police department, Willy's fondness for the shadows had been thoroughly put to the test.

None of which seemed to be bothering him now. He closed my office door, leaned up against it, and said, "I think I got a hot one. You want to join me?"

"We going somewhere?"

"I am. I think I found Lisa Wooten's supplier, but he's skipped town. He beat feet for the hills after the bodies started piling up, and I want to know why."

"What's his name?"

"Eric Meade. Lives out in the boonies on the Auger Hole Road, near the Marlboro end. I would've done him on my own, 'cept I knew you'd get pissed, not to mention he has a fondness for firearms." He smiled broadly at the last line.

I raised my eyebrows. "Think we ought to bring in more people?"

"Not if we want to keep this private. Plus, once he knows all we want is a conversation, he shouldn't be too hard to handle."

"Assuming he hasn't already shot one of us."

Willy waved that off. "No sweat. He's an ex-Marine, but I hear he's pretty peaceful. Got kicked out of the Corps because he lied on his application, not that he'd admit it. Anyway, I've got something I think I can use as leverage. I've dug up a candidate for your number one rat in all this."

It was clear this invitation was a one-time offer. The visit to Eric Meade would take place with or without me.

"Okay," I told him. "Have a seat and tell me who's the rat."

His eyes were shining with pleasure. "Walter Freund— from what I've been hearing, he makes Jamie Good look like he deserves his last name."

Chapter Twenty-one

The Auger Hole Road was fairly substantial by Vermont back roads standards. A perpendicular link running from Route 9, between Brattleboro and Bennington, to the Dover Road farther north, it wasn't something that tourists readily used, but it was well-known and well traveled by many locals.

That notwithstanding, it remained a twisting, narrow, tree-crowded gravel scratch on the map. And at night, dark and lonely.

At both ends, it actually had some pretty impressive homes—large old farmhouses, complete with outbuildings and open fields. Toward the middle, however, far from the conveniences of any community or major thoroughfare, the population thinned out, and didn't advertise much excess income. Land-locked trailers and weary shacks were the norm, often placed back from the road, and barely visible in the best of light.

Which were hardly the conditions now.

Willy drove silently, his eyes intent on the ice-smooth swath of road that wavered in our headlights. On either side of us, dirty snowbanks leaned against a thick palisade of trees, which flashed by like bars on a cage, thick and ominous. The night was so absolute as to feed the imagination, and the woods seemed like they were teeming with life, watching us go by.

I craned my neck over the dashboard to look up at the faint thin ribbon of sky directly overhead.

"Full moon," Willy said quietly. "Not that it matters out here."

"He live alone?" I asked.

"Supposedly. But you know how that can change."

The car slowed, and Willy began studying the side of the road. "I think we're close." He killed the headlights, plunging us first into total darkness, and then, as our eyes readjusted, into a thin penumbra between half sight and blindness. The car kept rolling, the absence of light making the sound of its wheels on the frozen dirt seem much louder.

"If Meade's as hinky as I think he is," Willy explained, "he's not going to like seeing any slow-moving cars."

I mentally reviewed the briefing Willy had given me in my office. Born to an addict who'd killed herself when he was five, Eric Meade had grown up as the poster boy for every rehab organization known to the state, from Alcoholics Anonymous to the Department of Corrections. According to Willy's sources, he had finally learned to cope by simply avoiding society, venturing into its treacherous currents only when strictly necessary.

Willy pulled as close to the bank as he could and killed the engine. "Okay. Foot patrol time."

He reached into the back seat, retrieved a small canvas case, and handed me an electronic instrument about the size and weight of an instant camera. "The on switch is on the bottom."

I found the small button he was referring to and slid it forward. A dim green glow emanated from one end of the device.

"Night-vision monocular," he explained. "Bought 'em from a catalog two years ago for a couple of hundred bucks each. I got sick of waiting for the department to buy enough units to pass around—plus, I just like having my own."

We both exited the car, with me still fooling with the scope, holding it up to my eye and admiring how well it revealed everything around us, although in a universally sickly green wash. "You use these much?" I asked in a whisper.

"Now and then. I bought that one for Sammie. Better than a date anytime."

I lowered it and glanced to where he was bent over, tightening a shoelace. I imagined him and Sam prowling the streets late at night, peering into other people's business just to keep tabs. I had no idea if that bore any semblance to the truth, but I could suddenly understand what Sammie saw in Willy and how Willy must be missing her since she'd hooked up with Andy Padgett.

He straightened and began walking down the road ahead, as quietly as the shadows around us, his scope turned off by his side, navigating by the tepid moonlight. He was military-trained and combat-tested, experienced in traveling behind enemy lines for days on end. This kind of world—dark, still, and filled with unseen menace—was as comfortable to him as a walk in the park. It was an adaptation that went a long way in explaining his character.

I fell into step behind him.

We walked like that for several hundred yards, until

we came to a barely discernible break in the snow-bank, more like a deer path than a driveway. Here Willy paused and waited for me to catch up. I could hear the creaking of the frozen tree trunks and the rattling of bare branches in the light breeze high overhead.

"This is it," Willy whispered, his voice as gentle as a sigh. "Runs about two hundred yards up to a trailer. Rumor has it he's rigged trip wires, so keep your eyes glued to where I put my feet. He knows what he's doing, remember."

"What're the wires attached to?" I asked, my curiosity unpleasantly piqued.

Willy shrugged. "You want to find out?"

He led the way down the middle of the path, night scope to his eye, moving like a careful cat, his body above the waist as smooth as a boat slipping through quiet water.

Once again, I followed, seriously rethinking all the decisions that had brought me here.

Willy stopped abruptly about one hundred feet along, and fell gracefully to one knee. Then he looked over his shoulder and gestured to me with his one hand, still holding the scope. I came up next to him.

"See the wire?" He pointed just in front of him.

I squinted into my own scope, taking my time, and eventually saw a thin discoloration—like a razor cut across a photograph—about one foot off the ground. I nodded.

Willy rose without comment, stepped over the wire, and continued on.

Ahead of us, behind a slight curve in the path, we could see the glowing green shape of a small trailer in the woods. Briefly, I lowered the scope, and found myself staring at complete and utter darkness. All the trailer's windows had been blacked out.

The scope back in place, I again saw Willy come to a halt. This time, he merely wiggled his fingers at me to move up.

I looked at the ground as before, and saw nothing.

"What is it?" I asked in a murmur.

He wordlessly pointed to a tree by the side of the path. I aimed the scope at it and saw a small metallic object about waist level—not very bright, but distinct from the rest of the tree.

Willy then pointed to our other side, where a second dim box was stuck to another tree. "Light beam sensor," he whispered into my ear.

We both gingerly ducked low and passed under the beam.

The rest of the way was unimpeded, and in about three minutes we were standing before the trailer's front door, listening to the faint mutterings of a radio from within.

"Now what?" I asked him.

"You go 'round back. For all this to make sense, there should be a vehicle parked there by a rear door, facing another way out of here. Just give me a thumbs up if I'm right, and I'll trigger that last alarm to flush him out."

I did as he said, picking my way with extra care around the edge of the hay bales ringing the trailer. At the far corner, I stuck my head out quickly, saw the rear of a four-wheel-drive pickup across from a back entrance, and withdrew to give Willy his signal.

I then retraced my steps, moving more quickly now, and took up position, gun drawn, behind the hood of the truck, hoping the intervening engine block might do me some good.

A minute later, without warning or sound, the back door blew open with a bang and a glare of light, and an enormous man-made shadow fell across the front of the truck.

"Police!" I shouted. "Don't move."

Everything went dark again. I blinked once, as if I'd imagined the whole thing, and realized that Meade had slammed his door as abruptly as he'd opened it, leaving me back where I'd begun.

Before I could move, I heard a second loud crash, this one followed by a yell and a heavy thud, accompanied by a vibration I could feel through my boots.

I ran, stumbling and slipping, around the side of the trailer and back to the front, and found Willy Kunkle kneeling by the head of a prostrate, bearded giant, his gun shoved in the other man's ear.

"Don't you even quiver, Eric, or I'll splatter your brains all over the front yard," I heard him say.

"You okay?" I asked Willy as I drew near. I stuck my head into the trailer and checked it for more inhabitants. It was empty.

"Oh, yeah," he said. "I figured he'd pull something like this once you yelled at him, so I hooked his snow shovel across the top step. He landed like a ton of bricks. Didn't you, Eric?"

There was no response from the man aside from his heavy breathing. I sympathized with his sense of betrayal—Willy had sent me out back knowing full well what to expect, even though common sense would have dictated putting the officer with two good arms in the primary position.

"Any weapon?" I asked.

"Not in his hands, but I wasn't about to go through his pockets."

It was a point well taken. Leaving Willy to cover, I cuffed Meade's wrists behind his back and checked his clothes, finding no more than a hunting knife in a sheath at his waist, which I removed and tossed within sight into the yard. "Clear."

I reached over, grabbed the big man's shoulder, and rolled him onto his back with some effort. "You Eric Meade?"

The face staring back at me was large, round, florid, and with a snow-covered beard reaching up almost to his eyes. It was the fierce and theatrical face of a Viking conqueror, which made the meekness of his reply all the more incongruous.

"Yes, sir."

"You okay?"

"Yes, sir."

"Can you sit up?"

"I guess, with a little help."

Willy and I each grabbed a shoulder and pulled. Slowly, the man's huge torso levitated like a log being tipped on end.

"That better?" I asked.

"Yes, sir. Thank you kindly."

His grateful politesse put a final stamp of absurdity onto the entire scene.

"Eric," I told him. "We're from the Brattleboro Police. We want to ask you a few questions. You haven't done anything wrong that we know of, so you're not under arrest, but we would appreciate some cooperation. You all set with that?"

"You just want to talk?"

"That's all."

"But we don't want any shit from you, either," Willy cautioned. "I don't want to have to blow your balls off."

Meade blinked once, tiredly, obviously more than familiar with that line of reasoning. "I won't give you any trouble."

I bent behind him, unlocked the cuffs, and stood back with Willy to see what he would do next. Sitting like a bear at a circus, Meade rubbed at his wrists, his legs splayed out before him. Then, with slow and deliberate forethought, he organized his limbs, got to his knees, and eased himself to an upright position, leaning on the trailer to do so. I guessed he had to be about six and a half feet tall and three hundred and fifty pounds.

"You want to come inside?" he asked.

Willy, looking like a ferret beside him, quickly moved up the two wooden steps ahead of him, throwing the shovel still wedged there to one side. "I'll go first."

I gave our host ample room, cautious of what one well-placed back kick could do, knowing Willy was already checking the contents of the trailer to make sure that wherever Meade moved, it wasn't toward any part of his reputed arsenal.

But the big man wasn't interested in harming us. Once inside the trailer, he lumbered toward a stained and torn recliner, next to a small radio and a dropped paperback romance, and settled down with a heavy sigh.

I closed the door behind me, suddenly conscious of the plaintive country music quietly filling the room. I pointed to the radio. "You mind?"

Without a word, he reached over and switched it off.

The room's warmth began to return, fueled by a propane heater. I opened my coat and sat in a chair near a small breakfast table. The trailer was a tiny one-room affair, broken into distinctly separate functions, but unlike most bachelor pads, neat, tidy, and largely uncluttered. Its most remarkable feature was the wall of weapons, far out of reach behind Meade's armchair. Arrayed like the display of some modern knight's banquet hall, rifles, shotguns, and handguns of all sizes were hung in fanciful patterns from one end to the other, interwoven with a sampling of Marine Corps patches, flags, bumper stickers, and memorabilia.

I nodded in its direction. "Nice collection."

"Thank you."

It was one of Vermont's oddities that the only gun laws on the books were federal ones, aside from a few largely ignored local ordinances mostly designed to impede deer hunting at night. Not only could anyone openly pack heat, including when they were strolling around downtown, but they could do so even if they were known felons. Thus Eric Meade's passion for collecting hadn't been stymied by a record of minor crimes.

"Must've cost a bundle."

He merely cast his eyes down onto his clasped hands. I was struck by his passive lack of curiosity, and at how it probably stemmed from a lifetime of catering to mindlessly nattering authority figures.

"How do you make a living, Eric?"

He didn't look up. "Odd jobs."

"Like selling drugs?" Willy asked him.

"Sometimes."

I gave Willy a surprised look. This was looking more hopeful all the time. "You been doing that recently?"

This time, he did look at me. "You caught me when I did it last."

Clever answer. I smiled. "Okay. Here're the ground rules. We need to have some questions answered, but it'll probably mean admitting to a few illegal activities. We're willing to cut you some slack there, assuming they're not too bad, but only if you're as honest as you can be."

"What's 'not too bad' mean?"

"You tell us you killed someone, or played a role in killing someone, the deal is off. You tell us you dealt a little dope to make ends meet, we'll give it a pass."

"This once," Willy amended.

"There's a big hole between those two."

"According to the rules," I said, "we're not supposed to make any deals without a state's attorney's say-so. We're sticking our necks out as it is."

A small look of irritation crossed his bland face. "What do you want, anyhow?"

I liked that—a small step toward us. "We want to know if you sold drugs to a girl a few years ago. Lisa Wooten."

His eyes narrowed and he looked from one of us to the other suspiciously. "She died, right?"

"Yes, but not because of anything in the dope. She just OD'd."

"But if I sold it to her, that makes me an accessory, doesn't it? You said you'd nail me for something like a murder. Wouldn't that be murder?"

"I'm not going to call it that," I told him, angry at my own clumsiness. "She was going to do herself in one way or another. No reason you should be blamed."

But he was like a dog with a bone. "The state's at-

torney might not think so. How do I know he won't
be coming here next?"

Willy had reached the end of his patience, as I was
afraid he might. He got up abruptly, swung his chair
around, and slammed it down directly in front of
Meade, straddling it so they were knee-to-knee. Despite his enormous size, Meade seemed to shrink back
a little into the cushion.

"Look, asshole," Willy said, "we're not here to dick
around. You either tell us what we want to know and
we keep it between ourselves, or I let Walter Freund
find out you been mouthing off, and you can discover
if all that firepower and all your stupid alarms out there
are going to do you any good. Does that make things
easier to figure out?"

"This is got to be illegal," Meade said, but his heart
wasn't in it. Willy's Walter Freund trump card had done
the trick.

Kunkle jerked his thumb at me. "Probably, if it was
only me. My reputation's worse than yours. But that
man wouldn't do anything illegal—goddamn saint."

Meade looked genuinely sad, as if his fate in life
were to be forever confronted with such hopeless puzzles. "All right. Yeah, I sold it to her."

"You mix the batch yourself?" I asked him.

"I always do—did. I don't want to hurt anyone."

I ignored the absurdity of that. "And how long had
you been supplying her?"

"A few months."

Willy moved his chair back and now asked in a less
threatening tone, "You were her only source?"

Meade hunched his shoulders slightly. "I think so.
She made a big deal about seeing me. If she'd had
somebody else, she probably wouldn't have."

If true, that let Brenda Croteau off the hook and supported the thesis that Owen Tharp had been set up.

"Tell us about Walter Freund," I said.

His face closed down. "What about him?"

I got up and began pacing the width of the narrow trailer, suddenly reminded of something only he would know. "Let me put it another way. The medical examiner who autopsied Lisa said that addicts usually OD because they take a dose they're no longer used to, either 'cause they couldn't come up with the money for a while, or they tried to go straight. In any case, their tolerance drops, and the next time they take their standard hit, it kills them."

Meade just watched me walking back and forth.

"You were Lisa's exclusive supplier, according to you. Given that fact, did you tnink her tolerance had dropped just before she died?"

"What's that got to do with Walter?"

I obviously had made another mistake by rementioning Freund's name prematurely. Like a dog distracted by a powerful scent, now Meade couldn't get his mind off it. That did tell me something about Walter Freund, though.

Tearing a page from Willy's book, I stepped close enough to him that he had to tilt his head back to look up at me. "Nothing yet. Keep with me here, Eric. You paying attention?"

I waited until he nodded. "Good. What about Lisa's tolerance?"

"She was buying the same amounts, if that's what you mean."

"Yes, I do. But if you were selling to her regularly, and in the same amounts, didn't it strike you as a little strange that she suddenly died?"

"I don't know. That's what they do. I thought maybe she'd mixed it with something else."

I remembered the autopsy that Bernie Short had faxed following our phone conversation. It had found Lisa Wooten's body chemistry free of all other toxins except a little alcohol. "Was that one of her habits?"

"I don't know. I just sold to her."

"Bullshit, Eric," Willy broke in, quick as a trap. "She's been dead for years, and you remembered her right off. She wasn't just a customer."

The big man squirmed in his seat. "She was nicer than the others. That's all."

"What?" Willy persisted. "She give you freebies?"

I thought he'd gone too far, but Meade surprised me by letting slip a flitting boyish smile.

"She did, didn't she?" Willy laughed. "You dog."

I sat back down, aware that with that one break-through, the whole mood had become friendlier. "Okay, so you were pals. Did she ever mix her drugs with anything else?"

"Not that I ever saw," he finally conceded.

"Who else was in her life? Any other boyfriends? Or were you it?"

The smile returned, but embarrassed this time. "Oh, no. She was just nice to me sometimes. Owen was her real friend. I liked him, too."

"Owen's a wimp," Willy declared. "What'd she see in him?"

Eric Meade frowned. "Owen was a good guy. Everybody just treated him like a loser. It wasn't fair. Lisa knew that. He and Lisa were kind of the same that way—real gentle."

It was the longest sentence we'd heard from him yet, and told me something of where his prejudices lay—which I now hoped to use to redeem my earlier fumble.

"Not like Walter, right? The wannabe Marine." I glanced at the military shrine on the wall behind him.

Meade became angry. "He's no Marine."

"He acts like one, strutting around. Looks like he gets pretty much what he wants, too. Popular guy, well liked, doing well financially."

Eric's face had darkened. "He's a jerk."

Willy laughed. "Oh, yeah. Some jerk. When we mentioned him a minute ago, I thought you'd shit your pants."

"I did not," Eric shouted, moving about in his chair.

"Come on," Willy kept up. "He's got the real stuff. The Corps threw you out. That's why you compensate with all these stupid guns. Walter's got what it takes—they'd take him in a heartbeat if he asked."

"That's a lie." Meade tried to lurch to his feet. Willy placed his hand against his chest and shoved him back against the cushion.

"Sit down. What's the big deal? Some people got it and some people don't. It's a fact of life."

"He doesn't got anything. He hurts people. That's why they follow him. He messes with their minds. He would never be a Marine."

I caught Willy's eye, and he instantly resumed his seat, as peaceful as if he'd never said a word. Eric Meade stared at him in surprise, his chest heaving with emotion, confused by the abrupt change of pace.

"Eric," I said gently, "it's okay. Take a few deep breaths. You must've really hated him for what he did to Lisa."

But I'd overplayed it. He looked at me doubtfully. "Walter did that?"

"He knew her, didn't he?" Willy asked calmly.

"Sure."

"He ever do drugs with her?"

"I guess so."

"He know you supplied her?"

"Sure."

"Was he hanging around more toward the end—near the time she died?"

Eric sounded contemplative. "Yeah, he was. He was paying her to sleep with him, and being real mean to Owen, too, like he wanted to break them up."

"Talking about Owen like I was just a minute ago?" Willy asked.

Eric looked at him accusingly. "That wasn't right."

"I know it wasn't," Willy admitted with unusual gentleness. "I wanted you to be honest with us, and I knew you were worried about Walter. I heard on the street you had a falling out with him, right after Lisa died. That's part of the reason you live out here now. What happened between you two? You challenge him for what he did?"

The big man was obviously baffled. "No. He just started coming after me. It didn't make no sense. I never bothered him. I hardly even knew him."

"But you did see him doing a head game with Lisa and Owen toward the end," I spoke up. "Why was he doing that?"

"I don't know," he said forcefully, his frustration climbing. "I didn't understand."

"Didn't understand what? That he was trying to steal Lisa from Owen? Why's that so strange?" I prodded him.

Eric ran his hands through his hair anxiously. "Because he wasn't. He was just sleeping with her—he didn't even like her. Right after she died, Walter was all of a sudden acting like Owen's best friend—giving him support and a place to stay." He shook his head and repeated, "It just doesn't make no sense."

Willy and I exchanged looks. It made sense to us, in more ways than one.

Chapter Twenty-two

I'm not sure I'm getting this," Gail said. "Who's Walter Freund?"

"We still have a way to go," I explained. "But I think he's the one who was pushing Owen's buttons—the guy you're after."

We were sitting in her office, late at night, just the two of us. The rest of the floor was dark, empty, and silent, imbued with that aura of abandonment that homes never seem to suffer.

"You're going to have to give Willy high marks here," I told her. "He went at it with a vengeance, especially after I told him how many rules we'd be breaking. To be honest, when you first came up with the Owen-as-guided-missile theory, my bets were on Jamie Good, what with all his groupies. But Walter's smarter and more manipulative, and we've got him positioning poor old Owen like a chess piece. Good, on the other hand, never had much to do with him."

"We're going to have to do better than that," Gail said glumly. She'd already told me it had been a bad day of sniping with Derby.

"Well, it's all circumstantial," I continued, "but we have a witness who says Walter was putting a wedge between Lisa and Owen just before Lisa died. And afterward, although he'd been treating Owen like shit before, he tucked him under his wing like a doting mother."

"Why?" Gail asked. "He couldn't have been grooming Owen to kill Brenda years before the fact. It strains credibility."

"We don't think he was—not specifically. We think he was either planning for a rainy day or just saw in Owen the chance to mess with somebody's mind. Knocking off Brenda by remote control was probably an experiment—and a successful one, as Walter would see it. After all, if we're right, he'd already done a variation of that with Lisa, so it definitely fits his character."

Gail frowned. "Hold it, explain that. I thought Lisa died of a straight overdose."

"She did, but I don't think it was unassisted. Bernie Short planted the idea that she may have lowered her tolerance through a period of abstinence, and thus over-injected herself by simply taking her usual dose. But now we've been told her drug use had been constant till the end. My bet is that Walter overloaded her last syringe without her knowing it and let her kill herself so he could gain control of Owen.

"After we found out about Walter's possible role in all this," I continued, "we talked to everyone we could about him, especially concerning the time period following Lisa's death. We confirmed he made a special project out of Owen, even having him move in for a year. And it was then that Owen started telling people Lisa had been poisoned, although no one heard him

say by whom, which makes me think Walter left that
role blank till later."

Gail sat forward, keenly interested. "Were there any
instances of Walter directing Owen to act against his
own welfare?"

I smiled, having already thought of that. "Not that
anyone's seen. Walter made sure the mind-control aspect of their relationship was kept mostly under wraps.
Actually," I added, "I feel a little guilty about that.
Early on, a girl named Janice Litchfield told me Owen
was 'Walter's pet,' and had attacked Walter once, using
a pen like a knife after Walter taunted him to do it. At
the time, I thought it just meant Owen was prone to
violence. Now I think it was more of a training exercise—like a handler making a dog go after a guy in a
padded suit. Janice told me Walter laughed right after
the supposed attack, and yesterday she added that Walter even hugged him, like he was rewarding him."

Gail shook her head. "Aside from Janice, who're
your witnesses?"

I pulled a short list from my pocket and gave it to
her. "It starts with a man named Eric Meade, who was
Lisa's supplier, and then runs down a few people Willy
and I have been interviewing over the past few days,
including Janice. I also ran it by the department shrink,
who says it's perfectly possible. Problem is, Walter's
got Meade so spooked, he's armed himself to the teeth
and has his house ringed with security devices, and I
doubt any of the others will be any less paranoid."

She took the list and laid it on her desk. "My God.
What's Walter's past like?"

I produced another sheet of paper. "Pretty bad. He's
thirty-five now and his record goes back twenty-three
years. His juvie records are sealed, but he hit the ground

running once he came of age—everything from disturbing the peace and speeding, to sexual assault, armed robbery, bank fraud, pimping, manslaughter, and some serious drug activity. Over twenty hits so far. He's the proverbial three-time loser, and he's currently on federal parole for a weapons charge, which is probably encouraging him to keep a low profile. All in all, a classic sociopath, and one well motivated to work from the shadows—or to use tools like Owen Tharp."

Gail sat back in her chair and rubbed her eyes. "You're sure Brenda Croteau didn't sell Lisa the dope that killed her?"

"As sure as I can be. As far as we know, they never even met."

Gail gave me a tired smile. "Well, I guess I asked for this one. I'm going to have to tell Jack I just came up with a late Christmas present for McNeil, without having anything to replace it except a bunch of psychological mumbo-jumbo. You mind sitting in when I break him the news? He's going to want to know the details."

I got up, leaned toward her, and gave her a kiss. "You couldn't just hang the bad guy and be done with it, could you?"

She caught my face in her hands and kissed me back. "Nope. It's not my job."

"No one would agree with you, but that's one reason I love you."

Jack Derby's office was a modest affair—a box in a string of boxes, lined up along a hallway on the second floor of a modern bank building. One wall was covered with two windows looking up Main Street toward the courthouse, while the others had either pastoral pictures or framed law degrees hanging on them. His predecessor had been more of an egomaniac, and while admittedly the SA's office had been housed elsewhere in his day, James Dunn had always made sure he got the biggest desk, the best view, and the grandest room to call his own. It made me wonder how Dunn would rearrange things in the unlikely event that he won in November.

In fairness to Jack Derby, who'd recently been getting on all of our nerves, he was certainly no egotist. He was a decent, hardworking, well-intentioned man who—I personally believed—had let his inexperience, an enormous workload, and a premature case of reelection jitters get the better of him. Which probably helped explain both his testiness and frazzled appearance, even though that election was still eight months off.

Nevertheless, as he sat opposite Gail and me the following morning, he didn't look as if he were going to let any deep-seated honorable character traits get the better of him.

"I can't believe you did this, Gail. I can't believe you'd be so totally out of touch with what we do here. To willfully dig up exculpatory evidence against a prime suspect in a capital case. I mean, my God, it boggles the mind. What the hell were you thinking?"

Gail had prepared for this. "I've said from the start there's more to this case than we're willing to admit. I have no doubt that Owen Tharp killed Brenda Croteau. I have a big problem leaving it there. My interpretation of our job, since you mentioned it, is to seek justice on behalf of the people—the innocent, the guilty, and especially the ones who for one reason or another fall in between. I absolutely believe that to just nail bad guys is a violation of the very premise on which this office is founded."

Derby stared at her in astonishment, opened his mouth to speak, hesitated, and then finally said, with visible self-restraint, "I think we'd better agree to disagree on that for the moment, and stick with the nuts and bolts. Joe, I know the ME said there was no poison in Lisa Wooten's last dose—Gail handed me that small grenade a while back—but are you absolutely sure Brenda Croteau didn't sell it to her?"

"We can't find a single witness who says she did," I answered carefully. "And we do have someone who says he was her supplier right up to the end."

Derby glanced at the report Gail had placed before him at the start of the meeting. "Eric Meade. How reliable is he?"

I put the best slant on it I could. "I think he's utterly truthful—not a devious man at all. He might not make the best witness if you were to put him on the stand, though. A little reclusive."

Derby stared at me a moment. "Swell." He checked the report again. "And Walter Freund—he's the guy you think killed Wooten to gain control of Owen, and then steered Owen at Croteau."

"We think so. According to witnesses, Wooten's intake hadn't altered over those last few months, and she was known to be a fastidious shooter. The only variable cropping up near the end was Freund."

He signed and pushed the report away from him. "Gail, let's be honest here. What've we got now we didn't have before?"

Her response was instantaneous. "Doubt."

He didn't react, but looked at me instead. "Joe?"

"I *would* like to look into Walter Freund."

He surprised us both by smiling slightly. "Okay, fine. Why don't we compromise, then? We have a bird in hand. Let's prosecute Owen Tharp for the double murder of Brenda Croteau and her baby. Then, once he can no longer hide behind his Fifth Amendment rights— and while you, Joe, have had a chance to build a case against Mr. Freund—we can use him as a state's witness and issue an invitation to Freund to join him in jail."

But Gail was already shaking her head. "Reggie McNeil'll drag out the appeals process for years if he can. Plus, nothing says Owen will turn against Walter in any case. If Owen did kill Brenda for Walter's sake, there's no way he'll squeal on him once he's already convicted. What would he gain by it? He'd be labeled a stool pigeon in jail and probably get himself killed. But if we approach Reggie and offer a deal for Owen in order to get Freund, that'll turn Reggie into an ally. It'll be a two-for-one slam dunk."

Derby began to respond, but Gail cut him off. "And I don't think the case against Owen is that strong, anyhow. When we went into this, we were looking at life without parole. Now that his state of mind has been called into doubt—"

"For which we have you to thank," Derby interrupted in turn, some of his earlier emotion returning. "My God, you're sounding like his defense attorney, Gail. Have you forgotten what this man did? Do you have to look at those photographs again?" He grabbed another document from off his desk and waved it at her. "And this motion from McNeil to suppress the confession. You want to hand him exculpatory evidence going to intent on top of this?"

I noticed a vein throbbing in his forehead as his face

reddened with barely suppressed anger. "I think you
are right, by the way, that we probably won't get life
without parole anymore. Is that justice on behalf of the
people? That we go gently with a stone-cold killer because he had a rough childhood, or we bend over backwards to help his defense because some bully told him
to kill two people, and he went ahead and did it? I
don't think so."

Gail's expression was as tense and closed down as
I'd ever seen it, but her voice, when she spoke, was
level. "I'll resign if you want me to."

His eyes widened. "Resign? What the hell—" He
stopped abruptly and studied her for a moment. "You'd
quit over this?"

"Only because I think we're ignoring the big fish
so we can make a meal out of a minnow. We *could*
have both."

He scratched his forehead, peered at me, and asked,
"She like this all the time?"

"Yes," she answered for me.

I mentally tipped my hat to him and reconsidered
my earlier harsh opinion. Instead of throwing us out,
as he easily could have, he settled back in his chair
and asked, "Okay—from the top. You have nothing
solid linking Walter Freund to Brenda Croteau. So why
couldn't Owen have visited Brenda, thinking—for
whatever reason—that she'd played a role in Lisa's
death, then gotten into an argument with her, grabbed
a nearby knife on impulse, and killed her with it?"

"I think that's what *did* happen," Gail said. "What's
bothering me is that it doesn't explain why all the lights
were on in the house, why pages were torn from her
journal, why the wounds were so numerous and sav-
age, and why there's no connection to Brenda living

beyond her means. Also, when Owen was picked up and his possessions examined, why was there a single drop of blood on one shoe and a small smear on the cuff of his jacket, when Brenda's injuries caused blood to spurt everywhere? And, last but not least, why was there a denim knee-print in Brenda's blood when Judith Giroux claims her nephew never wore jeans and that the slightly bloodstained pants she now admits destroying were khakis?"

Derby was looking confused. "What're you saying? He did it but he didn't?"

"I have to believe he did," she admitted. "The physical evidence is strong, he confessed to it, he knew where the murder weapon had been thrown. I would just like to know the answer to those other questions. Because I'll guarantee you one thing," she added. "If I'm thinking along these lines, with as little mileage as I have, Reggie NcNeil's cooking up a storm."

Derby stared at me sourly. "No one can say *you* don't have mileage in this area. Did any of these questions occur to you? Are new ones occurring to you as we speak? I mean, much as I hate to give Gail any credit here, I need to know if you're totally satisfied with this case."

"I'd like to find the answers to some of her questions."

He rolled his eyes. "Like the degree of frenzy reflected in the wounds? We know he acted out violently in the past. Hell—we know he killed this woman, for Christ's sake."

Gail wouldn't concede an inch. "I got to know the difference when I worked with women's counseling groups. Putting aside the possibility that Owen was trained to attack like some kind of vicious pet, the kind of acting out he'd done before was spontaneous, short-lived, and asexual—it fit a pattern. In the parlance, he's 'psychodynamically predisposed' that way. That's what Freund took advantage of, probably without knowing it. We found out that, as a kid, Owen would run out into traffic, or jump from heights and bust himself up, and as he aged, he developed the sort of violent behavior we first used to explain his attack on Brenda. But I now think we misread the signs there. The difference is that Brenda was stabbed seventeen times—way beyond some spontaneous acting out—and that the wounds have a sexual connotation to them. All those slashes to the breasts. Owen used a weapon of opportunity, which is perfectly plausible for his type, except that the psychosexual pathology I see in Brenda's wounds points to a man who came prepared to attack. A man with a past of sexual abuse of some sort, which Owen doesn't have."

Derby didn't respond, but both his silence and his expression were enough.

Gail added, "Of course, I'm not qualified. This is strictly speculative, but I bet we'll be hearing it again at trial from McNeil's experts."

He looked over our heads out the window for a moment, seemingly lost in thought, pondering no doubt things both practical and political. "Well, that's great," he finally said in a tired voice. "Between the two of you, it doesn't look like I have much choice. What's happened so far is bound to leak out. So, I better get the jump on Reggie, distract him with these exculpatories, and get our own psychological analysis done on Owen. After which"—and he pointedly addressed Gail—"I'll issue a statement emphasizing our search for justice on behalf of *all* the people." He shifted his gaze to me. "I want a plan of attack from you ASAP on how we're following up what was said here today."

In the stilted silence that followed, we both understood it was time to leave.

"One more thing," Derby said, just as we were about to cross the threshold. "Part of my agreeing to this is because I know how the shit would hit the fan if I didn't. That doesn't make me very happy. I don't want anything like this to happen again—ever."

He wasn't fishing for a response. I closed the door gently behind us.

The conference room was packed and the conversation at an unusually high pitch, given that the sun hadn't even broken the horizon.

"You see this?" Willy asked, waving a copy of the *Reformer* at me as I entered.

"Haven't had a chance yet."

"The Senate passed the Reynolds Bill. Biggest crock I ever saw. They want to call us the VBI, like we were a bunch of G-men."

"Who says you'd be one of them?" Sammie asked.

"Are you kidding?"

"They pass it as a cabinet-level agency?" I asked, moving through the crowd to the head of the table. I was impressed that Reynolds had met his deadline. Town Meeting Day—the first Tuesday in March—was next week.

"Yeah," Ron answered. "They'd have a Secretary of Criminal Justice, which'll probably go to Commissioner Stanton. The VSP, Fish and Game, the Alcohol guys, and everybody else will all be included, except the sheriffs and constables. They've been left out."

"And how," Willy added. "No one'll admit it, but it

sounds like the sheriffs are being reduced to a taxi service for cons."

J.P. was sitting back in his chair, his own paper neatly folded before him on the table. "Even if the House passed it, it would never work," he said quietly.

"Why not?" I asked, realizing I'd never once heard him speak on the topic, despite its popularity around the building.

"Simple economics," he said. "The bill states that all officers will be brought up to the highest pay levels now currently available, which would be the state police. That was obviously just to buy off their union. But right now, the state police budget is around twenty-five million dollars a year, almost the same as all the other municipal agencies in the state combined. The state cops number three hundred, more or less. The municipals come to twice that many. You do the math. And that doesn't include the costs of bringing all those people and all that equipment under one umbrella. They can talk saving money till they're blue in the face, like Reynolds did in the Senate, but this thing's one huge white elephant, whether you like the principle behind it or not."

Willy finally threw his paper onto the windowsill behind him. "Well, I think the principle sucks. There's no goddamn way this thing's going to fly, and if it does, there's no goddamn way I'll be part of it."

Sammie laughed. "Maybe the library'll take you back."

I rapped my knuckles on the tabletop to quiet them down. In addition to the entire detective squad, there were several uniformed officers attending, along with Gail and Tony Brandt.

"Okay, folks, this is going to be short and sweet.

Turns out we might have gotten a little ahead of ourselves handing the Tharp case over to the SA's office—understandable given the weight of the evidence. They'd like us to extend the investigation a bit more, based on a few inconsistencies they don't want used against them in court later."

Since most of the evidence against Tharp had been gathered under his supervision, J.P. was the first to react. "What inconsistencies?"

I tried putting him at ease immediately. "Nothing involving what we collected so far. If anything, we'll be needing more of it. There is no doubt whatsoever that Owen Tharp used a knife on Brenda Croteau. Where questions have cropped up is in answering how and why."

"What do we care about why?" Sammie asked.

"Because it runs to intent," Gail answered. "Owen may have been misled about Brenda's role in his girlfriend's death. He was told Lisa Wooten died because Brenda spiked her dope with poison. We've recently found out Brenda didn't sell her any dope, and that what Lisa used wasn't poisoned to begin with. She died of a straight overdose, albeit a big one. Also, we need to dig deeper into what happened at Brenda's that night. We all know a jury is detail-dependent. Those TV shows they watch make them eager for fingerprints and hair follicles and DNA, and—although it shouldn't be our concern—motive. If, as we're beginning to suspect, Owen might've been programmed to kill Brenda—which we can count on McNeil emphasizing in court—the jury might let him off unless we can come up with an alternate explanation."

"Programmed by who?" Ron asked.

"Right now," I answered him, "we're looking at Walter Freund. We also think he was responsible for Lisa Wooten's overdose."

There was a ripple of conversation around the table. One of the uniformed officers, Ward Washburn, asked, "Does this mean the SA is going after Freund instead of Tharp?"

"No," Gail said emphatically. "Absolutely not. Tharp is still on the hot seat. If it turns out he *was* manipulated by Freund or someone else, the charges against him might be amended, but only because we'd be dealing with two perps instead of just one. Please keep in mind that the quote-unquote *guided missile theory* is only that for the moment—no more."

More generalized chatter followed, which I interrupted. "Owen's on his way to the head shrinker right now, which may end up telling us a little more about what really happened that night. Our job is to pretend we never handed the case over to the SA in the first place—that the investigation is ongoing. Let's forget about the confession, which might be thrown out anyway—"

"What do you mean?" Sammie jumped in.

"McNeil's saying he was too cold, too freaked, and that I scared the shit out of him," Willy answered.

"Also," I said loudly, trying to keep things on track, "we need to reanalyze the hard evidence—see what else we can find." I looked at J.P. "That means going over the blood samples, the knife wounds, whatever prints you collected—the whole ball of wax."

"There was some tissue under one of her nails. We assumed it belonged to Tharp. Should I get that DNA'd? I hadn't bothered because of the expense."

"Yes. Go back over everything with a fine-toothed comb. Now remember, everyone, this means we're back to running two separate investigations—Tharp and Resnick. Both have equal priority. We've made good inroads on the Resnick case. Billy Conyer's little group of friends is feeling the pressure. We need to keep that up. Our advantage is that we no longer have to worry about stepping on the SA's toes over Tharp. On the other hand, given the way some of the people we're dealing with are popping up in both investigations, I have to stress two major points: coordination and documentation. I don't want a single one of you to move a muscle without clearing it through Sammie or me, and I don't want anyone to have a conversation, make an observation, or overhear a comment out there that isn't immediately logged with Ron. We have got to know at all times what everyone's doing. Is that absolutely clear?"

Everyone nodded. Willy, just as predictably, smiled enigmatically.

"I know," I continued, "that Walter Freund's name is familiar to most of you. He's someone we'd all like to see put away for good. That's another thing we have to watch out for. Our handing Owen Tharp over to the SA prematurely's going to cost us with the press and some of the politicians. The race for the primaries will begin after Town Meeting Day. And even though things won't get hot till May, after the Legislature calls it quits for the year candidates are going to be chasing every issue they can, especially our old pal James Dunn. So, one last request: Keep your mouths shut. Any reporter, any civilian you don't know, asks you any question at all, tell them 'no comment,' and let me know who they are. You all know what happened to Cary Bancroft. Let's not give him any company on the unemployment line."

The rest of the meeting was devoted to dividing the workload and apportioning responsibilities and schedules. I let Sammie and Ron run most of it, given their dual leadership roles, except for wrapping things up with a few words of generic encouragement.

As I was retreating to my office, however, I was approached by patrolwoman Sheila Kelly, an expectant expression on her face.

"What's up?" I asked her.

She kept her voice low. "I might have something that could be helpful—an old snitch I used to have."

I escorted her to my office and closed the door behind us. "Have a seat," I said. "Fill me in."

She got straight to the point. "She used to do me favors now and then when I was with the Burlington PD. About six months ago, I heard she'd moved down here. I looked her up, but she didn't want anything to do with me—said her new boyfriend would string her up if he ever found out she'd been a snitch. It didn't mean much to me at the time, but the boyfriend is Walter Freund."

Chapter Twenty-three

Her name was Alice Duprée. She was all of twenty—blond, emaciated, stoop-shouldered, her eyes bruised by too little sleep and poor nutrition. She had a fondness for leather clothes, body piercing, odd-colored nail polish, booze, and dope. She was also quiet, subservient, and conditioned for abuse.

Walter Freund's kind of woman.

For two weeks, we put her under surveillance, eight hours of every day, when she wasn't in Walter's company. The schedule was chosen not just for budgetary reasons—since the evidence linking Freund to Brenda's death was too slim to justify much overtime—but also because we were worried Walter might tumble to us faster than his more naive companion.

Walter, after all, was looking at time in a place like Leavenworth if he was ever caught dirty again. It made him a terribly cautious man. Putting him under surveillance was deemed a waste of time.

Not so Alice Duprée. She was needy, high-strung, easily bored, and alcohol-dependent. And Walter's job on the four-to-midnight shift at a paper plant outside

of town left her alone when many of those character-
istics played in our favor. During those two weeks, as
the evenings stretched into night—and her need to keep
awake for her man hinged on keeping herself busy—
we caught her on film drinking, smoking dope, getting
friendly with other men, and agreeing on tape to sell
crack to Sam's undercover impersonation of a newfound friend.

It was a somewhat otherworldly period of time for
me, split as it was between studying the self-indulgent
roamings of an aimless girl, supervising the increasingly frustrating investigation into Billy Conyer's last
days, and tracking in the press how the Reynolds Bill
was faring in town meetings across the state. Especially since it was all in addition to coming home every
night to a few gingerly handled hours with a woman
increasingly under pressure from her boss, who was increasingly impatient with me to produce results.

By the time we decided we had enough on Alice
Duprée to suit us, I was more than a little anxious she
would provide us the break we were craving.

The night the crack deal was to go down with Sam,
we had one officer tail Walter to work—to make sure
he stayed there—while Sheila, Willy, and I huddled in
the freezing, empty second-floor office of a warehouse,
watching Freund's dilapidated apartment building from
across the street.

At the appointed time, dressed in threadbare punk
regalia, Sammie appeared below, casually climbed the
steps onto the building's rotting porch, and disappeared
inside. Over our headphones, we heard her high-heeled
boots clumping upstairs, and watched through the
binoculars as her expectant hostess rose in response to
her knock on the door and let her in.

The deal was concluded so quickly and with such ease, it was almost anticlimactic. Alice's friendship with Sammie had been built on a specific offer. Once that had been dealt with, Sammie ceased to be relevant. Alice had eyes only for her newly won wad of cash.

Until Sam slipped a badge under her nose.

At that point, things did pick up a little, as Sheila had warned us they might. Over my headphones, I heard Alice scream, and saw her leap to her feet and strike out, only to be quickly reduced to a crooked pile on the floor, with Sammie's knee in the small of her back. At Sam's unruffled suggestion that we come on over, Sheila and I did just that, leaving Willy to cover.

We'd wanted no fanfare, had dressed down for the occasion, and so crossed the street at a leisurely pace, our arms interlinked as if heading to bed after a long day at the bar. We made it to Freund's apartment without meeting another soul.

That, of course, had been the main point of this exercise. Alice Duprée wasn't worth clogging up the system—not that we'd tell her that—but the digs she called home were something else. We were perfectly willing to lose our case against her in exchange for a little conversation and the chance to legally search Walter's room.

When we arrived, Sammie had perched Alice on the edge of the bed with her hands cuffed behind her and was talking to her, inches from her face, in a tone too low for us to hear from the door. From Alice's expression, however, I wondered once more about all the time Sammie had spent with Willy over the years.

Sammie straightened as I closed the door behind us, and moved to Alice's side.

She recognized Sheila and managed to say, "You

bitch," before Sammie clamped a hand on her shoulder and quieted her down.

I took a chair from near a scarred bureau, placed it before Alice, and sat in it. Sheila positioned herself on Alice's other side, close enough so that she and Sammie looked like an honor guard.

Alice's eyes widened as the space around her was completely boxed in. "What do you want?"

"Has Detective Martens read you your rights?" I asked, knowing full well she hadn't.

She hesitated before answering, probably looking for the trap. "No."

"Good. That leaves us some options, 'cause if she had, that would mean you were under arrest, and we'd have to cart you off to jail, take your fingerprints and mug shots, have you spend the night in our basement, and arraign you in front of the judge tomorrow morning. In short, saddle you with a criminal record that would haunt you the rest of your life."

"I don't give a shit about a record. All my friends have records and it don't hurt them any."

I smiled at her. "I doubt they'd agree. But—miracle of miracles—you've still got a clean slate. A couple of goes at Diversion for retail theft, a misdemeanor or two over your drinking, a dropped charge for malicious mischief. You're right on the edge, but so far you've hung in there. Until now, of course."

I paused to let the significance of that sink in.

"What do you want?" she repeated, her voice more plaintive than defiant.

"We'd like you to tell us about your roommate."

She went pale. "Walter?"

"Yeah. We're a little suspicious he's been up to things he shouldn't be. What do you know about him?"

"I know he's done stuff."

"What kinds of stuff?"

She apparently changed her mind. "Whatever. We don't talk about it. It's just part of life in the streets."

The phrase was so melodramatic, it sounded like she'd read it from a cue card.

Sheila said softly, "Alice, I know your folks. This life was your choice. Nobody drove you to it."

Alice's lower lip went out like a child's and she stared at her feet.

"I think you know exactly what kind of man you're living with," I said. "That's part of the appeal, isn't it?"

"He's a good guy," she murmured.

"He's a powerful one, and a dangerous one. He ever done things to scare you?"

Her silence spoke for her.

I extracted a folded piece of paper from my inner pocket and held it up to her. "This is a warrant to search this apartment, Alice, for any and all materials pertaining to the sale or possession of illegal drugs. What're we going to find?"

She tossed her head toward Sammie. "She set me up. It was entrapment."

I pulled several cassette tapes from another pocket. "These'll prove otherwise. You know how long we've been watching you?"

She stared at me, her mouth partly open.

"That's right. For hours on end, day after day." I pointed over her shoulder. "From right over there, across the street. And from other places, too. We have tapes, photos, video, the testimony of other undercover officers. We've been living your life with you for weeks, Alice. Think back over some of the things you've been doing."

I glanced up at Sheila and Sam. "Undo her cuffs and go ahead."

They both set to work searching the small room, moving quietly and efficiently. We'd timed all this to allow for plenty of leeway before Walter was due back. Alice watched them anxiously, like a kid whose secret horde is about to be uncovered.

"They're going to find something, aren't they?" I asked her.

"I got nothing to hide."

Sheila extracted her latex-gloved hand from a bureau drawer. A small baggie of crushed brown leaves dangled from her fingers.

"You may be right," I said.

I pulled one last item from my pocket, a manila envelope filled with five-by-seven photographs. I laid one on her lap.

"You know the drinking age in Vermont?"

She nodded.

I turned the picture around slightly, so we could both see it. "Pretty good shot. You can even make out the label on the bottle."

From across the room, standing in the open closet, Sammie smiled, "Joe."

She was holding a crack pipe.

I shook my head. "It's not looking good, Alice. You ever been to jail before? No. That's right. I forgot. Tough place. Overcrowded, too. Not enough room for young women to be housed apart from one another."

Alice began to fidget.

I put a second picture on her lap, of her and Sammie talking, hunched together like conspirators. "Show-and-tell," I said. "To go with the tapes."

Alice brushed it off her knee onto the floor with a spastic gesture. "I can't tell you anything. I don't know what Walter does. He's real private."

"Private, maybe. But you live with him. You notice things. Remember the night Brenda Croteau was murdered?"

She sat farther back on the bed, lifting her knees so she could slide all the way up against the headboard. I moved to her spot at the foot, still crowding her. "No."

"You do, don't you? What happened that night?"

"Nothing."

I took a wild guess. "Walter was late coming home from work."

"That's bullshit."

"Then why're you scared half to death? It was pretty bad, wasn't it? And he told you to keep your mouth shut."

"Nothing happened that night."

"You think I'm making this up?" I asked, hoping she wouldn't answer correctly.

"I'm not telling you anything. I don't care what happens to me."

"Because he'd beat you up? Or worse? It may be a little late for that." I placed a third picture before her. "He's pretty jealous, isn't he?"

She glanced at it and swayed slightly. "Oh, shit. You can't do this."

It was a photograph of her kissing another man.

"That's not what it looks like. He said he'd rape me if I didn't. I—"

I cut her off. "Walter's not going to believe that.

Alice, pay attention. Sheila's told us about Burlington. We can fix things up between you and your folks—get you straight again, get you back in school. This is not a dead end. You can get out. You just have to talk to us."

My pitch was more desperate than she knew. I had no intention of sharing what I knew with Walter. And, glancing over my shoulder, I could tell Sam and Sheila hadn't found anything more than what they'd already shown me—which meant the apartment contained nothing so incriminating against Walter Freund that we could move decisively against him.

Fortunately, Alice was beyond knowing such things, much less using them to her advantage.

"I got something," she blurted, making me release an inner sigh of relief. "A bag. He had it with him that night. He did come in late. He was real worked up. He treated me rough, tore my clothes, treated me like a whore. I followed him when he left with the bag, and I saw him throw it away in one of the Dumpsters. I got it out right after and hid it."

"Why?" I asked. The others were deathly silent, frozen in place.

"He pissed me off. He said stuff—it really hurt. All the shit I do for him."

"Did you look in the bag?"

"No. I was too scared. And then later, he said he was sorry and everything was cool, and I sort of forgot about it."

"Where's the bag now?"

"I got a hiding place in the basement."

"Will you show us?"

She was so nervous by now, she couldn't keep still. "I don't know. He can get real mean. I'm scared."

"I know you are, Alice, but it doesn't matter what's in the bag—you're out of here now. We'll put you somewhere safe, get you back with your folks. You can leave this behind you—tonight."

"Oh, God. I don't know."

I leaned for emphasis. "Alice, listen to me. You stay here, word of this will get out. Not from us, but some-one'll talk. That's the way things work. You know that, right? Word gets around, sooner or later. Somebody sees something, or somebody, and puts two and two together. You want to run that risk? You want us to find you like we did Brenda Croteau, in a pool of blood with your head half cut off?"

She covered her ears and began rocking back and forth.

I reached out and stopped her. Pulled her hands down. "Alice, show us the bag and let's get the hell out of here."

Without comment, she swung her legs off the bed and headed for the door. Sammie quickly updated Willy by radio, and we all three silently followed our skinny guide down the dark, creaking stairs, straining to hear anyone approaching, fearful we'd be interrupted with the prize almost within grasp. Alice led us to an earthen-floored basement, cold and damp and filled with shad-ows. We used flashlights rather than hit the lights, and Alice took us to a distant corner, behind a monstrous oil tank squatting on short metal legs.

Brushing aside cobwebs, crawling on our hands and knees, just she and I squeezed behind the tank and came to a stack of moldy bricks, which she began un-piling in a frenzy, sending up a clatter that rebounded off the cold walls.

"Slow down, slow down," I urged her. "It's okay now."

She finally reached into the middle of the bricks and pulled free a dirt-smeared black gym bag, which she thrust into my hands as if it were on fire. "There. Can we go now? Please?"

"You want anything from upstairs?" I asked.

She was crying now. "No, no. I just want to go. Come on, come on."

I placed my fingertips on her mouth. "Quiet, Alice. Keep it together. We're almost out of here."

We returned to the first floor, exited to the street, and crossed quickly to the warehouse opposite, surrounding Alice like bodyguards, blocking her from view.

Willy met us inside the door. "What'd you get?"

"Don't know yet," I told him. "Let's get to some light. Sheila, can you take care of Alice?"

She nodded and took the skinny girl off to where we'd parked one of our cars in a back bay, out of sight.

The rest of us crossed the dark, echoing room we'd entered and stepped inside a small interior office. Willy closed the door and turned on the lights.

I placed the bag on a dust-covered desk, pulled on a pair of latex gloves, and opened the zipper.

On top of a bundle of clothes and a pair of spattered sneakers were some blue jeans, one knee of which was crusty with old blood.

"Bingo," Willy said softly. "Who they belong to?"

"As far as we know," I answered, "they're Walter's."

Chapter Twenty-four

We didn't arrest Walter Freund, although there was pressure to do so among members of the squad. Instead, we sent a car to his house shortly after he'd returned home and had a patrolman question him about his girlfriend's whereabouts, implying she might have been involved in a crime and left town. The officer reported later Freund hadn't seemed too concerned.

The contents of the bag—the bloodstained clothes, the sneakers, and a vicious-looking but very clean hunting knife—were labeled, packed up, and sent to the crime lab for analysis.

Gail, Jack Derby, Tony Brandt, and I met on the afternoon of the next day in Derby's office to discuss what to do next.

Derby, seemingly recovered from his anger of our last meeting—I thought in large part because we'd brought him something useful—made a show of letting Gail represent their office in the conversation.

"You're comfortable not arresting him?" she asked us after I'd outlined how we'd come by the bag—barring a few details.

"We don't think he's going anywhere. He has to re-port daily to his parole officer, he doesn't know what we've found, and he thinks his girlfriend just got into a jam and split town. On our side, we don't want to repeat the mistake we made with Owen Tharp and move prematurely. Until the lab tells us otherwise, we can't prove if the contents of that gym bag have anything to do with him or Brenda Croteau."

"Would you have any objections to getting a non-testimonial evidence order for a blood sample from Freund?"

I thought about that for a moment. It was perfectly feasible. Freund had waded deeply enough into the "reasonable suspicion" category to allow a judge to grant such a request. And with Alice Duprée now out of harm's way, stirring up Walter's paranoia might not be a bad idea. It could push him to do something that might land him in hotter water.

"This to compare with the tissue sample collected from under Brenda's fingernail?"

"Seems like a good idea—it didn't match Owen," Gail admitted with a smile.

"Sure, I'll serve him with it," I answered. "What happens with Owen and Reggie McNeil while we're waiting for forensics?"

Gail deferred to Derby.

"We're meeting with Reggie in Judge Harrowsmith's chambers this afternoon. I'm hoping Reggie will see the value of holding his breath till we sort this out."

I asked another question that had been nagging me. "What did your shrink think of Owen?"

"Perfect fit," Gail said. "I just got her report this morning. She confirmed our guess he was a prime can-didate for manipulation. She couldn't ask him anything about the crime, of course—not with Reggie there—but in general terms, she found him both extraordinarily malleable and prone to devoting himself to whoever's treating him well at the moment. Supposedly, Owen's sense of gratitude is so psychologically rooted that it virtually stands in stead of a conscience. He's not wired too tightly, of course, which doesn't help matters, so he's also easily overwhelmed by people's use of language."

"What about the fits of violence?"

"They're there, but 'fits' is the operative word. She agrees with me that the carnage at the Croteau scene exceeds Owen's capabilities, even if he was artificially disinhibited with booze and dope."

That caught Derby off guard. "Hold it—I thought we were working on the theory that if the blood on Freund's belongings was Brenda's, then that merely placed him at the scene. Is the shrink suggesting he actually played a role in the killing?"

"That's what we're starting to think," I admitted, "but my question is, why did Walter get Owen involved in the first place? Why run the risk of having some simpleminded kid spill the beans later?"

"He hasn't spilled the beans, though, has he?" Gail answered.

She had a point.

"Still, the risk . . ."

"So Walter set Owen in motion," Derby hypothesized, "and then watched from the shadows to make sure he did the job right?"

"And possibly finished her off when he didn't," I suggested. "Now that we have two knives, I can ask the ME to try to match each wound to the blade that caused it."

"Why would Walter make it so complicated?" Derby wanted to know.

Gail shrugged. "Because he had the perfect fall guy. Because it fits his sociopathic needs. Because he almost got away with it."

That last crack obviously hurt. Derby scowled. "What a mess."

Tony broke his silence to disagree. "Maybe not—in a few days, we could have a nice, tidy little package that McNeil will be happy to help gift-wrap."

Derby looked doubtful. "Maybe. What bothers me about all this is that everything made sense when Owen was the sole killer. With the death of his girlfriend, he had the perfect rationale for killing Croteau." He looked at Gail balefully. "You're the one who's so hot on motive. What did Freund have against Croteau?"

If he'd had a sense of humor, the obvious response should have been that motive wasn't a prosecutor's concern. Gail, however, wasn't about to go there again, jokingly or not. She simply said, "Let's hope we find out."

I found Walter Freund in what seemed to be his home away from home, the Dirty Dollar—a true dump of a bar near where South Main meets up with Canal. Once the basement of a tenement building, the Dirty Dollar reminded me of the lower-class speakeasies I'd read about as a boy, where the bar had consisted of a plank and two sawhorses, and a seat was wherever you chose to fall down.

It wasn't quite that bad, of course. Building codes and licensing requirements had seen to that. And a long time ago some pretense had even been made to decorate the place. But the effort was so faded or in disrepair, and the lighting so poor in any case, that none of it really mattered.

Walter was sitting in a corner booth, his back against the wall, his feet extended along the bench, as if he were propped up in bed. On the battered table next to him were a pack of cigarettes, an overflowing ashtray, a small, closed notebook, and a glass of what looked like water, although the glass itself was too dirty to tell. He was a small man, cadaverously thin, with a long greasy ponytail and a yellowish complexion that reminded me of mushrooms.

I slid onto the bench facing him. "Walter Freund?"

"Lieutenant," he said, as if we'd known one another for years. In fact, despite his reputation, we'd never actually met. Neither of us extended a hand in greeting, and Freund kept his eyes sleepily focused elsewhere.

"Your name's been coming up quite a bit lately."

"So's yours," he answered.

I kept my tone conversational. "Oh, yeah? How's that?"

Walter gave a shrug so small, it was barely a quiver. "Busting Owen, shooting Billy, libeling politicians. I was thinking you maybe had Katz on the payroll—keeping you in the news. Must compensate for the lousy salary and all those hours. What do you make?"

I was impressed by the way he modulated his voice, making it almost theatrical. "Funny you should mention Owen and Billy. They were regulars here, weren't they?"

"Them and a lot of other people."

"You and Owen pretty tight?"

He glanced at me. "Kid's a retard."

"That doesn't answer the question."

His eyes narrowed just a fraction, then he went back to staring into space. "He was a wannabe—attached himself to whoever didn't shake him loose."

"Like you."

"What do you care who he hung out with?"

I ignored the question. "You may be right—we think he's a little simpleminded, too. Prone to doing what he's told, even when it gets him in trouble."

"No shit?" But he didn't sound surprised.

"You know anyone who used him that way?"

He shook his head. "I didn't pay attention. He sucked up to me a lot, but it just bugged me."

"So that's what people saw when you two were together? Him sucking up and you resisting?"

He smiled. "Okay. It wasn't that bad. I didn't know he was a psycho, though. I would've told him to fuck off if I'd known he was nuts. I mean, hell, he could've whacked me."

"He did come at you once. What did you do to piss him off so much?"

He seemed to consider that for a moment. "Don't know. I don't even remember it."

"You know Brenda Croteau?"

He took the change of topic in stride without comment. "Sure. Everybody did—one way or the other."

"Which way was it for you?"

He leered. "Oh, no. I wasn't going to stick it in that honey pot. She was just a barfly to me, and an ugly one to boot—that's it. Did the autopsy show she had AIDS? I bet she did."

"How 'bout Owen?"

"I didn't think he knew her—guess I got that wrong, huh?"

"Interesting. You two were glued at the hip. He

knows her well enough to kill her, and you don't think they were even acquainted."

He equivocated again. "Well—*acquainted*—sure, they were probably that. This is a popular place. All sorts of people see each other."

"What was the scuttlebutt when he killed her?"

"Not much. It's a weird world. Lot of bad shit happens."

I slid a document across the table at him. "Got something for you."

He picked it up as though it were a flyer stuck under his windshield wiper, and gave it a cursory glance. His eyebrows knitted slowly. "What the hell is this?"

"It's a court order for a sample of your blood."

"Why do you want my blood?"

"You can have it drawn at the hospital within the time frame stated in there. Or if you want, I can drive you there right now—get it over with."

"I got to do this?"

"So says the judge."

For the first time, he seemed at a loss for words. He stared at the evidence order before asking, "What's my blood going to tell you?"

"Your DNA, for one thing, plus all the information a urine sample does."

He laughed. "Oh, shit. I live to pee in a cup. Seems like that's all I do for you people. I can tell you now, you aren't going to find any drugs. No way I'm going to fuck up my parole doing that shit."

I slid out of the booth and stood up. "Then you got nothing to worry about."

He hesitated, obviously weighing his options. "What about DNA? They use that like fingerprints, right? For rapists and whatever?"

"Yeah. You leave a little of it behind and we find it, you might as well have left your driver's license."

Walter's confidence seemed to return. He actually laughed as he also got to his feet. "Just like a fingerprint. That's pretty cool. Lead the way."

I took him to my car and we drove to the hospital at the other end of Canal Street, less than a mile away.

"So why me?" he asked on the way.

"You knew Owen, Brenda. You been a bad boy in the past. You're actually pretty high on our list of suspects."

"Suspects of what? Owen whacked her."

"He knifed her. We don't think he killed her."

He was quiet for a while, watching the scenery go by. The snowbanks hadn't been replenished for several weeks. Winter was winding down, and its coat was shabby, tattered, and stained.

"I never heard she was raped."

I liked that his brain was circling this problem, trying to sort it out.

"She wasn't."

Another patch of silent thinking. "Then why collect DNA?"

"Oh. There was a ton of blood. Her head was almost cut off—by a hunting knife—probably one with a double edge, curved at the tip like a Bowie knife."

He turned away from the view to stare at me. "How could you know that?"

This time I laughed, pulling into the hospital parking lot. "Don't you watch TV? They don't make that stuff up. Those lab guys are incredible. Here we are."

I escorted him to the ER, got him hooked up to a nurse, who quickly and efficiently sat him down in one of the examination rooms, tied off his upper arm, swabbed the inside of his elbow, and extracted a tube of bright red blood—all in a matter of minutes. Throughout, I could almost see the wheels turning in Walter's head as he tried to calculate what he'd just given up.

Finally, rolling his sleeve down over a Band-Aid and putting his parka back on, he asked, "So they're going to compare my blood with what they found at Brenda's?"

"Yeah, among other things. You want a ride back downtown?"

He paused in the lobby. "What other things?"

"Well, DNA's funny that way. It's not just in blood or semen. It's almost everywhere in the body. It's what makes up our cells." I held up my fingertip. "There's DNA in every bit of skin, for example—in the roots of each hair. And you know how much they fall out— hundreds of them every day, supposedly."

Unconsciously, his hand snuck up and touched the side of his head. He jerked it away as if he'd found it trespassing.

"But it's not really hair we're interested in," I continued casually. "Turns out there was a small sample of skin under one of Brenda's nails—we think where she scratched the man who really killed her. That's what we're hoping this'll match." I patted the pocket where I'd placed Walter's vial of blood.

He stared at me, and then down to the pocket, his lips slowly compressing.

"Give you a lift back?" I offered again.

I could barely hear his voice, it was so low. "I'll walk."

*   *   *

I was watching TV when Gail got in that night, not too late. I heard her dump her briefcase in the kitchen, as usual, and kick off her shoes in exchange for the slippers she kept by the back door.

"Hot water's on," I shouted, and heard her preparing one of the curious-smelling concoctions she called tea.

A few minutes later, she entered the living room balancing a steaming mug and a plate of cookies on a tray. I cleared the coffee table in front of the couch.

"My kind of hors d'oeuvres," I said, grabbing one of the chocolate chips. "How was your day?"

"Pretty good," she said noncommittally. "What're you watching?"

I hit the mute button and reduced two people to reading lips over a greasy pan and a dishwasher. "The news. Just finished. I was trying to make up my mind to either veg out or make some dinner. I didn't expect you back so soon."

She laid her head back against the cushions. "I know. And I have a pizza being delivered. So you're off the hook. What did the news say?"

"Hot topic's our esteemed speaker, Mark Mullen, who's doing what everyone thought he would. Now that the Reynolds Bill is in his hands—which he never refers to by name—there's a whole bunch of hemming and hawing going on. The clip they showed had him touting the virtues of all us heroes in blue, and how the worst thing we can do to this precious resource we call Vermont is to overreact to an admittedly egregious situation, et cetera, et cetera. I smell some wicked deal-making in the air."

Gail sipped her tea. "There will be that. He has to pay lip service to the popular support that came out of those town meetings, while he replaces Reynolds's name with his own as the author of a solution." She sighed. "Pretty predictable. Even if he weren't competing with Reynolds for governor, he'd still be inclined to gut the bill and start over. It's his nature. He's been in the House for more years than anyone can remember, cutting deals, bringing opposites together, making or breaking friends and enemies—and in the process completely forgetting that sometimes you don't need to do all that crap. Sometimes a situation is so simple and obvious that it's worth your while not to mess with it."

"Occam's Razor," I muttered, remembering Reynolds's words in a different context.

"Exactly. But it ain't going to happen, 'cause even if it weren't his nature, Mullen *does* want the governorship. The point's moot."

"So what's he going to do?" I asked.

She munched on a cookie. "He can't bury it in committee or kill it legislatively. It's too popular. Somehow or another, he's got to make it his own. How is beyond me. He's been putting in some late hours with his cronies, though. How did it go with Walter Freund?"

"I think we shook him. He associated DNA with semen only, and maybe blood. I let slip at the end that it works with tissue also, and that we had a sample from under Brenda's nail. When I left him, he was looking like he wanted to throw up. I also described the kind of knife we found in his bag as the murder weapon. That caught his interest."

"Good," she said as the doorbell rang.

We rose to take in the pizza, pour drinks, break out a bag of chips, and bring everything back to the living room, which was still being entertained by a silent television set.

"Things back to normal between you and Jack?" I asked before taking a large bite.

"Pretty much."

"Is something up?" I asked with my mouth full, struck by her distracted tone.

She hadn't begun eating yet, and now looked at me squarely, as if bracing for a shock. "I got a job offer today—from Vermont StayGreen. They want me as part of their legal counsel."

My chewing slowed down. Vermont StayGreen was the state's biggest environmental group. A powerful combination of gatekeeper and lobbyist organization, it appealed to all sorts of nature lovers, from those wandering the hills with sandals and a guidebook to the more combative, who liked bringing the battle to the Legislature's door. They published books, periodicals, and pamphlets, organized grassroots campaigns against everything from gas pipelines and condo developments to snowmaking ponds and nuclear energy— and, to be fair, in support of forest management, nature trails, municipal conservation projects, and a raft of other things—and had political and financial connections as far-flung and diverse as Greenpeace and the Sierra Club. Given Vermont's cuddly image in the national consciousness, they had no trouble attracting a steady stream of backers.

They were, despite their detractors, a major political force in the state.

They were also headquartered in Montpelier.

I swallowed what I had in my mouth half-eaten, sensing at last that all the issues Gail and I had been circling lately were about to be addressed, if in an un-expected way. "That's quite an offer. What's it entail?"

"Be part of their legal staff. Maybe do some lob-bying. A lot of travel." She smiled halfheartedly. "Not to the Grand Canyon or anything. More like Washing-ton and New York and places like that. Still, it's a pretty big deal."

I wiped my fingers on a napkin and sat back, my appetite gone. "You must be feeling on top of the world."

"It is flattering. I didn't commit myself one way or the other, though. There're a lot of things to consider."

There was an awkward silence. The people on the screen yammered soundlessly on, looking like the cho-rus of voices in my brain—and just as effective.

"The timing's not bad," Gail said. "I mean, not over-all. I have to see this case through, of course. I did tell them that, and they said they'd taken that for granted. But I can't deny, the SA job hasn't worked out the way I'd hoped."

"Maybe you should run against Derby," I suggested lamely, irritated with myself that now that the moment had come, I didn't know what to say. While she was talking about a job, I kept thinking of us, although I knew that with time, we'd end up on the same page.

She laughed politely and played out the game. "Yeah, right. No—he's a little frazzled right now, but only be-cause he's nervous about being reelected. He's so much better than Dunn was, it isn't funny, but he's the last to realize it. He'll win in a landslide, and things'll set-tle down. I bet in the long run, he'll become one of the best SAs this state's ever had."

She thought a moment before adding, "He's not the problem—it's me. I think I got into this line of work for the wrong reasons. I'm not designed for it—all the God-like manipulations. It bothers me to cut a deal to avoid the cost of a trial, or to dismiss one person's crime so we can go after someone else. I understand the rationale behind it. But it doesn't feel right. And I'm not sure it does anything for the victims.

"And there's a glee to it that bothers me, too," she continued, making me realize how heavy a burden she'd been carrying all this time. "We talk about nailing people or hanging them out to dry, like they were rabid animals. It reminded me of why I stopped coming to police department picnics years ago—I hated hearing the people you work with reducing the world to scumbags and losers and bringing down bad guys. It sounded like a bunch of nasty kids playing with lethal toys. Part of the reason I became a prosecutor was that I thought I'd be standing above all that, helping put things back on an even keel by looking at them in a compassionate, measured way."

She stopped to smile, presumably embarrassed by her own naïveté.

I couldn't argue against her. I'd never heard any prosecutor speak with that kind of idealism. In fact, it was usually disparaged as missing the whole point of the job.

"Not very practical," she concluded, as if reading my thoughts. "Derby's made that pretty clear. I'm sure he kicks himself nightly for hiring me."

"I doubt it," I said supportively. "He probably sees the same potential in you that you see in him."

She stared out the window without comment.

"Are you going to take StayGreen's offer?" I asked.

"It's probably the right thing to do," she conceded. "It's taken me a long time to get my feet back under me. I know going to law school and joining the SA's office were mostly in reaction to the rape. I wanted to get even, I wanted to stop hurting, to become sane again. I even wanted to do something that would bring me closer to you—to what you did. I was feeling so disconnected to the world around me."

She looked at me again. "But that's been changing. I've begun to care again about the things that interested me before—politics, the environment, people's welfare—and it's made me feel a little trapped by some of the decisions I made to survive in the short run."

We were at that watershed point again, but now I finally understood what had brought her there. "Like our living together."

It wasn't phrased as a question, and as I said it, I took her hand in mine. "To be honest, it was always a little weird having you in the SA's office, knowing you like I do. It was fun talking shop, and I was incredibly proud of everything you did. But deep inside, I kept asking myself why you were doing it—and when it might wear off. Just like this arrangement." I waved my other hand toward the ceiling.

She sat there, seemingly unable to speak.

"It's been a healing process for both of us," I continued, feeling strangely at ease, "and with this Stay-Green offer, it just brings us back full circle—the hippie and the cop. The Velveeta-man and the granola-head. The couple nobody can cook for, or explain to their friends. Let's face it, we've been working against nature lately—way too conventional."

She laughed, if only feebly. "God, it feels good to get it out."

I kissed the side of her head, the smell of her hair so familiar.

"You know," she said, snuggling closer, "if I do take this job, it would probably mean spending most of my time in Montpelier, at least to begin with. I asked them about working from down here later, what with computers and all. They said that would be fine when the Legislature's out—like having a branch office."

She tilted her head back to look at me. "A while ago, you said that the reason we worked so well together was that we gave each other lots of space. You want to try turning the clock back a little—live apart like we used to, and see if we can't sort this out? I want this new job to be a *part* of making life normal again—but I want us there, too."

I hesitated, wondering how much we should tackle at one time. But she seemed so much like her old self again. "Since we're laying our cards on the table, I gotta admit, I have sort of missed having a place of my own."

She gave me a long kiss and then said, "I know. And I know this house was never really a home for you. But I'm going to hang on to it. Maybe you'll like it better as a place to visit."

I let out a long, bottled-up sigh, stretched out on the couch alongside her, and hit the off button on the TV remote, plunging the room into darkness.

The pizza would taste just as good cold.

Chapter Twenty-five

The good news was that both the medical examiner and the crime lab eventually confirmed that everything we'd sent them connected Walter Freund to the death of Brenda Croteau. His DNA matched the tissue under her fingernail, minute traces of oilstone grit were identical to those found on his Bowie knife—and made matching the various wounds to the two knives that much easier—and the soiled clothes had been stained by Brenda's blood.

The bad news was that Walter Freund had disappeared, influenced, no doubt, by my all-too-clever conversation with him.

A general be-on-the-lookout order was issued throughout the country and entered into the NCIC computer, and Freund's background was analyzed for leads on his whereabouts. But no one I knew was holding their breath. We knew Walter would resurface in the long run—people with his habits always did—but we also knew our efforts would have little to do with it. Sooner or later, he'd rob a store, beat up a girlfriend, buy some dope from an undercover cop, or even run a red light, and he'd be back among us.

None of which made me feel any better.

At least as far as Gail was concerned, things improved immeasurably. She and Reggie McNeil worked out a proposal lessening his client's charges at Walter's expense—pending Owen's full explanation of his role in Brenda's death—and Derby was forced to admit that, Walter's disappearance notwithstanding, this deal made him look a whole lot better than had he crucified Owen and never given Freund a second's thought.

Which was just as well, since when Stanley Katz broke the news of the deal prematurely, Jack Derby was able to claim almost full credit. And at this point, with her future discreetly in her pocket and the two of us back on track, Gail couldn't have cared less.

Unfortunately, the hinge pin for success was Owen Tharp, and nobody knew if he'd play along.

Gail and I drove up to the Woodstock correctional facility in early April to meet with Reggie and Owen and see if he'd help decide his own fate. Reggie had been spending weeks with him, revealing the evidence against Walter and telling him how Walter had manipulated him into sacrificing himself—trying, with time and effort, to wean Owen from his loyalty to the man who had killed his girlfriend and ruined his life. But according to Reggie, it had not been easy going.

The room we met in was bland, bare, windowless, and small, adorned with a single table and a few chairs, two of which were already occupied by Reggie and Owen when we were ushered in.

It was odd meeting Owen after all this time. The first and last time I'd seen him was in the middle of a snowstorm when we'd all been dying of hypothermia. Despite his importance in my life since then, he'd almost become an abstraction. Watching him sitting there now—pale, thin, and nervous—helped reduce all our machinations to a pathetically human level.

Introductions were made all around. No one bothered shaking hands. Owen didn't look like he had the energy for it, anyhow.

Gail placed a tape recorder on the table and depressed the record button, raising her eyebrows at Reggie. He shrugged his agreement without comment.

Gail recited the time, date, location, and the names of everyone around the table, and then asked Reggie if his client had been apprised of the reasons for this meeting. Reggie stated that was the case.

It was then my turn to address Owen.

"I'm sorry for all the mumbo-jumbo," I began, "but with any luck, this'll be the beginning of the end of this mess for you. They treating you all right in here?"

"It's okay."

"Good. Would you like a smoke or something to drink while we're doing this?"

He shook his head.

"Okay. We want to hear about your relationship with Walter Freund and how it led to what happened in Brenda Croteau's home the night she died. Why don't you start with Walter?"

Owen's eyes hadn't moved from the tabletop from the time we'd entered the room, and they stayed there now. "We were friends. I thought he wanted to help me out."

"How?"

"Just doin' stuff. I have a hard time that way. I don't see everything real clear in my head. He explained things."

"Like what happened to Lisa?"

"Yeah—later."

"Long after she died, you mean?"

"Yeah."

"How long? Months? Years?"

"Years. He told me he didn't want me to know at first, 'cause it wouldn't bring her back, and he didn't want to make me more unhappy. But he knew she'd been murdered all along, and he told me when he found out who'd done it."

"Is this what he told you, or what you still believe now?" I asked carefully.

He shook his head. "I know what happened now. He lied to me. He killed Lisa to foul me up."

"Is this something you know for a fact? Or is it something that's been told to you, and you think might be the truth?"

I noticed McNeil getting restless, but Owen beat him to it, looking up at me, open and guileless. "I know what you're thinking. I'm not too smart and I let people push me around. I know they all think I'm stupid, but I have a brain, and I see stuff, and I can figure things out. I see what Walter did. I believed him then, but I know he lied to me. He used me to kill Brenda like he'd use a car to run her down."

I was impressed. Reggie had done his work well. "Let's focus on the period leading up to that. Walter told you he'd discovered that Brenda had poisoned Lisa's dope. Did he say why she'd done it?"

"Just that she was a crazy bitch—that Lisa had stolen her boyfriend from her once, and she'd wanted revenge. Walter made her sound like a real nutcase—a hooker, a doper, a blackmailer, a thief. He used all sorts of words to put her down. Made her sound like scum."

"How did the subject of killing her come up?"

"We were getting pretty blown. That part's a little fuzzy. I remember being in Walter's office—that's what he called it—and him asking me if the world wouldn't be better off without people like her. Next thing I know, we were talking about how to do it. He talked a bunch about Lisa and how sweet she was. It really got me mad. I mean, I know it was wrong, but I really did hate Brenda then. Walter told me it wasn't a one-shot thing with her, either—that she'd done this junk to other people. Like a bloodsucker. He kept asking me, what do you do to a bloodsucker?"

He paused. He was back to addressing the table. "I don't really remember going there—just standing in her kitchen door, hearing her yell at me. I accused her of killing Lisa, and she started calling me names—puttin' me down like everybody does. But I kept hearing Walter in my head, too, telling me to shut her up. He told me she'd be like that, and he was right . . . It wasn't till she hit me that I grabbed the knife. It was just lying there. And then she went down. And I ran."

"Hit you how? With her fist?"

"No. She slapped me."

"Let's back up a little," I suggested. "If you went there to kill her, didn't you have your own knife?"

"I couldn't find it. Walter gave it to me, but I didn't have it in the house. I knew then I'd left it in the truck. But when I looked later, it wasn't there, either."

"And you have no recollection of how you got to Brenda's house? You don't remember driving there?"

He shook his head.

"Is it possible you were driven there by Walter?"

He looked up a second time, briefly. "I don't know. They're whole parts of that night that're just gone—

like they didn't exist. I dream about it sometimes, but that doesn't help either, 'cause the faces get mixed up. I have one where I'm hitting Lisa with the knife."

"In those memories, Owen—the real ones, not the dreams—how do you see Brenda? What's she doing to protect herself?"

"I dunno. Holding her hands up." He shuddered suddenly. "I don't like thinking about it."

"You've got to, though. You know you did this."

Reggie McNeil stirred slightly in protest and I nodded to him. "Owen, how much blood do you remember? Was it spurting all over, or just running out like it would from a cut?"

"There was a lot of it. I don't remember spurting."

"And when you left, was she still alive?"

"She was still yelling at me, down on the floor."

"Yelling?"

He equivocated. "Maybe not yelling. She was crying. She sounded real scared. The anger was all gone." His voice cracked at that last comment, and he lapsed into silence.

"Think back to the last memory you have of her, on the floor. Is she surrounded by blood? What does it look like on the floor?"

He gave me a baffled stare. "I don't know. Splotches—like when you cut something real bad."

"Not a big pool?"

"No—just a whole bunch of spots."

"Okay. Let's back up again. You said Walter called Brenda a blackmailer, along with everything else. Did he say who she was blackmailing, or why?"

He shook his head.

"And you also mentioned an office. Where was that?"

"Where the Dirty Dollar is, on the top floor. Nobody knows about it. It's not really an office. It's full of old junk. Walter just called it that. We'd meet there and talk. Sometimes, when I was in a jam, he'd let me sleep there, too. That was kind of fun."

"Was it was just you and Walter who knew about this place?"

"And Billy. I saw him there once, when I was leaving. He was coming upstairs."

"Billy?"

"Yeah. Billy Conyer."

I stood in the doorway of Walter's office—an abandoned, dusty corner room, mostly filled with old broken furniture, dilapidated shelf units, and piled boxes of unused municipal forms apparently stashed there by some neophyte clerk of the 1950s who'd overordered by tenfold and chosen to bury his sins.

In a corner, under two grimy windows, was a cluster of blankets, ratty pillows, two seats torn from a car, and a scattering of pornographic books, magazines, and some crumpled newspapers. The floor was littered with cigarette butts, used Kleenexes, stray pieces of clothing, and clumps of ancient accumulated dirt.

Willy, J.P., and two uniformed officers were just finishing their examination of it all.

"Find anything?" I asked.

"Nice timing," Willy cracked. "You show up to offer a hand?"

J.P. snapped off his latex gloves and neatly put them in his pocket. "Pretty much what you see," he said with an uncharacteristic smile. "There're some more clothes and dirty books in a carton, and we found a cashbox—

open and empty. Walter might've cleaned it out before he disappeared."

I glanced out the windows at Brattleboro's flat-topped skyline, rendered by the dust to look like an ancient photograph of some gritty industrial town. "Willy," I asked, "did you ever hear back from the lab on Billy's personal effects?"

"Like fingerprints on the banknotes? Yup, but none matching anything on file. And the rest didn't come to anything, either—rent receipts and bills, and a letter demanding back payment for some hundred-dollar wreck on wheels."

It sounded like a wash, but I sensed from the good mood of both men that they were holding something back. I entered the room and walked over to the carton J.P. had mentioned that contained more clothing and books. I kicked back one of the flaps with my foot and peered inside. "So what's the punch line here, guys?"

"Right here," J.P. said, obviously pleased with himself.

I turned to see him dangling an evidence bag by one corner, swinging it back and forth. "And that is?"

He smiled. "A bloodstained T-shirt. If there's a God, it'll match someone we know."

"Just heard from the lab. The blood on the T-shirt belongs to Phil Resnick, and the shirt's the right size and has trace evidence linking it to Walter Freund. You'll love this—the DNA you collected from him matches the sweat stains from the armpits."

I was sitting in a borrowed chair in the squad room, opposite the two cubicles occupied by Ron and Willy.

As I spoke, I fiddled with a rubber band I'd found on the floor.

"I suppose Walter could've used Billy like he did Owen, brain-jamming him to participate in Resnick's killing, but I kind of doubt it. Billy struck me as more of a fellow traveler. Owen was a plaything—a mouse to Walter's cat."

"You don't use a mouse as a hit man," Willy said doubtfully.

"You might if you're feeling too exposed," I countered. "A three-time loser on parole—and the T-shirt tells us Walter already had one body on his slate. In theory, Owen could've been the perfect remote-control killer—he'd do the job, get caught, and clam up out of loyalty to the only friend he has left in the world. Walter would be in the clear because nobody would think to connect him to it. It must have really bummed him out when he realized Owen had left the Bowie knife in the truck."

"No shit," Willy agreed. "So Walter went in after Owen peeled out of there—throwing the kitchen knife into the bushes—finished Brenda off, ransacked the place looking for whatever it was she was blackmailing him with, tore out the journal pages with his name, and split, leaving the lights on behind him, and the kid to freeze to death."

"With one additional detail," I said. "She would've survived otherwise. The ME's pretty confident the kitchen knife only inflicted the lesser wounds. That's why Owen only remembers splotches of blood, instead of the huge pool we found. Walter's problem was he had to kill her, but he couldn't get close enough without getting scratched."

"Which probably pissed him off enough that he almost decapitated her," Willy finished.

"It explains the savagery Owen lacks," I agreed.

"But it still leaves us not knowing what she was holding over him," Ron said, ever the pragmatist.

"Yeah," I mused. "The way he went through the place, it must've had a physical form, like a recording or a picture—maybe a document. It had to be more than just the journal, since that was on the desk out in the open. But we could be putting too much faith in that. She might've just known something about him."

"Then why tear the house apart?"

"To make sure there wasn't anything more, like another journal or some pictures. He couldn't afford the smallest link between them, especially now that his plan with Owen had gone wrong."

"There was the empty cashbox at his hideout," Willy pointed out. "Maybe he hid whatever he stole from her in that."

"Or maybe it just had cash." I fooled with the rubber band some more in silence and then changed tack: "At least we have an idea *what* she was blackmailing him about, even if we don't know how."

"Resnick's murder," Ron suggested.

"Right. If Brenda knew about that, it not only explains why he killed her, but why he tried to use a surrogate to do it."

"How did she know he killed Resnick?" Willy asked rhetorically.

I steepled my fingers in front of my mouth, the rubber band looped loosely around them. "Okay, let's go back—Billy, Walter, and somebody else knock Resnick senseless. Where we don't know, but presumably wherever he went after leaving the truck—or somewhere he could take care of those burns. That's the first place she might've seen them."

"Hold it," Willy said, as if glimpsing a vague light far off. "Why go so far back? How many people did we talk to who saw the three of them at the tracks? Half a dozen. Why couldn't Brenda have been there, too? She knew Walter. She might've recognized him by the way he walked or something."

"She didn't show up in the canvass," Ron countered.

Willy smiled broadly, suddenly looking very self-satisfied. "She was a hooker, right?"

Ron's mouth opened, but I answered for him. "And the four guys at the poker party were celebrating a birthday."

The sense of epiphany we all shared at that split second totally eclipsed from my mind that one of those four had been Sammie's Andy Padgett.

James Lyon didn't look comfortable, which suited me fine. He sat in the small interrogation room we had tucked into a corner of our bailiwick, facing the one-way mirror with his hands in his lap. He had nothing to read, no one to talk to, and no window to look out of. He'd been sitting in there for forty-five minutes, during which I'd periodically come out of my office, stepped into the closet-sized viewing room, and checked on his psychological progress.

I liked what I was seeing. Of the four poker players who had been interviewed following Phil Resnick's death, Lyon was the one Willy Kunkle had described as nervous. If we were right about what had gone on that night—in addition to the card game—I could now understand why. Andy Padgett was unattached—or had been up till then—Frankie Harris had been one of

Brenda's regular customers, Don Carter had the longest rap sheet and was therefore presumably a hard-ass, but Lyon—married, with kids, and as clean as a whistle—was another matter entirely. If anything untoward had occurred at that party, Lyon was going to tell us about it.

Eventually, I opened the door and stepped inside to face him.

I parked myself on the edge of the table, my eyes glued to an open file. "James Lyon," I pretended to read, my voice grim, "married, three kids, age thirty, you've worked at Span-Lastic for the past five years. No record, no parking tickets—says here you play on the softball team, too. All-American boy." I finally looked at him. "How long you been married, Jim?"

He swallowed hard. "I, ah . . . guess eight years."

"You guess?" I laughed harshly. "I thought you were supposed to know that stuff—get into trouble otherwise. Is it eight years or not?"

"Yes," he said hesitantly, and then added, "Why have I been brought here?"

I didn't answer him. "Eight years, three kids. Place must be like a nuthouse when you get home. Your wife easy to get along with?" I glanced back at the file, "Sherry?"

"Sure, and the kids aren't bad."

I raised my eyebrows. "A glowing report. In my line of work, that usually means a cover-up. You hiding something?"

He opened his mouth to answer, but I cut him off. "Tell me how long you've known Frankie and the boys. You play poker together often?"

He flushed red and stammered, "N-no. That was the first time I'd done it."

"Done it? Done what?"

"Play . . . cards."

I smiled. "Wasn't sure what you meant there for a second. Four guys out at a bachelor birthday party. One thing leads to another."

"We just played poker."

I looked at him for a long, measured ten seconds and then went back to the file. "Right. So how come you got invited?"

"I know Don Carter from softball. They'd asked somebody else for the card game, but he couldn't make it. I said I'd go to even things out. Sherry said it would be okay."

I nodded. "Well, I guess if we had to, we could ask her about that. She know you're down here?"

"No. She thinks I'm still at work." He feigned looking at his watch, although his shirtsleeve covered half its face. "I ought to be getting back, too. Did you want to ask me something about that man getting killed?"

I placed the file on the table, crossed my arms, and stared at him. "I want to know about the poker party."

He made a pointed effort to maintain eye contact, but I could see his Adam's apple working hard. "What about it?" he asked, his voice almost breaking.

"I want to know what happened besides card playing."

"We drank a little. It was a birthday."

"Any gifts?"

He hesitated. "There was a bottle—"

"Who from?"

His fingertips nervously brushed his chin. "I think it was Andy."

"What did Frankie bring?"

Sweat began to appear high on his forehead. "Frankie? I'm not sure—"

I interrupted again, "I'm sorry. I should've asked, *who* did Frankie bring?"

He just watched me.

I leaned over so my face was inches from his. "Jim, either talk to me now or talk to Sherry tonight. Does the name Brenda Croteau ring a bell, or was your hand too good to notice her?"

Interrogations are a little like dancing with a blind date—lots of preliminary subtle body language establishing boundaries and intentions. Jim Lyon made it easy—he merely doubled over sobbing.

I watched his trembling curved back for a moment, before announcing quietly but clearly, "Okay, time to come clean. I like what you tell me, this whole conversation stops here. Your choice."

He wiped his eyes with his fingers and took a couple of deep, shuddering breaths. "I'm really sorry I didn't tell you before. We were worried we'd get into trouble—that *I'd* get into trouble. I had the most to lose, being married and everything. They did it for me."

"Lied, you mean?"

"Yeah. We couldn't believe it—all you people suddenly there asking questions. It was like a nightmare. And I'd only said I'd go at the last minute. It was unbelievable."

I kept my voice at a monotone to try to calm him down. "Was it Frankie who brought her to the party?"

"Yes. You were right. She was Don's gift. Frankie even had her wear a red bow around her neck. I didn't know anything about it till they walked in. I wanted to get the hell out of there as soon as I saw her, but then I thought, how would I explain it to Sherry? I was stuck."

"Did you also figure, what the hell? And sample some of the goods?"

He looked genuinely horrified and began to fidget in his chair. "Oh, my God, no. That's what I was worried about. I'm totally screwed now, if word gets out. There's no fucking way anyone's going to believe me."

I placed a hand on his sweat-dampened shoulder. "Relax. You're doing fine so far. Don't fall apart on me. Tell me what happened, and in what sequence."

He worked to control himself. "Frankie got there late, I guess on purpose, to make a big entrance, and she was like I said, wearing that bow. There was a lot of laughing and drinking and talk, and after a while, Don and her went into the bedroom down the hall."

"And the rest of you did what?"

"We played cards and talked and drank . . . watched TV. Finally Don came back—"

"About when?"

"I'm not sure. After midnight, I think. I was so nervous, I sort of overdid it with the booze."

"Okay, so Don came back."

"Right, and then Frankie went to the bedroom to . . . you know."

"How long did that last?"

"I fell asleep around then. They woke me up to play cards—I don't know what time. The girl was gone. And the next thing that happened was you people came in asking questions about the guy who got killed by the train."

"And you saw nothing of that?"

His eyes grew wide. "I didn't lie there. And I swear I'm not lying now. That's everything I know."

"How about cooking up your cover story?"

He flushed again. "I'm sorry. That's right. Frankie

did see something through the window. Not the murder—just something he said was weird. And later, when the cops—I mean the police—were going door-to-door, we heard them coming. That's when Frankie figured what he'd seen must've been pretty bad. So we came up with the all-night poker story. We didn't know anything—Frankie told you the truth there. We didn't see fessing up to having had a hooker would make any difference. It would just cause trouble."

"You must've read about her in the paper when she was killed," I said, not bothering to hide my contempt.

"We were scared shitless. We talked on the phone about it—about going to the police and telling them what we knew. But what *did* we know? I caught hell from Sherry as it was when I got home. This could've ended my marriage." He paused and drew a long face. "Might still end it."

I rose to my feet, finally tiring of his self-involvement. "Not unless you tell her, Jim. I'm cutting you loose. I will tell you one thing, though—it's for her sake and the kids that I won't blow the whistle. Your covering your own sorry butt cuts so close to interfering with a police investigation, it barely shows daylight, and if I ever hear of you stepping out of line again—in any way, shape, or form—I'm going to make it my business that everyone finds out about this little conversation. Clear?"

He stood shakily, his shoulders stooped, and nodded miserably, which only made me want to kick him in the ass. "Yes, sir."

"Get the hell out of here."

He preceded me out of the door and disappeared. I stayed behind to slide his chair back under the table and turn off the light, and when I pulled the door shut behind me, I saw Sammie standing in the darkened viewing room, leaning against the wall, her face as still as stone.

"You been there long?"

"Long enough."

I scratched the back of my neck. "What're you going to do?"

"What do you think?"

I saw her point. Maintaining a love affair with a man who had kept vital evidence from the police, not to mention flat-out lied to her, would have been a little much to expect. I couldn't have done it in her place.

"You want the rest of the day off?"

"I don't know."

I stepped into the small room. "Get it over now, Sam. Go see him, clear the air, and then come over to my place later. We'll get a pizza or something, have a few beers, and talk about what shits men can be. Gail'll pitch in—I promise."

She tried to smile. "Thanks, Joe. I'll see how it goes."

I watched her walk into the squad room, grab her coat, and leave, moving like an exhausted, shell-shocked soldier. She was possibly the best cop I'd ever worked with—committed, passionate, driven to out-perform everyone around her. It almost broke my heart to see her served this way—the one time she'd taken a chance on a small bit of happiness.

Chapter Twenty-six

Gail, of course, had been right. Mark Mullen, Vermont's speaker of the House, following his supportive and glowing speech about law and order and the Reynolds Bill, immediately set about taking the latter apart, piece by piece.

He did this in time-honored fashion, spreading the responsibility far and wide among his colleagues, vowing he was improving the Senate's work by giving it the thorough and careful review it deserved.

At least his method was original. He pushed a resolution through the House creating a special committee—traditionally an advisory group—with full authorization to act in place of all the standing committees that would normally consider such a bill. Thus, instead of trying to manipulate several dozen people sitting on Appropriations, Judiciary, Government Ops, and the rest, Mullen simply handpicked a few representatives from each—and from both parties—and appointed them to the study committee. Their job was to analyze the bill, listen to testimony supporting and decrying it, and eventually report to the House membership for a full vote.

On the surface, it was both practical and efficient. It was also a good way for Mullen to maintain near-total control.

Once again, I was asked to Montpelier to act as an expert witness, which I only hoped I could do with total impartiality. As the months had slipped by, the law enforcement "super agency" bill had been sharply debated across the state, and my earlier desire to keep an open mind had begun to erode.

In this I was hardly alone. If nothing else, Reynolds had given birth to a genuine hot potato. In radio commentaries, newspaper editorials, and squad rooms across Vermont, this topic had been bandied around with passion and prejudice, and with little general agreement. Most interesting, however, no one had been seen rallying around the status quo. They couldn't agree on what exactly was broken, but everyone agreed it needed fixing.

It was a custom-made void for Mark Mullen and his ambitions, whatever end strategy he might have been considering.

Mullen had made of himself a living local legend—although one whose grasp on power was at a crucial juncture. Born outside Barre forty-five years ago, the youngest of two sons of a quarryman father, he'd been elected to the House while still in his early twenties and had stayed there ever since, eventually sitting on most of the committees, and finally—though a member of the minority party that year—being elected speaker, a quirky phenomenon almost unique to Vermont, and one the Republicans had since come to rue.

At the time, however, his selection had been no surprise. An instinctive consensus builder and a genuine "people person," Mullen paid minimal attention to party lines, orchestrating the Legislature less from the podium and more by intimate personal contract, although naturally most often to the advantage of the Democrats.

His early reign had not been without controversy—with predictable accusations of favoritism and grandstanding—but lately it had smoothed out to the point of becoming bland. His influence had begun to pall. Mullen's creation of this special committee, instead of letting the Reynolds Bill loose among the standing committees, had struck many as the action of a man both doubtful of his old clout and transparently eager to make a big splash.

My drive to Montpelier this time was very different from before, when the snow and recent ice had turned the countryside into a crystal palace. Now a strong feeling of change was pervasive in the countryside—the unlocking season, as some called it, was nigh—when winter's frozen grip began yielding to something just shy of spring.

This wouldn't have been the case during the legislative sessions of yore. Back then, the State House had called it quits by early April, so the mostly farmer/lawmakers could return to their fields and maybe get in a little late sugaring if they were lucky or lived up north. But times had changed and The Bill, as some sorrowful legislators were calling it, had delayed things even more, so that nobody was placing bets on when they'd be going home.

But while the mood in the State House was souring, its crush of humanity had steadfastly remained the same. The hallways were as crammed with people an inordinately large number of them in uniform the sense of tension was as palpable as befor

I was supposed to meet with the study c

one, but found that the schedule had gone routinely off track. So I located an old and decorous chair, tucked under the wing of one of the building's two sweeping staircases, and prepared for a long wait.

A tall, thin, angular man wearing a suit and a tangled mop of dark hair slid into the chair next to mine—Commissioner of Public Safety David Stanton.

"Hi, Joe," he said, leaning over to shake hands. "Long time."

"Yup." I gestured at the stream of people passing before us. "You pretty pleased with what you set in motion?"

Still smiling, he watched me closely. "I set in motion?"

"Reynolds wouldn't have started all this without the governor's blessing, and Howie wouldn't have given it without consulting you. That makes you the logical choice for the next Secretary of Criminal Justice."

"He consulted me, sure," Stanton agreed coyly, ignoring my conclusion. "But this is Reynolds's baby. Not mine."

"Oh-oh—that mean you're looking to jump ship?"

He laughed. "You're worse than the news guys. I have no idea where this is headed."

"I'm not against it heading somewhere," I said to reassure him. "And I never expected the Legislature *not* to tie it up in knots. But I was thinking as I drove here that the debate's been pretty interesting— up a few closets a lot of people might've liked

heriffs?"

ly—all that local control baloney. I've those official press releases about interagency cooperation compared to the real thing. This has ripped off some of the camouflage."

Stanton cut me a look. "Sounding pretty cynical, there, Joe."

I shook my head. "I'm happy it's getting shaken up—long overdue. I just hope things don't end up exactly where they were."

He stared at the floor, nodding silently in agreement.

I became aware of a shadow to my left, and turned to find a young page awkwardly standing by my chair. "What's up?"

"Are you Mr. Gunther?"

I admitted as much.

"Speaker Mullen would like to meet you in his office."

Stanton laughed softly. "Watch your step there, Joe."

I got up and patted his shoulder. "You, too. For what's it worth, I think you'd be good in that job."

I followed the page upstairs to the second floor, through the vast, empty House chamber with its brilliant red carpeting and enormous bronze chandelier festooned with statues of nude women, snakes, and eagles. We climbed the low stage at the front, circled the carved, pulpitlike speaker's podium, and almost ducked under a large, low-hung portrait of George Washington into a narrow hallway connecting the old building to a new addition housing a modern cafeteria and Mark Mullen's office.

There, barricaded behind a small reception area guarded by a secretary, I found the speaker stretched out across an old leather tilt-back chair, his feet planted on his antique desk, talking on the phone. He smiled as the page faded away, waved me to a chair, and quickly wrapped up his conversation.

He then rose, leaned over, shook hands, and said, "Joe Gunther. I'm sorry we've never met till now. Heard a lot about you. Appreciated what you said when the Senate called you in. You want some coffee?"

"I'm fine, thanks."

"I'm also sorry we had to drag you up here again, but I told 'em I didn't think we could do this thing justice if we didn't get some of the brains in on it they'd had the first time around."

"There going to be big changes?" I asked innocently.

He didn't duck. "Count on it. You don't throw out over two hundred years of tradition without pissing a few people off. Reynolds was living in a dream world if he thought otherwise. You two buddy-buddy?"

"Hardly."

"Good, 'cause he's in for a wake-up. The Senate has no idea what's going on in this state. They see a few dead babies, all the headlines, they run a poll, and next thing you know, they're talking about a mandate from the people. It's a joke. The people don't know any more about the problem than they do. It is a problem—I know that just like you do—but to solve it, you need expert advice, to find out what you can do and what you can't. Simple as that—and hard as that, too. People don't take kindly to politicians saying, 'This is the way it's going to be.' You gotta give 'em a sense they're part of the process." He paused and then smiled. "But, shit. You know all that. What do you think we ought to do?"

I had to hand it to him. He was affable, gregarious, informal, and inviting—a very likeable mix—and very unlike his rival in the Senate. He also spoke with the practical assurance of a veteran, and left his listeners thinking they were dealing with a man who would use the tools at hand to get the job done. The amount of Mullen's blarney probably didn't differ much from Reynolds's, but it was a lot more pleasant to listen to.

"So you agree with Reynolds that a big change needs to happen?"

"You kidding? That's the downside of two hundred years of tradition—it's two hundred years old." He laughed. "Sure it's screwed up—everybody guarding his own little patch of dirt. Dumber than hell. But how do you change it?"

I realized it wasn't a rhetorical question. "Maybe shoot for the middle ground? Somewhere between seventy agencies and one. And standardize communications and procedures so we all play out of the same book. I don't really know, either," I admitted uncomfortably, "but it's pretty clear the more we share, the better off we are. Programs like CUSI, NUSI, and single dispatch centers like the one in Chittenden County could be used as models."

He was nodding vigorously. "Right, right. That's it. Use what we got as examples. That way, law enforcement's leading its own instead of being pushed into something by a bunch of politicians."

The same page who'd escorted me here reappeared in the doorway.

"They want him downstairs?" Mullen asked, jumping to his feet.

"Yes, sir."

He shook my hand again as I headed out. "Give 'em all you got, Joe. No time to hold back. Good talking to you."

With that staccato pep talk echoing in my ears, I followed my skinny guide back through the building, this time to the second floor of the north wing, where the House held its hearings.

It had been an odd encounter to no apparent purpose, although I was conscious of feeling that, like a bull going up for auction, I'd just been given the once-over by the money behind the bidders.

I returned to Brattleboro that evening, after two hours with the study committee. The experience had been appropriately more chaotic than during my encounter with the senators, since the contradictory special interests had finally broken cover to wield their influence. But one thing I did come away with was the conviction that Reynolds's clean if simpleminded bill would reemerge as a shredded shadow of its previous self.

The car phone went off as I was nearing the interstate's Putney exit, north of Brattleboro.

It was Ron. "Looks like that intel meeting you attended a few months ago paid off," he said. "I just got a call from Budd Sheeney in Hinsdale. He's been showing Resnick's picture around since you handed it out, and he thinks he might've found something. He's being a little coy—probably worried we'll steal the credit unless he talks to you himself."

I sighed at the mentality, memories of where I'd just left fresh in my mind. "Where is he?"

"I didn't know where you were, so I didn't set anything up."

"Call him back. I'm fifteen minutes out. I'll drop by the station, pick you up if you want, and we can go straight to him."

"Don't worry about it," he answered. "I don't need to come. I'll get back to you with a location."

I was almost in Brattleboro when the phone buzzed again. "Hinsdale High School parking lot," Ron said. "He'll be waiting for you."

Hinsdale, New Hampshire, is right across the river from Brattleboro, so integrally linked to it that the relationship is essentially symbiotic—they have a greyhound racetrack that our citizens regularly patronize, while our Putney Road commercial strip—complete with a sales tax New Hampshire has so far avoided—still serves as their primary shopping place. The best example of this close tie can be found with the local Wal-Mart. When Vermont was making a stance as the nation's only Wal-Mart-free state, the company defiantly planted an outlet within view on the Hinsdale side of the Connecticut River. Over time, not only has such proximity not gutted Brattleboro's downtown, but Wal-Mart had been forced to ask its rival's board of selectmen to accept the residue of a slipshod, malfunctioning sewer system instead of trucking it daily to who-knew-where. Brattleboro had politely refused.

The actual village of Hinsdale lies several miles southeast of the bridge—a quiet, none-too-prosperous town, once dominated by the quasi-obligatory nineteenth century mill and now looking for a substitute cash cow to help it survive. Home of several substantial trailer parks and mile upon mile of residential roads, Hinsdale had become a bedroom community for those looking for less expensive housing and New Hampshire's lighter touch in the taxation department.

The high school was located just north of the village, at the back of a broad expanse of fields and parking lots. There, reflective under one of the bright sodium lights, was a marked cruiser, its muffler emitting a tenuous plume of vapor. I pulled up next to it, nose-to-tail, and rolled down my window to talk to Budd Sheeney, elbow-to-elbow.

"How're you doing, Joe? You didn't waste any time."

Budd was a large man in his forties—big-bellied, broad-shouldered, sporting the straight bristle mustache so common to police officers. A Hinsdale boy from birth, he'd gone straight from the school surrounding us to the police department and had been there ever since. He knew everybody as though they were blood-related, and was as comfortable in this community as a bullfrog in a pond.

"I was just coming into town when Ron called me," I answered. "I hear you have something on Phil Resnick."

"I got a tickle, yeah. Wasn't sure how high that was on your list anymore."

I didn't know if I should believe that, but I didn't see any harm in letting him play Santa Claus. "Pretty high, Budd. I'd appreciate any help you can give us."

"Not a problem," he answered casually. "It's one of those guy-who-knows-a-guy things, though, and I haven't checked it out. But according to my source, someone looking like Resnick was seen at Sandy Corcoran's place around the time you're interested in."

"What makes you think it was Resnick?" I asked.

"You said he might've been burned. Supposedly, this one's face and hands looked like one big blister."

That stopped me. I remembered the ME saying that the chloracne reaction to the chemicals would have taken several days to develop—and that at the time of exposure, Resnick probably wouldn't have done much more than wipe the stuff off without giving it a thought. "You have a precise date on this sighting?"

Sheeney shook his head. "The reference I got was 'a few days before' you found that body, whatever that means. Supposedly the guy was seen looking out of one of Sandy's windows."

"Sounds good," I said. "What's the story with Sandy Corcoran?"

"Standard bad girl, but no headline-maker. She's been clean for about eight months. Did a little time for drunk and disorderly back then, when she took a bottle to her boyfriend's head—not that he noticed or cared. But it was in the racetrack parking lot, so we had to do something about it."

I thought for a moment. "Okay. Could you round up a search warrant? I want to be able to move on her with full guns when the time comes. I'll have Ron call you tomorrow to coordinate. That okay?"

Sheeney nodded gravely, now officially integrated. "You got it."

Sandy Corcoran lived in a small, peeling house on Route 63 heading out of Hinsdale village. Neither in town nor in the suburbs, it hung like a tattered thread on the border, near a couple of others like it, just shy of where the road opened up to countryside and woods.

When I parked the car a hundred yards below it and killed my lights, it was almost seven o'clock the night following my talk with Sheeney. Willy and J.P. were in the car with me. Sammie had taken a few days off and hadn't been seen or heard from since.

I saw Budd Sheeney's bulk loom up ahead of us, his outline caught by the dim lights from the house behind him.

He crouched by my door as I rolled down the window. "She's inside, alone. Got back from work about an hour ago. I have a man watching the rear."

"Then let's get going," Willy said, and swung out of the car.

We walked quietly up to the building's front porch, littered with the remnants of a winter's worth of cordwood, now reduced to a few logs and a dunelike pile of bark scraps. The air was still and surprisingly warm—a hopeful harbinger of long-awaited spring.

Sheeney knocked politely on the front door.

We heard footsteps against a backdrop of TV noise, and a shadow passed across the curtain next to us. "Who is it?"

The voice was neither soft nor fearful. I remembered the comment about Sandy laying a bottle across her boyfriend's head.

"It's Budd Sheeney, Sandy. Wondered if we could talk to you."

The door swung open, splashing us with light. Before us stood a tall, muscular, statuesque black-haired woman, dressed in tight jeans and a tank top. Her feet were bare and her eyes hard. She had a tattoo of an eagle on her well-muscled shoulder. "Who's we?"

Budd gestured in our direction. I answered, "Joe Gunther—Brattleboro Police. We're investigating a homicide, and thought maybe you could help us."

"I haven't killed anybody."

"No one said you did, Sandy," Budd said. "Can we come in?"

"It's not that cold. We can talk here."

I took the warrant Budd had handed me earlier and gave it to her. "We'd like it better inside."

She took it from me but didn't bother opening it. She stepped back. "You fucking guys."

We took that as an invitation and filed past her into a cluttered living room, piled with clothes, several old pizza boxes, and an assortment of cast-aside magazines. The walls were decorated with Harley and rock star posters, a plastic cat clock, and an out-of-date calendar advertising a beach in Hawaii.

"I got nothing to say, you know?" she continued. "And I don't know shit from any homicides." She pointed at Sheeney and smirked. "Ask him. He watches me enough of the time. He could probably tell you more about what I done than I could."

"How 'bout the night of January sixth?" I asked, ignoring that Sheeney had actually blushed a bit, "when the body of Phil Resnick was found on the railroad tracks in Brattleboro?"

The only reaction I registered was a slight hesitation in her answer. "I don't know nothin' about that." She then followed with more bluster, pointing at J.P. and Willy, who were quietly poking around the room, heading off elsewhere into the house. "What the hell do you think you're doin'?"

I walked over to the TV and switched it off. "Read the warrant, Ms. Corcoran. We're here because a judge agrees that you're up to your neck in trouble. Have a seat." I motioned toward the couch.

"Eat shit," she said.

"Your choice," I continued. "We happen to know Phil Resnick was brought here shortly before he was murdered. When he was dumped on the tracks, he was already unconscious, probably because he'd been hit on the head." I made a show of pausing a moment before adding, "Which is something you like to do, don't you? Beaned your boyfriend not long before Resnick got his. State's attorney will like that pattern."

"You're so full of shit," she said, but I thought her enthusiasm was beginning to flag.

"Not this time." I jerked my thumb over my shoulder. "You know what they're looking for?"

"Whatever it is, they won't find it."

"Not a single drop of blood?" I asked. "Not a fingerprint? What about his clothes? He was dressed like a bum when we found him. You don't strike me as the neatest person around. If you forgot to remove, or vacuum, or wipe off even the tiniest bit of evidence, we'll find it. After that, your life will be hell. Remember, we're across the state line here. This'll involve cops, prosecutors, and judges from both New Hampshire and Vermont if you don't play ball. You could spend a lot of time in jail."

She seemed to freeze a moment, then her face bunched up and she came at me, flying across the room like an enraged panther. Caught off guard, I braced myself for the worst.

But Budd Sheeney knew his people. Just as I was raising my hands to defend myself, Sheeney's massive bulk cut across my line of vision, enveloping Corcoran's body and whisking it away like a gust of wind might a leaf. They both landed with a tremendous crash against a side table, a tangle of arms and legs, wrestling and rolling on the floor until Sheeney was able to pin her face down and pull her arms up behind her back. Willy and J.P. appeared at separate doors, guns drawn, just as Budd was slapping on the cuffs, comfortably sitting on her muscular backside.

I squatted by her head. Her nostrils flaring, she sent up little puffs of dust from the floor with her breathing. "You assholes."

"Talk to us, Sandy. We got you on attempted assault. Won't be long before there's more, including murder. I can't believe it's worth it."

She closed her eyes briefly. When she reopened them, her voice was calm and measured. "If he's finished enjoying himself, get this ape off my butt and help me up."

Sheeney did the honors, smiling broadly, and steered Sandy Corcoran over to the couch, checking its cushions first for weapons.

She sat down with a wince, her hands pinched against her back. I settled opposite her on the coffee table. "Your choice."

She stared at me angrily. "He was here, but I had nothin' to do with killin' him."

"Who did?"

She hesitated. "Walter Freund."

I felt a small release valve open up inside my brain, and I fought the urge to smile, helped by a sudden concern. "You know where he is now?"

She shook her head. "I haven't seen him since that night. That was the deal. I didn't want any more to do with his bullshit."

"Tell me what happened."

"Take the cuffs off."

Sheeney laughed. "Not likely."

She flared back up. "I'm cooperating, all right? My wrists're killin' me. I already said I know what happened."

I glanced at Sheeney and nodded. He crossed over to her, reached behind her back, and undid the cuffs. She made herself more comfortable, rubbing her wrists. "Walter called me one night and said he needed to stash somebody for a while. We did each other favors now and then. The timing was okay, so I said fine. He shows up with this guy. His face is all red and puffed up and kind of slimy in places. His hands, too. It was disgusting. I told Walter to fuck off—that I wasn't no hospital. I thought it might be catching—all this shit you hear about in the news."

"Did it look like Walter was helping this man, or forcing him to be here?"

"He was helping him. The guy was hurtin', and complaining about some son-of-a-bitch who'd done it to him. Walter told me he'd been splashed with chemicals. They'd even raided a Salvation Army bin to replace his clothes. He looked like a bum."

"The son-of-a-bitch have a name?"

She smiled slightly. "That was it, far as I heard. What were those chemicals anyhow? I always wondered."

I ignored her. "Was Resnick threatening to get even?"

"He was pissed, all right. But he was too sick to do much about it."

"Was there any indication of where Resnick had been staying before Walter brought him to you?"

She looked at me curiously. "Before? I don't know anything about that."

"How did Walter get you to change your mind?"

She laughed. "He doubled the price. Plus he told me it wasn't catching. The damage had already been done."

"What happened then?"

"Nothing at first. He stayed here a couple of days, tried to take care of himself. I don't know 'cause I was at work."

"Did he use the phone?"

"That would've been a neat trick. I don't have one."

"What kind of shape was he in?" I pressed her. "Did you think he was going to die?"

Her eyes grew round. "Shit, no. He was burned, is all, like with scalding water or something. It hurt like a bitch. I did buy him some ointment I got at the store. He used a ton of that stuff, and either it helped or he just started getting used to the pain." She shook her head. "He was fine otherwise." She paused. "At least while I saw him. I mean, I know some of that crap'll really do you damage—cancer and what all—but that would've been later, right?"

"What happened to change things? Why did they go from helping him to killing him?"

"I don't know. That's why I told Walter we were done afterward. They showed up the next night and just popped him one with a hammer. Just like that. He went down like a dead cow. I mean, Jesus, one minute they're talkin', next minute they're draggin' his ass outta here like he was meat. I went ballistic."

"You keep saying, 'they'. Who did Walter have with him?"

"Some little shit. Called him Billy. I didn't know him."

"They kill the guy?"

"Not then they didn't. Billy asked Walter if they checked for a pulse. The guy was alive when they all left."

"That was it? There weren't three of them?"

"Nope." She began studying her nails.

I leaned forward slightly. "Don't quit on me now, Sandy. Who was the other man Walter brought with him?"

She suddenly gave up, staring me in the eye. "I never saw him. He stayed in the car. I figured he was Walter's boss, or at least someone who had something over him."

"Why's that?"

She looked contemptuous. "Well, for Christ's sake.

It ain't rocket science. Walter's already in deep shit—on parole and all. He didn't need to be poppin' people off. So he was pissed. When they were dragging the guy out of here, he kept bitchin' about how he didn't have a say in it—that he was stuck between a rock and a hard place. He wasn't a happy camper."

"Neither Walter nor Billy mentioned any names?"

"No. Billy was a moron, anyhow. Kept lookin' at my tits like he didn't know what they were. Probably didn't."

Sheeney laughed shortly. Sandy leered at him. "You do, don't you, though, lardass? Too bad you'll never get a piece of 'em."

"Sandy," I interrupted. "You were about to hold back a minute ago. Were you thinking you could still get something out of this—put the squeeze on this third man?"

She smiled ruefully. "Seemed worth a try."

"How were you going to find him?"

She shrugged. "Shit, I don't know. I figured find Walter, you find that guy, right? Worth a shot."

I couldn't argue the logic. "Right."

Chapter Twenty-seven

Sandy Corcoran's simple recipe for using Walter to find whoever had ordered Phil Resnick killed had one obvious, glaring flaw—and with our inability to locate Walter, our investigation finally rolled to a complete stop, despite a national distribution of his picture and description.

Happily, our misfortune wasn't contagious. Gail and McNeil finally found enough common ground to work out a deal. Owen Tharp agreed to a fifteen-years-to-life sentence for second-degree murder, making him eligible for parole in twelve years, which Jack Derby spun into a bragging point as the summer campaigning began picking up speed. In the face of a few media grumbles about Walter—as with a cartoon showing Derby à la Teddy Roosevelt with his foot on a dead rabbit, and a grizzly escaping over the horizon—the candidate merely blamed us for not getting our man. The press wasn't all that interested, in any case.

Tempers cooled between Gail and Derby also, allowing her to graciously serve notice that she'd be moving to the StayGreen job by summer's end, and with sad predictability the flight of Walter Freund and the fate of his two lower-class victims slipped off the front page.

Our squad was left to pursue all the deferred day-to-day business that had piled up when things were hot and to deal with the fact that, posturing aside, Derby had been right—we hadn't gotten our man. Not a week went by when we didn't meet to discuss Walter's open file—and to wonder what might be in it that we simply couldn't see.

And that wasn't our only aggravation, although it topped the list. As spring gave in to summer, the Reynolds Bill saga reached the level of comic opera, affecting every cop within the state along the way.

Mark Mullen's strategy of disassembling the bill and remaking it in his own image reached a climax in late May, when his special committee finally reported to a restless and bored Legislature that—aided by many witnesses, much thought, and the application of old-fashioned pragmatism—it had taken Reynolds's radical notion of replacing those sixty-eight agencies with a single cost-saving unit and had "amended" it by slapping on a sixty-ninth.

To be called the Vermont Bureau of Investigation— a dismissive nod to Reynolds that while his plan had been gutted, he'd come up with a great name—this new creation was to do what the Vermont state police's Bureau of Criminal Investigations had been doing for years for those communities lacking full-service departments. A loosely structured, minimally bureaucratic entity, VBI was to handle all so-called major crimes, including, among others, murder, rape, kidnapping, armed robbery, and arson with death resulting. Operated by the Department of Public Safety's now legislatively mandated and funded Criminal Justice Services, and reporting directly to the attorney general—who could at his discretion dole out prosecutions to the state's twelve state's attorneys—VBI was to have full reign throughout the state, directed by statute to assume responsibility of all major crime investigations, regardless of which other agency was handling them to begin with. Thus, from the state police down to the lowliest constable, everyone was to give the big cases to VBI. Agencies could keep their detective squads—the lesser-ranked crimes, of which there were plenty, would still need local addressing—the state police would maintain its BCI, and all uniformed forces would pretty much keep their traditional roles, with a renewed emphasis on community policing. Commissioner Stanton would not become a cabinet secretary.

In short, it was the ideal political solution, designed to look good on paper, sound good on the stump, and drive the people it affected the most totally insane. Not a single cop I knew liked it.

Not that Reynolds gave in without a murmur. Although the House okayed Mullen's compromise bill—largely because they were eager to get home to their jobs or start running for reelection—it still had to go to a conference committee, where Reynolds got to make his final pitch.

As his cherished bill had begun to unravel, he'd taken advantage of Mullen's transparent maneuvers to wrap himself in a martyr's cloak, decrying for weeks on end the death of common sense. So when the time came for three senators to meet with three representatives to hammer out the final bill, he offered himself for service. The Senate's president—also the lieutenant governor and another contender for Governor Howell's office—was the man whose job it was to make those three appointments. But while he couldn't in all decorum deny a slot to the chair of the Judiciary Committee—and the author of the original bill—he could and did saddle him with two Senate colleagues who sided with Mark Mullen's view of reality.

So, at five-against-one before the conference committee even met, the outcome was preordained. Reynolds was reduced to making one last speech to his colleagues in the Senate, mourning the loss of a potentially high-quality, well-trained, efficiently run organization to a disparate clutter of unevenly trained and experienced officers reporting to a crowd of over five dozen bosses. It was clear, brief, and delivered with great heart, and when he was finished, there was a genuine tang in the air of an opportunity missed despite all his listeners' knowing it really hadn't stood a chance from the start.

The new bill soon passed. VBI became law, the various bureaucrats in charge of it disappeared to turn it into reality, and all of us in law enforcement waited until January, when things were slated to come on line, and our fates to be decided.

The press kicked it around for weeks, first siding with Reynolds, then trying to predict the future, and eventually—tentatively—conceding that maybe Mullen hadn't been so self-serving after all. Echoing the speaker's own mantra that Reynolds had been hunting flies with an untested, high-cost artillery piece, editorials began agreeing that Mullen's proposal had cut to the root cause of the problem—the consolidation of resources and information for the purpose of solving major crimes. With time, the vision of a steely-eyed corps of bright, tough, statewide Untouchables began to take hold of the public's consciousness, overriding all concerns about how such a unit could be gracefully blended into a profession famous for its inbred sense of turf.

In the end, along with everybody else in the department, I yielded to the resigned fatalism common to all military-style organizations. I remembered with irony that Jim Reynolds himself had told me early on that in the long run, the cops would do as they were told.

Acceptance of all this was made easier by improvements at home. With Gail coming to terms about her future, she seemed to slip free of the rape's last tentacles. She was happier, felt freer to wander and quicker to laugh, and suddenly found time in the day to relax and have fun. Not wanting to miss any of this, I left work whenever I could, and Gail and I took advantage of the early warm weather to go for walks, drives, and hikes, and started—in leisurely fashion—looking for some bachelor digs for me. The whole experience—with a few minor stumbles along the way—brought both of us back emotionally to where we'd been years before.

It also made watching Sammie Martens that much harder.

She hadn't had any choice but to break up with Andy Padgett. As she saw it, he'd violated a moral code she used as her primary guide. But her commitment to what he'd represented had been deep, and his betrayal had hit her hard. After returning from an accumulation of sick days and vacation time, she'd gone back to work like an automaton—regularly, predictably, and utterly without spirit. Willy, protectively out of earshot, if with no more sensitivity, complained it was like working with the living dead.

I began hoping either for a break in the Walter Freund case or another to replace it, just so I could give her something to sink her teeth into.

About halfway through the summer, I got my wish.

I was standing in my office, tidying up before day's end. The windows were open, the warm air was steady and clear, and I was looking forward to renting a Sunfish and sailing with Gail on a nearby lake.

Until J.P. walked in, a broad smile on his face.

"What're you so happy about?" I asked him.

"This." He held up the semiautomatic we'd recovered from Billy Conyer the night he'd died. "I've been going over every scrap of evidence we have—checking fingerprints we hadn't bothered with, running records of everybody we talked to, staring at witness statements till I was blue in the face. I knew there had to be something we hadn't thought of."

I pointed at the gun, all too familiar with what he'd been going through. "And?"

"Ballistics," he said simply. "Ron figured it out. We checked the serial number at the time and got nowhere, so we figured the gun was a dead end. But we never did a ballistics check to see if any bullets from it were on file at the crime lab. They have hundreds of them up there, all dated and cross-referenced—a bunch without guns to fit. Turns out they had one for this."

I slowly sat down, thoughts of summertime leisure quickly replaced by that familiar adrenaline. "Go on."

"Three years ago, a gas station was held up off Interstate 89 south of Montpelier. A twenty-year-old named Richie West stuck a gun in the attendant's face and told him to empty the till. Either the attendant didn't move fast enough or he did something stupid he wouldn't admit later, but a couple of shots were fired and he got whacked on the head before West took off into the night—just as an off-duty cop was pulling in for gas. The cop didn't know what had happened till too late to give chase, but he remembered the getaway car, and the state cops had Richie in cuffs within forty-five minutes."

"Don't tell me," I suggested, "the gun was missing and the bullets they dug out of the wall match what we got off Billy Conyer."

"Right—one of them actually went through a bunch of lined-up motor-oil bottles and ended in perfect condition at the bottom of the last one. They grilled West for hours. He never fessed up about the gun. Said he tossed it out the window after the robbery. They looked, but it never showed up."

I took the semiautomatic from him and weighed it my hand. "Sound familiar? Young man clamming up for someone else? How often you think we run into that outside the movies?"

J.P. leaned against my doorframe. "Basically never—not once the deal's on the table."

I returned the gun. "Where's Mr. West now?"

"St. Albans. I called up there to ask what kind of guy he was. They said he's real quiet, almost repressed. A loner. I also talked to someone in the Washington County state's attorney's office—they prosecuted him—and what they described sounded like something between Owen and Billy Conyer."

"You ask them what he was like before he got caught? Past associates, criminal history, family?"

"Yeah. That part's more predictable, and more like Conyer's. But we'll probably have to talk to some of those folks face-to-face if we want to find a connection to Walter Freund. His name doesn't appear on the record."

I smiled at him, the urge to grab hold of this case coming on strong. "Why not start at the source? Let's talk to Richie himself."

The Northwest State Correctional Facility outside St. Albans is located in a long, shallow valley, and as we approached it from a distance later the following morning, after a three-hour drive, the razor wire surrounding it gleamed and glittered in the sun, making it appear faintly otherworldly, as if some glimmering, ephemeral presence had set a halo around a collection of low redbrick buildings.

The halo is anything but that, of course. St. Albans is one of the more heavily guarded of Vermont's prisons, and although not maximum security by federal standards, it is close enough to house some of the worst we have to offer it.

From the outside, though, it looks relatively benign, the wire notwithstanding. Surrounded by rolling green countryside, it is designed to look like a cross between a reform school and a nondescript housing project.

I'd chosen Sammie Martens to accompany me, hoping the trip would give us a chance to talk. So far, all I'd gotten had been monosyllabic responses punctuated by dead silence.

We were brought to an undersized room with a table in its middle and were soon introduced to a thin man with a shaved head and a single dark eyebrow running straight above hollowed-out, furtive eyes. He looked like his stay here had not been the best of therapies.

We sat opposite him. "Mr. West, I'm Lieutenant Gunther. This is Sergeant Martens of the Brattleboro Police Department. We're facing a situation back home we thought you might help us with."

"I never been to Brattleboro."

"That may be, but one of your possessions has."

He'd been staring at the table between us. That made him look up.

"The gun you used during the robbery," I explained.

His single eyebrow dipped in the middle as he scowled in concentration.

I continued. "We had to kill a man who came out shooting at us. The gun in his hand was the same one you had that night at the gas station—the one you claimed you threw out the window."

He sat back in his chair and allowed a half smile. "I guess those things happen."

"Especially if the same man supplied the same gun to both of you. Where did you get that gun, Mr. West?"

"I don't remember."

"How're they treating you in here?"

His eyes narrowed at the sudden change of subjects. "Like shit."

"Reason I ask is that if the powers that be are told the right things, they might start thinking you supplied the weapon that was used in the attempted murder of a police officer."

He looked outraged. "You can't stick me with that. I threw it out the window."

I pretended to check the contents of a folder I'd brought in with me. "So you said. You also said you didn't commit the robbery, were nowhere near the gas station that night, and a bunch of other bullshit. You've got zero credibility here, Richie. Basically, if we hand this over to the prosecutor, you're screwed, and your stay here gets extended God knows how much longer. Aiding and abetting an attempted murder."

He scratched his forehead. "I didn't *do* anything."

"You did, though," I corrected him. "You gave the gun to Walter Freund after you ripped off that gas station, and he gave it to the guy we had to kill. It's a direct link, Richie, A, B, C. Simple as that. You hear what happened to Walter, by the way?"

He fell for it, much to my relief. "What?"

"He's on the lam. We nailed him on two homicides, and now the U.S. marshals are hot on his heels. He's going up for more time than he's got years left in him. You might as well forget he ever existed."

"You're full of shit."

I pulled a copy of the *Reformer*'s front page out of the folder. "Guess you don't watch TV," I said, having already been told of his habits, and slid the article across to him.

He picked it up, read the headline about Freund and stared at the picture, and then let it drop back onto the tabletop. He looked crestfallen.

"It's over, Richie. He won't be there to help you when you get out—in fact, he used that gun to give you one last poke in the gut. Unless," I said, "you start getting chatty. After all, the opposite can be true about my talking to someone. Help us out, and maybe life can be made a little better for you in here."

He didn't say anything.

"You gave the gun to Walter, right?"

"Yeah." His voice was a monotone.

"You know, Richie, if it's any comfort, you're not alone. You might even be the lucky one. Walter set up two other people we know of. Now one of them's dead and the other's looking at worse time than you are, for helping kill a woman and her baby. Walter may have seemed like your only friend back then, but he was in it purely for himself."

"You're just seeing one side."

I didn't argue. He'd lost enough already. "I know. We don't always have a choice. For what it's worth, I'm sorry it got you in here, and I'll make sure to tell the SA if you help us today. Parole comes up soon."

He looked vaguely hopeful. "Thanks."

"Tell me something," I added conversationally. "Where were you and Walter hanging out when you got nabbed?"

"Around Barre. I was working at Thunder Road the summer we met. He had a job there, too."

Thunder Road was Vermont's only paved stock car track—a quarter-mile oval placed in a bowl on the side of a mountain with an incredible view—and a magnet to locals born to the car culture. My brother Leo had driven there years ago, with me cheering him on from the pits.

"Boy," I said, "there's a name from the past. I used to go up there all the time. Were you working with a crew?"

The first signs of life stirred as his eyes lit up. "Yeah. I drove, too—street stocks."

"No shit? That's great. Who'd you work for?"

"Danny Mullen. He was into late models, but he had a street stock he let us run—a Toyota pickup. Wasn't much to look at, but moved like a raped ape."

I fought to contain my own excitement and not let him see the importance of what he'd just said. "That's great. They're on today, aren't they? Every Thursday? Wonder if Danny's still involved."

Richie West was by now almost totally relaxed. "You

kidding? He's like addicted to it. He'd have to be dead to miss a race."

I got up, leaned over, and shook his hand, more grateful then he realized. "Maybe you can join him back up there before too long. I want to thank you for being straight with us, Rich. Try to keep your nose clean."

Sammie Martens was prodded out of her silence as we walked down the hall, heading back toward the parking lot. "Danny Mullen—that any relation to the speaker of the House?"

I gave her a broad smile. "His brother."

Chapter Twenty-eight

The return drive from St. Albans was as animated as its counterpart had been glum. From being virtually mute, Sammie was almost back to her old self again, as stimulated as I was by the unexpected mention of Danny Mullen's name.

"What a weird twist," she said once we'd regained the interstate. "How do you think Danny connects to all this?"

"Maybe not at all," I had to admit.

"You saying it's a coincidence?" Her voice was incredulous. "Pinning Resnick's death on Reynolds would've directly benefited Mark Mullen. Danny probably told his brother to use Walter for the job. I mean, look at the sequence: Mark Mullen's coming off the peak of his game—running out of time to become governor. If he doesn't move now, when Howell's retiring on his own, he'll not only lose his best shot at that job, but probably the speakership, too, since his support's eroding fast. Then all of a sudden, Reynolds pops up as heir apparent, complete with headline-grabbing bill. No wonder things escalated from a screwed-up break-in, to a rumor campaign, to finally pinning a murder rap on the guy. Mullen must've been desperate."

"He didn't seem desperate when I met him," I said. "And he doesn't look in bad shape now, just using old-fashioned politics. The Reynolds Bill is dead, his version of it is gaining more and more acceptance, and he's rising in the polls. If anything, the rumor-mongering and the klutzy murder frame *helped* Reynolds early on. He started running out of gas after they'd been proven false."

Sammie was so worked up she was almost bouncing in her seat. "That's the way things turned out, maybe, but the Mullens didn't know that at the time. You're not just going to write off Danny's involvement, are you?"

"No. But I'm not going to jump to the conclusion that the speaker of the House murdered some truck driver to get the drop on a political opponent. What Richie West told us is definitely interesting and needs chasing down, but you've got to admit, we're going to have to work to make a case out of it."

Sammie crash-dived into her previous mood, staring out the side window without uttering a word.

"You ever been to a racetrack before?" I asked, hoping to bring her back.

"No."

"Thunder Road's right on the way. We could make it a cultural experience."

She turned and looked at me, smiling slightly. "You think Mullen'll be there?"

"You heard the man—he never misses a race. Maybe he'd be up for a little chat."

* * *

Thunder Road is located in the hills above Barre, covering one hundred and sixty acres. It represents a Vermont never seen in the tourist brochures, and yet captures better than most the true essence of the state. It is an irony that Vermont is so well-known for skiing the locals can't afford, maple sugar they have to sell, and photo-op cows that have all but disappeared. In fact, Vermont is a blue-collar state, only minimally agricultural, marked by marginal incomes, low education investment, small manufacturing, and heavy welfare rolls. Unemployment isn't too bad, but the kinds of jobs those numbers represent are not the stuff of careers. When Vermonters are asked what they do for a living, more often than not they answer, "Everything."

Thunder Road was made for them, and it is fitting that it sits above a hardscrabble, working-class, melting-pot town built around the extraction of granite from the surrounding mountains. Stock car racing really boomed in Vermont following World War Two, when energy, optimism, and access to cars were suddenly rampant. There were some eighteen tracks in the state back then, creating a gypsylike aura of tough, hard-driving, independent, family-supported racers that wandered from event to event, putting up with brutal, primitive, often dangerous conditions, all for the thrill of a near-death experience, a resurgence of the camaraderie born in battle, and a few bucks in winnings. It quickly became a tradition passed from father to son—and lately, to daughter.

It also became a financial phenomenon the locals couldn't exploit. Before long, the southern states had taken over the sport, using more money, better PR, and far better year-around weather to transform a madcap backfield pastime into a multimillion-dollar national passion.

Nowadays, there are just three racetracks in Vermont, two of them dirt. Thunder Road is the best of a small bunch.

It is also unassuming. Driving into one of the several grass parking lots, hunting for an open slot, I was struck once again by the small footprint the track made on its surroundings. The few buildings—housing ticket sellers, food concessions, announcers, and the like—were modest wooden structures built of plywood and two-by-fours. The track itself was paved, as were the access roads and the pit area, but they were all hemmed in by woods, fields, and grassy hills instead of any commercialized development. And the stands—a spread of concrete steps reminiscent of an ancient Greek amphitheater—were set into the flank of a steep grassy slope running the length of one side of the track. The total effect was more reminiscent of a semi-permanent community picnic site than of a forty-year-old institution visited by up to five thousand spectators per night.

But that rural quaintness was visual only. To the ear, there was no mistaking what the enterprise was all about. Sam and I got there late, as the light was beginning to fade, and the races had been running for several hours. The air reverberated with the scream of high-test engines, the squeal of tires, and the rattle-and-pop of other cars waiting in line for the next event. The breeze over the parking lot was thick with the acrid smell of burnt rubber and exhaust.

Sammie and I walked to the entrance gate and showed our shields to the ticket-taker.

"Is Danny Mullen around tonight?" I asked.

She smiled brightly, seemingly unfazed by our identities. "Yup. Never misses a night. You'll have to find him yourselves, though. God knows where he's at. Unless you want to use the PA."

"No, no," I quickly answered. "He's not racing?"

"He pretty much gave that up. He's got a team, though. You could ask them—they're parked with the other late models, up against the hill."

"Walter Freund around, too?" Sammie asked suddenly.

The woman looked at us blankly. "He a driver?"

Sam shook her head. "Never mind."

As we followed the edge of the access road leading to the pit area, I asked her, "You think Walter's here?"

"Not really. Just thought I'd ask. What did she mean by 'late models'?"

"They race three classes of car here: street stocks, which are four-cylinder jobs mostly run by local teenagers. Intermediates, which they call 'Flying Tigers,' I guess from World War Two days—they're a little pricier and have some high-end equipment on them—and the late models. They're what you see on TV. They come from all over, travel the country in special enclosed trailers, do about forty races a year, and basically try to make a living at it. They start at around twenty-five thousand dollars and have full support teams. When I used to help my brother Leo try to commit suicide this way, it was all pretty crude—no brakes, no rules, no floorboards, and some chicken wire to stop you from flying into the woods. Nowadays they use computers to calculate the jacking bolts, suspension, fuel loads. It's all geometry and physics, and they fool with it nonstop, all night long. Not the street stocks, though," I added, as we passed several of them being worked on by their youthful tenders. "They're pretty much reduced to playing with tire pressure." I pointed ahead. "Those are the ones I was talking about."

We were approaching a long line of large, enclosed, low-slung trailers, their gaping mouths looking like whales poised to swallow the cars crouching before them. Under an assortment of colorful flags advertising STP, Chevrolet, NAPA, and others, groups of men and women in overalls scurried around the cars. Several of them had radios clipped to their belts, with wires running to headsets slung around their necks.

Sammie nodded toward one of them as he jogged by. "What's with the radios?" A sense of intense purpose was palpable all around us. Everyone was serious and focused, with minimal laughing or joking. To our right, barred from sight by the embankment holding the curve, the racetrack emitted an undulating high-pitched howling.

"Each of the drivers is connected to a spotter. As the cars go around the track, the spotters tell the drivers who's ahead, whether they're clear to cut back into line, and other things the driver can't really tell. They're moving at eighty-five miles an hour sometimes—twelve seconds every lap. Takes concentration. Here's Mullen's car."

We stopped before a dark blue car bedecked with advertisements, its flimsy hood open to reveal a huge engine unlike anything available in a normal car. The steering wheel had been removed to allow easier access for the driver.

This time, I didn't show my shield to the young woman coming out of the trailer with a tool in her hand. "Danny around?" I asked.

"Yeah. Up in the stands somewhere."

We walked along the rows of cars to a chain-link

fence enclosing the concrete stands mounted into the hillside. A white-haired deputy sheriff stood by the open gate.

"Hey, Rob," I greeted him as we drew near. "How you been?"

His craggy face split into a wide smile. "Joe, by God. Haven't seen you in years. How you been? How's Leo?"

"He's fine. Still cutting meat over in Thetford, living with our mom." I introduced him to Sammie and asked if he'd seen Danny Mullen. He directed us to the upper reaches of the stands.

We climbed the paved path bordering the stands, shading our eyes against the floodlights above the crowd. The higher we got, the more the track dropped away below us, until we could see the entire layout, strung with bare bulbs, circled again and again by a mad pack of jostling race cars filling the air with their screaming. The two curves of the track were nicknamed the Launching Pad and the Widow Maker, and as each car approached either one or the other, I remembered various accidents I'd seen here over the years—miraculously none of them fatal.

I closed my eyes for a split second and let the sounds alone hold sway, recalling how the street stocks squealed more than the late models, since their wheels were configured like those of a regular car. Late models are designed only for tracks like this, and have their right front wheels canted in at an angle to put more rubber on the road during a tight left turn. At eighty miles an hour, the pressure on that one wheel can reach two tons. The point of the exercise, of course, is better contact, which means late models don't squeal as much as their smaller, lighter, more home-built counterparts.

From the sound alone, therefore, I knew I was hearing the same kind of car Leo had worked on in the family barn for hours on end, dreaming of the day he'd qualify for the big leagues.

"What're you doing?" Sammie's voice in my ear cut through the cheering, the nonstop loudspeaker chatter, and the deafening sound of the engines.

"Sorry—reminiscing." I looked once more at the vehicles below, noticing how each driver seemed isolated and alone in his or her cockpit, as if maneuvering a spaceship through an asteroid shower.

I resumed climbing alongside a crowd remarkable only for its normalcy—all blue jeans, T-shirts, and baseball caps, with a smattering of older folks, the men sporting suspenders stretched over comfortable guts.

We didn't have any luck finding Mullen. The current race came to an end, a "Victory Lane" banner was quickly rigged on the track facing the crowd, and the announcer grabbed a mike and proclaimed the teenage winner, who was so enthused he leapt onto his car and jumped up and down on the roof. The whole ceremony was over in minutes flat, the banner was removed, and before we'd reached the bottom again, the pace car, sporting a flashing yellow light bar and a boldly painted "Cody Chevrolet" sign, was already positioning to lead the next field of cars, this time late models.

As we cut away from the stands and passed before the crowded concession booth, heading back toward the gate, I saw Rob gesture to us from his post. I waved back as he yelled, "He just went by. I told him you were looking for him."

But in that instant, I was no longer thinking about

Danny Mullen. Attracted by Rob's yelling over the line of cars behind him, a man straightened from laboring over a late model's engine and looked up in our direction.

It was Walter Freund, dressed as one of Mullen's pit crew.

Sammie saw him, too, and immediately began running.

Freund's reaction was fast and lethal. He sprinted toward us, reached Rob in five steps, and chopped him on the side of the neck, felling him like an ox. He then pulled the old man's revolver from its holster.

"Gun," I yelled at Sammie ahead of me.

Sam swerved as Walter aimed and fired a round, her feet slipping on the inclined walkway and causing her to slide like a home-base runner into several men coming out of the rest room. I crouched quickly, steadied my elbow on my knee, and drew a bead on Walter. Too many people were standing behind him for me to risk a shot.

"Police. Drop the gun," I yelled.

Instead, he shot carelessly at me and then broke for the car parked next to the one he'd been working on, temporarily losing himself in the crowd.

I jogged up to Sammie, who was already fighting off several helping hands. "He's gone for a car."

We bolted for the gate, where Rob still lay prostrate, surrounded by a confused crowd of gawking people. The gunshots had blended without notice into the sound of crackling exhausts, so many who'd actually seen Walter fire still didn't understand what had happened.

I paused long enough to check Rob's pulse. His other

hand reached up and swatted me away. "Get the bastard," he said, "I'm fine."

There was a small explosion of sound from where Walter had disappeared, and a yellow late model suddenly leapt backward into the service road paralleling the pits, scattering people like chickens under attack. I saw Walter's grim face through the plastic windshield as he wrenched the steering wheel around to straighten the car out.

He had but one way to go. Due to the line of cars behind him and the crowd clogging the service road, the only outlet was the entrance to the track. Spewing twin clouds of acrid blue smoke, his car burst toward that direction, almost hitting Sammie and me as it sped past.

Incongruously, we both gave chase on foot, guns out, topping the small embankment enclosing the track just as Walter slewed onto its surface, cutting off the pace car and causing the entire pack behind it to scatter, brakes and tires squealing. To the sound of several collisions, I reached the pace car's passenger door, pulled it open, and yelled at the astonished driver, "Police. We have to stop that man."

Sammie piled into the back seat as I slid into the front, and the driver—a young man with a sudden broad smile on his face—took off much as Walter had moments before.

Again, our quarry's options were limited. He couldn't make the loop and head back out the entrance chute, since a tangle of race cars was now blocking his way. The grandstands, a tall fence, and a hill cut off other potential exits, so, about halfway down the length of the track, he did the only thing left to him—he cut violently to the right, vaulted over the lip of the track, and took off across the grass toward the parking lots, two rooster tails of dirt marking his progress.

Laughing by now, our driver followed suit. I could hear Sammie behind me being thrown around like a rag doll.

"Seat belt, seat belt," I yelled at her over the engine noise, while I struggled to follow my own advice. "What's your name?" I asked the driver.

"Sean. Glad to meet you. He kill someone or something?"

We hit a trough, and I smacked my head against the roof. "Yeah."

His hands still on the wheel, he said, "Use the radio. Tell them to call for backup."

He had a portable radio wedged under his thigh. I grabbed it, keyed the mike, and said, "This is a police emergency. Call the cops and tell them we have an officer down and are in pursuit. We need assistance."

The laconic reply was, "Got that. VSP's already been notified."

Ahead of us, Freund leapt onto the roadway and fishtailed toward the parking lots. Moments later, with a sickening crunch from underneath, we did the same. Sean let out a yell and hit the gas.

"This thing going to hold together?" I shouted, grabbing the dash.

"Hell if I know, but I've always wanted to open 'er up."

We barreled down between a row of parked cars, grateful to be on a smoother surface, even if it was still dirt. I kept my fingers crossed no pedestrians would suddenly appear. In the straightaway, Walter widened the gap between us.

"Don't worry about him losin' us," Sean declared.

"Why not?" I asked skeptically.

"'Cause he won't be able to turn right worth shit."

Those words were still in the air when Walter reached the end of the lane in front of us, cut right to make the corner, and went sailing into a row of cars, sending a shower of sparks into the night air. That canted right front wheel, solely designed for left turns, had bit into the dirt with all the effectiveness of a skinny bicycle tire. We were back on his tail as he recovered and regained speed.

The next stretch played to his favor, however, going downhill in a wide left turn, at the bottom of which the surface returned to asphalt. We were nearing the exit to Thunder Road, and the state highway beyond.

"Let's hope your friends are on their toes," Sean said, "'Cause this boy's options are just about to open up."

Walter seemed to sense the same thing, while simultaneously catering to his vehicle's one drawback. As he hit the end of the entrance road, he predictably turned left.

I grabbed the radio again. "Anyone out there?"

The response was scratchy, the range being only a mile or so. "Go ahead."

"We've gone left out the entrance. Tell VSP to set up roadblocks."

Nothing came back except static.

"Guess we're on our own," Sammie said from the back.

Sean needed no more urging to apply the speed. I hoped his skill matched his ambition as I felt my back press against the seat—especially as we topped a rise, all four wheels off the ground, and saw Walter ahead of us swerve to avoid an oncoming pickup truck.

Either his lack of skill or that front wheel did him in. He fishtailed slightly, puffs of blue smoke curling from his rear tires, and then he began to slide. As Sean hit the brakes and started us into our own controlled skid, I saw Walter's car give the pickup a glancing blow and go sailing across the ditch. He smashed into a tree about five feet off the ground and landed with the finality of a dictionary hitting the floor. As we shuddered to a halt not fifteen feet behind him, only slightly out of true with the road, I was suddenly aware of both silence and stillness, even before Sean killed his engine.

I stepped out, glanced over at the pickup's astonished driver, still frozen with his hands on the wheel, and crossed the ditch to Walter's car. It was shattered, flattened, surrounded by debris, and utterly, totally at peace.

Sammie was right behind me. "You see him?"

"Not yet," I said softly.

I approached cautiously, gun drawn, aware of sirens closing in from afar, and crouched low so I could see through the passenger window. Walter Freund was holding the steering wheel in a lethal embrace, his rib cage seemingly welded to the car. Blood was everywhere.

He hadn't had time to fasten his seat belt.

I straightened and turned to Sammie. "Of the three men who killed Phil Resnick, it looks like we're down to one."

Chapter Twenty-nine

We returned to the track after the state police took over the crash site. The evening's events had been canceled and thousands of departing spectators were being detoured through various exits, forcing Sean to inch along in a parody of his earlier glory. By the time we got back to where the late models were parked, Danny Mullen was long gone and his crew was tight-lipped about his whereabouts.

I found it a frustrating end to a day that had begun far more hopefully.

In contrast, Sammie seemed curiously upbeat. "Too bad Walter committed dumbicide, but at least now we know who to focus on."

Since I remembered she'd been on a tear to go after Mark Mullen earlier, she now had me guessing. "Danny or Mark?"

She stared at me. "Danny. You know goddamn well he tucked Walter out of sight 'cause he was on the payroll. No frigging way that's some kind of fluke."

I didn't disagree. "What about his brother?"

"Same thing. They're in it together. One guy does

up-front showboating, the other one breaks legs and
raises the money. All we need now is enough to justify a warrant for all his paperwork, and I bet we get
him cold."

I remained silent in the face of her enthusiasm. "You
don't think so?" She challenged me.

I hesitated before answering. "I don't doubt Danny's
got dirt under his nails, and I don't doubt Mark wants
to be governor. I do wonder how neat and tidy it all
is."

Sammie was dismissive. "But it is neat and tidy. That's
what's fouled us up from the start—Phil Resnick, Owen
Tharp, Brenda Croteau, Walter Freund, Billy Conyer. All
of them were like cobwebs hitting us in the face, keeping us from seeing the root cause of it all. If you take
it back to the Mullens, it gets real simple."

I thought back to what was the biggest objection to
William of Occam's famous razor in his day—that if
the answer to a problem was arrived at by extracting
or excluding all pseudo-explanations, who was to decide which of those was superfluous and which had
merit? Might the process not become too simplified
and miss a vital truth?

I decided to hold off debate and take advantage of
Sammie's reborn energy to get her to open up a little.

"I'm glad you got the bit back in your teeth."

That caught her by surprise. She looked out the side
window at the passing darkness for a while before finally saying, "Yeah, well."

"I owe you an apology," I continued. "I think I'm
partly to blame for what happened between you and
Andy."

She switched her gaze to me. "How?"

"After I talked to him about hanging out at the Dirty

Dollar, drinking with Billy Conyer and the others, I dropped the ball. I knew Brenda used to go there, too. It would've been logical to find out if they knew each other—I did ask him, but only in passing. I should've checked into it. If I had, it might've made things easier for you."

She merely shrugged. "I doubt it. Any way you look at it, he lied to me. Wouldn't've mattered when I found out."

"You really loved him." It wasn't a question.

"Whatever that is."

"Don't be so cynical. It doesn't make you a sucker because you fell for the wrong guy. Everything in life takes practice, otherwise every teenage hot flash would end up in a lifelong commitment."

She flared up a little. "I'm not a teenager."

I kept silent, hoping I'd uncorked things enough that they'd start flowing on their own.

After a pause, she added, "It just felt so right. He was really good company."

"You sure you were right to dump him?"

She surprised me by sighing tiredly. "Yeah. You know, it's funny, saying what good company he was. It's almost like hearing someone else talking. He wasn't that good company. To tell you straight, he was mostly just terrific in bed. And I was really horny. Sounds pathetic, but that's what I miss the most right now. I never did have what I see with you and Gail—the deeper stuff."

I laughed. "Better not go too far with that. We're looking for a place for me to live right now."

She stared at me in total amazement. "What?"

I flapped my hand dismissively in the air, "It's not that big a deal. We're putting things back to where they were before she was raped. If anything, it's a sign of restored health. We lived apart all those years because we knew we were probably too independent to share the same roof. Not that it was a bad experience—it was actually kind of nice—but you got to stick your neck out sometimes to make things work. Gail's strong again, and she needs her space."

"And you?"

I thought of how poorly words stand in for one's feelings sometimes. Reducing all that Gail and I were going through to a few snippets of rationalized thinking made it feel trivial and painless, which it definitely was not.

But Sam didn't need to hear that right now.

"It works for me, too. That house was always a little big for my taste, and it looks like Gail'll be commuting a lot to Montpelier when she starts up with StayGreen. I think I'd be better off with a small place I can call my own. I've been missing my old habits. I like to play music and read. I've been thinking of setting up a woodworking shop, like I had when I was a kid."

Sammie still seemed shocked by what I was admitting.

"You know," I told her, "sometimes the trick to making a relationship work is realizing you don't have to see eye-to-eye on everything. You don't have to like the same things, or keep the same hours, or have the same ambitions. You don't even have to live in the same house. If you admire and respect and love one another, the rest is just details that can always be worked out. I think a lot of people fall apart because they get tangled up in a skirmish they turn into a major battle."

"You telling me something here?" she asked a little sharply.

"I doubt it's anything you don't already know. You're an aggressive, type-A perfectionist. That's good on the job—a bit of a pain sometimes—but you got to learn to shift gears when you're at home. Didn't you like staying home when you were with Andy, just putting your feet up and watching TV or whatever?"

She didn't answer. The hurt she was feeling was eloquent enough.

My concern that Sammie was overrating the Mullen brothers—to the exclusion of all others—was eased the next morning when Harriet told me over the intercom that a woman was waiting in the hallway to see me.

I stepped outside to find Sandy Corcoran sitting on the park-style bench we kept there for people awaiting Breathalyzer tests or to settle their parking tickets. She was still rigged out in black—heavy boots, a leather jacket, and several chains looping this way and that—but her demeanor was significantly more civil.

"Hey, Sandy," I greeted her. "What's up?"

With a hint of medieval clanking, she reached into one of her pockets and handed me a key. "Belonged to Walter. With him dead, I figured maybe you should have it."

I held it in my palm. It was obviously to a safe-deposit box. "He give it to you to hold?"

"I guess. He called it his insurance policy and told me to hide it where no one could find it. 'Cept him, of course."

"You know what it is?"

She shook her head and stood up. "Don't want to, neither."

With that, she thudded down the hallway.

* * *

It took some doing finding the bank that owned the key, and even more on Jack Derby's part to legally fit the key to the lockbox and take hold of its contents. When he did, what we had was a single cassette tape.

Given what we'd all been through so far, it seemed only fair to share the tape's contents with everyone involved, so the premiere took place in Derby's conference room, with most of my squad, most of his office—including Gail—and Tony Brandt attending.

J.P. waited until we'd settled down before hitting the play button.

Walter Freund's voice filled the air. "I got him out of the motel, like you said. He's stashed at a friend's place."

The other voice was obviously on the far end of the phone line. "What's he saying?"

"Same thing—he wants to be taken care of."

"Or?"

"Or nothing. He wants to be checked out. He's scared he'll get cancer or something. He looks like shit. And he's probably right—that junk rotted his clothes, for Christ's sake."

"I don't care how he looks. I want to know if he's getting an attitude."

Walter paused. "He's not happy."

"Well, pacify him. I gotta check my options."

The line went dead. The tape kept rolling.

After a click, Walter said, "I didn't hear that."

"What're you, stupid? I said kill him. We don't do that, he takes us all down—everyone. The son-of-a-bitch's been dumping shit for me for years. He knows places, people, the whole operation."

"Why not just take care of him, like he asks? He doesn't look like he's going to last too long anyhow."

"That's just the point. If he knows he's cooked, and we let him out of the bag, he'll shoot his mouth off. What's the problem here? You want to go to jail?"

"No, no. I want assurances."

The other voice exploded. "You fucking peckerhead. We're talking about killing a man. You want me to write you a note saying it's okay, so the cops won't bust your balls? Give me a fucking break."

"I'm a three-time loser on parole. They don't need to prove anything to send me away. My PO gets even a whiff of this, I'm toast."

"You're toast if you don't do it, Walter. I'll see to that."

There was a long silence. "I still want assurances."

The sigh at the other end was clearly audible. The voice, when it came back on, sounded like an indulgent father's. "Tell you what. I'll do it with you. That satisfy you?"

"It helps. What do we do about the Mob?"

"What Mob?"

"He's connected. He told me so. Shit, you know that. You hired him."

"It's part-time. They won't give a fuck. He's not even Italian. He's like a contract worker. Who cares what he does on his own time?"

"You want to risk that?"

I expected another outburst, but the other man paused instead. Almost a minute elapsed before he finally said, "We'll pin it on somebody else."

"What? Who?"

"Reynolds. You screwed up the break-in. We'll use this instead. Find out what Reynolds drives and get hold of a look-alike. We'll get rid of Resnick some-

where public and pin it on Reynolds—sic the cops and
the Mob on him both." He laughed.

Walter sounded genuinely baffled. "I don't get it."

"You moron. Just get the car. I'll come down and
put it together for you. In the meantime, make goddamn sure Resnick doesn't disappear. Can you do that
much? Not fuck up? Or is that pushing you too far?"

"Up yours. I done a lot of shit for you. I don't need
to hear this."

"Fine. Don't, then. Just sit on Resnick and I'll be
down."

The tape went quiet. J.P. fast-forwarded it, listened
to more silence, repeated the process, and found the
rest of it blank.

Everyone in the room sat back. I realized we'd all
been unconsciously leaning forward, as if to hear better.

"Cool," Willy murmured.

"It's a smoking gun, all right," Derby agreed, "once
we find out who belongs to the other voice."

"I can tell you that," Tony said. "I met him once,
at a party for his brother. It's Danny Mullen."

We took our time getting an arrest warrant for Danny
Mullen. Working with the state police Bureau of Criminal Investigation, we assembled evidence from the outside in, starting with his whereabouts on the night Resnick
died and then securing items like phone records, fingerprints, business documents, and anything else we could
think of that might link him to the murder. Included in
this bundle was a thumbprint that matched one that
Willy Kunkle had found on Billy Conyer's wad of fresh
bills and, more ominously, a work boot whose sole impression was a perfect mate to the subdermal footprint

that Bernie Short had discovered under Phil Resnick's skin during autopsy. In addition, forearmed by a comment made on Walter's audiotape, we pursued and uncovered evidence of an illegal haz mat trucking operation that Danny had been running for almost fifteen years.

By the time we did put the cuffs on Mullen's wrists, Jack Derby was confident he had a winnable case on multiple levels—and an all-but-guaranteed victory against James Dunn in the primary.

Not that the fate of a lowly SA could compete with the publicity stirred up by Danny's jailing. He—and his relation to a gubernatorial candidate—dominated every front page in New England, and in many cases beyond.

This was not solely due to their simply being brothers, although that was bad enough as far as Mark Mullen's political handlers were concerned. Far worse was the revelation by one of Danny's nervous employees that as we'd been assembling facts against Danny, he'd burned a box of documents labeled with Mark's name—not a good sign in a man claiming that the sole tie between himself and the speaker was familial.

Unfortunately, there was little we could do about this report after the fact. As far as we could prove, Danny had ordered and participated in the killing of Phil Resnick without the knowledge or complicity of his brother.

The press did not suffer such constraints. To them, Danny's actions were so obviously linked to his brother's political ambitions as to make the truth of the connection a foregone conclusion—proof or no proof. As a result, as Primary Day loomed near, Mark Mullen's previously assured victory—even given his humiliation of Jim Reynolds over the law enforcement bill—began to look weak in the knees. Reynolds, for his part, simply kept to the high ground he'd staked out with his speech following the conference committee. It was a little hard watching him act the martyred saint, but I couldn't help enjoying the irony of the situation. Reynolds had started his run for governor on the murdered bodies of innocent children, and was now regaining momentum on the corpse of a Mob-connected truck driver—all while standing like a hero amid the ruins of a bill that had never stood a chance from the start. As one editorial put it, the man had achieved nothing, and was about to ride that fact to the state's top job.

Reynolds, however, wasn't my concern. Mark Mullen was.

It was too much to believe that Danny's bonfire hadn't involved more than old business papers and embarrassing love letters, as Danny had claimed when confronted. Unfortunately, that point was now moot. The task ahead was to distinguish whether Danny had acted on his brother's behalf spontaneously or on Mark's outright bidding. The first would allow Mark to claim face-saving innocence, the second would not. We needed to know for sure where the line was drawn.

And so we dug into Mark Mullen's life as we'd just finished doing with his brother's. And almost as soon as we started, we rediscovered a name from the recent past.

I was on the phone with the sheriff of Orleans County, where the Mullens had grown up, asking him what he knew about Mark, when he suggested instead, "You ought to talk with Win Johnston. He came pokin' around months ago askin' the same questions. He's probably way ahead of you—could save you a bunch of time. You know him?"

"Oh, yeah," I admitted, already looking up Win's number.

I called him moments later. "Win, it's Joe. I think we ought to talk."

He laughed quietly, needing no more of a preamble. "I was wondering how long it would take you. Chelsea Royale in half an hour?"

Gail often claims that I've trained my system to survive solely on Dunkin' Donuts. It's a joke, of course, made somewhat cruel by the recent closing of the downtown outlet of that gourmet chain—conveniently a stone's throw from the office. But in fact, it's Mom's Meatloaf at the Chelsea Royale that I'd happily mainline well into my dotage, especially if followed by apple pie.

The setting, admittedly, adds greatly to the appeal. The Chelsea Royale, located on the edge of West Brattleboro, almost directly opposite the state police barracks, is as close to a real diner as is available nowadays. The original shiny steel railroad car stands proud and distinct—complete with old neon sign—although adulterated somewhat by the usual modern attachments of an additional dining area, bathrooms, and a kitchen. And it is justifiably popular, offering not just the kinds of food that fill me with joy and make Gail roll her eyes, but more offbeat fare for more sophisticated palates. It was a credit to Win and our friendship that he'd suggested it for a meet.

Unfortunately, I'd already had lunch at my desk, and had to settle for the pie and some coffee.

Win Johnston was a pleasant-looking man, neither fat nor thin, short nor tall, with the kind of face people could never recall, and a manner and voice best described as bland. When he was a state cop, he could make almost anyone open up. Now as a private investigator, he could nose around without drawing attention or leaving much of an impression. He was very good.

He joined me in ordering some pie for himself.

"Nice work you been doing," he said once the waitress had delivered our orders.

"Which might've been speeded up if you'd shared a little."

He smiled and cut into his pie. "And violated a contract in the process."

"Can you tell me now what you were up to?" I asked.

"Some of it, sure. Not all." He took time to savor a mouthful with a contented smile. I didn't press him.

"The initial investigation you know about," he finally resumed. "To dig into that office break-in. But it wasn't quite as unfocused as I implied when you asked me. Reynolds suspected Mullen from the start. He'd known for a couple of years the two of them were in competition, and that sooner or later things might turn nasty. The break-in was like a warning shot."

"Which Mullen are you talking about?"

"Either one. They're joined at the hip. Danny feels he owes his younger brother pretty much everything, so there's not much he wouldn't do for him, and Mark's come to rely on his always being there. They're like two halves of a pair of scissors that way."

"Very poetic," I said sourly. "Does that make Mark a killer, too?"

"I don't know," he answered candidly. "I suppose it's a possibility."

"You sure you don't know?" I asked pointedly.

"Me? Yes, I'm sure. I'd be straight about that."

"Tell me about the break-in, then. You called it a warning shot. Was that its intention?"

"Oh, no. Our guess is it was something like Watergate—plant a bug or two for a little competitive eavesdropping. I found out later Danny had bought some miniature audio equipment through a mail-order catalog."

"What about the open filing cabinets?"

Win raised his eyebrows, looking bemused. "Like Jim told you—sloppy housekeeping. As far as we know—or at least according to Reynolds—there were no signs that whoever jimmied that door ever got into the office. Your boys scared 'em off."

I moved on, curiously disappointed. "Why is Danny so beholden to Mark?"

He chewed thoughtfully for a few seconds before admitting, "That I can't say."

The body language was eloquent enough, but I asked anyway. "Can't or won't?"

"Won't. That part is confidential and involves nothing prosecutable."

I didn't push him. He'd said what he could, and I wanted to keep him talking.

I retreated to firmer ground. "We have a tape proving the office break-in was Danny's doing, and you just mentioned his buying some bugs, but given their closeness, you think Mark was behind it?"

He took a sip of coffee. "That's one of the amazing things about them. According to people who've known them since they were kids, they've always been like Siamese twins, at least when it comes to sharing information. But I dug till I thought I'd disappear from view, and I couldn't find any business documents linking them together, or anyone who'd been privy to their private conversations. I read about the papers Danny was supposed to have burned—it didn't surprise me he could fit them all into a single box. Probably wasn't half full. As far as I could tell, everything was spoken, and kept strictly between the two of them. They were like their own secret society, with Danny handling the money and Mark the power."

"Be interesting if Mark wins the election."

Win nodded in agreement. "No argument there. Of course, there's no proof any of it's true." He paused and then added, "On the other hand, Danny had no qualms about killing someone for the cause. I suppose that shows a certain prejudice."

I laughed with my mouth full.

Win smiled at my reaction, but then became serious again. "I don't know, Joe. All I've learned tells me you're on the right track, trying to connect Danny to Mark on this killing, but I'm damned if I know where you'll find the evidence."

We both ate in silence for a while, chewing as much on the information as the food. I suddenly paused in midbite, however, struck by an odd revelation. "You know something weird?" I told him. "I've never even met Danny Mullen. It's almost like he was the puppeteer in this whole thing—pulling the strings, but always out of sight."

"You'd like him," Win said. "He's like his brother that way. Very good-natured, very approachable. I guess it goes without saying he does have a temper, though."

I couldn't argue with that. The voice I'd heard on that tape recording had hardly been good-natured.

"What're you doing for Reynolds now?" I asked after another pause. "You implied you're still under contract."

Despite our both being trapped in a booth together, I could almost sense him stepping back. "Yeah, I'm checking a few odds and ends. Mostly wrapping things up. The primary's almost here, so it won't be too much longer."

I gave him a long, level look. "You're not going to tell me, are you?"

He smiled benevolently. "You know the rules, Joe. If I find anything you can move on, I'll call you in a heartbeat."

We finished our snack, exchanging gossip and updating one another on what we were up to. Win observed that the way Gail was going, she'd probably wind up governor herself someday, and I didn't disagree.

After we parted, however, I didn't wait to get to the office to act on what Win had refused to tell me. Driving back toward downtown, I called Ron on the cell phone.

"I just had coffee with Winthrop Johnston. He's been digging into the Mullens. I think he's found something he won't talk about. It's nothing criminal—he would've fessed up to that—but I want to know what it is. Get everyone working on this, including the BCI people, and let's see if we can track who's he's been talking to."

"Why bother if you know it's not criminal?" Ron asked.

"Because he wasn't hired to put Mark Mullen in jail.

He's just looking for dirt that'll get Reynolds the election. If we dig a little deeper in some of the same holes, we might just get lucky and find something to prosecute."

Chapter Thirty

Marcia Wilkin lived in Bristol, Vermont, a small town northeast of Middlebury, tucked into a steep-sided narrow gap between the Hogback and South mountains, and hard up against some of the most dramatic, rugged areas the Green Mountains have to offer—Camel's Hump, Sugarbush, and Mad River Glen among them. Driving out of the Champlain valley toward the axlike incision splitting this solid wall—under a flat, gray skillet of ominous, snow-laden clouds—I felt I was about to be swallowed alive by a dark and looming menace so vast and intractable that no one would bother looking for me once news of my disappearance leaked out.

It was now late November, closing in on a year since we'd discovered Phil Resnick across the railroad tracks in the middle of the night. A year in which law enforcement in Vermont had been threatened with total overhaul and undergone a major readjustment, in which a bright political star had clashed with one of the state's Democratic standard-bearers—and begun a battle they were waging even now—and in which a stack of dead bodies had been attributed to ambition, paranoia, and greed, but whose final rationale had yet to be explained.

And which had stimulated this trip.

According to our research, Marcia Wilkin had not only known both Danny and Mark Mullen as young men, but—we strongly suspected—maintained powerful and secret ties to them to this day.

Unfortunately, that still didn't give us much. Danny Mullen, in jail awaiting trial for murder, hadn't said a word since the day he'd been cuffed. It was only wishful thinking on my part, therefore, that Marcia Wilkin had the answers Danny was refusing to divulge. But by now—weeks of interviews, computer searches, and brainstorms later—it was all I had left to go on.

It had been a generally riotous fall. The September primary hadn't followed anyone's forecast. Most people I knew had entered the polls confident Mark Mullen would carry the day—despite all the bad publicity—only to discover the next morning that Jim Reynolds had won. Saint Sebastian, riddled with the arrows of his opponent's devious ways, had pulled off his message of principle over politics.

But whether convinced that Reynolds was no paragon of either purity or innocence—a suspicion I shared—or merely yielding to his own thwarted ambition, Mark Mullen had thrown over the applecart of convention, declared himself an independent candidate, and stormed undeterred toward the November general elections, to the outrage and consternation of his party.

The chaos attending this move had revived national interest. Once again, articles, news reports, and TV shows were featured daily about the man-who-would-be-governor—come hell or high water—and whose brother was suspected of murdering on his behalf, turning the whole political contest into a carnival.

Little did we all realize that we were only two-thirds into a three-act play. With the same quirkiness that had once stimulated the state's voters to elect a Democrat, a Republican, and an ex-Socialist each to Congress, they once again befuddled the pundits by splitting the vote four ways in November. The Republican, given no real chance to begin, limped across the line in third place, just ahead of a Liberty Union candidate, who, by miraculously winning fifteen percent of a disgusted electorate, further inhibited either Reynolds or Mullen from capturing a majority, although Reynolds did end up with the higher popular count.

But the rules were clear. According to the state's constitution, a winner had to collect more than fifty percent of the vote. Shy of that, a legislative joint assembly got to choose from between the two top candidates. Mullen and Reynolds were to face off one last time in early January.

And convinced as I was that Mark Mullen had more than passively benefited from his brother's scheming, I also had to admit that he'd survived so far not just because of the average Vermonter's love of the absurd, but because, at long last, he'd stepped out from behind the machine of his own making and identified himself to the people as one of their own—born poor, proud, and willing to fight against the odds. As questionable as were his integrity and his goals, Mark Mullen on the stump came across as the genuine article, as homespun and honest as Reynolds appeared lofty, rich, and arrogant.

Not that I had any doubts that when it came time for the two men to lobby their erstwhile fellow legislators prior to the January vote, Mullen would come out on top. Not only was he a better back-room manipulator than Reynolds, but he'd just finished being the titular leader of one hundred and fifty House members. Reynolds had merely been one of thirty Senators, even if an important committee chair. It reminded me that while Saint Sebastian survived those arrows, his enemies had his head in the long run.

To pay him his due, I had liked Mark Mullen from the moment we'd met, and I suspected he actually hadn't played any part in Resnick's death. Most likely, his knowledge of Danny's malfeasance was limited to financial chicanery, and Danny—stimulated either by frustration or who knew what quirk of allegiance—had stepped over the line on his own. Many a politician had sprung from a contaminated source. Who was I to say Mark Mullen might not similarly defy convention?

As I climbed the last gentle hill into Bristol, however, I knew it to be a fatuous debate, as easily argued from one side as from the other. The bottom line depended on what evidence I might or might not uncover, and on the vagaries of one hundred and eighty assembled legislators. Gut reactions and/or logic no longer had a place.

Marcia Wilkin's home was a pleasant, well-maintained Cape with an immaculate yard and a new car in the driveway.

The first thing I heard upon ringing the bell was an urgent but feeble scratching on the other side of the door, followed by footsteps and a woman's voice saying, "Watch out, Stan—door coming at you."

I was met by a short, comfortably round woman, whom I knew to be in her forties, accompanied by a cat sitting by her feet like a statue.

"Hello," she said.

I held out my hand. "Hi. My name's Joe Gunther. I'm from the—"

She lost her smile and ignored the hand. "I know who you are, Lieutenant. What do you want?"

"To come inside if I could. It would spare you some heating oil."

She stepped back silently and I walked around the cat, who sniffed my leg as I passed. On impulse, I crouched and extended the backs of my fingers for him to sniff.

"He doesn't like strangers," she said.

The cat hesitated, came forward, and butted his head against my knuckles, purring loudly. I turned my hand and cupped his cheek, scratching him under the chin.

Marcia Wilkin relented slightly. "He doesn't usually do that. Do you have a cat?"

"No, but I was raised on a farm. I like animals." I brought my other hand into action, rubbing his back and really winning him over. "You called him Stan?"

"That's right—Stan the Cat."

I looked up at her. "The only other Stan I know is a newspaper editor. A real pain in the neck."

She laughed despite herself. "So's this one when he wants to be. You'll find out if you keep doing that. He won't leave you alone."

"That doesn't sound so bad," I said, straightening up. Facing the front door, hanging on the wall, was a three-foot long, elaborately carved wooden sign reading, "The Ellis Hastings House." Beneath it was a small table with an open Bible resting on a cushion.

I indicated the sign. "That's nice work. It mean anything?" I waved a hand around me. "All this is too new to be historical, isn't it?"

She gave me an odd smile. "Doesn't have to be ancient to have history. I like a house with a name."

"Hey," I said, looking down. Stan had reared up to rest his forepaws against my leg, seeking more attention.

"I warned you."

I bent over to ruffle his ears. He closed his eyes contentedly. "I'm sorry my showing up has made you unhappy, Ms. Wilkin."

It might've been the cat acting as ambassador, but she finally relented. "I shouldn't have been so rude. Let me take your coat."

I shucked it off and handed it to her. She hung it on a peg on the way to the living room and gestured to me to sit in one of two facing sofas. The room was large, neat, and furnished—it looked to me—straight out of an expensive Ethan Allen catalog.

As soon as I sat down, Stan jumped into my lap, drilling his forehead amorously against my chest.

"If he starts bothering you, I'll put him in the other room," she offered, sitting opposite me.

"No, that's fine. I enjoy the company."

"That sounds a little lonely."

I looked up at her. She was composed and serene in a matronly manner, but with careful, intelligent eyes. I was surprised by her insight and her ease in airing it—first impressions had slighted an obvious depth of character. "Sorry."

"Don't be. Your job is partly to blame. I bet people talk to you a lot like I did."

I went back to tending to Stan, pondering how to proceed. Obviously unintimidated, Marcia Wilkin was either trying to keep me off balance or merely displaying the habits of a self-confident woman who felt she had nothing to fear.

I decided to push her a bit. "I suppose you know why I'm here."

She ignored the bait. "Not really."

"You knew who I was."

"I know what you've done to Danny Mullen, and that you're part of a conspiracy to keep Mark from being governor." It was said matter-of-factly, without passion.

I studied her a moment, my hands resting on the cat, who'd settled down in my lap to doze off. "I did help put Danny in jail. That's my job. As for Mark, I guess I'm damned whatever I say. For what it's worth, driving into town, I was thinking how much I genuinely liked him. I really do hope I can give him a clean bill of health—but I'm stuck till I get all the facts."

She frowned, as if holding a private debate. "Maybe you *should* tell me why you're here."

"You know the Mullens well?"

"We grew up together."

"But it was more than that, wasn't it? I'd heard you and Mark had once been a couple."

She smiled thinly. "You hear all sorts of things. We were friends."

I let that go, despite what my research had told me. "It doesn't really matter. None of my business. I just wondered what they were like when they were younger. I mean, would you have guessed back then that Danny could've done what he did?"

"He hasn't gone to trial yet, has he?" she asked pointedly.

"No, but regardless of what the jury's allowed to

hear and finally decides, I know the case against him. He did kill that man."

"So you say."

"I'd like to hear why, though. We're not supposed to worry about that—we catch 'em red-handed, that's pretty much it. But given how close Danny is to Mark, the question begs asking."

She half opened her mouth to say something, and then shut it again, seemingly angry with herself. "Then you better ask them."

"You seem like you're wrestling with something, Ms. Wilkin."

She inhaled a deep breath and let it out slowly. "Maybe I'm just having a hard time staying polite."

I doubted that, and so took a chance. "Would you like me to leave?"

That caught her off guard. "No, I'm sorry."

I tried a different approach. "Look, let me be honest with you. I know you don't like my being here, I know your ties with the Mullens run deeper than just friendship, and I know a private detective named Win Johnston's been bugging you about all this. We don't live in a world where too many secrets survive anymore. We've been taking apart the Mullens' life for months now, trying to separate what Danny did from what Mark may have known. You've popped up as having deep, long-lasting financial ties to them—for well over twenty years. We know they've been supporting you all that time."

Her face had hardened during this, so I quickly added, "I don't want to make anything of that. I'm here as a guest only, to ask for your help—not to harass or threaten or anything else. I just wanted you to understand I wasn't being coy or playing games."

That wasn't entirely true, of course. Of all of the people we'd connected to the brothers, only Marcia Wilkin had stood out for her very lack of clarity. Born in their hometown and a classmate of Mark's all through school, reportedly ending up as his lover, she hadn't had any known ties to either one of them since—and yet had been living all this time without a job or any obvious source of income. What I'd just rattled off had been pure speculation.

And yet she still didn't throw me out.

Instead, she said, "Go on."

"As I see it, Ms. Wilkin, my only job here is to make sure the right thing's done. Your loyalty to Danny notwithstanding, I think you know he's not innocent. We all make mistakes, sometimes pretty big ones, and sometimes we make them out of misguided affection. That's what I think happened to Danny. He got carried away—things escalated. Before he knew it, he was in over his head. He didn't kill that man because he's evil. He killed him because right then, at that moment, he'd convinced himself it was the right thing to do—that he was acting for the one person in his life who means everything to him.

"What I need to figure out is where Mark fits into it, regardless of what the prosecutor does, or of what I think of Mark personally, or even whether he gets to be governor. Because until I can get that settled in my head, I'm going to have to keep digging. It's the way I am."

She smiled slightly. "Just for yourself? I doubt that. One thing leads to another, Lieutenant. I won't help you be Mark's jailer."

"I wouldn't expect you to. Maybe you could just help be his conscience."

I was about to continue, but the look on her face made me stop. She seemed suddenly drawn into herself, as if the inner debate I'd suspected she'd been having all along had finally taken her over.

The silence dragged on, the cat continued sleeping peacefully, and I slowly became aware of every small sound in the house. Finally, she raised her eyes to mine, smiled ever so slightly, and said quietly, "I think I would like you to leave now."

I placed Stan on the pillow next to me, brushed myself free of cat hair, removed my coat from the peg by the door, and let myself out.

On the face of it, I was leaving as empty-handed as when I'd arrived. On a deeper level, however, I felt oddly as if I'd accomplished something substantial, the meaning of which for now eluded me.

I returned to Brattleboro from Bristol along the scenic route, enjoying the fading day and the emergence of the stars. I'd seen my conversation with Marcia Wilkin as the last turn of a wheel before it comes to a final stop. If anything had been accomplished there, it was now going to be played out elsewhere by someone else. After ten months of digging, I felt—perhaps disingenuously—that I'd reached daylight, or at least enough of it to deserve a sense of peace. Driving for hours along smooth blacktop, the trees, farms, and villages becoming an endless blur to either side, I reviewed the year's events meditatively and tried to convince myself that while little had worked out the way I'd imagined, the final results were mostly acceptable.

I stopped to have dinner in a small café in Poultney. Eating at a table by the window, I watched the traffic go by as if from a fish tank, trying not to feel remote and ineffectual. Occasionally pedestrians turned toward me in passing, drawn by the neon sign flashing above my head, their faces alternating from pale gray to tepid pink, emphasizing my lack of success.

Gail had left for her job in Montpelier, driven to the next stage in her life as by a migratory urge, dissolving a pattern I'd been adjusting to since we'd moved in together. And despite my encouraging her, and having occasionally longed for a return to the "old days," I was now having to deal with only a subtle imitation of the past—and at an age when such evolutions were made slowly and with doubt.

With Gail's practiced help, I'd found a place to live on Green Street, just a block away from my old apartment. It was a radically different setup—a two-story carriage house out back of a large building that was home to a family of four. The carriage house had a garden, huge windows, a brick wall with a chimney, lots of exposed wooden beams. It was a place that felt like a home.

Gail had joined me the first night I moved in. We'd made love in the bedroom upstairs, and on the rug in front of the open wood stove. I'd made her spaghetti out of a box, with sauce from a jar—my kind of vegetarianism. We'd watched an old movie on TV, huddled under a shared blanket on the couch. And after she'd left, and I'd cleaned the place up to some music on the radio, I'd felt better than I thought I would. Just as she'd reached a point where she could recollect her strength and set out to achieve new goals, so I began to think I might find comfort in surroundings all my own again.

In the end, I'd come to believe our undocumented marriage had been a pleasant, worthwhile, and honorable failure, doomed less by incompatibilities and more by the simple fact that we each needed privacy as much as we needed one another. In a suitable paradox, our separation had finally brought us closer together. Once again situated as we'd been years earlier, we'd been relieved of the question of what life might be like if we moved in together—and burdened by knowing what that knowledge had cost.

Arriving in a dark and quiet Brattleboro much later, I parked at the back of the shared driveway off Green Street and entered my new home, still enjoying the novelty of its unfamiliar odors. Seeing by the light filtering in through the windows, I crossed the downstairs to a door leading to a small attached barn and entered what I was hoping would become a source of rejuvenating comfort. One of the things that had attracted me most to this place had been the opportunity—for the first time since I'd left the family farm—to have a fully functional woodworking shop.

Aside from reading, which I did as much as possible, I had no real hobbies. Work had consumed most of my waking hours, later yielding occasionally to spending time with Gail, especially lately. But that was now over, and I had hopes of reaching back to my past to revive a pleasure I hadn't visited in too long. As a boy and a teenager, I'd worked, first under my father's guidance, and then, after he'd died, by myself in a cow shed on the Thetford farm where Leo and our mother still lived, running ancient cast-iron saws, lathes, and drills, turning out everything from uninhabitable birdhouses early on to some pretty sophisticated furniture later. But since leaving home, I'd never tried it again.

With typically nurturing invasiveness, Leo had encouraged my yearnings. He'd taken time off from his butcher shop, and from caring for Mom, to help me move in, arriving with a truck full of the same equipment I'd used all those years ago—refurbished and overhauled and gleaming like new. It had taken a whole day just to set up the shop, but the results had been akin to receiving a transfusion.

Now the machinery sat strategically placed around the open floor of this small, warm, renovated barn, waiting to carve out a whole new line of creations. I was pretty sure I'd make a mess of things early on, but the comfort I felt merely watching these tools under a row of bright lights—silent, shiny black, and resolute—more than compensated for any lingering apprehension.

There was a gentle knock on one of the windows. I crossed over to the sliding door that led to the driveway and opened it enough to see Sammie Martens standing in the cold.

"Come on in."

She slipped inside and leaned her back against the wall, taking in the scene before her. "Wow. You weren't kidding about this."

I slid the door closed again. "Nope. And it's all my old stuff. My brother brought it down so I could take another stab at it."

She took a few steps forward and laid a hand tentatively against the cold, hard flank of a band saw. "It's beautiful—like out of a museum."

"It's old enough to be. All cast-iron, solid as rock. It's the kind of equipment they used to have in lumber mills. My father picked it over the years, sometimes bartering, sometimes buying it secondhand."

I realized she was now looking at me, a small smile on her face. "You sound like a proud father yourself."

I laughed and motioned her over to the door leading back to the living room. "Yeah—well—old dog, old tricks. You want something hot to drink? I just got back from upstate. I was thinking of fixing some hot chocolate."

"Hot chocolate?" She hesitated as she passed before me. "Sure. Why not? I haven't had any of that since I was a kid."

I turned on a few lights as I walked toward the kitchen, which was separated from the rest of the room by a long, low counter.

"How was your trip?" she asked, perching on a stool and watching me work.

"Pretty much a dead end. I'm all but positive Marcia Wilkin's holding back, but nothing I said would budge her. Unless something pops up we can use as leverage, I don't see what else we can do. We'll just have to wait till Mark gets elected governor, and then see what that draws out of the woodwork—if anything."

"Well," she said philosophically, "it's not like we have a case building against him, anyhow. Just a bunch of suspicions. The really bad guys are all behind bars."

I was shifting things about, preparing the kettle, getting the cups out. "Yeah. Would've been nice to tie up that one loose thread, though."

Sammie didn't respond, and after a few moments of silence, I turned to look at her. She was staring off into space, her face small, pale, and sad.

I reached out and touched her shoulder. "You okay?"

She smiled wanly and laid her hand on mine, giving it a squeeze. "I should ask you the same thing."

"I think so," I answered. "I've been debating with myself all night. Maybe that's why I was in the woodshop—sort of getting myself reanchored to something. I know we've just gone back to the way things were— even with her working up in Montpelier—but I miss what we had."

"Tell me about it," she said wistfully.

"You still think about him a lot?" I asked.

"Not him—*it*," she answered. "I know now he wouldn't have worked out, for a whole bunch of reasons, but I really liked that closeness with someone."

The kettle began to whistle. I spooned out the chocolate, poured in the water, added a little half-and-half, and set the end results in front of her. "I have whipped cream."

Her face brightened. "No kidding?"

I got the canister out of the fridge and shot a small iceberg into her mug. She took a careful sip, putting a dollop of cream on her nose, which she wiped off with the back of her hand, laughing.

I thought of how we represented far sides of the same spectrum—she at the start of adult life, and I much closer to the end.

"You looking for someone else?" I asked after a while.

Her mood had lightened, her tone become jauntier. "Shit, no. I'm still walking wounded. I think I will in the long run, though. I can see what people are talking about now."

"This won't be the last time you get hammered," I cautioned.

"Oh, I know. That's what made me think it was such a crock. I used to watch my parents duke it out and think, no way I was going to fall into the same trap. But I'll give Andy that much—for all his bullshit, he showed me what it could be like. And you and Gail showed me, too."

I looked at her, surprised, hardly thinking we set an example for anyone. "You're kidding. We live in separate towns, for Christ's sake."

"But you love each other, even so."

I sipped my drink silently, reflecting on how simple she made it sound—and on how she might be right.

After a moment, I resurfaced from my thoughts. "I never asked—why did you drop by tonight?"

She held up her mug and smiled. "For this."

Chapter Thirty-one

The year had come full circle. It was January again, the ground was covered with snow, and I was back in the State House, elbowing through a throng of people. This time, however, Gail was beside me, beaming with enthusiasm, fueled by a renewed passion for working in the political storm.

"They say he has it wrapped up. He's been twisting arms, calling in markers, making all sorts of deals. He looks like he hasn't slept in days—been working on pure adrenaline."

We were crushed together, navigating the hallway like tandem kayakers in a raging stream. All around us the air was filled with similar conversations, the showdown at the joint assembly being the only topic in town.

I'd come in the day before, and spent the night at Gail's new condo, drawn not just by curiosity—although that would have been enough—but also by an invitation from Dave Stanton, the commissioner of Public Safety. He'd asked me to meet him outside the governor's office on the second floor shortly before the big vote was scheduled to take place.

Gail's running commentary was still going strong as we reached the black iron staircase and began working our way up. "Reynolds has been just the opposite—damn near invisible. People say he's been holding secret strategy sessions, but no one I've talked to has been approached for their vote, so I'm damned if I know what the strategy's supposed to be."

The governor's office faces the top of the western staircase, and I saw Stanton framed in its doorway, craning to see over the crowd. He waved at us as we came into view. "Joe. Gail—good to see you again. Governor Howell said we could use his office. Why don't you come in?"

Gail glanced at me and raised her eyebrows questioningly. "He didn't say it was private," I whispered.

We followed him through the small reception area into the largest, least appealing office I've ever visited. It was huge in all regards, with enormous windows and a two-story ceiling. The paintings and furniture were grandly historic, and the restored plaster on the walls and ceiling elegant and ornate, but the overall impression was of those old Soviet banquet halls on TV, where heads of state were photographed shaking hands, their smiles prefabricated and their eyes cold.

It was, in all fairness, a ceremonial office. Howell's real one was across the parking lot in the Pavilion Building. This was used for large photo ops and political meetings when the Legislature was in session. But with just the three of us in its midst, especially after Stanton had closed the massive door with a thud, the most impressive thing about it was its emptiness.

It apparently struck him the same way. He looked around like the sole visitor at a royal mausoleum and shook his head. "Sorry about the setting. It was the only private place I could think of."

"No problem," I said. "What's up?"

"It's a job offer. We were wondering if you'd like to join the new bureau."

Reynolds and Mullen had both made the same invitation—to join an organization that had yet to exist. I'd dismissed their offers as standard political smoke, since neither one of them had actually been in a position to hire me.

This man was, and the job was now real.

I was flattered by the offer, and despite two dress rehearsals, surprised. I was no spring chicken, and had assumed the new VBI would be staffed largely by the thirtysomething crowd and mostly drawn from the state police.

I decided to respond cautiously. "Who do you mean by 'we'?"

"There's a candidate review board. I'm its head. The offer would be pending a physical exam and a background check, but if what I see now is what you got, I don't think that'll be a problem."

"Have you formulated a structure for this unit yet?"

"It's been slow, but we're getting there. It won't be top-heavy. We're dividing the state into five regions—the four corners and the middle—and the people assigned to them will live in those regions, but they'll be free to wander wherever the job takes them. Right now, we don't see much ranking. The point of the exercise is that this represents the best and brightest—you shouldn't need a bunch of supervisors looking over your shoulders. You'll report to a head either in Burlington or Waterbury—probably the first, so people won't think you're state police—and he'll in turn report to the attorney general. Details still need to be worked out, and we're looking for input from the first draft of candidates, but that's basically it.

You'd keep all the seniority and benefits you've built up in Brattleboro, plus get a big boost in pay and get into the state's retirement and health coverage programs, all of which will be portable when you leave."

I walked over to the island-sized desk near the middle of the room. It was covered with an enormous sheet of glass and had dozens of photographs pinned under it like fish under ice. "You're not having face-to-face interviews like this with every candidate, are you?"

Stanton laughed. "No, you're one of the few. Most applied as soon as they heard about it. We noticed you weren't among them, so we all agreed I should make a personal approach. This isn't an oh-by-the-way offer, Joe. We'd really like you on board."

I turned to him. "I appreciate that, Dave, and I'm honored. There must be a hell of a lot of people in line."

"There're quite a few."

"And I suppose the applicant list is confidential."

His face betrayed a dawning wariness. "Yes."

"Are either Sammie Martens or Willy Kunkle on it?"

He hesitated.

"The reason I ask is that Sammie Martens is one person I think you ought to consider closely—more than me."

He relented. "We will, Joe. She is on the list. Just make sure she doesn't find out I told you. She thinks she's betraying you personally by trying to leave the PD."

I wasn't surprised, at either the ambition or the attending guilt. "What about Kunkle?"

He tried ducking the issue. "Every candidate will get the same scrutiny. Yours is just a special case."

"Meaning he's not on the list."

Stanton shifted his weight as if his feet were overheating. "He didn't apply. We can't just arbitrarily pull names out of a hat. I have to assume he doesn't want the job."

"I didn't apply, either."

His expression changed to one of irritation. "You want it or not?"

"Yes, if you'll consider Kunkle. I'll make sure he applies."

"The deadline's passed."

I just looked at him.

"Jesus. The man's a head case. Everyone knows it. This is an elite unit. I don't want to start it off with a total flake."

"People are being judged on their qualifications, right? Not on whether you like them or not."

"Of course."

"Then all I'm asking is for him to be considered. If you won't do that much, then you can cross my name off, too."

Stanton let out a long sigh. "Okay, but if, by some miracle, he does make it, he's your baby—wherever you decide to call home, that's where he'll be assigned. That much I *can* control. Then it'll be up to you to ask me later to have his butt fired."

I slapped him on the shoulder. "I don't think I'll be doing that, and if, as you say, he does make the cut, I also think you'll be pleased with the results. He'll make you proud."

"If he does, I'll consider the priesthood."

"By the way," I asked him, standing by the door, "since we've totally blown the confidentiality of this process, did either Ron Klesczewski or J.P. Tyler apply?"

"No. You going to round them up, too?"

I could tell from his tone of voice he was over the worst of it—plus the fact he was now smiling. "They're probably happier where they are. Ron's a small-town boy, and J.P. would feel overrun by the mobile crime lab people. I was just curious."

I opened the heavy door and ushered Gail out, pausing on the threshold to look back at him. "Dave, I do appreciate the offer, and the slack you're cutting me."

He waved me away. "I know. Don't worry about it."

A few minutes later, Gail and I were maneuvering our way through the jammed reception room parallel to the House chamber, aiming for where Gail had reserved two spots near the west wing entrance, to the left of the speaker's podium.

"That was a hell of a stunt," she said angrily. "You damn near killed your own chances. And he's right about Kunkle. He'll be making the whole outfit look bad before you know it."

"I don't think so," I answered mildly, not surprised by her outburst. "If he agrees to apply, I think they'll be impressed. He'll do a good job."

"But why risk it, Joe? Why do you always bail him out? All he does is treat everyone like shit."

"Willy's very good, and if he doesn't get a shot at this, he'll be out of a job. If I join VBI without him, there'll be no one to stop Tony Brandt from letting him go, especially with Brandt's big emphasis on community policing. Sooner or later, Willy will offend someone, and that'll be all Tony needs. After that, Willy'll probably rediscover the bottle, get into some barroom brawl, and maybe even wind up in jail. He deserves better." We'd reached the back staircase. "I have to go pee. I'll find you in a bit."

I disappeared before she could argue any more.

The men's room downstairs is toward the front of the building, around the corner from the president pro tem's office. As I came off the bottom step and headed that way, I saw a small group of people quickly entering the office—among them the pro tem, Jim Reynolds, and Marcia Wilkin.

I stopped dead in my tracks, my need for a bathroom replaced by a thought that hit me like an electrical jolt.

I turned on my heel and ran back upstairs, noticing the crowd had abruptly thinned out, indicating that things were about to start in the House. In the hallway leading to where Gail had staked her claim, however, the going was much slower. I squeezed and elbowed my way along until I finally reached her, positioned just inside the doorway, with a perfect view of the podium, the chamber, and the viewing gallery high along the curving back wall.

The scene made me think of a Hollywood set, packed with a cast of thousands—a vaulting, ornate, ancient-looking room, filled with row upon row of people. The gallery was jammed, the walls lined with spectators, every desk filled. The evenly spaced chairs along the front wall, flanking the speaker's podium onstage, were occupied by the senators from the other chamber, looking like firing squad targets without blindfolds.

I gave it all a cursory glance before asking Gail, "You have your cell phone?"

She stared at me. "You going to call someone? Now?"

"Yeah."

She silently reached into her purse and handed me the phone. As I punched the keypad, I heard the lieutenant governor bang the gavel on the podium.

Ron Klesczewski answered on the second ring. "Ron, It's Joe. You gotta do something for me."

"I can't hear you too well."

"Too bad. I can't talk any louder. Check the computer for the name Ellis Hastings." I spelled it for him.

"What's the context?" he asked. "Criminal record?"

"I don't know. You're going to have to look at everything you got. I think it's really important, though, so do it fast."

"No sweat. Where are you?"

"Montpelier. I'm on a cell phone." I gave him the number.

"Okay. I'll get right on it."

Gail looked at me as I hit the disconnect button and kept the phone in my hand. "What're you doing?" she whispered. In the background, the lieutenant governor was intoning the rules of procedure prior to ordering the vote for the next governor of the state of Vermont.

"I just saw Marcia Wilkin downstairs, in close company with Jim Reynolds. It made me remember something I saw in her house—a name. I think she's what Reynolds has been cooking up against Mullen this last week." I pointed a finger at the gallery high and across the cavernous room. "Look."

Defying conventional decorum, Mark Mullen entered one of the gallery doors, stepped down to the rail overlooking the chamber, and remained standing there—like Caesar overseeing the forum. A small ripple of commentary flowed across the crowd.

The lieutenant governor banged the gavel and instructed the assembled legislators to mark their paper ballots. There is no electronic voting in Vermont—too high-tech. This count was going to be done by hand, on the spot, since only one hundred and eighty votes were being cast.

I glanced anxiously at the phone, increasingly convinced that what I'd tumbled to could directly affect what was happening before my eyes. As if reading my mind, it chirped loudly, causing several people nearby to scowl at me.

"Yeah," I whispered loudly.

"I can barely hear you," Ron said, "but here goes. It's not much. Ellis Hastings died twenty-five years ago, victim of a hit-and-run. They never caught who did it."

A second general murmur passed around the room. I looked up and saw Jim Reynolds appear at the other gallery door, across the chamber from where Mullen was still standing.

Mullen turned at the commotion, saw Reynolds, and smiled, bowing slightly. Reynolds gestured to the open doorway behind him, and Marcia Wilkin stepped in.

Mullen froze in place. His hand stopped halfway into a dismissive wave, his expression calcified, his smile looking suddenly grotesque.

Across the way, Marcia Wilkin moved to the rail herself, touching it with her fingertips to steady herself, and then slowly, emphatically shook her head twice at Mark Mullen. She then turned on her heel, walked past Reynolds, and vanished through the door she'd entered by. Mullen half collapsed, half sat on the railing, his face ashen.

In the swelling of voices that followed, I spoke more loudly to Ron.

"Where did Hastings die?"

"Route 12, just outside north Montpelier. He was crossing the road at night, apparently looking for a lost cat."

"Cross-check the date and time of his death. Find me a crime that occurred the same time and in roughly the same vicinity. I'll hang on."

The phone to my ear, I watched Mullen wearily signal to one of his cronies, write him a note, and dismiss him. He then rose to his feet like a man of eighty and half stumbled up the few steps to the exit. Moments later, his messenger appeared at the main door to the chamber with the sergeant-at-arms and they walked down the center aisle toward the startled lieutenant governor. The envoy then delivered the note to the podium and quickly retreated, as if he'd just pulled the pin on a grenade.

Which, in a sense, he had. The lieutenant governor cleared his throat, declared that candidate Mark Mullen had withdrawn from the race, and instructed the assemblage to cast their votes accordingly.

Now it was I who could barely hear Ron on the phone above the bedlam. "Joe?"

"Louder, Ron."

"A grocery store in East Calais was robbed that night. Nobody was caught."

"They get away in a car?"

"Yeah."

"Headed south?"

"Yeah. What the hell's going on up there? What's that noise?"

I paused to watch the press people running for the doors. "The end of a career."

Chapter Thirty-two

No official explanation was ever forthcoming from Mark Mullen. To all questions about why he had withdrawn from the race, he merely said he wanted to help his brother in his time of need. Marcia Wilkin was never seen again in Montpelier, or in the company of now Governor James Reynolds, and to inquiries concerning her—or her identity—he and his associates responded with uncomprehending silence.

None of which stopped me from dropping by Win Johnston's home in Putney a few days following the joint assembly. He met me at the door with his characteristic gentle smile, and welcomed me to share a cup of coffee in his sunny kitchen.

"I had a small private bet with myself about when you'd come by."

"Who won?"

He laughed and shoved both sugar and milk across the counter at me. "What would you like to know?"

"You free to talk this time?"

"To you? Confidentially? Absolutely. I would have

been earlier than this if Mullen hadn't turned into such a loose cannon."

"Desperate man, desperate measures, I suppose. Which begs my first question: Did he know of or play a role in his brother's activities?"

Win looked at me thoughtfully. "I would've told you about any actionable crime I'd discovered. I told you that. But basically, I've reached the same conclusions you have. I think Danny killed Resnick because he went over some kind of edge. Maybe fraternal competition, maybe he just wanted to show he could make a big decision on his own. We'll probably never know. As for Mark being aware of Danny's other illegal activities, I'm sure he was. Danny was Mark's cash cow, and they had to've both been in on it. But they were careful, neat, and organized—until Danny cracked.

"Meaning," he added as he lifted his mug to his lips, "I don't have one shred of proof."

"I'm guessing Mark ripped off the East Calais grocery store twenty-five years ago, and then ran over Ellis Hastings during the getaway. Am I right?"

He nodded. "Mark and Danny both, with Marcia in attendance. It started as a dare, according to her, but after the hit-and-run, they were instantly in over their heads. It was a watershed event in several ways. It broke up the romance between Mark and her, cemented the bond between the two brothers, and saddled all three of them with a secret that worked like a cancer on them forever after. From starting out as three teenagers on a lark, they ended that night as three co-conspirators for life. Only this last time, it was Mark who went over the top, fighting too hard to become governor. That's what forced Marcia to step forward."

"Why so late in the game?" I asked.

"You should know. She only made up her mind after you had that little chat with her. Ticked me off when I heard about it, given all the time I'd wasted on her. You must have a knack with the ladies."

"Not likely."

He shrugged. "Well, you did with her. As long as Mark was speaker, doing good for the state and its people, Marcia could justify keeping silent. The statute of limitations for the hit-and-run had long since passed, Mark was highly regarded, and just between you and me, I don't think Marcia minded the life of a kept woman, especially since she didn't have to do anything to earn it.

"But then things went off track. Danny was implicated in the Resnick killing, which Marcia didn't have a hard time believing, and Mark started obsessing on the governorship. The more driven he became—through the primary and the general election—the more she began to doubt that she should stay silent. Shortly after you dropped by, she supposedly called Mark and pleaded with him to drop out. I guess he really let her have it, calling her a self-serving bloodsucker and all sorts of other stuff. She's a pretty religious woman, probably as a result of that night, and she took it pretty hard. She did a lot of thinking, tried contacting him several more times—he wouldn't even talk to her— and finally, stimulated by something you'd said to her, she called me. What you saw under the dome was the end result."

"So she was ready to spill it all?"

"Yup, and obviously Mark believed her. She'd left him a final message about what she was going to do. He called her bluff and lost."

"You think this story won't leak out somehow?" I asked.

"Only you, me, and Marcia know the truth. The deal with Reynolds was that not even he could be told. His job was to appear in the gallery, gesture her in, and benefit from the end result. It was a show of blind faith on his part—and the only rabbit he had in his hat, anyhow. To this day, he has no idea what it was all about, or even who she is, and I've told him not to bother digging."

A long silence fell between us as we each lapsed into reflection.

"Amazing thing, this thirst for power," I finally said.

"Yeah, and you can bet it's still alive in Mark. He'll be starting from scratch, but I'll guarantee you he'll be running for something again soon—it just won't be governor."

He smiled suddenly. "Rumor has it you've gotten ambitious, too."

I made a face. "Yeah, I suppose so. I'm not real comfortable with it yet. All I've done is apply—I still haven't heard back. But I'm not sure I'm up for a whole new organization, anyhow—new colleagues, new bosses, new routine. I'm feeling like a pretty old dog right now. 'Nervous' might be a better word."

"You'll be okay. I think it'll be good for you. I *know* you'll be good for them."

It was a nice thing for him to say—typical of the man. But as I drove back to Brattleboro later that afternoon, my doubts lingered on, both about the job and my motivations for wanting it. I had a pretty good idea how VBI officers were going to be treated by every other law enforcement agency in the state. If ambition was in fact what was fueling me, then the flak I fully expected to encounter might end up being categorized as just desserts.

I had cast the die, though, so time would tell. To that degree, things were pleasantly out of my hands.

But I hadn't forgotten the condition I'd set to Dave Stanton, and while I had no idea what Willy Kunkle might say, I was determined to make him the offer.

The timing had to be right, though, for both of us.

I wasn't going to approach him at work. That seemed totally inappropriate. And that night, as I fine-tuned my woodworking equipment and honed my collection of chisels, I realized that part of my caution stemmed from the consequences of a possible rejection. If he turned me down, I'd be forced to reconsider my own course of action, and by now, almost guiltily, I was beginning to look forward to the challenge.

Around ten, I gave in, killed the lights, got in my car, and drove across town to Kunkle's house. It was snowing gently, not too cold, no wind at all—a perfect winter evening. A soft and elegant coat of pure white was draped over everything horizontal, including the tops of all the outermost tree branches. The snow glistened in my headlights as if salted with flakes of mica.

No lights were on at Kunkle's, which was unusual for a night owl like him, but the surprising explanation was parked in his driveway. Nose-to-nose with his own beaten-up Ford was another car, also covered with snow, making the house look like any other average young couple's.

The car was Sammie's.

I drove by without stopping. My conversation could wait, and if this sign was any evidence, it might turn out to be easier than I'd thought.

More
Archer Mayor!

Please turn this page
for a
bonus excerpt
from

THE MARBLE MASK

a Warner Book
available
wherever books are sold.

"JOE. YOU STILL THERE? TALK TO ME, BUDDY."

I didn't open my eyes. It was so dark I felt if I did, more light might fall out than enter, sapping what little energy I had left. I remembered having the same sensation once as a kid, when my brother Leo and I had hidden in one of my father's grain boxes in the barn, closed the cover over us, and shut out all light and air. Lack of oxygen hadn't been the issue, though—we were out of there, pale and laughing too loudly, long before suffocation became a threat.

It was darkness that had defeated us—invasive, all-absorbing, reaching in through our wide-open eyes to extract whatever was keeping us alive. Squeezing my lids shut had been like hanging onto a cliff edge with my fingertips.

Which paradoxically made me wonder if suffocation could be a problem here, entombed as I was. Certainly I felt sleepy, which I'd heard was one of the signs, but then that counted for cold, too, and God knows I was cold.

"Joe? We need to know if you're still okay. Give us an

indicator at least—hit the transmit button a couple of times if you don't feel like talking."

I really didn't. I was talked out—talking to them, talking to myself. I wasn't even sure where the radio was anymore. I'd shoved it under my coat when I'd pulled my arms out of the sleeves to turn my parka into a thermal straightjacket and better preserve my body heat. Besides, assuming I could find it, I doubted my fingers could operate the damn thing. That was probably why they'd told me to just hit the transmit button—they were guessing I was almost gone.

I thought about that for a moment, which was no mean feat in itself. My mind had been wandering for hours, easily bringing up images of my parents, life on the farm, Leo, times during combat I'd thought were the coldest a man could endure.

Until tonight.

But pondering the here and now was both a challenge and a bore—an impediment to more pleasant things. The vague memory that I hadn't lost the radio at all, but was still holding it in a numb and senseless hand, barely caused a flicker of concern. I was far too busy leafing through my life's album, evoking sunny, hot, open places.

And pictures of Gail.

I saw her above me, straddling my hips as I lay on the floor, her eyes narrowed, her mouth open just slightly. There was a faint shimmer of sweat on her upper lip as she raised her arms slowly, smoothly, and stripped off her T-shirt.

"Joe? It's Willy. Hang in there, pal. You croak, they'll nail me for sure. Don't be so goddamned self-centered."

What a guy, I thought—always the right word at the right time. What must his parents have been like?

I tried retrieving that last image of just seconds ago, remembering only that it had been of something pleasant and warm. I was beginning to feel warm again myself, in fact. At long last.

"Won't be too much longer," Willy resumed. "They say the storm's almost over—at least enough to try another sortie. Give us some kind of signal, though, will you? This playing coy shit is driving me nuts."

He'd always been an impatient man—always in a hurry and with nowhere to go. Not like Sammie, for example, equally driven but headed straight up the professional ladder.

Gail was ambitious, too, although a lot more complicated—one of the reasons we no longer lived together. Not that the love could be diminished—no matter the test.

I furrowed my brow, or thought I did. Sam and Willy and Gail and I were becoming blurred in my mind. Maybe there were similarities I'd never glimpsed before—he and I sort of stuck in our ways, the two women either using us as anchors, or fighting the pull of our inertia.

Surely there had to be more to it than that.

The radio spoke again, sounding like the last man to

enter a noisy, crowded room—too far off to be understood.
And I had too much to ponder anyway.

Let it go, I thought. Let me be.

Three Days Earlier

"VERMONT BUREAU OF INVESTIGATION——JOE GUNTHER."

"It's Bill. You're sounding very official."

I looked across my small sunlit living room at the snow-covered trees outside, feeling more unemployed than official. "Try hopeful. This is the first time I've used this phone since you guys put it in last month. Is this a good-news call?"

"Good and bad—we've got a job, but you're going to be flying damn near solo."

Bill Allard was the chief of the newly formed VBI. Purportedly an exclusively major crimes unit with statewide jurisdiction, but as yet nonexistent except on paper, it had become a victim of the Department of Public Safety's face-saving "analysis paralysis."

"What've you got?" I asked him.

"You hear about the hiker who froze to death on Mount Mansfield?"

"Vaguely. There was something about it on the radio yesterday."

"The Stowe PD was trying to keep it under wraps, making it sound like an accident, but the medical examiner just ruled it a homicide. Anyhow, someone must've leaked it, because at the governor's weekly news conference this morning, a reporter asked if VBI was going to be called in. He didn't turn a hair, said, 'They're on it as we speak,' and went on to the next question. I scrambled to have the AG call Stowe's chief and offer him our services before the press told him he'd already accepted."

"The state police'll love that."

"Love it or not, it looks like we're out of the closet."

I was a little less sanguine. "Or Doctor Frankenstein's lab."

Sammie Martens took her eyes off the road to stare at me. "What the hell was he thinking?"

I shrugged and pulled out into the fast lane to pass an eighteen-wheeler slowly grinding its way uphill. We were shouldered in between Vermont's Green Mountains on one side and a serpentine river on the other, heading west on the interstate toward Burlington and the chief medical examiner's office.

"He was being governor," I explained. "Someone popped him a question and he answered accordingly. He didn't have to be thinking of anything so long as someone made it look like he was. Not that I'd complain," I added. "Without this, God knows when we might've been activated."

"What do we know about the dead guy?" Sammie asked.

"Not much that makes sense. He was found frozen stiff high on the mountain, presumed to be a lost hiker with a Canadian ID, but missing a few body parts and according to Allard not looking at all like your run-of-the-mill tourist—whatever that means. Bill only said there was something about him that had everybody wondering. So now it's up to Vermont's version of the Untouchables to fill in the blanks, with or without resources, manpower, infrastructure, or equipment."

"Untouchables, hell," she said half to herself. "Unheard of is more likely."

I didn't agree with her there. Even if nonfunctional, we were almost as well known as Ben and Jerry's ice cream, at least locally—and as popular as the plague with every cop in the state.

The Vermont Bureau of Investigation had been the Legislature's reaction to a hot-button killing the year before, in which a communications breakdown among several police departments had led to a known criminal's remaining free until after he'd killed two kids. The original pipe dream—pushed by the same man who'd been elected governor on the strength of it—had been to replace the state's sixty-eight separate law enforcement agencies with a single coherent force. Instead, hounded by a lobbyist free-for-all, the Legislature had compromised by creating a face-saving sixty-ninth—a small, elite unit which, unlike the state police's Bureau of Criminal Investigation—BCI— whose ranks were filled only by state troopers, would be staffed by the cream of the crop from all departments.

But only if they supported it.

As with most grand visions, VBI was being seen so far as a device to steal away every department's top people and best cases.

The irony was that initially, I'd been one of those critics. A career veteran of the Brattleboro PD and the lieutenant in charge of its detective squad, I'd watched with disgust as an interesting trial balloon had been deflated by confusion and lack of support. When the time had come to fill VBI's ranks, I hadn't even applied.

Now I was its field force commander—the number-two man. A leap of faith I hadn't quite finished rationalizing.

Sammie seemed to be puzzling along similar lines, as well she might, being another newly anointed VBI special agent who'd been cooling her heels at home ever since. "What're we supposed to do here? Take over the case? None of this is turning out the way I thought it would."

I shook my head sympathetically. "Until I'm told otherwise, I'm looking at us more like the forensic lab, or the arson guys, or the bomb-disposal squad. We deliver manpower, expertise, contacts, and our own prosecutor to whoever asks for us, and we leave them with the collar, the kudos, and the headlines if we're successful."

"The Lone Ranger," she muttered, "making the town sheriff look good."

"Kind of," I agreed. "If we do it right, we'll get all the tough cases, act pretty much autonomously, and let whatever department head requested us handle the reporters, politicians, and the cranks. It's a cop's dream come true."

Hearing it out loud made it sound pretty good.

"If you weren't sure what this was," I asked her, perhaps hoping she wouldn't ask me the same question, "why did you sign up?"

Sammie flushed slightly. I knew she'd applied to VBI early on without telling me, while still on my squad in Brattleboro. She was smart, tough, persistent, and normally loyal, which I knew was embarrassing her now. But she'd always been hard-driving and ambitious, and I'd never expected her to stay with us forever—all of which was moot anyway, since I was once again her boss.

She began hesitantly. "I thought I could maybe learn a few things." She groped for something more meaningful in the face of an obviously different reality. Finally, she gave up. "It looked like an interesting opportunity."

I took her off the hook. "Me, too. Does what I just described help?"

She reflected a moment and then smiled. "It *sounds* great. You think it's realistic?"

I laughed. "Beats the hell out of me. How we perform right now'll probably tell us."

The ME's office in Burlington is tucked into a corner of Vermont's largest medical center, a happy beneficiary of the state's efforts to lock horns with competing hospitals in bordering New York and New Hampshire. Once located above a dentist off campus, Dr. Beverly Hillstrom's office was now extraordinarily well appointed and the source of considerable pride. Which was entirely fitting—over many years, and despite Vermont's small size and tight budgets, she had created one of the most efficient and highly respected medical examiner systems in the Northeast. These modern facilities were a long-overdue reflection of that.

She greeted us as soon as we were announced and escorted us down a gleaming hallway to the autopsy room at the far end, making well-mannered small talk along the way. Tall, slim, and Nordic in appearance, Hillstrom was of indefinable age and unmistakable bearing. Having worked closely together for years, we still referred to one another by title, and not once had she shared a single detail of her personal life. Yet the depth of our friendship was without doubt. She'd proven it many times, extending me courtesies she rarely granted others.

Titles, however, were causing her a problem right now.

"Lieutenant—in point of fact, that's no longer accurate, is it?" she asked as we neared the wide, blank door of her autopsy room.

"Not technically. I don't mind if you want to stick with it."

She shook her head. "No, no. That wouldn't do. How should I address you?"

I was still ambivalent about that. "It sounds a little silly, but we tore a page from the FBI book—officially I'm a Special Agent in Charge, or a SAC. Not that I'm in charge of anything yet. Why don't we just make it 'Mister,' with the understanding that I'd really prefer 'Joe.'"

She swung back the door and ushered us over the threshold, frowning slightly. "No. Mister is fine."

The room before us was broad, deep, bright, and neatly arranged, with a skylight overhead and two operating areas extending from the wall like twin boat slips. Laid out on one of the metal tables was a body so unusual in appearance, it looked more like a lab experiment than an autopsy candidate.

Standing next to it were two men, Hillstrom's long-time lab assistant Henry, and Ed Turner, a state trooper assigned to this office as its law enforcement liaison.

Turner raised his eyebrows as we entered, and greeted us with a reserve I knew we'd better get used to. He was, after all—and until or unless these prejudices were sorted out—a member of a "rival" agency. "Well, look at this—the feds that aren't. What're you doing here?"

I laughed and shook his hand, sensing Sammie tense beside me. "Just helping out the Stowe PD. How've you been keeping?"

Hillstrom, sensitive to matters of turf, quickly took over.

"We have an approximately mid-forties male, in good physical condition aside from a few missing parts, who appears to have suffered a single fatal puncture wound to the heart, although we'll have to wait for toxicology to rule out anything additional. The body itself has thawed out," she explained further, "although some of the organs are still a little hard. We're trying to speed things up by flushing them with warm water, but I don't want to move too quickly."

Sammie had been studying the open body with professional interest, staring down at its unusually dark red interior. Hillstrom's finding, however, made her look more carefully at the chest. "He was stabbed?" she asked.

Her confusion was understandable. The ME's patient was anything but traditional—its skin was red fading to a leathery brown, instead of the usual sickly yellow, its eyes were strangely sunken and dry, and its nose, ears, and fingers were dark, as if dipped in soot. It also was missing one arm and both feet, the amputations so clean, they looked cut through by a razor. But there was no sign of any violence aside from some bloodless scratches on the side of his face.

"You're reacting to how he looks," Hillstrom responded. "That's what stumped the Stowe police and the local assistant medical examiner, I'm embarrassed to say. It's also what led them to think that he might have just been a hiker who got lost and died of natural or environmental causes, perhaps scraping his face in the process."

She pulled on a pair of gloves, moved closer to the man's chest, and parted a few strands of his chest hair, revealing a tiny hole in the skin the size of a ruptured pimple. "There's the point of entry."

Sammie leaned so far over that her nose was inches from the wound. "What was it? It almost looks like a small-caliber bullet wound."

"He was run through," Ed Turner answered, "like with a shish kebab skewer."

I could see from Hillstrom's expression that she disagreed with the allusion, but she merely changed the subject. "Another interesting detail can be found with the victim's extremities, including the ears." She lifted his one remaining hand. "Notice the shriveling of the fingertips—its weatherbeaten quality?"

"Almost looks like a mummy," Sammie softly observed.

Hillstrom smiled broadly. "Very good, Agent Martens. That's exactly right."

"Implying he's been around for a while," I suggested.

"Longer than you think, I bet," Turner added, his earlier reserve now gone.

He crossed over to a pile of clothes on a nearby table and spread the top garment out for examination—a curiously constructed wool herringbone jacket with a belt across the back. It was worn, tattered, and faded. "Look at his duds."

Sammie glanced at it from where she was standing.

"Looks like something out of a pseudo good-old-days catalogue."

Turner shook his head. "Not pseudo. We're thinking it's the real McCoy. Check out the rest of it."

We gathered around him as he displayed it all—wool pants and shirt, cashmere sweater, silk underwear. It reminded me of an old movie about a debonair city slicker going country for the weekend.

I reached out and fingered the material. It was coarse and brittle despite its high quality, and much of it was in shreds, especially along the same side as the scratches on the body's face. "How old is it?"

Turner laughed. "Wild guess? Nineteen forty-five, six, or seven—in that range."

"You having a good time?" Sammie asked testily. "How're you so sure?"

He waved a hand in apology. "I'm sorry. This one's just so far off the charts. Here." He extended a small plastic bag to her from a sampling of similarly protected documents. Inside was a single piece of thick paper.

Sammie studied it a moment, turned it over, and finally gave it to me. "It's a Canadian driver's license, expires nineteen forty-seven. Name of Jean Deschamps."

I glanced at it. "That's it?"

Ed passed the other documents around. "No, no. He had all the usual stuff—money, business cards, kid's photos, picture of a guy in uniform, what looks like an ancient credit card for a Sherbrooke oil company, presumably for his car. There's also an identity card with his photograph, birth date, and address. It all looks like it came straight out of a museum."

"Let's see the paper money," I requested.

He handed me another envelope. "There's about five hundred dollars, Canadian," he said. "Good for a short vacation."

I didn't need to check for dates to know the currency predated 1952. Queen Elizabeth's profile was conspicuously absent from any of the bills, in favor of her father, King George VI.

"Not right after the war, it wasn't," I countered. "Adjusting for inflation, that's worth close to three thousand dollars, and even that's misleading, since three thousand back then bought a lot more than it does now." I waved my hand at the pile of clothes. "And those aren't for hiking—they're just dandified countrywear."

"I think so, too," Beverly Hillstrom said from behind me.

I turned to her. "So, what are we looking at? A man dead for fifty years, or something disguised to make us think so?"

"The answer," she said, "might lie in the depth of his refrigeration. Generally in hypothermia cases, we can either see or regain some degree of flaccidity shortly after we take possession of the body, even with the complication of rigor mortis. Here we had a subject frozen through and through at something around twenty degrees below zero, centigrade—a unique situation in my personal experience. And I would say that what Agent Martens identified as mummification is also in part what I would call old-fashioned freezer burn.

"Finally, add that to the equation," she waved her hand at the clothes and documents, "along with the three amputations and the postmortem scrapes on his face, and I would venture that our friend has not only been in this state for a very long time, but that he was brutally handled recently, resulting not in the severing but the breaking off of some of his anatomy. I studied the points of separation carefully, and they show little sign of the weathering the rest of the body's suffered, and no signs whatsoever of slicing, chopping, or sawing."

"Pretty unlikely Mount Mansfield had much to do with any of this," I suggested, mostly to myself.

Beverly Hillstrom smiled slightly. "I would agree."

"What about the amputations?" Sammie asked.

"One hypothesis," Hillstrom answered, "might involve dropping. If the frozen body hit a rocky outcropping or an icy surface at the proper angle, parts of it could break off or even shatter upon impact, as with a marble statue. That would also explain the lacerations and the torn clothes."

I looked over at Ed Turner. "Did the Stowe PD search the area?"

He nodded. "They didn't find anything."

"The body could have been dropped prior to its final delivery on the mountain," Hillstrom suggested. "Mr. Deschamps was not a small man, and in that condition must have been quite difficult to handle."

"So we might find an arm or a foot in a Dumpster somewhere," Sammie ventured.

I glanced around the room, restless with all this abstract musing. Until I recalled a small reaction of Hillstrom's earlier.

"What do *you* think caused that puncture to the heart?" I asked her.

She returned to the side of the presumed Mr. Deschamps and placed her finger gently on his chest. "It may not be possible to prove, but my suspicion is that it looks odd because it's rare—another indicator that all this happened long ago. I think he may have been killed by an old domestic standby, both in fact and in the movies: an ice pick. You don't see many of them nowadays. And certainly not as a lethal weapon."

To read more, look for *The Marble Mask* by Archer Mayor.